The Smart One

Ellen Meister

AVON

An Imprint of HarperCollins*Publishers*

HarperCollins books may be purchased for educational, business, or sales promotional use. For information please write: Special Markets Department, HarperCollins Publishers, 10 East 53rd Street, New York, NY 10022.

FIRST EDITION

Designed by Elizabeth Glover

Library of Congress Cataloging-in-Publication Data

Meister, Ellen.
   The smart one / Ellen Mesiter. — 1st ed.
       p. cm.
   ISBN 978-0-06-112962-9
   1. Sisters—Fiction. 2. Domestic relations—Fiction. 3. Murder—Fiction. 4. New York (State—Fiction. I. Title
   PS3613.E4355S63 2008
   813'.6—dc22   2008016193

08 09 10 11 12 OV/RRD 10 9 8 7 6 5 4 3 2 1

The Smart One

Also by Ellen Meister

SECRET CONFESSIONS OF THE APPLEWOOD PTA

For my parents

I would like more sisters, that the taking out of one,
might not leave such stillness.
—*Emily Dickinson*

Chapter 1

"And why do you want to relocate to Nevada, Ms. Bloom-rosen?"

Air conditioning, I wanted to say, but I dabbed the per-spiration from my upper lip and bit my tongue. I wasn't sure this principal from an elementary school in Clark County, Las Vegas—who had already endured hours in a stifling classroom at Columbia University so she could interview recent gradu-ates of Teachers College—was interested in New Yorkers of the smart-ass variety.

Principal Belita Perez folded her hands, waiting for me to answer. I glanced at the sweating can of Diet Coke on the desk in front of her and wondered how she'd react if I told her the truth—that I wanted to relocate so that I could get as far away from my loving albeit judgmental Long Island fam-ily as I could, that they were smothering me with unrealistic expectations, that once you'd been labeled "the smart one" as a child, your potential was considered limitless, and the only way you could live up to your early promise was to become a brain surgeon, marry a rocket scientist, and create two per-fect children who were bright enough to get their own game show called *Are You Smarter Than a Preschooler?* and that if you didn't, that if you fell short of that in any way, you were a disappointment. A failure.

A loser.

Mrs. Perez clicked her pen, waiting to transcribe my response. I considered saying, "I'm eager to work for a district that's so progressive, yet committed to the highest standards of education." But that was the textbook response most of her other interviewees probably gave, and I wondered whether a more mature and creative answer would make her remember me, perhaps shed light on the odd anomalies in my résumé. I was, after all, almost a decade older than most of her other candidates. No doubt she wondered why I graduated from college with a bachelor's degree in graphic design and spent ten years flitting from one job to another before going back to school to earn my master's in education.

Would it be inappropriate to explain about my divorce? Should I tell this woman with the pale-pink manicure and cream-colored suit that it took walking in on my husband performing cunnilingus on a pretty young schizophrenic artist named Savannah to rock the fragile foundation I'd spent so many years building? Would she understand that it required a trauma of that magnitude to make me finally see the truth and understand that I had wanted to be a teacher all along, that it was what I was meant to do?

I had always loved school. I loved raising my hand as high as I could when I knew the answer (which I usually did) and the feeling I got when the teacher pointed at *me*. I loved the whole *schooliness* of it—the smell of pencil shavings and paste, the smoothness of the pages between the covers of fat textbooks, the big round clock on the wall that made the softest *dit-dit-dit* as the minute hand moved.

I didn't, however, always love my teachers. Some of them were wonderful enough to worship. But there were a few who struck me as truly sinister, choosing certain boys and girls in the class to hate. It was painful to watch, and utterly confusing. Why, I wondered, couldn't Mrs. Gaddis simply show Stuart Weingarten how to multiply fractions instead of parading his D-minus paper in front of the whole class? Did she think that humiliating him would help him pass the next test? It seemed obvious to me that this would push him farther away from learning anything.

I thought hard about kids like Stuart Weingarten. They reminded me of those broken dogs I saw on charity canisters at checkout counters, and I fantasized about fixing them. I imagined myself as Stuart Weingarten's teacher, sitting patiently with him and explaining fractions in a way he could understand. There would be a moment of reckoning when he got it, and his whole sorry life would change. He'd wear better clothes and have cleaner hair, and the other boys would stop calling him Stupid Weingarten.

But back then, being a teacher seemed neither ambitious enough to meet my family's expectations for me nor rebellious enough for me to be able to consider myself irreverent. Becoming an artist seemed just the ticket. I could be eccentric, exotic, opinionated. To me, the artiste was someone who possessed some inner knowledge everyone else aspired to. It was perfect.

Besides, I reasoned, I could draw, so how hard could it be? Thus, I went to college majoring in fine arts, which I soon learned was a mistake. I did okay in art appreciation, as there was studying and knowledge and time periods involved, but the creative classes were a bust. My charcoal sketches, for example, were passable—accurate and precise. And I even enjoyed the process. But one glance at the creativity in the other students' drawings let me know I was in over my head.

I was too stubborn to admit I'd made a mistake, so I told

myself that changing my major to commercial art was simply the practical thing to do. I needed to support myself, after all, and had my whole life to become an artist in my spare time.

The result was a professional disaster—a string of entry-level jobs I could never commit to because they didn't truly satisfy me. I was, among other things, a photographer's assistant, a junior graphic designer, an assistant studio manager, and even a freelance illustrator. I might have enjoyed that last one if the thought of being a cheat hadn't put a knot in my stomach. I had cleverly developed a stylistic approach to my illustrations that masked my weaknesses as an artist, and I lived in fear that someone would find out. Eventually, the freelance jobs simply dried up, and I was once again without a career.

Throughout all this, I told my friends that my dream was to move into a loft and get back into oil painting, which I had once actually enjoyed. But part of me knew I'd never follow through with this, so I did the next best thing. I married an artist.

Mrs. Perez looked bored. She took a sip of her Diet Coke and I worried I was losing her. My answers to her previous questions had been intelligent, if a little dry. Perhaps I should make the air-conditioning joke after all, loosen things up a bit.

But what if she was a humorless type like my ex? Jonathan was always so serious. I've tried, in the years since we've been apart, to picture him smiling, but all I can conjure is that blinky, hurt face he gave whenever I made a joke, as if the idea of humor was something that wounded him.

Even on that day I came home from my job as an assistant layout artist to see strange limbs in the loft above my head, he remained morose.

"Hey," I had said stupidly.

A blond girl I recognized from the gallery scene downtown

sat up in my bed. They called her Savannah the Schizoid. Jonathan was clearly up there with her, but I couldn't quite make out where he was or what he was doing.

"Fuck," the girl said, and reached between her legs.

It took a second for me to realize she was tapping Jonathan on his head to get his attention. He lifted his face and looked down, the area around his mouth slick from her dainty little artist's box.

"You're not supposed to be here," he said.

"And you're not supposed to be *there*," I answered.

That wounded face, blinking. I had gone and made a joke, implying that there were things in this world less than serious.

The road from the sting of betrayal to the sweet realization that I had been headed in the wrong direction was a short one. Freed from the burden of Jonathan's biased scrutiny, it quickly dawned on me that I'd spent my entire adult life lying to myself about what I really wanted to do. So I stepped right over his arrogance as well as my family's attitude that teaching elementary school was simply aiming too low and, armed with a small cache of guilt-induced largesse from my trust-fund-bridled ex-husband, went back to school to get a master's degree in education.

And now, at last, I had the chance to not only answer my calling but to do it in an environment where I'd be appreciated instead of judged.

Principal Belita Perez put her soda can down on the desk and fanned her face with my application, waiting for me to tell her why I wanted to relocate to Nevada.

At last, I smiled. "Who needs this frigid New York weather?"

Chapter 2

As I stood waiting to catch the express bus back to my apartment in Forest Hills, Queens, I listened to an undergrad next to me speaking Spanish *mas rapido* into her cell phone. Even after all those years of getting As in high school Spanish, all I could pick up was *mi hermana*, my sister. I imagined she was talking *about* her sister, not *to* her sister, but I couldn't help wondering if I'd be chatting it up with one of *mis hermanas* if my cell phone hadn't broken the week before. Would I call Clare, my older sister on Long Island, and tell her I had just interviewed for the job of my dreams and thought I had a good shot at getting it? And if I did, would she be happy for me or as judgmental as she was that day I told her that I was going back to school for my master's in education?

I was sitting at Clare's designer table in her designer kitchen when I broke the news. Our younger sister, whom we call Joey but whose real name is Joanna, was in the chair next to mine, jiggling her foot and drumming the table, unaware of how obvious it was that she was buzzed on coke and about to jump right out of her skin. Clare was at the counter with her back to us, arranging a display of organic chocolate-chip cookies on a platter.

Clare, I should explain, is a member of the PTA who car-pools and has mental algorithms for calculating which type of manicure is appropriate for which occasion in which season, yet didn't know Afghanistan was a country until it had been in the headlines for a month. I can't blame her for this. She was always the beautiful one and got heaps of attention for it. The message instilled from the time she was small was that appearance trumped everything, and it formed the core of her character.

In a way, that message formed the essence of my character too, though to opposite effect. I think I must have sensed from the time I was small that I could never compete with Clare in the looks department. So I carved out a niche for myself in the family by taking on the role of the smart one. Then, when Joey came along, she had to find some other way to stand out. With the roles of pretty and smart already taken, Joey became the wild one.

"How long to get the degree?" Clare had asked.

"Probably two years," I answered.

She pushed the plunger on her French press and poured coffee for us. "You think you'll stick with it?"

I tried willing her to turn around so she could see me roll-ing my eyes. "Of course I'll stick with it," I said. "This is some-thing I've wanted all my life."

She sighed and put everything on a tray, which she brought to the table. As she set it down carefully, she gave Joey a *what-are-we-going-to-do-with-her* look. But our little sister's eyes were darting around the room as she bobbed her head to a song only she could hear.

"Didn't you say the same thing about flower arranging?" Clare asked me.

I gritted my teeth. Why was she so dense? "No, of course not."

"I seem to remember you being pretty excited about that. Like it was just the thing you were waiting for. Or the photography thing. Remember what you said about that? 'I think I finally found my medium, Clare,' that's what you said."

I cringed, knowing how unconvincing it would sound if I said this was different. So I just asked Clare what was up with her hair, which looked more tricolor than usual. A low blow. The hair thing was an issue between us. Back in my loft days, I wore my hair Joan Jett black, and Clare called it my "goth period." But I had been going for that downtown I'm-such-an-artist-I-never-go-out-in-the-sun look of severe dark hair against white skin. Admittedly, the effect was more anemic than artsy, and I'd since let my natural brown hair grow out. Clare was always trying to get me to put in blond highlights, and one day I snapped that I didn't want to look like a Long Island soccer mom. It was probably unfair of me to get mad rather than admit I had some vanity about my hair. God forbid I let on that I had a bit of pride about my natural chestnut highlights. No, I had to position myself as being above such shallow concerns. That way, I didn't have to worry about coming up short against my beautiful sister. Part of me resented that Clare, with all her sensitivity, couldn't see through my facade of studied nonchalance. The other part of me would have been mad if she *had*. A paradox, I know. But we're sisters so I guess it's part of the package.

Clare touched the back of her head in response to the tricolor remark. "He put in lowlights. You don't like it?"

Guilty, I backpedaled. I didn't want to make her weep again. "I'm an idiot about fashion, you know that. It's tres chic, I'm sure."

"You know what *I* think?" Joey said.

Clare and I turned to our younger sister, who was busy wiping her nose with the back of her wrist, as if we wouldn't notice all her sniffling as long as she didn't reach for a tissue.

"Do I have a choice?" I said, sighing.

Joey dug her spoon into Clare's designer sugar bowl and shoveled two mounds into her coffee cup. "I think," she said, stirring harder and faster than she needed to, "that wiping kids' asses all day isn't all it's cracked up to be."

Clare sighed and touched my arm. "I think you'll be a good teacher, Bev," she said.

I smiled, grateful that someone in my family had tossed me a bone.

"I just hope this isn't another phase," she added.

I hope Joey cracks your damned cup, I thought.

My parents hadn't reacted any better to the news that I was going back to school for a degree in education. Even though my excitement had been as obvious as a *New York Post* headline, they couldn't muster a pica of enthusiasm. My doctor father had said, "An *elementary* school teacher?" in a voice that implied he couldn't even conceive of such a thing. Like I was moving to Antarctica to start a branch of blubber-eating Hare Krishnas.

"Maybe she can work her way up," my mother offered, "and eventually teach high school. That wouldn't be so bad."

Back in my apartment, I played my answering machine messages as I riffled through the stack of mail I had brought in. The first call was from my mom. She and my dad were in Florida staying with their friends, the Waxmans, who were our next-door neighbors on Long Island. Like most Jewish New York couples of a certain age, however, the Waxmans followed an instinctive migratory pattern every winter, fleeing the driveway-shoveling responsibilities of the suburban Northeast for the country club lifestyle of Florida's swanky coastline condos. This year, they were staying straight through the summer, as they had decided that their particular nesting area—a hacienda-styled garden apartment in Boca Raton—was suitable for year-round habitation.

My mother's voice on my answering machine sounded a little shaky. "Everything's okay but. . . ," she said, and sighed. "Just you call me right away, dear. Everything is fine, though."

I dropped my mail onto the counter in my pint-sized kitchen and dialed the Waxmans' Florida number immediately, as I knew that the only time Mom bothered saying everything was fine was when it wasn't.

"It's Bev," I said, when I reached her. "What's the matter?"

"Nothing, but . . . well, your father slipped on some wet tile by the pool here and it seems he broke his ankle."

"Is he all right? Is he in a cast?"

She said that he was indeed in a cast and would have to stay off his feet for a while, delaying their return home. She handed him the phone before I had a chance to ask any more questions.

"You okay, Dad?" I asked.

"Herman Resnick is down here now," he said, referring to one of his old doctor pals, an orthopedist. "Had prostate cancer and now he jogs six miles a day."

"He set your ankle?" I'd been chasing my father's cryptic dialogue up alleys and around corners my whole life, but it was still dizzying.

"Herman? He hasn't practiced in years."

"He referred you to someone?"

"You should see the offices they have down here."

I took that as a yes and asked to speak to my mother again, who whispered that she thought he was secretly *delighted* to have the chance to relax. But there was one tiny problem, she explained, and it required my attention.

Upon their return to New York, my parents were supposed to take care of some practical details involved in selling the Waxmans' house next door, like unlocking it for prospective buyers and dealing with realtors, only now they wouldn't be around to do it. The proposed solution was for me to move into my parents' house until they returned at the end of the summer.

"The end of the summer?" I asked. "Is Dad laid up for that long?"

"Yes, well," my mother said and paused, "we might take this time to look for a place of our own down here."

She said it like she was breaking some difficult news to me, as if her thirty-five-year-old daughter might just fall apart at the thought of living in a different state from her parents. This was probably the perfect opportunity to tell my parents I had just interviewed for a job on the other side of the country, but I would resist the urge. After all, if the job didn't come through, I'd be even more of a loser in their eyes.

"That's great," I offered. "You and Dad will love it there. But I don't know about staying at your house. It's kind of a weird time for me."

Truth was, my lease had expired and I was living month-to-month in my apartment. The landlord had been trying to get me to sign on for another two years, but I kept putting him off as I tried to figure out where I might be in the fall.

"I left the Waxmans' house key in the cute little green cup in the kitchen," my mother continued. "You know the one I mean? Shaped like a frog?"

Of course I knew what she meant. I made that cup myself when I was in second grade. It was my first experience with a kiln, and I recalled the thrill of seeing the transformation of my handiwork from a raw creation covered in a dull gray coat to a work of art, glazed in a shiny green finish as brilliant as emeralds. My art teacher, Miss Butler, made an appropriate fuss over it, and though she probably did the same for everyone, my heart swelled with a special kind of pride. I had created a thing of beauty.

I picked up the stack of mail again and looked through it. Along with a couple of bills, two credit card solicitations from Capital One, pleas for funds from several different charities, and a Pottery Barn catalog, there was a letter from my landlord's attorney.

My mother sighed. "I don't know what else to do."

"What about Clare?" I said. After all, my older sister lived on Long Island just a few miles from my parents.

"Clare?" she asked, as if the suggestion was preposterous. "She's got the *kids*."

The kids, of course. Clare couldn't be expected to do anything that would compromise her time spent parenting. I opened the cabinet where I kept my drinking glasses and reached into the back for a bottle of Advil. I spilled two pills into my hand and swallowed them dry.

"I suppose Joey's out of the question?" I asked.

"She has enough on her plate, Beverly."

I took that to mean we shouldn't do anything to jeopardize the progress she had made in her drug treatment program. She'd been clean for over a year and we were all holding our breath.

I wondered aloud why the Waxmans' son, Kenny, couldn't take care of the house, and my mother explained that he was still in Los Angeles. This didn't surprise me, as it wasn't hard to keep track of his career through the occasional IMDB search. Though we lost touch after an animosity had developed between us as teens, I was well aware that Kenny had spent the past decade as a comedy writer in Southern California.

"And anyway," my mother continued, "I figured you had nothing to do now. Aren't you all done with school?"

Still cradling the phone under my chin, I walked from the kitchen and into the living room, which also served as a breakfast nook, dining area, den, and music room. I sat down at the table and ripped open the envelope containing the lawyer's letter. Apparently, I either had to produce a signed lease or vacate within ten days. I knew it was mostly bravado—evicting a tenant isn't all that easy. But did it make sense to put up a fight when my mother's alternative was presenting itself like some karmic gift? It wouldn't, after all, be that hard to put my stuff in storage and move into my parents' house while I sorted out my life's next move. Still, it felt like a humiliating step backward.

"Well?" my mother nudged. "You do have the summer off, don't you?"

I sighed and told her I did.

"And in the fall you start teaching full-time?"

"Yes," I said enthusiastically, wondering if she would ask me what my plans were. It was, I knew, a moment of weakness, but I made the impetuous decision that if she asked, I might just open up after all, letting her in on my excitement over the job in Las Vegas and all it offered. According to Mrs. Perez, the city was growing faster than the education system could keep pace with, so they were offering some extraordinary opportunities. Even without a degree in special education, candidates could get to teach a self-contained classroom of special-needs kids. If I was lucky enough to get one of the job openings—which I'd find out sometime within the next few weeks—I could even get a second master's degree at night and the district would pick up the tab. Since I'd been on the fence about whether I wanted to teach in a regular classroom or a special-ed setting, the idea of leaving this option open excited me. Surely my mother would be happy for me. Surely.

"I might have this great teaching opportunity," I prompted.

"So you can do it!" she squeaked.

"What?"

"You can stay in our house?"

I put my forehead down on the cool surface of the table and reminded myself that I should never get my hopes up about my family's reactions to the things that mean the most to me.

I folded the letter from the attorney and tore it slowly in half.

"What was that noise?" my mother asked.

The wind being sucked from my sails, I wanted to say. Instead, I asked her if she still kept the green froggy cup on the shelf by the sink.

Chapter 3

Ultimately, I decided to sell off some of my furniture and cram the rest into my parents' garage, so less than two weeks later I found myself sitting on the hood of my car in front of my childhood home, peering down the street to watch for the moving truck.

It was a sunny morning, and the metal of the car reflected the heat back into my sit-bones in a way that felt almost therapeutic. I leaned back and tilted my face toward the sun, feeling spectacularly young. I was back in time at my parents' house. There were no responsibilities calling me down off the car. And all I had to do was wait. Wait for the moving truck. Wait for the Waxmans' realtor to call. And, since I had arranged to have my mail forwarded to me at my parents' address, wait for the letter from the Las Vegas school district to arrive.

My new cell phone was in my back pocket digging into my butt, so I took it out and placed it next to me. I had finally relented and bought a new phone, despite how furious I'd been at Horizon Wireless. I had vowed to myself I was done with them, but when faced with the fact that I was giving up my apartment, my address and my land line, I simply couldn't bear relinquishing my cell phone number.

What got me so angry in the first place was that Horizon refused to honor the warranty on my previous cell phone. It had stopped working when the connection for recharging it broke, and since it was only two months old I was confident Horizon would fix it for free or just give me a new one. But when I took it to their store, a technician looked into the little hole where the charger plugs in and told me the repair wasn't covered under the warranty.

"Why not?" I had asked.

"Physical damage isn't covered."

"Well, what kind of damage *is* covered?" I demanded. "*Emotional* damage?"

He shrugged, and I railed, insisting that the phone broke because it had a design flaw, not because it had been dropped or abused in any way, but he remained expressionless. I asked to speak to a manager, and the technician paged Mr. Delp, a young man who bore a striking resemblance to Oklahoma City bomber Timothy McVeigh. I took this as a bad sign. Delp examined the phone and said, "I'm sorry. Physical damage isn't covered."

"That seems to be the party line," I said.

"Excuse me?"

"Would it help if I told you the phone has been having self-esteem issues ever since the new iPhone came out," I said, trying to get him off script, "and was so emotionally distraught it tried to take its own life?"

"What?"

I was exasperated. "Look, instead of trying to rip me off, why don't you just tell me what you can do for me."

The terrorist doppelgänger then proceeded to try to sell me a more expensive phone and a pricier contract with fewer minutes than the one I already had, at which point I calmly explained that the only way I would buy a more expensive phone and sign a pricier contract with fewer minutes was if it included a two-month stay at the Tuscan Villa of a certain potbellied-pig-loving Hollywood hunk, all the Godiva chocolate truffles I could eat, and a free pass to scratch a key along the car doors of every member of the Horizon Wireless Board of Directors.

He wouldn't even negotiate.

Sadly, when circumstances forced me to relent and go back to the store, even the pricey offer they made was no longer available, and I was forced to buy a still more expensive phone. I consoled myself with the thought that it had so many features I could probably get it to cook me breakfast and wash my car, if only I could make my way through the instruction manual.

I touched my phone to make sure it was well balanced on the hood of the car. Didn't want to risk physical damage again, after all. I heard a child's voice shout, "Haley, slow down!" and looked up to see two helmeted girls on bikes pedal past me. As I watched them turn the corner and ride toward the front of the neighborhood— probably to the schoolyard where there was a huge playground—I remembered how frequently I made that same journey with Kenny Waxman, my next-door neighbor and constant companion for the first decade of my life. We didn't drift apart until some time in fourth grade, when boys decided that proximity to girls was a threat to their newly discovered masculinity. A few years later I developed breasts, and Kenny rematerialized. Whenever I walked Stephanie, a miniature schnauzer Clare and I named, Kenny seemed to be loitering outside his house. He pretended to see me by accident and would walk the dog with me in a noncommittal way, as if he wasn't really joining me, but relaying important pieces of information while moving. Walking backward with his hands thrust deep in the pockets of jeans, he'd fill me in on critical school gossip he couldn't believe I hadn't heard.

"Berkman's husband died," he said one day, referring to one of the eighth grade teachers. "Plowed his T-Bird into a tree."

"Really?"

"I can't believe you didn't know. Everyone was talking about it, even the teachers. Michael Vine said he probably did it on purpose so he wouldn't have to look at his wife's ugly face anymore."

I thought Michael Vine was one of the most obnoxious boys in the eighth grade and said so out loud.

"Yeah, he's pretty bad. But he's okay, I guess."

At thirteen, that kind of contradiction seemed perfectly logical.

"Still," he added, "too bad about the car, huh?" He smiled and looked at me to see if I'd laugh, which I did. Kenny could be pretty funny.

When we got back from the walk, he said good-bye and started to leave but stopped. He turned to face me, his hands still in his front pockets.

"Are you going to Sandi Silverman's party?"

I momentarily froze. It was a loaded question and we both knew it. Sandi Silverman was throwing a make-out party. That was one piece of gossip that hadn't escaped my notice.

Confused and self-conscious, I crouched down to give Stephanie a pat. I'd known this guy my entire life and suddenly a whole new feeling was coating my insides, like that commercial for cough syrup. Only I wasn't sick. At least I didn't think I was, though I was getting awfully flushed.

"I don't know," I said, trying to act casual. "Are you?"

"Yeah, I am." He moved his head like he was trying to shake his hair out of his eyes, only his hair wasn't in his eyes. "You should come."

And so I did. When I entered Sandi Silverman's living room

in a tight red shirt that outlined the apprentice bumps on my chest, I wasn't surprised to see Kenny sitting on a sofa across the room. His eyes went from my face to my little breasts and stopped there. Then his expression changed to something I didn't recognize at the time but would later identify as lust. Kenny was picturing me naked.

He looked back at my face and patted the sofa next to him, signaling me to come over. It occurred to me that he had come to the party early to claim the best make-out spot in the living room.

I looked around. Kids were already going at it in every corner. I knew that if I accepted his invitation to sit down I was saying yes. There probably wouldn't even be any conversation.

I wanted to kiss Kenny, but I was nervous. I'd only ever kissed two boys before, and that was during a game of spin the bottle over the summer. There'd been no embraces, no petting, and no drum thumping in my chest.

I tucked my hair behind my ears and crossed the room.

"Hi," I said, sitting down next to him.

"You look nice." He said it straight to my chest, his eyes narrow. He looked back at my face. "What do you have when you've got fifty thousand pounds of bananas in one hand and a hundred gallons of ice cream in the other?"

I shrugged.

"Very big hands."

It wasn't funny, so I didn't laugh. But it struck me that Clare would have. I wondered if I would ever be any good at flirting.

And then he was on top of me. It was so fast I didn't know what was happening. I expected a movie star kiss, long and languorous and romantic. What I got was a rigid tongue stuck deep in my mouth and a face pressed so hard against mine I could hardly breathe. And with all his weight on top of me, my lungs were compressed, so what little air I could manage to get in had no place to go. I tried to shift my position, but he had me too tightly pinned. He didn't respond to taps on his back, so I put my hands on his shoulders and pushed. He was unyielding.

When he finally came up for air and took his mouth off mine, I told him I couldn't breathe. He looked surprised to hear my voice, almost as if he didn't expect me to be there. He paused before reacting, like it took the information a few moments to travel up to his brain. Then he picked himself up a few inches and I took a big gasp of air into my lungs.

"Kiss me softer," I whispered. I didn't want any of his friends to hear. A boy could get teased endlessly if anyone heard a girl say something like that to him.

He did, and I thought nothing in the world could possibly feel that good. The bulge in his jeans pressed against my crotch, and it was as if everything I'd ever felt in my entire life was concentrated in that one spot below my pubic bone. I wanted it to go on forever.

Then I felt his hand on my stomach, inching its way toward my chest. A kind of panic set in. This was something I wasn't supposed to let a boy do. Not yet. I was a good girl, a straight-A student. I knew the kind of girls that let boys feel them up at our age. They cut classes and got Fs and giggled incessantly. If you passed by the assistant principal's office, you usually saw a couple of them slumped in chairs, nonchalant about the trouble they were in.

"Don't," I said.

Kenny didn't listen. His hand edged higher.

"No," I said, grabbing his wrist. But he fought me, and his hand moved up despite my pushing it back as hard as I could. I was shocked by how much stronger than me he was. No amount of force on my part could keep his hand down, and then it was there, on my new little breast, squeezing and squeezing as if it could yield juice.

I thrashed and fought, but Kenny was determined. I figured he had made up his mind that he would feel my breast at the party and nothing was going to deter him.

"Stop! Stop!" I said, this time wanting the others to hear. I thought another kid might come to my aid, but the only response was a few giggles and a boy imitating my cries. It sounded like the obnoxious Michael Vine.

How could Kenny do this to me? We had been friends forever. I pictured us sitting on his father's car talking for hours, and a sickness as pervasive as grief made me go slack. I felt like the couch would dematerialize beneath me and I'd get sucked away. I welcomed it.

Then I heard a shrill laugh from the next room. It sounded like Shelley Mosely, one of the stupidest girls in our class, and a fury rose up in me. I was not Shelley Mosely. I was *not*.

I started to struggle again, a new strength adding power to my muscles. I was Popeye and rage was my spinach. I gave Kenny the strongest shove I could and . . . nothing. He was so much stronger than me that even my supercharged anger wasn't enough.

That made me even madder. I bit down hard on Kenny's lower lip and wouldn't let go, even when I tasted blood. He pinched my arm hard and I released him.

His face loomed over mine with his hand covering his mouth.

"Oo crwazy bitch!" he said, unable to form the sounds with his injured mouth.

"Get off me!"

He said a word I couldn't understand. It sounded like *pood*, but I later came to realize it was *prude*, which he muttered under his breath the next time we passed in the hallways at school.

I glared back and spit out the vilest name I could think of calling him.

"Rapist."

And that was it. We established a ritual greeting that would continue through the rest of junior high school and keep our hostility strong.

By the tenth grade, Kenny had drifted into the sleaziest drug clique in our school. Somehow, that made me angrier. All that wasted potential. He was the smartest, funniest boy I knew, and he was burning up his brain cells and his life.

But I moved on and stopped fixating on Kenny Waxman. At least that's what I was telling myself. Truth was, I had merely channeled all that hurt and anger into pity, making Kenny a pathetic figure. I wondered if his parents were as tortured by his behavior as mine were by Joey's.

Then, late one Saturday night during my senior year, as I was walking the dog past the Waxmans' house, a car came screeching to a halt in front of me. Kenny stumbled out, and I heard the driver tell him to fuck himself.

"After I finish with your mother," Kenny said, and slammed the door shut. The car sped off.

I kept walking and tried to ignore Kenny, but he saw me and called out.

"Bev! I'm so gl-happy to see you."

His voice was louder than it needed to be. And it sounded strange to hear him say my name. He hadn't called me anything but *prude* for nearly five years.

"Hello, Kenny."

He planted his feet far apart for balance. "I'm totally fucked up," he said.

"I noticed." Stephanie's legs started to tremble in the cold night air and I stooped to pick her up.

"Vine's being a dick."

"Why doesn't that surprise me?"

Kenny explained that he was supposed to go back to Michael Vine's house for a few hours until whatever he was on wore off, but they had some big fight. He asked if he could hang out with me for a while.

"Please, Bev. My father'll kill me if I walk in this messed up."

The idea of helping Kenny appealed to me. I liked to think my powers of persuasion could convince him to change the course of his life and be more like me. So I said yes, and by the time we crossed the threshold into my house, I already had an image of a new, clean-cut Kenny sitting in the cafeteria with my friends, impressing everyone with his wit. He'd be happy and fulfilled. And naturally, he'd be forever grateful to me, his savior.

"I'll make coffee," I said, unclipping Stephanie's leash.

Kenny let himself drop onto the living room couch. "You are so great, Bev."

My younger sister, Joey, was spending the night at a friend's house, and everyone else was upstairs, asleep. So it was just me and Kenny, having coffee together like grown-ups. Or, the way it seemed to me at the time, like one grown-up and one screwed-up teenager.

He tried to explain how bad things were at home. "Sam's a lying piece of shit," he said, referring to his father. "Don't ever fucking trust that man. He doesn't give a crap about anybody but himself."

It was hard for me to reconcile the ordinary next-door neighbor I knew with the monster Kenny described. I assumed he was like my own father—caring, but wrapped up in his work.

"I'm sure he loves you, Kenny," I said.

He let out a wild laugh. "You live in la-la land, little girl."

I looked down into my coffee. Here I was, trying to be an adult, and Kenny still thought of me as a naive fool. A prude. At seventeen, I thought nothing could be further from the truth. I considered the fact that I was a virgin a mere technicality and had that callow confidence teenagers get, allowing me to believe I understood more about the world than just about anybody.

"I'm smarter than you think," I said.

Kenny cocked his head and squinted at me, his blue-green eyes rimmed in red. "I'm an asshole, aren't I?"

I knew he was thinking about how badly he had treated me at that party and all through junior high.

"Sometimes," I admitted.

"I just don't want to be like him," he said, and started to sniffle.

His father. I didn't know whether to tell him he *wasn't* like him, or that his dad really wasn't that bad. So I just put my hand on his back and told him it was okay.

He started to cry then and put his head on my shoulder. He smelled like pot and wine and Pert shampoo.

"I don't know why you're so good to me," he said. "I was such a prick."

I hadn't seen Kenny cry since we were practically babies, and even though I knew it was the drugs and alcohol, his weeping broke my heart. I gave him a reassuring hug.

"It's okay," I said. "It was a long time ago. And anyway, all junior high boys are assholes."

His body shook in such a way that he could have been laughing or crying. He said something muffled that I couldn't make out.

"What did you say?"

He sniffed hard. "I said you're perfect, Bev. You're a perfect girl. That's what you are."

"I'm not," I protested, but even as I said it, I understood that he wasn't saying I was flawless. He was saying he knew exactly who I was, and that he accepted everything about me. He was saying I was perfect for *him*.

I tried to speak, to tell him I felt the same way about him, but before I could get anything out, his mouth was on mine and his heavy body was pushing me down onto the couch.

Kenny had learned how to kiss since that first bumbling attempt in junior high, and I couldn't help but compare him to skinny Lewis Lambert, the boy I had just broken up with. Kenny's lips were soft and relaxed, his body broad and heavy. I felt like I was kissing a man, not a boy, and the sensation was luscious.

We kissed and kissed, getting hotter and hotter, until we heard Joey's key in the door. She tromped in unaware and went right past us into the kitchen.

"I thought you were sleeping at Anna's," I said, sitting up and straightening my shirt.

Joey stopped and turned around, looking slowly from me to Kenny and back to me. She laughed a deep, stupid laugh. She was stoned.

"The nerd and the turd," she said, and laughed again. She turned and went back into the kitchen.

"You really believed I was sleeping at Anna's?" she yelled from the kitchen.

I heard my parents' bed creak upstairs and was pretty sure Joey had woken them up.

The refrigerator door slammed shut, and Joey emerged from the kitchen with a bowl of cold macaroni and cheese, which she was picking at and shoving into her mouth with her fingers. "You've really got your head up your ass. You're as gullible as *they* are." She nodded toward the stairs to the bedrooms.

"I'd better go," Kenny said, and rose to leave.

I looked up at him. "You okay?"

He nodded. "I'll call you," his whispered.

As he opened the front door, Joey yelled out to him. "Hey turd, I know someone who can get you some killer hash if you're interested."

Kenny looked at me quickly, his face red with shame. I thought he was embarrassed by my sister's display, but realized later it was the color of betrayal. The offer of hash was more appealing than a relationship with me. As it turned out, the betrayal didn't stop there.

But that was eons ago. I shifted my weight on the hood of the car and opened my palms toward the sky as if the warmth of the sun could erase my past and lead me to a new future in a new place where none of this mattered. I hoped the letter from Principal Belita Perez would arrive soon.

I heard an engine and looked up to see if it was the moving truck, but it was just a car with a noisy transmission headed my way. My butt was starting to slip off the hood of the car, so I repositioned myself. Alas, I managed to accidentally hip check my cell phone, which skittered off the car into the middle of the street . . . right into the path of the oncoming car.

I jumped off the hood, but it was too late to run into the street and grab the phone without risking my own life. So I just stared, holding my breath, hoping the car might graze past it. But the driver's signal was on. He was pulling over and headed right for my phone.

I tried to scream "Stop!" but nothing came out, and I watched in horror as my shiny new state-of-the-art Horizon SlimBlade crunched beneath the front tire, then flipped over for a second assault by the rear.

The driver parked in front of the Waxmans' house. I took a deep breath, wondering if I'd be able to keep myself from going for his jugular even though he probably had no idea he'd driven over anything, let alone an insanely expensive piece of electronic equipment that could practically end hunger and bring peace to the planet. Then the door of the car opened and a broad-shouldered man got out.

I stopped and stared. He was blond. He was tan. He wore a loose white shirt rolled up at the sleeves and a familiar crooked smile that made my heart flip over like a squashed cell phone.

"Bev Bloomrosen," he said, as if I was the last person he expected to see sitting in front of my house.

I walked into the street to retrieve my damaged phone. Then I turned to face him.

"Kenny Waxman."

Chapter 4

"Jeez," he said. "You haven't changed a bit."

You have, I wanted to answer. His blue-green eyes were now framed by a bronze face and a body that looked carefully sculpted, machine-enhanced pectorals straining elegantly against the fabric of his shirt. He was handsome, sure, but it was instantly clear to me that his penchant for drugs had been replaced by an obsession with fitness. He had, I figured, become a shallow Los Angelino, his values shifting from self-immolation to self-worship. But his nose was still a bit too large for his face, so at least he hadn't given in to the Hollywood plastic surgery epidemic, which was sucking the humanity from perfectly good faces.

I thanked him for lying and went to shake his hand. He gave me a hug instead. His hair smelled like vanilla.

"I never lie," he said. "I'm much more likely to piss people off with my honesty."

"What are you doing here?" I tried to sound detached. I didn't want him to think he could charm me. "I thought you were in Los Angeles."

"I came in for business. I'm staying in the city but I promised Renee I'd help out with the house while I was in town."

Renee. Kenny hadn't quit the habit of referring to his parents by their first names. He looked at the mangled phone in my hand. "Did *I* do that?"

I nodded.

"You'll let me pay for it, of course."

"Don't worry about it," I said, wishing he'd be a prick about it so I could be angry with him.

"I know you'd rather stay mad," he said, "but I'm going to buy you another one."

How smug of him to think he could still read me so easily. That he was right chafed me even more.

Kenny went on to explain that he had spoken to a realtor who would be stopping by any minute with a couple that wanted to see the house. I folded my arms.

"I'll leave it to you, then," I said, annoyed that I hadn't been kept in the loop on this. What was I there for if someone else was taking care of the damned real estate matters?

"Wait," he grabbed my arm with his big bronze mitt. "Stick around. Make sure I behave myself."

"I don't seem to be very good at that," I blurted, and immediately wished I hadn't. Now he'd think he still had some meaning in my life.

Kenny, of course, wasn't about to let that slide by. He took a deep breath and stared hard at my face. I cringed.

"That was eighteen Yom Kippurs ago," he said, referring to the day Jews atone for their sins. "You think we can move on?"

I could have shrugged him off, pretending I didn't care, but he'd see through that. Besides, why should I let him off the hook? He'd kicked in my heart and never even gave a damn.

"Not everything has a statute of limitations," I said.

"You're as prissy as ever."

Screw you, I thought, but didn't want to give him the satisfaction of hearing me say it.

He put his arm around me and kissed the top of my head. I wanted to move away. I *meant* to move away. But it felt so heavenly to be leaning against him that something in me liquefied, which in turn short-circuited my under-insulated wiring.

"I missed you," he said.

I smelled his shirt. Dear God, did he wash it in pheromones?

"Let's go inside," he said softly.

"Inside?" I repeated, wondering if he meant it as a proposition. I was so flummoxed I couldn't trust my own perceptions.

"I want to make sure the place is presentable," he said.

I took a step back and regained my wits. "I'd, *uh* . . . better wait here for the moving truck," I said. No sense putting myself in a position where my hormones could get the better of me.

"Isn't this the whole reason you're here—to help sell the house?"

He played the responsibility card. No fair. I followed him into the house, where everything looked still and vacant, as if the Waxmans had been living there going about their business one second and vanished the next. Then I noticed a coating of dust on the surfaces and a musty smell in the air.

"Open the windows," I said, and went into the kitchen to look for something to dust with.

"I meant to take a ride over here during the week to do this," I explained as I wiped down the countertop. "But I got a little behind."

He looked at my backside. "That's true," he said, stroking his face, "but you make up for it with your sparkling personality."

I stifled a laugh. "Save that for your TV show." I had read

that Kenny was writing for an awful situation comedy about a teenaged robot.

"If I ever wrote something that funny they would have fired me instantly."

"Oh, right. I forgot. You Burbank types are all frustrated geniuses muzzled by the corporate machine."

"Not me. I'm thrilled to be surrounded by moronic syco-phants who can suck all the creativity from a room faster than you can say 'target demographics.'" He opened a cabinet and retrieved a bottle of glass cleaner, which he sprayed on the bay window. "What about you? I heard you're going to be a teacher. I think that's perfect for you."

Did he mean for a priggish, uptight prude like me? Or was he being genuine? I looked over to try to read his face, but his back was to me.

"Your parents must be proud," he added.

"Ha."

He turned to look at me, scratching his chin as if it would help him understand. "What do *they* think you should be doing?"

"I don't know. Marrying a rich guy like Clare did? Perfect-ing nuclear fusion?"

"There's the rub. If you'd been a fuckup in high school like I was, they'd just be happy you were pursuing a career that didn't have its own section in the penal code."

I took the Windex from Kenny and sprayed the Formica kitchen table. "How's your father?" I asked as I wiped it clean. My parents had told me that Kenny's father, Sam, had rapidly progressing Alzheimer's disease, and I wondered if he was aware that his son had emerged from his adolescent rebellion to become a successful adult. I was curious about Kenny's insights but also wanted to know if he still hated the man.

"He has more bad days than good ones now," he said.

"I'm sorry."

"Couldn't have happened to a nicer guy."

And there it was.

"How are *your* parents?" he asked.

"Same as always," I said, and braced myself, sure he was leading up to a question about Joey. I wouldn't have minded it coming from someone else. In fact, everyone asked about Joey. But I didn't even want to hear Kenny say her name.

"And the rest of the gang?"

I have to admit, the guy had good instincts.

"Clare is Clare," I said. "She has the whole perfect soccer mom life going on." I paused, deciding whether or not I should say something about Joey. I glanced over at him. He was silent, trying to scrape something off the bottom of the window with his fingernail. Outside, the dogwood tree was in full bloom.

"I'll dust the table in the foyer," I said, and walked out of the room.

He followed after me. "Bev," he said, putting a hand on my shoulder.

I knew something heavy was coming and didn't want to deal with it. I kept my back to him and started dusting the hall table.

"I don't think I ever apologized to you," he said.

"You have nothing to apologize for." I paused. Why were we even talking about something that happened so long ago? "I had no claims on you."

That much, I figured, was true. I had no reason to think that passion in my living room meant anything. He was stoned and drunk and I was a warm body next to him. So why did I still feel so enraged over the scene I walked in on several days later in Joey's bedroom?

"But you were hurt."

"Don't flatter yourself."

Kenny sighed. "Here's the thing. I was a self-destructive kid. My impulse was to run the other way from anything that could possibly be good for me. You understand?"

Charity. *Ugh.* I noticed a cobweb above the mirror and flicked it with the rag. I saw his reflection behind me, waiting.

Why did he need my forgiveness? So he could go back to his Hollywood life telling himself he was a wonderful guy, albeit with a colorful past? I didn't think he deserved such a squeaky clean slate. I turned to face him.

"What do you *want* from me?"

"I just don't want you to be angry with me anymore."

"Is that what you're worried about? That I'm angry with you? I had ten melodramatic moments over Kenny Waxman when I was seventeen years old. It's water under the bridge." There. Not forgiveness. Indifference.

He folded his arms and squinted as if he wasn't buying it. I turned toward the front of the house and heard a noise from outside.

"Is that a car door?" I asked.

Kenny went to the window by the front door and looked out. "Two cars," he said. "The first one's the realtor, I think. Looks like the buyers followed behind." He paused. "Wuh-oh."

"What's the matter?"

"This could be a problem."

I went to the window to see. A very tiny man and woman were emerging from the car, which had to have been specially equipped for such a small driver.

"Midgets," Kenny said.

"Little people," I corrected.

"This is bad," he said. "Very, very bad."

"Why?"

"I'm an impaired human being, Bev. My PC switch is stuck in the off position. I'm in deep trouble."

"Nonsense."

"I feel about ten different jokes threatening to erupt."

"You may *not*." I used my most teacherlike voice.

"It's beyond my control."

"Kenny, look at me." I grabbed him by the shoulders and stared deep into his eyes like I was talking him down from a drug high. "Dignity and respect, okay? They deserve it as much as anyone else."

"But they're so *little*," he protested.

I tried my best to frown in disapproval. How awful for these people if this big, handsome lug of a guy made jokes at their expense.

"Please," he beseeched. "Just one *Wizard of Oz* joke?"

"No," I said firmly, like I was dealing with a child.

"You mean I can't even ask the realtor if she's the good witch or the bad witch?"

The doorbell rang. I wagged my finger in his face as a warning and opened the door.

The realtor introduced herself as Linda Klein, and the couple as Mr. and Mrs. Goodwin. The wife had warm blue eyes that nearly matched the turquoise stones in her hammered silver necklace. The husband had longish hair and a firm handshake.

Kenny called the realtor *Glenda*, and I jabbed him with my elbow.

After they looked around the house, opening and closing cabinet and closet doors, Linda Klein took them outside to look around the property. As soon as they shut the door behind them, I turned to Kenny.

"Don't blow this," I said. "They seem interested."

"You're being short with me."

"Not funny."

"Think I can convince them the linen closet is a fourth bedroom?"

"Stop it."

"If they make an offer, can I tell them they're a little low?"

"Are you through?"

"Baby, I'm just warming up."

I told him to sit down and keep his mouth shut and went to the kitchen window to watch the scene outside. Mr. Goodwin seemed to be looking into the crawl space under the house, frowning.

"He's not happy," I said.

Kenny looked up. "Which one is he, then?"

I shook my head and looked back at the scene outside. I remembered playing in that yard when we were young. Kenny and I would hide in the bushes or the shed, and his house-keeper, Lydia, would look around calling our names as if she couldn't find us. It was obvious that she knew where we were, and that it was all a big game of pretend. When she got to our hiding spot we'd pop out and shout, and Lydia would feign surprise. We adored her.

Inside, she gave us oatmeal cookies drenched in chocolate syrup—her own invention—and would laugh at how messy we got. She wore red lipstick and had teeth like a movie star, but her hair always struck me as an unfortunate mess. I would look up at Lydia as she wiped my face, thinking how pretty she'd look if she went to the beauty parlor like my mom.

I remembered being in Kenny's backyard one sticky summer afternoon when we were a little older—maybe eleven or twelve. There was a group of us from the neighborhood, bored as hell. Too old for kid games but too young for any real flirting, we fell into a game of tag almost nostalgically. I got thirsty after a while and wandered into the kitchen for a drink of water. An air conditioner in the window blasted cold air into the room, drying my sweat too quickly and covering my flesh with goose bumps.

Lydia sat at the table with a pen in her hand, staring at a piece of paper.

"Writing your mom?" I asked, rubbing down the skin on my arms. I knew she had family in Hungary and wrote to them often.

"Not today, my dear. Today I write to my lawyer who gets me green card, but *ach!* I have much trouble to write English."

"Can I help?"

"Maybe, yes." She picked up the page and read from it. "*Today your letter is get to me.* Is that right?"

"Not exactly," I said. "Just say, 'I got your letter today.'"

She smacked her head. "Oh yes! I make me so difficult when I write English. I need more power of the brain."

"You're doing fine," I said. "Your English gets better all the time. What else do you need to tell him?"

"I need to tell that yes, I will to be in court on September 15 as he says, no problem."

I asked her to show me the letter from the lawyer so I could be sure she understood what he was saying, and then I helped her compose the rest of her very simple message. It was fun showing a grown-up what to do, and I liked seeing her write the sentences in her exotic European handwriting. When we were finished she said, "You are natural teacher, Beverly Bloomrosen," and kissed me on the forehead. She seemed so sincere that it warmed me to my toes.

Still, as lovely as it was to know Lydia thought I had a special talent, I couldn't completely let it in. At eleven, I wasn't yet in my arty phase, but the throes of an Electra complex. I thought my father was a god then, and wondered if I could grow up to be a doctor like him. I wasn't completely confident

I would be able to shed my fear of needles and send it off to Goodwill like the clothes and shoes I had outgrown, but I liked telling adults I was going to be a doctor, and saying it with conviction. They were always so impressed. Except for Lydia, that is.

"I'm going to be a doctor," I said.

Lydia folded her letter in thirds and slid it into an envelope. "Doctor is good," she said as she licked the seal, "but teacher is good also, no?"

I wondered if being a teacher had more prestige in Hungary than it did here. I knew a lot of kids who went around saying they wanted to be a teacher when they grew up. Kids who were, in my opinion, pretty unimaginative. Of course, they were doing the same thing I was—trying to impress grown-ups. But they got it wrong. Saying you wanted to be a teacher didn't elicit much more than a pat on the head and a condescending, "Very nice." But saying you wanted to be a doctor made them look at you differently.

How easily this immature need to impress later gave way to my plans to be an artist. I sighed, trying to suppress my shame over wasting so many years of my life pursuing the wrong dream for the wrong reason. It was so obvious to Kenny's housekeeper that I was meant to be a teacher. Why on earth did it take me so long to come to the same conclusion?

"Whatever happened to Lydia?" I asked Kenny.

He shrugged. "They told me she went to work for a family in New Jersey. We never heard from her again."

"That must have hurt."

"I *still* think about her. It was never the same after she left."

"I wonder why she didn't keep in touch."

"That's the weird thing," he said. "When she lived with us, she gave me a handmade card for every birthday, every holiday. I treasured them, kept them in this special shoebox I never threw out. In fact, I bet it's still under my bed. But then when she left, nothing. Not a call, a card, a single letter."

He looked sad, as if the old pain was so close to the surface it didn't take more than the lightest tap for it to come bobbing into view. Feeling an urge to comfort him, I stepped forward, but the back door opened and Mr. Goodwin emerged, telling the realtor he thought there was a lot to like in this house. Mrs. Goodwin agreed but added that she thought it was "a little small."

I took a step back and stared into Kenny's eyes with a stern *don't-you-dare* look. He put his hands up as if to say, *I'm not even touching it.*

The realtor approached me. "Mr. Goodwin noticed a rip in the screen door and a broken gutter," she said, looking down at her clipboard. "Also, there's some sort of industrial drum in the crawl space out back. Looks like it's been there for years."

"It has," Kenny said. "That thing's been under the house since the extension was built."

"Do you know what's in it?" the realtor asked.

Kenny shrugged. "I think some contractor left it there. It's so heavy no one's bothered to remove it."

The realtor leaned toward me as if imparting some special secret. "It really *should* be discarded," she said.

I nodded. "I'll see what I can do."

As the Goodwins and the realtor got ready to leave, Kenny stood and put his arm around me like we were husband and wife. Mrs. Goodwin turned and asked me if I could tell them how to get to the nearest supermarket.

Kenny put his mouth to my ear and whispered, "Tell her to follow the yellow brick road."

Chapter 5

"How does he look?" Clare asked as she turned the giant page of a wallpaper sample book. We were in a home decorating store looking at patterns for her daughter's bedroom.

I pictured the smile on Kenny's face when his tan, broad-shouldered self emerged from his car, sun-streaked hair reflecting the light like some corny shampoo commercial. I tried to concentrate on his large nose, still crooked from a baseball he took to the face in a Little League game. I did not want to be seduced by his looks. Or his charm. Or the feel of his warm breath on my ear when he leaned in close and whispered to me.

"Well?" she nudged. "Is he still—"

"Very L.A.," I interrupted.

"Handsome?"

"I hadn't noticed."

"Liar."

"Stop playing matchmaker," I said. "One, he's not my type. Two, he lives in California and three . . ." I paused to think.

"What's three?"

"Three is I can't stand him. Can we change the subject?"

My sister closed the book with a thud and dropped it into

her mounting rejection pile. She opened another wallpaper book and sighed. "They're all so precious, you know? Maybe we're looking in the wrong category."

I stared down at the page in front of me, which had a whimsical pattern of monkeys with slightly grotesque faces. What could this artist have been thinking? It grated on my nerves, already worn thin by Clare's stupidity. Did she remember *nothing*?

"Besides," I said, "he fucked Joey."

"I thought you didn't want to talk about it."

I smacked the page in front of me. "Don't they realize it's stuff like this that gives kids nightmares?" I slammed the book closed, furious at myself for not being able to get the hell over something that happened so damned long ago. After all, I wasn't seventeen anymore, so what difference did it make? I'd been through a dozen boyfriends, one husband, four apartments, six cell phones, and at least fifteen pairs of sneakers since then. Why was Kenny Waxman still a pebble in my shoe?

Clare stared at me, her eyes looking as if they were about to spring a leak.

"I'm sorry," I said. "I guess I'm just too agitated for this right now."

"We can do this another time." Her voice had that cheery but strained sound she used when trying to hide her distress. I tried to see if she was actually crying, but she put her head down as she rummaged through her purse. Clearly, she didn't want me to see her face. Guilt tugged at my abdominals.

I opened the book again. "No, it's fine. Let's just get through these piles at least."

Clare and I had so little in common that accompanying her on this errand seemed like one of the few things we could do together. I figured I could apply my sense of aesthetics—such as it was—toward helping her make a wallpaper decision for Sophie's bedroom. When I thought about it, though, Clare was the one with an eye for decorating. I was just tagging along.

"Sorry I'm so edgy," I said. "I guess I'm just stressed waiting to hear about . . ."

"About what?"

I bypassed the upsetting page with the grotesque monkeys and flipped to the back half of the book, where I found a pattern with wavy yellow stripes against a white background. I brought my face closer to the stripes and realized they were textured in a bricklike pattern.

"A new job I interviewed for."

"A teaching job?"

"Of course a teaching job. For God's sake, Clare. Did you think I'd lost interest after spending two years getting my master's?"

"Don't get snippy. I'm just asking."

I turned the page and found the same wavy pattern but in emerald green. I ran my fingers along the page to feel the texture of the softly raised stripes. "Thing is," I said, "it's in Las Vegas."

"What?"

"Don't get mad."

"You're moving to Las Vegas? Why?"

"It's a great opportunity."

She slammed her wallpaper book closed. "You want to get away from us. You think it's your family's fault that you're . . ." She paused. I turned and stared and saw pink rise up in her face.

"That I'm what?" I said. "That I'm a loser?"

"I didn't say that."

"You were about to."

"Bev, please. Think about this. You'd be so lonely out there. Everyone you know is here."

Exactly, I thought. My chance to get a fresh start in a world where everyone sees me a bright and dedicated teacher, instead of as a lifetime of wasted potential.

Admittedly, the whole concept of the Fresh Start was like an addiction for me. A lot of people are terrified by change—or at least uncomfortable with it. But to me it's exhilarating. The idea of changing jobs or moving is like staring at a clean canvas I can paint any way I want. It's one of the reasons being a teacher is such a perfect career for me. The Fresh Start is built in, a permanent fixture. Every year it's a new sea of faces—scared or eager, silly or serious, bright or challenged—each needing something different from me.

And since I was taking this major step, I wanted the cleanest canvas I could find. Staying in New York would mean layering over my past. Moving away was my shot at creating a bright new life for myself. And what better place to do that than the city that tears down its past every few years and starts anew?

"I've thought about it tons," I said to Clare. "And besides, nothing's definite. I interviewed a couple of weeks ago and I'm waiting to hear."

"And if it doesn't come through?"

I flipped more pages in the wallpaper book and came to a section of boys' room wallpapers, all race cars and skateboards with jaunty stripes. I closed the book and pushed it aside.

"I have other options," I said.

She bit her lip, and I sensed that she didn't quite believe me, so I told her about my fallback position. I had been offered a job at the school in Queens where I did my student teaching. It was local—only about a half hour away from where we sat—and

I worried that she would root for me to take it, possibly even hope that the Las Vegas position wouldn't come through.

Clare's eyes widened. "Oh?"

"The art teacher is leaving next year," I said, "and the principal thinks I'd be perfect." Even as I said it, I realized Clare would think so too, so I quickly explained that it felt like some ludicrous compromise of trying to blend my old interests with my new ones. I wanted this fresh start to be completely separate from my artistic ambitions. Plus, I wanted to be a *teacher* teacher, with a classroom and a blackboard (or the high-tech equivalent) and the opportunity to create my own lessons.

Of course, there were things about the art teacher job that appealed to me too. I loved the way kids tended to open up when they were engaged in something tactile, and I enjoyed coming up with projects that would stimulate their creativity. Plus the Queens school offered the kind of diverse population I had always envisioned myself teaching. But the idea of moving away and starting anew tipped the scales heavily toward the job in Vegas. Surely, the art teacher position would look to my family like yet another halfhearted career choice, and I'd have to bear the burden of their disapproval. My self-esteem just wasn't up to it.

"The letter from Las Vegas better arrive soon," I said to Clare, "because the principal in Queens is going to want an answer on the art teacher job."

I pulled another wallpaper book from the pile and opened it. A few pages in I found a girlish floral pattern that was more jewel-toned than the muted Monet-inspired palette of all the other florals, and I thought it had a lot of life. I showed it to Clare.

"Not half bad," she said.

I pointed to a light coral in one of the flower petals. "You could pick that up in the carpeting."

She shook her head and pointed to a darker shade, more orange-red than coral. "*That* would be the carpet color."

Damn if she wasn't right.

The door opened and an older woman entered the store—a neighbor who had lived down the block from us for years.

"Look," I whispered to Clare, "that's Mrs. Bianco."

Clare eyed her and grimaced. "*Ick!* She looks like an *oven* mitt."

I stifled a laugh. Mrs. Bianco wore a bright blue blouse that was quilted in horizontal lines.

"A Coke says she asks about Joey first," I whispered.

Long ago, Clare and I had come to the realization that there were two kinds of people from our past—those who asked about Joey first and those who asked about our parents. Our younger sister had been enormously famous for about fifteen minutes, when the rock band she was the lead singer for had a Top 40 hit. They were never able to re-create their success, and the band succumbed to infighting and drugs. Clare and I knew it was a typical one-hit wonder story, but to our small Long Island town it was a big deal indeed. And the power of celebrity was so strong that even people who knew us as kids would get this glazed-over look in their eyes when they asked about Joey, as if just brushing that close to fame delivered them someplace transcendent.

"Hello, Mrs. Bianco!" Clare called.

Mrs. Bianco emitted a small gasp and approached. "Helen," she corrected, the smoker's rasp of her voice more gravelly than ever. "Please. You make me feel like an old lady."

"Oh, not with those legs," Clare said, smiling.

God, but she was charming. Clare wore social graces like a silk evening gown. If I tried the same thing, I'd just trip over the hem.

Mrs. Bianco giggled girlishly and said she wished Mr. Bianco thought so. Then it came. "How are you, girls? How's Joey?" Her eyes glassed over in that familiar way.

Clare banged me with her knee, and then gave Mrs. Bianco—*Helen*—the bare facts we gave everyone, saying that Joey had given up music for a few years but was now thinking about getting back into it. What she left out was that for nearly a decade Joey had done nothing but get stoned and go from living with one loser boyfriend to another. After one of her band members, Tyrone, died from an overdose, she decided it was time to do something that would decrease her chances of killing herself. So she checked into rehab and got off everything. Now she had a part-time job working in a recording studio and, we assumed, ambitions to get back into singing.

Mrs. Bianco had probably heard at least some of the rumors about our little sister's problems, but she was polite enough to simply say it was great to see us, and to please send her regards to Joey.

"Mom and Dad are fine, by the way," I whispered to Clare as Mrs. Bianco walked away. "Thanks for asking."

When we finished looking at wallpaper books, Clare drove me home. I wanted to be sure I was there when the gardener arrived, because I needed to talk to him about moving the Waxmans' industrial drum to the curb. On the way there, though, it started to drizzle, and Clare wondered aloud if he would even show up.

As we rounded the corner past the Waxmans' house, I noticed that the front door was open and told Clare to pull over. I didn't see a car parked out front and couldn't imagine who was inside.

"I'd better go investigate," I said, descending to terra firma from Clare's massive SUV.

My sister followed behind me. I peered through the screen

door and she pressed her face against the rippled glass of the sidelight window.

"See anything?" she asked.

"No, but I think I hear music." I opened the door. "Hello?" I called.

No one answered.

"Could it be Kenny?" Clare asked.

I shrugged.

"Maybe we should call the police."

"It's likely just a realtor," I said. "Kenny probably gave someone the key and never told me."

I stepped inside and noticed that the music seemed to be coming from a radio in the kitchen. As I cautiously approached, I wondered if Clare was right about calling the police. What if there was someone dangerous in the kitchen, someone armed?

Though my heartbeat raced as I neared the kitchen with Clare following behind, it pleased me that I was being the brave one. It was a powerful feeling. But it also occurred to me that I could wind up being the dead one.

When I reached the doorway, I stopped. A lone slim figure with bouncing blond curls stood leaning against the counter, her hand deep inside a box of Cheerios.

"Was the porridge too hot?" I asked.

Chapter 6

Joey extricated her hand from the Cheerios and wiped it on her pants. "Hi, Bev." She looked past me. "Clare, what are you doing here?"

"What are *you* doing here?" Clare asked.

"I had some time to kill and thought I'd come visit Bev," she said. "I was sitting outside waiting for her to come home and it started to rain. I didn't have a key to get into our house, but I remembered that the Waxmans kept a key under the hammock stand out back, and voilà. You guys want some Cheerios?"

"You can't just go breaking into people's houses and eating their food," Clare said.

"Please," Joey tsked. "It's not *people's* houses. It's the Waxmans'. We're practically family."

At that point I could have asked about incest, considering what she and Kenny were doing that day in her bedroom, but fighting with Joey was one of my least favorite activities. Even when I won arguments with her, I managed to feel like I'd lost. It was the way she had of shrugging off any topic as if you had to be an idiot to even care.

"You look good, Joey," Clare said.

And she did. Being off drugs had brought color back to her

face and life back to her eyes, which were catching the room's light and reflecting it back. She had that smug look again, like she knew this great joke she'd share with you if she decided you measured up. I figured that was part of her sex appeal; men always wanted to be admitted to that club. No doubt Kenny would still find her hot as hell, and I wondered what would have happened if Joey had been the one to run into him instead of me. Would they have ripped each other's clothes off and gone at it?

"You do look good," I agreed.

"Gained five pounds," Joey boasted, flexing her scrawny bicep as if it would prove how hearty she was.

I noticed that Clare looked grim. She'd been struggling with her weight her entire adult life, and often said how unfair it was that her sisters were naturally slim, practically assless. Joey seemed oblivious to Clare's anguish, and I couldn't help wondering if it was more passive-aggressive than genuinely clueless. Joey often managed to get in some digs with what passed for innocence.

"Mrs. Bianco says hello," I told her.

"Helen? *Hunh.* She used to scream that I would get my *comeuppance.*"

"You used to get high in her backyard," I said. "What did you expect?"

"Never. I got high with Maryanne Jackman next door and we would throw our burned-out roaches over the fence into her yard. It was hilarious."

I rolled my eyes. "Good times."

A crack of thunder interrupted our conversation and Clare looked out the window. Rain poured from the roof in sheets. "No way the gardener is coming today," she said.

"Figures," I said, frustrated that I couldn't get that out of the way.

Joey asked what the big deal was about the gardener, and I explained about moving the industrial drum to the curb for garbage pickup.

"I bet we could do it," Joey said. "The three of us together."

"Too heavy," I said.

"And it's pouring," Clare added.

Joey shrugged. "It's only water."

"What about the lightning?" Clare said. "And the thunder?"

"Storm's moving away," I said.

"Remember Lydia?" Joey asked. "Remember how she used to say, 'There's no time like the presents'?"

I smiled, remembering her gentle, if slightly ungrammatical, wisdom. "I think she was the only grown-up who listened to what we had to say."

Clare folded her arms. "Then let Lydia move the damn drum in the rain."

Joey flashed me her wicked grin, grabbed my hand, and headed for the back door. Her passion for fun was infectious, and giddiness tickled at me as I pulled Clare along the way.

"Forget it!" Clare said, resisting. "I'm wearing new shoes."

I tugged harder at her hand. "You're *always* wearing new shoes. C'mon. Marc will buy you another pair."

"At least let me find an umbrella."

And so it was that the three of us stood bent at the waist, under the umbrella Clare held, staring into the crawl space beneath the Waxmans' house. I said that if we went under there and toppled the drum onto its side, we'd probably be able to roll it out. Clare refused to get on her knees, as she was wearing linen pants that she insisted cost more than two hundred dollars. Joey, of course, was game.

So Clare held her umbrella and watched as Joey and I went

to work. We got on our hands and knees and crawled under the house, where it smelled musty and squirrelly and felt uncomfortably tight. It made me understand the foreboding feel of claustrophobia. Even though I knew it couldn't happen, I felt like we'd run out of oxygen any minute. I wanted to get out of there *fast*.

Toppling the thing wasn't as easy as I thought. It was hard to get leverage when we were both on our knees. Joey and I put our hands against the top of the drum and shoved with all our might. I was just about to demand that Clare come in and help us when the drum finally went down with a thump and a slosh, letting us know the thing was filled with liquid. The lid held on tight.

We rolled it out, and when we at last cleared the bottom of the house, I rose to take some air into my lungs and loosen the tightness in my chest.

"Your turn," I said to Clare. "I'll hold the umbrella for a while."

Instead of getting on her knees, Clare bent over at the waist so she wouldn't be dragging her pants through the grass. Good thing too, because in another five feet they would have to push the barrel through an oval of earth that had once been Mr. Waxman's tomato garden, but which was now simply a huge, soupy mud puddle.

Clare stopped when they got to it.

"Wait a minute," she said. "I'm not going through that. I'll ruin my shoes."

"Your shoes are already ruined," I said.

"And look," she said, holding up an index finger. "I broke a nail."

I rolled my eyes. "Call 911."

She tried to grab the umbrella. "You take over for a while," she said.

I held it back out of her reach. "No, I'll take over for Joey if she wants, but you have to pull your weight."

"Why don't you two princesses go inside for a cup of tea and I'll just do it myself," Joey said as she pushed.

"You're going to let her do it all alone?" I asked Clare.

"Are you?"

"Screw you," I said to Clare, and handed her the umbrella so I could help Joey get the drum through the mud. In a huff, Clare walked over to Joey's side to hold the umbrella over the two of them. The next thing I knew, the umbrella went flying through the air, carried by the wind over my head. Clare made an effort to reach it and then, in what seemed like slow motion because I anticipated the whole thing but could do nothing to stop it, she tripped over Joey's foot, landing belly first into the mud.

Joey and I locked eyes, momentarily horrified.

"Oh my God!" Clare said, "I'm ruined!" She picked herself up and stood, dark mud covering her expensive blouse and pants from top to bottom. It dripped in slow plops to the ground.

"*Ew,*" she said, looking down. "This is *so* not funny."

Joey and I locked glances and then simultaneously exploded with laughter.

"Stop it!" Clare cried.

That just made it funnier. We collapsed into one another.

"You two are so immature," Clare insisted, but even as she said it, I saw a smile playing around her lips as she finished the sentence. She looked down at her clothes, pulling the sticky shirt away from her body. "I guess I do look kind of ridiculous," she said.

That's when Joey straightened herself out and took several steps back.

"What are you doing?" I asked, but it became evident soon

enough. Joey took a running start and then dove into the mud like a baseball player sliding into first base.

"Try it," she said, looking up at me.

I backed off. "No way."

But Joey shot Clare a conspiratorial grin, and it was clear I had no choice in the matter.

Chapter 7

After getting the industrial drum to the curb, I told my sisters we should go straight back to our house to get showered and changed, provided they didn't mind borrowing my clothes. Clare insisted on retrieving our handbags first, so we went into the mudroom in the back of the Waxmans' house and stopped.

"Now what?" I said. "We can't exactly go traipsing through the house like this. Renee used to have a heart attack if we wore our shoes past the front door. This would kill her."

"No worries," Joey said, stripping to her underwear faster than most people could say hello. "I'll get the handbags. You wait here."

"Get us some towels too," Clare said.

Joey nodded, left her soaked clothes and shoes in a pile on the floor, and ran upstairs toward the linen closet.

"You're not going to want to get back into those muddy things!" Clare shouted after her. "So find something to wear while you're up there—borrow something of Renee's!"

Clare turned to me, her face looking lovely even smudged in black mud. In fact, the contrast of her glamorous cheekbones against the gritty filth was striking. And the colors were an inspiration, as if all the browns and blacks of the scene paid homage to her cinnamon irises, standing out against the white of her eyes. Suddenly, I had an itch I hadn't felt in a long time. The itch to paint, to capture a very specific aesthetic thought on canvas. I wondered if I could experiment with transposing the concept that beauty is only skin deep by putting the grotesque on the surface and letting beauty shine through from beneath, turning the whole into something glorious. Had that already been done? Probably. And anyway, I wasn't nearly talented enough to pull it off, so it would be a useless exercise.

"I need to ask you a favor," Clare said. "I was about to bring it up in the store, but the sight of Mrs. Bianco in that oven mitt knocked it out of my head."

"Shoot."

She held a tip of hair in front of her face and shook off the mud. "You can say no. I don't mean to put you on the spot."

"Just spit it out."

"I enrolled in a continuing-ed class this summer. Modern American Lit. But it's only offered in the afternoon and I'll need someone to watch Dylan and Sophie for a few hours."

"What about Marta?" I asked, referring to her Salvadoran housekeeper.

"She's taking a little time off," Clare explained. "Next week she's going back to South America to visit her family."

I could have explained to Clare that she got Marta's continent wrong—that El Salvador is in Central America, which is part of North America. I sensed, however, that it was a bad time to correct her, and let it go.

"Continuing ed? American Lit? Where did this come from?"

"You think my life is all PTA luncheons and shopping."

"It isn't?"

Clare's lower jaw tensed. "If you can't do it, I understand. I can probably hire a sitter."

I sighed, guilty. Why was it so hard to predict when Clare would institute her zero-tolerance policy for good-natured teasing?

"No, I'd love to do it for you, Clare. And you know how I feel about your kids."

She thanked me and got busy trying to rub the mud from her hands.

I folded my arms and looked at her. As far as I could remember, Clare never showed any interest in literature beyond keeping abreast of the trendiest bestsellers. Something was going on that she didn't want to tell me about. Why the sudden desire to broaden her horizons?

"Everything okay at home?" I asked.

"Fine! Why does there have to be a problem for me to want to take a lit class? You think you're the only one in this family with an IQ for God's sake."

I apologized and changed the subject, saying I thought our little sister was doing well. She agreed that Joey seemed clean and on track. We both wondered when we could stop worrying that she'd backslide and wind up on drugs again. Those dark days were so recent, so fresh, that it was hard not to feel terror at the thought of revisiting them. Joey herself said it was by the grace of God that she wasn't the one who wound up dead on the floor of a friend's house, a truth that followed us around like a storm cloud on a string.

A few minutes later we heard Joey's quick footsteps coming back down the stairs, accompanied by a curious rustling sound.

In a moment, she was at the door of the mudroom, no longer in her underwear. My voice caught in my throat as I took in what she was wearing: a rose-colored ball gown, with a glittery beaded bodice and billowing skirt.

"Joey!" I said. "For heaven's sake!"

She seemed quite pleased with herself. "Isn't this a pisser?" She threw towels to me and Clare, then twirled around.

"That's the gown Renee wore to Kenny's bar mitzvah," Clare said as she wiped the mud off her face. "Why on earth did you put that on?"

"I can't believe you remember where she wore it," Joey said.

Clare rolled her eyes. "Who could forget? It was ridiculous then and it's ridiculous now. Looks like a cheesy pink wedding gown. Take it off, Joey."

"But I *like* it," she whined.

"Hate to be a . . . *er* . . . stick-in-the-mud," I offered, wiping off my own face, "but you really *shouldn't* be wearing Renee's couture gown."

Clare snorted and rolled her eyes. "Couture, right."

"Fine," Joey said, all attitude. "Hold this." She planted a box of tampons in my hand and started to unzip the dress.

"You have your period?" I asked.

"No." Joey dropped the gown to the floor and stepped out of it. "I found that in Renee's lingerie drawer and knew she had to be hiding something in it."

"How did you know that?" I asked.

Joey stood with her hands on her hips, more comfortable in a skimpy bra and panties than most people are fully dressed. "Please," she said. "Renee hasn't had her period in years. Why would she still have a tampon box?"

"Your mind works in mysterious ways," Clare said.

"All those years as a druggie," Joey explained. "I spent a lot of time thinking up hiding places for my stash." She pulled the box from my hand and opened the lid. "See?" she said, showing us the contents. "Looks like a letter or something."

"Put it back," I said.

"*Nuh-uh*," Joey said. "No way. Not until I've read it."

"Joey," I said, trying to grab the box from her.

She turned her back to me and extracted a thin blue page that looked like it had been folded and refolded many times. "It *is* a letter!" she exclaimed, staring at it. *"Dearest Samuel,"* she stopped and looked over her shoulder at Clare and me, her mouth wide open. "A love letter to her husband!"

"Samuel?" I said. "But Mrs. Waxman always called him Sam or Sammy."

"Maybe it's not from her," Clare said, moving toward Joey and looking over her shoulder. "Maybe Mr. Waxman had a *lover.*"

"C'mon, put it away," I said. "This is none of our business."

"If you don't want to hear it, go stand in another room," Clare said. "I *have* to know what this says."

I tsked and crossed my arms. This was wrong, a terrible invasion of privacy. But if Clare and Joey were going to hear the letter, I sure as hell wasn't going to miss it.

"Get on with it," I said to Joey.

She read, *"Today I am happy because I know that you love me. If we cannot be together, God has His will and I have grace so accept. Your love is precious gift I will forever keep. In this life, we can only be happy if we open our hearts to know what is a blessing."* Joey looked up at us. "Philosophical," she commented, nodding in assent, and continued reading. *"As maybe you guess, God has given me another gift. Your life grows within me now and that is more glorious even than what we have beetwing us."*

"Beetwing?" I asked. "She sounds foreign."

"She sounds pregnant," Clare said.

Joey squealed with glee and went back to reading. *"I understand if you want me to go away now. I will never wish to be a burden to you or to your family. But know that I love you, and already I love this child, and will be devoted to you both forever and ever."*

Joey stopped and looked up at us.

"Is that it?" Clare asked.

"That's it." She looked down at the page. "It's not even signed."

"Let me see it," I said, and Joey handed it to me. I looked down at the curly European script and a chill danced up my spine. Could it be Lydia's handwriting? It looked so very much like the script I saw her write that day at the kitchen table.

But my brain didn't want to process what that meant. I was stuck seeing Mr. Waxman the way I did when I was ten. He was an old man, somebody's dad. He couldn't have had an affair with Lydia, could he?

But it made sense. If he got Lydia pregnant, he might have forced her to leave. It would explain why she disappeared so suddenly from Kenny's life. Sam Waxman might have paid her for her silence.

"We should show it to Kenny," Joey said.

"No!" I said. "Absolutely not."

"Why?"

"First of all, it's none of our damn business. We shouldn't even have read it. Second, he doesn't need more fuel for hating his father."

Clare looked over my shoulder at the letter. "I wonder who it's from."

"Maybe somebody who worked in his factory," I said, feeling only slightly guilty about throwing them off with a red herring. After all, the situation didn't need more drama, and it was going to be hard enough to keep Joey from telling Kenny. If she knew I suspected the letter was from Lydia, I'd have to gag her and bind her and lock her away.

"Maybe a neighbor," Joey said.

Clare lit up. "Like Mrs. Bianco!"

"Dawling," Joey said, imitating Helen Bianco's smoker's rasp. "I can't keep my hands off your pepperoni. You make me so hot I could . . ." Here she pretended to succumb to a disgusting smoking jag and Clare laughed in delight. I was too distracted by the terrible thought of Lydia's predicament to join in the fun. What had happened to her? She was a poor immigrant in a strange country with no friends or family. Where did she go? Who did she turn to? Did she go back to Hungary?

I glanced back at the letter to see if there was a date, but there wasn't. I did some quick math and figured it had been about twenty years since Lydia left. If the letter was indeed from her, Kenny might have a grown-up brother or sister somewhere.

The thought gave me a shiver, compounded by the fact that I was still wearing wet clothes. I started to tremble.

"You look cold," Clare said.

"I'm freezing."

"Let's go home and change," she said. "Joey, go borrow something more appropriate from Renee's closet so we can go next door and get showered and cleaned up."

"I'm on it," Joey said, dashing from the room.

"Wait!" Clare shouted after her. "Put the gown back! And the letter!"

Before Joey could answer, the doorbell rang.

Clare looked at me. "Who could that be?"

I shrugged.

"I'll get it!" Joey shouted, her footsteps trampling back down the stairs.

"Not in your underwear!" I called, knowing full well Joey wouldn't listen. I quickly folded the letter and stuck it in my bra—the only dry spot on my body—then pulled off my shoes and socks and rushed from the mudroom, but it was too late. By the time I got to the front door, it was wide open and Joey stood there, in her panties and bra, talking to the Goodwins.

"Look," she exclaimed, "midgets! Aren't they cute?"

At that moment, I wished I had the power to disappear. Or spontaneously combust. Anything but have to endure the chagrin of seeing the Goodwins suffer such a horror of insensitivity.

"Joey!" I admonished. "I'm so sorry," I said to the couple. "She doesn't always think before she speaks."

Mrs. Goodwin waved the comment away. "Nothing we haven't heard before."

"Besides," her husband added with a wink, "we think she's cute, too." He looked from me to Clare, who had followed me from the mudroom, and said, "You two, however . . ."

Clare covered her mouth with her hand, horrified. "God! I can imagine how we must look!"

I explained what we had been doing and why we were caked with mud. All the while, Mr. Goodwin stared quizzically at Joey.

"I just realized why you look so familiar," he said, pointing at her face. "You're Joey Bloom from Phantom Pain!"

Joey ran her hands through her mud-caked curls and nodded.

"I knew it!" he said. "'Tiger Attack' was a monster hit. I loved that video— must've watched it a hundred times!"

Joey barely smirked. "Thanks." She shrugged.

Mr. Goodwin stuck out his hand. "I'm Teddy Goodwin," he said, "and this is my wife, Alicia."

"Teddy works in the video business," Alicia Goodwin said. "He's in postproduction."

"Cool," Joey said.

"In my spare time I'm also a songwriter," he added. "Kind of a hobbyist, but I have some edgy rock tunes." He fingered the fringe of hair that extended just past his collar, as if he were suddenly conscious of this modest symbol of hipness. "Do you still sing?"

Joey took a step back, planted her feet apart, and belted out the beginning of "Tiger Attack," her band's one-hit song, in a voice so strong I was momentarily stunned:

"We didn't go to Paris or on any damn plane ride, but I showed him how to sweat when the radiator died!"

Man. If Joey's drug habit had taken its toll, you'd never know it by her singing voice. She still had that haunting tone and seismic force, but her control was better than ever. And there was something else there, something I couldn't quite put my finger on.

"Powerful," Teddy said.

"Jeez, Joey," I added. "That was amazing."

Clare agreed.

"Would you sing the whole thing?" Alicia asked.

That was all the encouragement Joey needed. She ran to living room, which was right off the foyer where we stood, and jumped onto the coffee table. Teddy pulled a tapered candle from a holder on the shelf and handed it to her, standing on his tiptoes. Grasping it upside down, she used the candle like a mike and launched into the song from the beginning, gyrating her hips and swinging her head like she did in the video. I could almost hear the drum beat, the guitars. Her charisma was undeniable. But there was a layer there that didn't exist when she sang with the band. It was an emotional connection to the song, a willingness to go to the deepest part of herself and put it out there. It was riveting. Best of all, everyone seemed enthralled by the performance—they were connecting with her magic.

From the corner of my eye I spotted some movement outside the sidelight window next to the front door. It was Kenny, getting out of his car. I hesitated for a moment, deciding what to do. I knew that if he walked in the door the spell would be broken, the performance interrupted. Joey was in such a special place that I thought it would be a shame if she didn't get to finish out the song. So I quietly slipped out the front door and waylaid Kenny.

"You can't go in yet," I said, pushing my hand against his chest for emphasis.

"Why? What's going on?" He stepped back and took in my appearance. "And what the hell happened to you? You look like a sewer rat."

That stung, but I couldn't argue. My muddy hair was plastered to my head and my wet, filthy clothes hung down from my body like they were trying to get away.

"I know," I said. "It's a long story. Just try to hang out here for a minute. Joey is performing for the Goodwins."

Kenny smirked. "The Goodwins?" he said. "Joey must be thrilled."

"Why?" I asked, knowing full well I was stepping into one of his jokes.

"Because all she ever needed was a little audience." Kenny approached the window and looked in. "God, she's practically naked!"

I looked through the window at my rock star sister, pushing her soul up from her pelvis to her throat and past the makeshift mike toward her rapt audience, and tried to shake some mud off my pants.

Deal with it, I thought. He's going to choose Joey over you, like he did last time. Why wouldn't he? She was talented, charismatic, wild.

And anyway, my feelings for Kenny were probably just

physical. He was, after all, gorgeous. Maybe not Roman statue
gorgeous, but close enough. So what if I was attracted to him?
I was a normal, healthy woman who hadn't been laid since
I dated Bart Flaum, the mattress salesman whose mustache
dripped food when he ate.

I still can't figure out why I dated that guy. Was I so filled
with self-loathing, or was I simply looking for someone completely opposite from my ex? Jonathan was an artist, with no
appreciation for jokes. Bart was a joke, with no appreciation
for art. Sure he was sweet and thought I was a goddess, but the
guy framed bumper stickers and hung them on his walls.

And I let this man go down on me.

For some reason, this thought made me acutely aware of how
dirty I was, and I couldn't imagine what crazy explanations
Kenny must have been imagining. I told him the whole story
about moving the industrial drum out from under the house,
and how my sisters ganged up to force me into the mud.

"And I thought they loved me," I joked.

"They do love you," he said seriously. "But they're jealous
of you."

Of me? Had someone kicked him in the head?

"Hardly," I said. "I'm the loser of the family, remember?"

He moved a lock of hair from my forehead and I thought
he was going to kiss me. His lips parted the tiniest bit, and
I imagined the warmth inside his mouth, the slickness of his
tongue, the heavenly feeling of his broad chest pressed against
mine. My panties were getting even wetter than my clothes.

"The loser of the family?" Kenny said, his face inches from
mine. "Oh, Bev, for a smart girl you are such a dope."

"Clearly you're an expert on family relations."

Me and my sarcasm. He took a step back and set his jaw.
"Don't bring my father into this, okay?"

So I sabotaged the moment. Likely my subconscious was

just smarter than I was and knew what a terrible mistake I'd be making. Our history was too complicated to attempt a meaningless sexual encounter before he jetted back to Los Angeles. Though, admittedly, the thought that he wanted me lit my libido like a Grucci fireworks show at Jones Beach.

In an attempt to shake off the hormonal launch sequence activated by my sex-starved imagination, I changed the subject, telling Kenny the Goodwins' visit had taken me by surprise. "I didn't know they were coming for another look today until they got here," I said.

Kenny sighed, as if he were physically releasing the anger he just felt. "Me neither."

"I thought that's why you came."

"No, I came because I'm going to be staying here in this house for a while. My things are in the car."

"Don't you have to get back to L.A.?"

He shook his head. "Actually, no. I've been meaning to tell you—the reason I'm in town is because I'm talking to some folks who may be crazy enough to hire me to write for them. I could be in New York to stay. "

Whoa. Kenny was moving to New York? That cast his interest in a whole different light. I'd been thinking he saw me as a quick lap around the block, but since I hadn't told him I was hoping to move to Las Vegas, he had every reason to think I'd be around. Did this mean he was really interested? And did it matter?

"I didn't know," I said. "Is it a TV show? Something I've heard of?"

He smirked and nodded. *"Letterman."*

I gasped. *"Letterman!* That must be your dream job."

"Nothing's definite yet," he said. "We could be in negotiations for weeks. That's why I gave up my expensive hotel room in the city today."

"You're moving into your parents' house?"

"Just temporarily." He touched my shoulder with the back of his hand. "We'll be next-door neighbors again."

I didn't know how to react to that. It left the possibility of some kind of relationship wide open—at least for the summer—and I needed time to take that in. I changed the subject by asking him how he got his foot in the door with Letterman's people, and he explained that he had worked on a couple of episodes of *Everybody Loves Raymond,* one of Letterman's projects, so they knew him. I feigned surprise; I didn't want him to know I had kept track of any part of his career. But the truth was I knew more about the trajectory of his résumé than I wanted to admit, even to myself.

"We should go inside," I said. "Sounds like Joey is coming to the end of her song."

Chapter 8

We opened the door just in time to join in the applause. Joey started to take a bow, but when she spotted Kenny she leaped from the table.

"Kenny!" she squealed, throwing her arms around him.

Oh yeah. It was a good thing I didn't kiss him. These two could be going at it again within hours. She released her embrace and stepped back so he could get a good look. Clearly, she was offering herself to him. I shivered, the chill from my damp clothes soaking through to my bones.

"I would say that I don't get to see enough of you," Kenny said as he surveyed Joey's half-naked body, "but under the circumstances . . ."

Joey laughed. "How have you *been*, K? I hear you're a big man in Burbank."

"Oh yeah, a giant among—" he stopped and looked at the Goodwins and then at me. "I mean, I can't complain. Not that I don't want to, but there's a clause in my contract. How are you? I heard you were in rehab."

Joey beamed. "I'm clean!" she said seriously.

Silence hung for a palpable second and then everyone burst into laughter, which seemed to warm the room. It also had the effect of severing Joey's stranglehold on Kenny's attention. He greeted Clare warmly and said hello to the Goodwins.

Teddy raved about Joey's singing, then he turned to her and asked if she had ever thought about trying to make a solo career for herself.

She made a face and shook her head. "Not into it."

"Another band, then?" he asked.

Joey stuck out her tongue to suggest the idea was sickening.

"Well, if you change your mind," he said, "I wrote this song I think would be perfect for you. If you ever want to hear it, let me know."

"Perfect for you," his wife echoed. "You'll fall in love with it."

"I'll keep it in mind," Joey said, and folded her arms, indicating that the subject was closed.

I looked hard at Joey to try to determine if she was being truthful or not. She was always so driven I had assumed she wanted to get her singing career back on track. I chided myself for not having discussed this with her. She could have been dealing with some significant fears about exposing herself to drugs. I hoped she could get past that. I hated to think of her talents going to waste. But of course, she was with Tyrone when he OD'd and had watched him die. It drove her to rehab, and I supposed it could have also driven her to re-evaluate what she wanted out of life.

One thing I knew for sure—if she still wanted a career in rock and roll, she'd go after it.

Once, as a kid, she announced her intention to go to church with some of her Catholic friends. She said she wanted to know if the God in their church was the same God who was at our temple. My parents didn't buy Joey's spiritual curiosity and forbade it. They fought and fought, Joey insisting she just wanted to know about God, my parents yelling that she just wanted to go church because she thought that's where the cool kids went.

"You don't want to be Jewish anymore?" my mother asked, wringing her hands. Clearly she took Joey's request as a personal affront.

"I just want to know if God's in *St. Paul's*."

My father interrupted, "And how will you know, eh? You think God is going to *speak* to you?"

"I'll just know."

"Bah! You want to impress your friends!" my father said, in one of the rare occasions when he raised his voice.

My parents wouldn't budge, and Joey stomped around the house, furious, for days. I didn't get involved in the argument because I wasn't sure who was right. Now I can see that they both were. Joey did indeed have an insatiable curiosity. She was the kind of kid who had to look under every stone (and in every tampon box) and try everything at least once. If she got a question in her head, she wouldn't relent until she got an answer. On the other hand, the reason she had such a burning curiosity about St. Paul's in particular was that her hard-edged friends went to Mass there. She probably wanted to see if they knew something she didn't.

Then, early Sunday morning, she climbed out her second-floor bedroom window and jumped to the ground, breaking her ankle. She got up and limped to St. Paul's to attend Mass, the area above her shoe swelling to the size of a bowling ball. It had to have been agonizingly painful.

I don't know if Joey discovered anything about God in a Catholic church, but I know the rest of us learned that nothing would ever get in the way of Joey going after what she wants.

I put my hand on her back and announced to the group that

I hated to break up the party, but my sisters and I needed to get back to my house to shower and change. She returned the gesture by putting her arm around me.

Teddy asked how we planned to dispose of the industrial drum at the curb. When I told him that we intended to leave it there for the garbage truck to pick up, he clucked in disapproval. "They won't pick that up. Not without knowing what's in it."

"Why not?" Clare asked.

"Because it could be toxic chemicals. If you want the sanitation department to take it, you have to open it yourselves."

Joey clapped her hands. "Cool! Let's do it now."

The thought of doing anything other than taking a hot shower and getting into dry clothes made me shudder. "We have to get cleaned up," I said.

"But look," Joey said, pointing to the window. "It stopped raining."

"That doesn't make me any less cold and wet and filthy."

"Bev's right," Clare said. "We should get showered and changed."

Joey tsked. "You two are such old ladies."

And you're such a two-year-old, I wanted to say, but instead I reminded her that it would still be there in an hour. Then I asked Kenny if he could get something from his mother's closet for Joey to wear so we could run next door. Joey folded her arms and pouted.

Teddy said he and his wife would be gone by the time we got back, and told Joey and Clare it was lovely meeting them.

"Don't you want to see what's in the drum?" Joey asked.

"We just don't have the time, dear," Mrs. Goodwin explained.

"Then let's do it now!" Joey demanded. She looked at the rest of us. "Please."

Kenny looked at me and shrugged, as if to say he had no choice, and I shrugged back, agreeing. After all, how long could it take? He announced that he'd go upstairs to get something for Joey to wear, and asked if someone could go into the mudroom and find a screwdriver to pry off the lid.

"I'll do it!" Joey said, and dashed to the back of the house.

Moments later, when she returned, she was indeed carrying a screwdriver. She was also wearing the pink ball gown.

"For heaven's sake, Joey," Clare chided.

Kenny, descending the stairs just as Joey entered, spotted her. "I was going to offer you these old tennis shorts," he said, holding up some clothes, "but I guess a gown's appropriate too. You can't *be* overdressed for these gala industrial drum openings."

I looked at Clare, who simply threw up her arms in defeat. Joey clapped her hands, delighted, and together we all went outside and watched as Kenny wedged the screwdriver under the lip of the lid and tried to pry it off.

"It's like opening Al Capone's vault," Joey said.

"That was empty," I said. "Remember?"

"I mean the suspense."

"Doubt there'll be anything very dramatic inside," Kenny grunted as he pushed on the screwdriver. He used both hands and forced his weight into it. Was anything happening? He stopped and pulled out the screwdriver, holding it up for everyone to see. It was bent. The lid held fast.

"Well?" he asked. "Any suggestions?"

The sun peeked through the clouds and I was glad for the warmth. My hair was drying and I felt like my body was absorbing some healthful vitamin D. And Kenny. Kenny was starting to glisten, with dots of sweat seeping through the front of his thin T-shirt, highlighting his sculpted pectorals. Goodness. It really *was* starting to heat up. I shook my hair out to try to distract myself from what I was feeling, but when I looked up he was staring straight at me, as if he knew what I was thinking and refused to let the moment pass. I held his gaze and something happened. It was as if his look penetrated so deeply that my boundaries vanished and my very cells were becoming unglued. I felt my body opening to the forces of nature, letting the heat of the sun enter through the top of my head and move downward, while the coolness of the earth rose up through my feet. The two fronts were about to meet and explode in a storm somewhere south of my equator when someone spoke.

"You can't just do one spot," Joey said.

Kenny looked at her. "Huh?"

"You can't just do one spot with the screwdriver," she explained. "You have to go all the way around the lid."

"Oh," Kenny said as he glanced back at me quickly. "I don't think that'll make a difference." As proof, he stuck the screwdriver in another spot and pushed down, to no avail.

"Do you have a claw bar?" Teddy asked.

"A what?" Kenny asked.

"A claw bar," he repeated.

Kenny scratched his head. "A claw bar? What do they serve there? And do they have karaoke?"

"Yes, but you can only sing *Eagles* songs." Teddy winked.

Kenny smirked. "Is that in case there's a *talon* scout?"

Teddy laughed. "A claw bar is like a crowbar, with a special kind of tip."

Kenny shook his head. "Nope, I don't have one. But wouldn't an ordinary crowbar do just as well?"

"It might." Teddy nodded hopefully.

"I don't have one of those either."

We all laughed, and Kenny admitted he was teasing and that there probably was a crowbar in the basement. He said he'd go look and asked if anybody else wanted to give the screwdriver a try while he was gone.

"I'll give it a shot," Teddy said.

Kenny handed him the screwdriver and headed back into the house. Teddy wedged the tool into another spot and pushed down so hard his face turned bright red from the exertion. Alicia's hand went up to her chest in alarm. I thought she was going to tell him to stop before he hurt himself, but she didn't and I was glad. I could imagine how emasculating that would be for him.

He stopped to rest, which he clearly needed, then tried again. Standing on his toes, he pushed his weight onto the screwdriver, and his face flushed even redder and started to sweat. I was beginning to get genuinely concerned for his health and considered whether I should speak up. Would he get insulted? Possibly, but wasn't that better than risking a collapse?

But he paused on his own before I had to say anything. "Getting warm out here."

"Let's get you a cold drink," Alicia said.

He nodded and handed the screwdriver to Joey before going back into the house with his wife. Then it was just us sisters.

"What they were doing wrong," Joey said, as she stooped to pick up a large rock, "was not getting the tip of the screwdriver wedged in enough."

She held the screwdriver under the lip of the lid, and banged on the other end with the rock.

She tsked. "It's not going in."

"Try angling the handle upward," Clare offered.

Joey did that and gave the handle a hard knock with the stone. There was a tiny sound, like a whisper of air.

"Did you hear that?" she asked. "It sounded like some air escaped." She made a face. "Oh, man! I *smell* it."

I moved closer and caught wind. "Ooh," I said, "chemicals! Goodwin was right."

"Don't even bother opening it," Clare said. "What's the point?"

"You've got to be kidding me," Joey said, as she pushed her weight down on the screwdriver handle. "We've gotten this far." The lid budged upward the tiniest bit. Joey removed the screwdriver and inserted it in another spot a few inches away. She banged it in with the rock again and pressed down hard.

"Somebody help me," she said.

I went behind her and put my hands over hers.

"Push," she said. "Push!"

"I don't want to crush your hands."

"Never mind. Just push."

Clare moved in next to me and put her hands over mine. Together, the three of us pushed down as hard as we could until we could see the lid actually rising. The chemical smell was almost more than my empty stomach could bear. I wanted to stop but I could see that my sisters were intent on finishing the job.

"Okay," Joey finally said. "Stand back. I'm going to lift the lid off now."

"Be careful," I said. "It smells toxic."

"Maybe you shouldn't touch it with your bare hands," Clare offered.

"No worries," Joey said, grasping the lid with both hands. She gave a hard yank and pulled it off, tossing it onto the grass.

The odor made my eyes tear, the nausea swelling in a ghastly wave. Still, I couldn't help but glance inside at the brackish liquid that filled the drum, as it did indeed look like there was something inside.

I noticed a filmy coating on top. Holding my nose, I brought my face a little closer for a better look. It wasn't a film, but a mass of floating fibers.

"That looks like *hair*," Joey said.

I tsked. "It's not hair, for heaven's sake."

"And what's *that*?" She pointed to something whitish beneath the surface.

Clare and I moved in for a closer look.

Joey knelt down and picked up a twig. She stuck it into the liquid and poked the white shape. The hair-like fibers on the surface swayed as the thing she disturbed bobbed up from the fluid.

I was certain it wouldn't be anything more interesting than a piece of old wood or some other building materials. After all, Kenny had said it was probably the contractor who built the extension that left the barrel there.

But I stared intently, hoping we could identify it in short order so that I could get back home to shower and change. I'd had enough of this nonsense.

Then the thing broke the surface of the liquid and came into full view. There was a moment of silence followed by a collective gasp. The reality of what I saw hit me just as the emptiness of my stomach, the weakness of my knees, the power of the odor, and the force of my nausea overtook me. My world started to spin like that scene in *The Wizard of Oz* where Dorothy's house turns and turns in the force of the twister. As my world darkened, colorless images went flying by my field of vision: Clare slipping in the mud . . . Joey clambering into that tight crawl space . . . the distinctive handwriting of that hidden letter. And then, just before the screen went black, one final vision I didn't have to imagine because it was right in front of me, bobbing up from the dark liquid like a signal for help.

A human hand.

Chapter 9

I awoke in gauzy thickness, dreamlike. My surroundings were familiar but incomprehensible. Was this my house? How did I get here? The room was dark, appearing in shades of gray, but out the window the sky was that piercing blue you see only after a thunderstorm, and I thought I glimpsed something miraculous. Was it a rainbow? A real rainbow? I lifted my heavy head and stared straight out to be sure. It was! Then I blinked and saw a confusing vision. On the bright green lawn in the distance I saw what looked like Glenda the Good Witch, complete with pink gown and screwdriver-shaped fairy wand. I covered my eyes with my hands as I lay back down and thought, *this can't be.*

"Are you okay, dear?"

The voice startled me. I had thought I was alone. She sounded familiar but not like family. Who was she? And why couldn't she just go away? I didn't want to talk to anyone. I just wanted to look out the window again and see Glenda, who I thought might be able to help me escape from some bad place I sensed I was in.

The woman moved closer. "Bev, can you hear me?"

Without opening my eyes I sensed that she was a little person. And there was another one like her hovering over me.

Little people? Glenda? Rainbows? What was happening to me? Did I go to sleep and wake up in Oz?

I spread my fingers and peered out at the face of the woman speaking, trying to concentrate. *You know her*, I told myself. *Think*.

"You passed out," said the man next to her. "Kenny carried you in."

Kenny. Kenny Waxman. I lifted my head again, trying to force past the fog. I noticed I was on the couch in my living room.

"Do you remember what happened?" the woman asked.

A distant siren got louder and I glanced toward the window. The rainbow was gone. So was Glenda.

"Is she out there?" I asked.

"Who?" said the little man. "Is *who* out there?"

"Glenda."

"Glenda?" asked the little woman.

"With the pink gown and the wand."

The little woman took my hand in hers. "That was Joey, your sister. Do you remember? You girls opened that . . . that industrial drum."

A sick feeling seized my stomach with a cramp, followed by a wave of nausea. Yes, I remembered, but I didn't want to. I wanted to go back into the dream where I had landed in Oz.

"Teddy, see if there's some orange juice in the fridge. We don't want to lose her again."

"I'm okay, Mrs. Goodwin," I said.

"Alicia," she corrected. "We'll get your blood sugar up and you'll feel a whole lot better. When was the last time you ate?"

"I don't know. I'm hungry though."

"Crackers too, Teddy," she shouted to the kitchen.

"Are you a nurse?" I asked.

"No," she said. "I'm a psychotherapist."

Good, I thought. Then help me forget what I saw just before I passed out. Or convince me it was an imaginary vision. Just don't tell me it was real.

"In the drum," I mumbled.

"*Shh.* We'll talk about that in a minute. First see if you can sit up without getting dizzy."

I sat up and put my feet on the floor. Teddy brought me the orange juice, which I sipped slowly. He offered me crackers, and I took a tiny bite.

After a while Alicia asked, "Now, are you feeling better? Do you want to talk about what you saw when you opened the drum?"

No, I didn't. I wanted to pretend it never happened. But a glance out the window revealed the truth. Four police cars had pulled up in front of the Waxmans' house, and an officer was wrapping yellow tape from tree to tree around the property.

"Bev?" she said gently.

I rubbed down the goose bumps on my arm and handed the empty juice glass to Mr. Goodwin. I cleared my throat and looked down at the floor. *Speak,* I said to myself. *Just say it.*

Alicia Goodwin squeezed my hand and told me it was okay. I could rest if I wanted.

I shook my head and finally spit it out. "A body," I said.

She took a breath. "Yes," she said gently, "there was a body."

"Do we know who?" I looked into her eyes, afraid I already knew the answer. I touched my chest where the letter Joey had found was still tucked inside my bra. *Please,* I prayed, *let me be wrong.*

"I'm sure the police will work very hard to figure that out," she said.

As if on cue, the doorbell rang, and I hoped it wasn't the police. I wasn't ready to make a decision about whether to tell them about the letter. After all, what if I was wrong? What if I was just addled and confused? I didn't want to implicate Sam Waxman in a murder if it was just a case of my imagination working overtime.

But if I didn't tell the police about the letter, would I be guilty of something? Would it mean I was withholding evidence in a murder case? I took a deep breath to the count of four and told myself it would be okay. If I simply deferred handing over the letter, I wouldn't be guilty of anything.

But what if my sisters had already told the police about it? Then I'd *have* to hand it over. And what if the detective was cagey like the guys on TV, and didn't tell me he knew, waiting to see if I would come clean on my own?

Come clean? Why was I thinking like a criminal from a bad movie—as if the coppers might burst in and say, "The jig is up." I put my head in my hands. I didn't even know what a jig was, let alone know how to determine when it was, in fact, *up.*

I heard Teddy chatting at the front door and got a clammy chill. I looked down at Alicia's hand, patting my knee, and pictured blood circulating through veins and arteries, nerve endings alive with electrical impulses. Then I envisioned that dead white hand, inert as a shadow on the moon. Could it have been Lydia's? Had it pumped chocolate syrup onto a plate of cookies? Written a confusing note to a lawyer . . . or a desperate letter to a lover about the baby growing inside her?

Picturing Lydia dead and crammed into whatever liquid preservative was in that barrel sapped my already limited reserves, and that familiar weakness crept back.

Teddy Goodwin and a police detective entered the room.

"You just went pale as a ghost," Teddy said, looking at me.

Alicia turned to face me. "Head between your knees," she said.

"Do you feel well enough to answer some questions, Miss?" the detective said, bending toward my face.

"Name's Bev," I said from between my knees. "Can we do this later?"

"Of course," he said, and told Teddy Goodwin he'd leave his card.

Chapter 10

Later, after I was feeling better and the kind Goodwins had left, I took a hot shower and changed into clean clothes. I heard my sisters let themselves in.

"Upstairs!" I called.

Clare and Joey tromped up the steps, helped themselves to clean towels, and took turns showering in the other bathroom while I blow-dried my hair. The volume of the dryer served to drown out everything but my thoughts, and I wondered how I would tell my sisters about the connection I made from Sam Waxman to the letter, from the letter to Lydia, and from Lydia to the dead body without sounding like I had suffered permanent brain damage from my little fainting spell.

I came into my bedroom to find them rooting around in my drawers for clothes to borrow. The room felt a little crowded; I had replaced my childhood twin bed with the queen-sized one from my apartment, and it took up most of the floor space. Unlike Clare's old room, which had been converted to a nursery when Dylan was born, and Joey's old room, which became a big storage closet after her furniture was donated to a needy cousin, my room remained largely unchanged from the day I left for college and stripped it bare of posters. The walls were pale purple and the windows had lilac and gray curtains that had matched my old bedspread. The furniture was this aesthetic horror in shiny white contempo enamel that my mother thought was Trump-chic in the eighties.

I looked out the window at the Waxmans' house. There were still police cars parked out front but now they were joined by three news vans. A woman reporter with a microphone stood talking into a camera with the house as backdrop.

"The media have arrived," I said.

Joey rushed to the window next to me. She was topless. I pulled the curtain over to cover her.

"They're probably going to want to talk to us," she said, scrunching her curls.

"I hereby designate you our official spokesperson," I said, and looked at Clare for confirmation.

She shrugged. "Fine with me. I look like a cow on camera."

Joey went back to rummaging through my dresser drawers. "Do you have a solid tank top?" she said. "Something dark?"

I opened another drawer to see what I had for her. "What did they do with the body?" I asked.

"Took it away in an ambulance," Joey said as she pulled an old concert T-shirt from my drawer. She made a face and put it back. "Said they would do an autopsy."

"They tell you anything else?"

She shook her head.

Clare took a sleeveless black shell from my drawer and held it in front of herself. "It was a woman." She put her hands inside the shirt to see how much give it had, and placed it back in the drawer. Wise move. My own modest breasts barely fit in that shirt. Clare's porn star D cups didn't stand a chance.

"They told you that?" I said.

"I heard them talking. The detective was speaking to the ambulance driver and said, 'She's damn well-preserved.'"

"I kind of figured," Joey said. "A man wouldn't have fit in that drum unless he was chopped up or something. Let me see that black shirt." Clare handed it to her and Joey pulled it on. "I wanted to go back into the house to use the bathroom, but they wouldn't let me. Said it was now a 'crime scene.'"

Clare added that no one would be allowed in until they removed the yellow tape, and I wondered aloud where Kenny was going to stay. "He was planning to sleep in the house tonight," I said.

Clare closed the drawer she'd been looking in and opened my closet. "Maybe he went back to the city," she said.

"That cute cop took him to the station to grill him." She faced the mirror and tugged on the front of my shirt. "Do you have anything lower cut?"

"What cute cop?" Clare asked.

"The dark-haired one who wasn't wearing a ring. Detective Miller. Think he's Jewish?"

"Since when do *you* care?" I asked.

"I'm just saying. Why is it a big deal if I care if a guy is Jewish?" She took off the black shirt and tossed it onto my bed.

"In college you slept with half the international dorm," I said. "I think you conquered more countries than Genghis Khan." I folded the shirt and put it away, then handed her a plum-colored Lycra tank top I almost never wore.

"Maybe I'm on a different path now."

"Yeah, right," I sneered. "I'll call Grandma Elsie today and see if we can make a match for you. I hear Lazar Wolf is available."

She ignored me and put on the tank top. It looked sexy as hell on her. She stared at the mirror, admiring herself from the front and the side.

"You can have it," I said, anticipating her question.

"You sure?"

I nodded.

"Do you have any skinny black jeans?"

I frowned. She knew I did because I wore them all the time, but I was reluctant. I really liked those pants.

"I'll give them back," she said. I must have looked dubious because she added, "I promise."

I went to my closet and fetched the jeans she was talking about. "They're my favorites," I said as I handed them to her.

She sat down on my bed and pulled them on. "You'll get them back." She flipped her hair over her head and went to work scrunching it from underneath.

"Feel free to lend me something you hate," Clare said.

I laughed and fished out a beige shirt with red piping from my drawer. "How about this?"

I knew it was kind of ugly, but I wasn't prepared for Clare's reaction, which was to put her hand to heart and gasp as if she was in cardiac arrest. "Oh, Bev. They wouldn't force someone in *prison* to wear that shirt."

"Is it that bad?"

"Please." She pulled it from my hand and dropped it in the trash.

I took the shirt from the wastebasket and put it back in my drawer. "This is not an episode of . . . whatever you call that show you like so much."

"Trust me," she said, "if this were an episode of *What Not to Wear*, Stacy would burn that shirt and Clinton would bury the ashes."

Joey went into the bathroom and helped herself to my makeup. Minutes later she was out the door and in front of the Waxmans' house. Clare and I watched from the window as a reporter rushed to her. Joey arched her back and looked very serious as she spoke to the woman, whom I recognized as a field reporter for NBC. Joey pointed to the backyard and the curb as she spoke, obviously explaining how we had moved the drum. By the time she came back upstairs, Clare had gone into our mother's closet and found clothes to wear that weren't too terribly offensive, and I was lying in the middle of my bed examining the letter again.

Joey flopped down next to me. "I'm going to be on the eleven o'clock news," she said.

"What did you tell them?" Clare asked.

Joey shrugged. "How we brought the drum to the curb and all that. You'll see."

My little sister, Joey, worked a camera like magic. It awed me. She could be funny, charming, sexy, disarming, alluring, sassy, and adorable all at once. I once asked her how she did it and she told me you have to dig deep inside to where your self-love resides. "If you believe you're hot shit," she had told me, "even just for those ten minutes you're on camera, they will too."

"Is that mom's skirt?" Joey asked Clare.

"Shut up, Joey," I said. Clare was too curvy to fit into any of my pants, and I thought Joey was rubbing it in.

"What did I say?"

I changed the subject and asked if the TV people recognized her.

"The cameraman did and told the reporter. It'll be interesting to see how they spin that."

"I bet they'll find that stock shot of you with a tiger," I said, "and flash it on the screen before the segment."

She laughed. "And the voice-over will be, 'Has-been Joey Bloom finds body deader than her career.'"

I smiled and glanced at Clare to see if she was on the same page or stinging from Joey's previous remark. She seemed more distracted than upset. I patted the bed and she sat down.

"Maybe it'll be your chance for a comeback," she said to Joey.

"God forbid." Joey took the letter from my hand. Her expression changed as she studied it, and I braced myself, waiting for her to say something.

"I know this is going to sound weird," Joey said.

I cleared my throat. "Probably not as weird as you think."

Clare picked up a brush from my nightstand and ran it through her hair. "What's not weird?"

"This letter to Sam," Joey said. "Do you think it could have any connection to the dead body?"

"Of course not," Clare said.

"Think about it," Joey said. "If he got a woman pregnant and she threatened to tell his family . . ."

"You watch too much TV," Clare said. "Sam Waxman is not a murderer."

"How do you know?" Joey asked.

"Because he's Sam Waxman. He went to temple on Saturdays. He played bridge with Mom and Dad. He made plastic flowers for a living. That is *not* the profile of a murderer."

"I'm not so sure," Joey said. "What do you think, Bev?"

They both looked at me. I think they sensed I had something to say. I kept my head on the pillow as I took the letter from Joey and held it in front of my face. Clare lay down next to me, and the three of us studied it.

"Does this handwriting look familiar to you?" I asked.

"Should it?" Joey said.

I closed my eyes and pictured the letter Lydia had written to her lawyer. It was a draft on notebook paper, written in longhand. I remembered how exotic her curvy European capital letters looked and how evenly sized her lower case ones were. I opened my eyes and stared at the page in my hand. It looked exactly as I had remembered Lydia's script.

"Doesn't it look . . . European?" I said.

"European?" Clare asked. "It looks, I don't know, old-fashioned."

"Maybe," I said. "Maybe that's all it is."

Joey rested her head on her elbow and looked at me. "Are you going to tell us what you're thinking, or do we have to beat it out of you?"

I sat up, holding onto the letter. I wanted to get off the bed and walk around so I could deliver the news facing them, but they had me sandwiched between them. I stared at the letter again.

"I think Lydia wrote this," I finally said.

"What?" Joey sat up and took the letter. "Lydia? You think Lydia had an affair with Sam?"

Clare sat up too. "Disgusting!"

Joey stared down at the note. "You think Sam got Lydia pregnant?"

I nodded.

"You don't think he . . ." She looked at me and her expression changed. "You think the body in the drum could be Lydia?"

"I don't know," I said.

Clare took the page from Joey and examined it. "Nonsense."

"But she disappeared," I said.

"That doesn't mean he killed her," Clare said. "If he got her pregnant, it would make perfect sense for her to leave. How could she possibly stay?"

"But the timing," I said. "Lydia disappeared right around the time the Waxmans built that extension on their house."

"The same time the drum appeared in the crawl space," Joey added.

"And Kenny said he never heard from her again," I said. "Don't you think that's telling? They'd been so close. Wouldn't she have kept in touch?"

Clare rubbed her forehead. "You're making so many assumptions. This letter could be from *any*one."

"You're right," I said. "But if it *is* from Lydia . . ."

"Then that hand," Joey said.

That hand. The earlier queasiness I felt started to creep back again. I put my head between my knees.

"You okay?" Clare asked.

I pulled myself into a tight ball, remembering how I used to play hide-and-seek in Kenny's backyard, making myself as small as possible so I wouldn't be seen from behind the bushes. I could almost hear Lydia's voice as she pretended to look for me. "Where are you, my dear girl? Have you gone forever?" Now I was tempted to answer back, "Have you?"

Chapter 11

Clare insisted we weren't dressed well enough to go out for dinner, but at last agreed to a casual Mexican restaurant. The place was noisy and crowded enough to numb my mounting anxiety over the fact that we had spent our childhood living next door to a murderer . . . and that our parents were currently sleeping in the room right next to his.

"How did Mom and Dad sound?" I asked my sisters. They had called Florida while I was unconscious.

"Pretty wigged out," Joey said. "But not nearly as hysterical as Renee."

I could only imagine. Renee would have had a nervous breakdown over us trekking that mud inside. News of a dead body under her house had to push her right over the edge.

The hostess told us we could have a seat by the bar while we waited for our table.

"We'll wait by the door," I said. Truth was, I was desperate for a frozen margarita, but I didn't think it was fair to put Joey in that environment.

"We'll sit by the bar," Joey said.

Clare turned to her. "Are you sure?"

"Please. This is Disneyland compared to what I'm used to.

In fact . . . ," she said as she reached into Clare's handbag for the car keys, "I'll drive home."

Joey knew that Clare and I were both lightweights. And indeed, I started to feel the effects of the alcohol about halfway through my fishbowl-sized drink. By the time Joey brought up the subject of the letter again, I was struggling to keep my IQ above room temperature.

"How sure are you about the handwriting?" she asked me.

"Handwriting?"

"How sure are you that it's Lydia's?"

"I don't know."

"We need to be sure," Joey said. "We should compare it to a sample."

"You want a sample of Lydia's handwriting?" I asked.

"You have one?"

"No."

Soon after that we were led to our table. When the waitress arrived with our enormous sizzling platters, I stared at mine, watching the steam rise as I replayed the conversation I'd just had with Joey, trying to fill in the piece my subconscious was nudging me to remember. I picked up a tortilla, filled it with whatever was in front of me, and took a bite.

"Oh!" I cried, a little louder than I'd intended.

"Too spicy?" Clare asked.

"No, I just remembered—Lydia *did* leave papers behind! Kenny told me he kept a shoebox filled with cards from her."

"Do you think it's in the house?" Joey asked.

I paused for a moment, and recalled that Kenny had said it was under his bed. "Yes," I said, and Joey grinned. "Why are you smiling?" I asked.

"Because you have a key."

Joey stopped Clare's mammoth SUV in front of the Waxmans' house. "Place looks dark. Where did you say he kept
that shoebox?"

I was in the front seat next to her. "Under his bed."

"We can't go in," Clare said from the back. "There's a big
yellow *X* over the front door."

"It's only tape, for God's sake," Joey said.

Clare leaned forward to get closer to us. "We'll get in trouble," she whispered, as if someone could hear.

"Who's going to know?" Joey got out and shut the door.
Clare and I did the same. I glanced around. There were no
police cars, no cars of any kind.

"Don't you see what it says?" Clare asked, pointing to the
taped up front door. "Police line—do not cross, police line–do
not cross, police line—"

"I got the picture," Joey said, "but we're not going to *cross*.
We're going to go *under*."

"What do you think, Bev?" Clare asked.

I wasn't drunk enough to believe that Joey's Clintonesque
differentiation between *cross* and *under* would convince anyone in a position of authority that we didn't know we were
doing something wrong. But I wanted to go inside and get that
shoebox filled with letters. I imagined us back at my kitchen
table, under the bright overhead light, comparing bona fide
samples of Lydia's handwriting against the mysterious letter.

I needed to know.

"I guess it wouldn't be such a big deal to go in." I turned to
face Clare. "But why don't you wait here? Joey and I can get
it. We'll be back in a minute."

Clare looked relieved, and Joey and I approached the front
door. I slipped my key into the lock and pushed the door open
without disturbing the yellow tape, which was affixed to the
door frame. We got down on our knees and crawled beneath

the X, then shut the door behind us. The house was dark except for a gentle glow from the kitchen, which I knew came from a small florescent bulb over the stove. The only sound was the soft electronic *whir* of the refrigerator.

"I need to piss," Joey said.

"Now?"

"While you guys were busy with your margaritas, I drank three cups of coffee. My bladder is ready to burst."

I rolled my eyes. "Go ahead. I'll go upstairs and see if I can find the shoebox."

"Just don't turn on any lights," she said.

"Why not?"

"Because if anyone outside sees lights go on, they'll know someone's in the house."

"Then you'd better see if you can find a flashlight in the kitchen," I said. "It's going to be pitch-black up there."

I tiptoed up the stairs. I don't know why I felt compelled to be quiet, but there was an eerie stillness to the house and I couldn't shake the feeling that we were breaking the law, and that if we weren't careful, someone would catch us.

When I got to the top of the steps, I could make out that the bedroom door to Kenny's room was open. From where I stood, the interior was black velvet dark. I walked toward it with my hands out like a blind person. At the doorway, I got down on my knees so that I could crawl to the bed without worrying about bumping into anything or tripping. I felt along the carpet until I got to what I knew was the tailored bed skirt that hung from the frame. I lifted it and felt around beneath the bed. *Ridiculous*, I thought, *to do this without a flashlight.* Still, I reached my arm all the way under the bed so that my shoulder met the frame and my hand was as close to the other side of the bed as I could get. I rubbed the carpet all the way to the head of the bed. Nothing. I started to work my way back down toward the bottom of the bed when I thought I heard something creak.

"Joey? Did you get a flashlight?"

Silence.

"Joey?" I repeated.

I heard the sound again and froze. It wasn't coming from outside the room.

It was coming from the bed.

I listened hard, trying to convince myself no one was in the room with me and that the sound I heard was simply the bedsprings responding to my arm bumping against the bed frame. I replayed the scene from outside. There had been no cars parked out front. If someone was in the bed, they had taken great pains to conceal their presence.

I was on my belly, my ear pressed against the carpet, and my heart pounded so hard I could hear it through the floor. I held my breath and lifted my head. The bed was still. Had that creak been my imagination? I listened and heard something else, something softer. It sounded like steady bursts of air. *Wuh-wuh-wuh.*

It sounded like . . . breathing.

Okay, I thought, this is the moment in the horror movie where you scream at the screen, "Get the hell out of the room!" But I was literally petrified. The darkness was so complete and my fear so paralyzing that I couldn't move even an inch. At least not without wetting myself.

The last time I had felt that scared was when I was in ninth grade and heard a piercing howl from my backyard that was at once heartbreaking and terrifying. It didn't sound like man or beast. It certainly didn't sound like our schnauzer, Stephanie, whom I had let out just a short while earlier. It was late at night, and I was studying for a math test while the rest of the family slept. I had opened the door to the yard and stood staring into the darkness, scared that some strange predator had eaten Stephanie alive. I heard someone pad down the stairs and turned to see my father standing behind me in his bathrobe.

"What's that noise?" he asked.

"I don't know."

"Is Stephanie out there?"

"She was."

He put his hand on my shoulder. "I'll get a flashlight."

We stood side by side as he ran the beam across the yard until at last we saw the source of the horrible wail. It *was* our Stephanie, lying on her side, clearly in such horrible pain that she emitted a sound we had never heard before.

"Be careful," my father said, as I rushed across the yard to her. "Wounded animals will bite."

I was crying by the time I reached her. "What's the matter, girl?" I said as I kneeled beside her. She lifted her head and wailed. My father pointed the flashlight on her and I saw what it was—the clip of her backyard tether had pierced the part of her hind leg where a bit of flesh served as webbing between anklebone and tendon.

"How could this have happened?" I cried.

She nipped at the air as I got closer, but my dad was calm and slow.

"Easy, Stephanie," he said, as he knelt. He put his hands on either side of the dog's head, holding it steady as rubbed behind her ears.

"See you if can ease that clip out," he said to me.

At the time, I thought it was crazy that I was the one performing the surgery when my father was a doctor. But of course, he didn't want me to risk being bitten. And so, I held Stephanie's leg and carefully, slowly extracted the clip. Then my father picked up the dog and carried her inside.

"I guess she didn't want to be tethered and was tugging

against it when her leg got caught," my father said as he cleaned and bandaged her wound.

That sounded logical except for one thing. I hadn't tethered her. I had simply let her run free in our fenced backyard, which I knew I wasn't supposed to do, as she liked to pee in a spot by the fence that bordered the Waxmans' yard, and Sam complained that the urine was killing his grass. Months before, my parents had instructed all of us girls not to let the dog run loose in the back, but to make sure she was tethered on the opposite side of the yard. I usually complied, but it was late at night and I figured everyone was asleep and I could get away with it.

All these years later and I still hadn't solved the mystery of Stephanie's injury. At least not until now. Lying on the floor in the Waxmans' house, scared half to death, I finally understood that my next-door neighbor might have been psycho enough to hurt my little dog.

The bed creaked again and before I could pull my hand from under it and run from the room, something grabbed my wrist. I screamed and tried to pull away.

Joey came running up the stairs.

"Help!" I called.

"What's going on?" she said from the hallway.

I turned my head toward her and could see only the beam of the flashlight, first in my eyes and then as it traveled upward toward the bed.

"What are you doing here?" Joey said.

A voice from the bed spoke. "What are *you* doing here? You scared the shit out of me. Who's under the bed?" The hand released my wrist.

I scrambled to my feet and stood beside Joey, staring down at Kenny looking like a giant in his childhood bed.

I put my hand to my heart in an effort to quiet the kettle-drum player on methamphetamines who continued to pound away in my chest. Joey shined the flashlight on our faces so Kenny could see who he was talking to.

I tried to speak. "I . . . we . . ."

"We didn't know you were here," Joey said.

It's only Kenny, I told myself as I took a long deep breath to calm down. *You're safe.* I repeated this mantra several times and my heart rate started to slow.

Kenny sat up and clicked on the small lamp next to his bed. He was bare-chested, possibly naked under the thin blanket that covered his lower half. The percussion instrument that was my heart had just settled into a neat four-four beat when it morphed to a set of congas, and the tempo changed to some kind of Latin rhythm that reverberated southward in a mambo that would have made Ricky Ricardo jealous.

Kenny explained that he didn't feel like checking into a hotel and figured no one would know if he sneaked in and slept in his own bed. He had parked his car around the corner.

"I was going to ask if I could crash at your house," he said to me, "but you weren't home."

Even in the dark, I knew Kenny could sense that I was blushing. I looked down, and Joey started to talk, explaining that we were looking for the shoebox of cards and letters Lydia had written to him.

"Why do you want that?" he asked.

Joey looked at me to see if I wanted to explain that part.

"You tell him," I said.

Joey nodded. "There was this tampon box in your mother's room," she began.

Chapter 12

Back at my house, Kenny and I sat at the kitchen table as he scrutinized the letter. It was late and my sisters had gone home.

"What do you think?" I asked after waiting and watching as he silently studied it.

"That prick," he said without looking up. He sounded more sad than angry.

"Are you surprised?" I asked, wondering if Kenny had ever guessed that his father cheated on his mother.

He kept his face down and rubbed the stubble on his cheek, clearing his throat in that way guys do when they're trying not to cry. When he looked up at me, his eyes seemed so tired.

"Do you remember when my mother broke her arm?" he asked.

"She fell carrying a load of laundry or something?"

"That's what we told people. You want to know what *really* happened?"

I wasn't sure I did, but Kenny continued. "This woman called the house—one of the girls from the factory. That's what he called them, 'the girls.' Anyway, I answered the phone and it was someone I remembered meeting because she was young and pretty. Her name was Halina. I asked if she wanted to speak with my dad, and she said, 'No. I wish to speak with your mama.' So I gave my mother the phone and she put it to her ear but barely said anything. Then, when she got off, she went to talk to my father. I couldn't hear what they were saying, but after a few minutes he screamed, 'I won't have this conversation!' and stomped upstairs. My mother ran after him, crying 'For God's sake, Sam, how *old* is she?' He said, 'It doesn't matter how old she is, she's a liar.' My mother didn't believe him, and I had the feeling it wasn't the first time they'd had a conversation like that, probably not the first time she found out he'd slept with one of 'the girls.' The fight escalated until he told her she was an ungrateful bitch and utterly useless and how many women with one kid needed a full-time housekeeper, blah, blah, blah." Kenny paused to grab a tissue and blow his nose. "My mother got hysterical," he continued, "and screamed that he didn't love her and her life was over." Kenny stopped and looked at me, as if to make sure I was paying attention. "Then I heard it—a dull thud followed by an enormous crash. My mother screamed and I ran up the stairs. She was on the floor—their huge old dresser on her arm. She looked so terrified. I can still see her face. 'Don't just stand there,' my father yelled, as if it were *my* fault. 'Help me pick this up.'"

I pictured it—poor Renee pinned beneath the heavy wooden dresser, and Kenny pretending he believed it was some freak accident, just to keep the peace. I didn't know what to say. "I had no idea."

He shrugged. "So, no, I'm not surprised he had an affair." Kenny picked up the letter again. "And wouldn't be surprised if . . ." He trailed off like he was disappearing into his own thoughts.

"Do you think . . . does it look like Lydia's handwriting to you?"

He laid the letter on the table in front of him and straightened it out. "I don't know," he said, biting his lip. "I need to see those old cards again."

"What do you think happened to that shoebox?"

Kenny told me that it probably wound up in the attic with all the other old junk. He said he would have a look tomorrow and I asked if I could come along. "If you want," he said, and looked so sad I regretted making such a chirpy offer, like it was some kind of happy adventure. I rose and approached him so he would know I understood how hard this was. It was awkward to hug him, since he was sitting, but I bent over and put my arms around him. He hugged me back and we stayed like that for several minutes. I released him and moved to take my seat again, but he grabbed my hand and pulled me onto his lap.

I never really understood the whole sitting-on-the-lap thing. To me, it was about as sexy as getting weighed, and made me nearly as self-conscious, as I regretted that last fajita I ate and tried to position myself against gravity. It did nothing to ease my mind. In fact, the more I tried to get comfortable perched on Kenny's thighs, the more I realized how undignified I felt. It made me wonder if other women felt as I did. Would Clare and Joey feel infantilized on a man's lap? Or would they throw their arms around his shoulders and snuggle into his neck? I cursed the roll of the DNA dice that bestowed my sisters the flirting gene and not me. Granted, I had gifts they lacked. But what good was a talent for getting the fifty-point bonus in Scrabble when you were trying to score in a different way entirely?

"You don't seem comfortable," Kenny said.

Relieved, I stood. He held onto my hand and rose too. We were face-to-face and he touched my cheek. The gesture made me weak. It was so much more emotional than physical that I couldn't ignore that there was something beyond pheromones driving the pulse between my thighs. He moved his face in and I closed my eyes. I wasn't going to fight it. The rush was too exhilarating, the pull too intense. To hell with the past. I wanted to get naked with Kenny Waxman.

He pressed his lips to mine and our tongues touched. He pulled me closer so that we were body against body. My breathing got fast . . . and faster still when he put his face on my neck. I heard his cell phone ring on the counter behind me and ignored it. It kept on, though, and he released me. I picked up the phone, glancing at the caller-ID window before passing it to him. It was Jocy.

He looked at it, and I hoped he would just put it down, but he answered. "Hi," he said. I took a step back, my heart starting to shrivel. It was just a single-syllable word, but there was an intimacy to his voice I couldn't ignore. "I did," he went on. "I think so. No, tomorrow I'll look for it." He pulled the chair from the table and sat down, ready for a lengthy conversation. I stood there for a few moments, waiting. But he didn't give me any sign that he would wrap up quickly and so I murmured, "Good night," and left the kitchen.

Earlier, before my sisters left, we had all discussed Kenny's sleeping arrangements and agreed he shouldn't be in his taped-off house, and that his original idea to spend the night at my house was a better option. Kenny and I hadn't worked out what room he would sleep in, but now it became clear that it wouldn't be mine. How foolish I was to believe that kiss was more about feelings than proximity. If he had been sitting at the table with Joey instead of me, well, never mind. I gathered bedding from the linen closet, left it on the sofa for him, and went upstairs.

The next morning, Clare called looking for Joey. Apparently, our little sister's PDA had fallen out of her purse in Clare's front seat the night before.

"She's probably wondering what happened to it," Clare said. "I called her house and her cell, but she didn't answer. Do you know where she is?"

"No idea," I said, just as Kenny walked into the kitchen. "Do you know where Joey is this morning?" I asked him.

"Joey?"

I rolled my eyes. "Yeah, you remember. Skinny ex-rock star you spoke to on the phone half the night."

"Wasn't half the night."

"Are you being evasive?"

"Me? Evasive?" He opened the pantry and looked inside. "What's good for breakfast around here?"

"Kenny knows where she is," I said into the phone, "but he won't tell me."

"You think she's okay?" Clare asked.

I glanced at Kenny, who had pulled out a box of raisin bran and went about opening cabinet doors looking, I presumed, for a bowl. Since he didn't seem concerned, I figured whatever she was up to didn't involve hypodermic needles or trips to the South Bronx to hook up with certain suspiciously entrepreneurial friends.

"I'm sure she's fine," I said to Clare as I pulled a cereal bowl from the cupboard and handed it to Kenny. "But if you really want to be nosy, why don't you check her PDA?"

After I got off the phone with Clare, I set about making coffee, trying to understand what, if anything, was going on between Kenny and my younger sister.

"There's nothing going on between Joey and me," he said, as he spooned raisin bran into his mouth.

"How do you do that?" I asked. "How do you always know what I'm thinking?"

"I read you like a newspaper," he said, reaching for the *Times*.

"Oh yeah? What am I thinking now?"

"You're trying to figure out if I'm telling the truth about Joey and me."

I smiled, happy that he got one thing wrong. Maybe I wasn't so transparent after all. What Kenny missed was that in some way I got him as much as he got me. I knew he wouldn't lie. He could be evasive. He could be secretive. But telling the truth was like a compulsion. Lying made him feel caged.

"I promise," he said emphatically, "nothing is going on between Joey and me."

I put a cup of coffee in front of him and thought, *not yet.*

The Waxmans' attic was only accessible through a ladder that pulled down from the ceiling in the hallway, so Kenny held it steady while I went first into the dark, dusty space. He followed behind and pulled the chain on a naked single-bulb fixture that hung from a beam.

Bending over to clear the low ceiling, I looked around, covering my mouth with my hand to protect it from the dust. There wasn't as much up there as Kenny had expected—just a few file boxes with old tax returns, several bins of the plastic flowers his father used to manufacture, and the empty cartons from what appeared to be recent purchases. So we went down to the basement to have a look around. In contrast to the dry, chalky heat of the attic, the basement was cool and clammy and seemed to be the repository for thirty years' worth of crap destined for a garage sale. There were at least a dozen shoeboxes on a bookcase by the bottom of the stairs, but they contained things like nails and screws, old silverware, extension cords, gardening gloves, cabinet hardware, knitting needles, and old eyeglasses.

"Don't your parents throw anything out?" I asked, trying on a pair of white cat's-eye glasses.

"Not even dead bodies," he said. "You look glam in those."

I quickly put the glasses back in the box.

After we finished searching every corner of the room, Kenny surveyed the space, scratching the back of his neck. "They moved everything around," he said. "There's a lot of stuff I haven't seen, like cartons of clothes and books, and my mom's boxes of photographs and keepsakes."

We checked the garage, but it was a pretty pristine place, containing Kenny's old sled and bicycle and Sam's gardening tools, snow shovels, lawnmower, and not much else.

"I'm out of ideas," Kenny said.

"You don't think your mom threw it out?"

"Not unless she looked inside . . ." He moved a bag of potting soil and looked behind it as I waited for him to continue. He turned to me. "I didn't just stash letters in there."

"What did you stash—" I stopped myself. "Drugs?"

He shrugged. "I was a teenager. It was a handy spot."

"Oh, Kenny. Couldn't you do any better than that? Joey used to hollow out books, take the switch plate off the wall. I once even found her unscrewing the top of her swim trophy."

"I wasn't that creative. Besides, subterfuge doesn't come naturally to me."

"So what are you going to do?"

"I *really* want those letters."

"Me too."

"I guess I'm going to have to ask my mom where that box is," he said, and walked to the corner of the garage where his bicycle leaned against the wall. "Remember how we used to ride to the park?" He squeezed the tire, which looked soft and airless.

"And the schoolyard. You once fell coming down that ramp."

"Because I was riding with no hands. I was showing off for you."

It shouldn't have meant a thing. And yet, the thought that Kenny had once cared about impressing me had a physical effect on my heart muscle, which contracted as if it had been poked.

Chapter 13

The next day, per Kenny's instructions, I made a photocopy of the letter Joey had found and drove to Clare's house with the original. We had arranged to go to the police station together to turn it over to the detectives.

"I called Joey two more times," she said as she got into my car. "I left messages saying she should meet us here if she wants to come along."

"Should we wait a few minutes for her?" I asked.

Clare bit her cuticle. "She's been missing for more than a day."

"She's been *incommunicado* for more than a day," I corrected.

"You're not worried?"

Until that moment, I'd been more focused on Joey's relationship with Kenny than whether or not she could be off getting high somewhere. In the past, though, any time Joey disappeared it always meant the same thing, and I had to consider whether she might have fallen off the wagon.

The last time she vanished into the void was the worst. Just before she went missing, we had a fortieth-anniversary celebration for Mom and Dad at a fancy Long Island steakhouse.

Everyone was there—Clare and her family, Grandma Elsie, and me, with a date I'd just as soon forget. After waiting for Joey for an hour, we stopped stalling and placed our orders. She finally showed up when we were about halfway through our entrées. Dad was the first one who spotted her coming into the restaurant. I know because he faced the door and was in the middle of shoveling a forkful of creamed spinach into his mouth when his complexion went blood red. I turned around and saw Joey, looking like she'd risen from the dead and hadn't bothered changing her clothes. She was junkie thin, her eyes hollow and dull. An oversized green sweatshirt, stained down the middle, threatened to devour her. Joey's drugs of choice were crack cocaine and alcohol, and when she swaggered like this, I knew she was high on the latter.

"Joey," my father said.

"You couldn't fucking wait for me?" she asked.

I glanced at Grandma Elsie who seemed utterly confused. I looked back at Dad, whose blood pressure was so high I worried the top of his head would blow off.

"There's no reason to use language like that, Joanna," my mother said.

"I want a steak," Joey said.

No one spoke. I think we were all waiting for my father to make the decision. Finally he said, "Sit down, then," and she did.

The waitress tried to hand Joey a menu but she waved it away. "Just bring me a porterhouse and a shot of tequila," she said. I doubted she would even eat a bite. The rest of us tried to continue chatting as if we could save the party if we just pretended nothing was wrong. Joey didn't speak again until we were placing dessert orders.

"What would you like, honey?" the waitress said to her.

"Another tequila," she said.

"No more alcohol," my father said.

My sister put her hands on the table as if she was about to stand and make a scene, but she changed her mind. "Okay," she said. "No more alcohol. Just give me money."

Grandma Elsie opened her purse and took out a ten-dollar bill.

"Don't," my father said.

Joey put her hands back on the table and stood, clearly deciding the time was right for her scene. She faced my father. "Give me *money*."

"How much do you need," Grandma Elsie said, holding up the bill.

"Two thousand," Joey answered, staring straight at my father. "I need two thousand dollars."

He wiped his mouth with a napkin. "Get yourself into rehab and I'll give you all the money you need."

Joey waved his comment away. "Fuck you," she said. "Fuck all of you. Except you, Grandma." She kissed the top of Grandma Elsie's head, snatched the ten-dollar bill from her hand, and headed for the door.

"I hope you're not getting behind the wheel of a car!" my father said, rising.

I'm not proud of this, but at the time I thought, *Let her go. Let her get herself killed so we won't have to deal with this anymore. We'll all be better off.*

As the weeks went by and no one heard from her, the thought that she might really be dead sent me into an emotional tailspin. I felt guilty for hoping she would die, but at the same time a part of me wondered if the best outcome I could hope for was a quick death. I just couldn't imagine Joey getting herself sober again.

Then, over a month later the phone rang after midnight, waking me from a deep sleep. *She's dead, I thought. She's dead.* And it was as if the earth had opened and I was falling into a dark hole. My baby sister. I wanted to hold her and tell her I loved her.

But it was my dad on the phone. Joey, he told me, was okay. She had called him from the hospital where Tyrone, whom we all knew, was pronounced DOA. Joey had at last agreed to check herself into a treatment program.

And now she was missing again. I felt the familiar mix of anger and worry stir in my belly.

"Should we drop by her place?" I asked. For the past several months (with some financial help from our father) she'd been renting part of a small house near the Sound.

"I'll call her one more time." Clare reached into her purse for her cell phone.

"Wait a second," I said, looking into my rearview mirror. "Is that her?"

Clare and I both turned around and peered at the motorcycle approaching. We couldn't make out who the driver was, of course, but you don't see too many bikers in Clare's neighborhood, let alone yellow-helmeted ones. So we were pretty certain who it was. Sure enough, it came to a stop behind my car.

I opened my window. "Where've you been?" I said, when Joey pulled off her helmet.

"You know, the usual. Shooting up, turning tricks."

"Funny."

"I've been calling and calling you," Clare said as Joey got into the backseat.

"I got your messages. That's why I'm here."

"You can't disappear like that," Clare said. "We get worried."

"You have to have a little faith in me."

Clare gave me a look and I was glad to see there was anger

in it. It made me feel better to know I wasn't the only one who was pissed off.

"Joey," I began, wanting to tell her that saying we should have faith was stupid and dismissive and insensitive of all the suffering she'd caused. Instead I said, "We need to talk about the letter," and went on to explain that we shouldn't tell the police my suspicions about the handwriting.

"Why not?" Joey asked.

I pulled away from the curb. "Because they might ask if we have any samples of Lydia's handwriting to compare it to and I don't want to tell them about the shoebox. At least not until we find it and Kenny can clean his old drugs out of it."

"He kept his drugs in a shoebox?" Joey said. "What a rookie."

The parking situation at the Nassau County Police Headquarters in Mineola was so bad I considered turning around and leaving. I never would have imagined crime was such a popular industry on Long Island. Besides the white-collar offenses our stockbrokers became famous for in the nineties—and our few notorious cases, like the Joey Buttafuoco–Amy Fisher mess—I thought it was a pretty quiet region. Criminals, I understood, didn't like to commute, and tended to limit their nefarious activities to the five boroughs. Ask anyone who's suffered the Long Island Expressway at rush hour and they'll tell you it takes patience of biblical proportions to make it past exit 39. If ancient kingdoms had had expressways instead of moats, they wouldn't have needed canons and armor.

By the time I found a parking space we were four lots and nearly a half mile away from the building.

"Remember," I said, as we trekked across hot asphalt. "We don't know anything about the handwriting and we certainly don't know anything about any shoebox."

"What shoebox?" Joey said.

Inside, a sergeant at the front desk took our names and called upstairs. A few minutes later, Detective Miller came to get us.

"Hi, Detective!" Joey said, arching her back.

"This way ladies." He led us to an elevator, and the farther away we got from the front door, the cooler the building felt.

"What's your first name, anyway?" Joey said to him as we approached the interview room.

He pushed the door open for us. "Sheldon. Have a seat. I'll be with you in a minute."

"Sheldon!" Joey squealed as the door shut behind him. "I *told* you he was Jewish."

The room was windowless, with a mirror along one wall and a long rectangular metal table in the middle. A fluorescent fixture overhead cast a sickly light.

"I can't get used to religion being a criterion for you, Joey," I said as I sat.

"You had very different standards before," Clare added.

"What standards?" I said. "Personal *hygiene* wasn't even an issue. Remember Phil?"

Clare shuddered. "Mom sprayed Lysol after he left the room."

Joey approached the mirror and cleaned the melting mascara from under her eyes with a fingertip. "Isn't he dreamy?" she said.

Clare looked horrified. "Phil?"

Joey tsked. "No, *Sheldon*."

I'm not sure I would have described Miller as dreamy, but he was good-looking enough, with dark, intelligent eyes and an appealing smile. His black-brown hair receded from his forehead enough to add a little wisdom to his otherwise boyish face.

Joey flipped her hair over her head and scrunched it. Then,

to my horror, she stuck her hand inside her tank top to lift her boobs for maximum cleavage.

"Joey," I whispered. "For heaven's sake—that's a one-way mirror!"

"Oh yeah?" she said. "Well, if they're watching, I may as well give them something to see."

She stood up and grabbed her shirt from the bottom.

"No!" I yelled, but she just laughed as she lifted her shirt and flashed whoever might be on the other side of the glass.

"Sit down!" Clare said, covering her face in embarrassment.

"Hey, I'm just trying to lighten the mood."

"You're trying to get Miller's attention," Clare said.

"So what if I am?"

"There's a right way and a wrong way," Clare said.

I pulled my chair toward the table. "You girls realize they can probably hear every word we're saying?"

"I have nothing to hide," Joey said.

I let out a snort. "Clearly!"

We were all laughing when the door opened and Miller entered with another officer.

"Ladies, this is Detective Dunn," he said.

"Were you watching us from the other side of the glass?" Joey asked, still smiling.

"Should I have been?"

"Depends what you like to see . . . *Sheldon*."

Dunn snickered. Miller retained his composure, which I suspected was his way of flirting with Joey. He seemed pretty damned sharp and probably knew exactly how to play her. His aloofness seemed to be working like an aphrodisiac on my little sister. Not that her libido needed any help, but still. I started to get a feeling about these two.

"Can I get you ladies a cup of coffee?" Dunn asked.

We politely declined, and the detectives sat down at the table opposite us. My mood shifted right back to somber.

"I understand you have something to show us," Miller said.

"I was trying to," Joey answered with a grin. "But you weren't watching."

I was growing impatient. "Enough already," I said. "This is serious." I took the wrinkled blue letter out of my purse, flattened it on the table, and pushed it across to Miller.

He took a pencil from his pocket and dragged the letter to him with the eraser end. "What is this?"

I looked at my hands, feeling stupid for not having had the sense to keep my fingerprints off it.

"I found it in Renee Waxman's bureau drawer," Joey said. "Stuffed inside a tampon box."

Detective Dunn, who had puffy cheeks and looked like an African American version of actor Paul Giamatti, tilted his head to the side so he could get a look at the letter. "Why were you looking through her drawers?" he asked Joey.

"It was just after we got the industrial drum out from under the house," she explained. "We were all covered with mud and I was going to borrow something to wear."

"And you thought you'd find something to wear inside a tampon box?"

"I was just being nosy," Joey said. "Mrs. Waxman is too old to need tampons, so I thought she might be hiding something in there, and I was right."

"She'd make a good detective," Dunn said to Miller.

Joey cocked her head cutely. "I'm good at a lot of things."

Detective Miller kept a serious expression and read the letter without touching it. Then he pushed it to his partner with the pencil eraser. After Dunn read it, they exchanged the subtlest of looks.

"Why didn't you turn this in earlier?" Miller asked.

"We didn't think of it," I said.

I held my breath, waiting to see if they accepted the explanation.

"Why do you think Renee Waxman saved this letter?" Miller said. I exhaled. It seemed like he was directing his question to Joey, and she answered.

"My guess? She probably found it somewhere and never even told him she had it. She might have been waiting for the courage to confront him about it."

"That's a long time to wait," Miller said.

"Mrs. Waxman was always very timid," Clare said.

Dunn pushed the letter back to Miller, who used the pencil to move it into a plastic bag.

"Is Sam Waxman a suspect?" Joey said.

"We'll ask the questions," Miller said.

Dunn nodded and got right down to business, asking me when I first noticed the industrial drum under the house and if it had ever been moved. He also wanted to know why we had brought it to the curb, and I told him all about the Goodwins and how I was helping to take care of the selling the house. He took notes, although I was sure they had already obtained this information from my sisters and Kenny. Then he asked a question that seemed out of left field.

"What do you know about Sam Waxman's manufacturing business?"

My sisters and I looked at each other, surprised.

"He made plastic flowers," I said, trying to remember what I knew.

"He did," Clare corroborated. "And those foam blocks they stick them in? He made those too."

"Why do you need to know that?" Joey asked.

Miller took a deep breath, and I thought he was going

to chastise Joey for asking another question, but he gave a direct answer, "We're trying to determine who would have had access to formaldehyde, which is used in certain types of manufacturing."

"That's what that smell was," I said. "The body was preserved."

Clare made a face like she was going to vomit. "Why would a murderer want to preserve a body?"

"To keep it from stinking," Joey said. She squeezed her nose for emphasis.

"Oh God," I said. "I just remembered something." They all looked at me. I put my hands flat on the table while I considered whether there was any reason to keep my revelation to myself. The table felt cool beneath my fingertips and I considered pressing my forehead against it for comfort. Instead, I looked directly into Miller's dark eyes.

"Sam *did* have access to formaldehyde," I said. "He used it in his factory."

"How do you know?"

I turned to Clare. "Remember Pickles?"

She thought for a second. "In the jar," she said.

I nodded, and explained to the confused detectives. "When we were kids, Kenny Waxman had a preserved dead mouse. His mom was too neurotic to actually let him have a live animal, so he joked about it like it was his pet. But I remember that he told me he had preserved Pickles himself, using formaldehyde that his father had brought home from the factory for him."

Dunn scribbled furiously, while questions ricocheted around my head. Was the formaldehyde connection alone enough to charge Sam Waxman with murder? Where was the shoebox with those samples of Lydia's handwriting? And perhaps most important of all, was the woman in the drum pregnant?

"Detective," I began, trying to think of a way to phrase the question that wouldn't earn me a sharp rebuke.

"Yes?"

I stopped myself, realizing that even if he *was* willing to answer the question, I wasn't sure it was something I was ready to hear.

"I have to use the bathroom."

Miller said that was fine, and that we were done, anyway. He turned to my sisters. "Unless there's anything else you ladies want to tell me?"

"Just one thing," Joey said.

I looked at her, wondering what other information she might have.

"Yes?" Miller said.

She smiled. "What are you doing tonight?"

He held up the baggie containing Lydia's letter. "Looks like I'm going to Florida to talk to 'Dearest Samuel.'"

Chapter 14

"What do you think she's up to?" Clare asked, after we had dropped Joey at her bike and watched her speed off. My older sister had suggested a trip to the mall and a quick bite, but Joey had begged off without explanation. "And why is she so mysterious?"

"I don't know."

Clare looked pained. "I have such a bad feeling, Bev. When she gets secretive like this. . ."

I stared off in the direction her motorcycle went. "Should I follow her?" I asked.

Clare nodded enthusiastically, so I sped to the corner and stopped. I spotted Joey's bike at the end of the block making a right, and proceeded slowly, maintaining a distance between us.

"She might be heading home," Clare said when Joey left the neighborhood and turned north on Glen Cove Road.

I followed behind, going slowly enough so that two cars got between me and Joey. Soon enough, it became apparent that she was indeed going home. After she turned the corner onto her block, I pulled over and waited a few minutes before driving on. I parked down the block from the house she rented. Her motorcycle was in the driveway.

"She's already inside," Clare said, putting on sunglasses.

I laughed. "You're a regular master of disguise, Clare."

She remained somber. "I think we should wait here and see if she comes out again."

"For how long?"

"Shh."

"Why are you shushing me? No one can hear us." I put the car in gear. "This is ridiculous. I'm leaving."

"Wait!" she said. "Look!"

A dark sedan parked in front of Joey's house and a man with a reddish beard and a briefcase got out. He wore a base-ball cap, which looked incongruous with the white button-down shirt and tan khakis he wore.

"Who *is* that?" Clare asked.

"Probably the other tenant," I said. Joey rented one-half of a two-family house.

"Pull up!" Clare commanded.

I inched forward so we could see which door the man entered. To my surprise, he pushed Joey's buzzer. I stepped on the gas.

"Who do you think that was?" Clare asked after we passed.

"He looked like an accountant or something. Maybe he's doing Joey's taxes."

"Who does their taxes in July?"

"Maybe she filed for an extension."

Clare shook her head. "If it was something innocent like that she would have told us. She would have said, 'I have to get home because I have an appointment with my accountant.'"

I would have argued with Clare, but this mysterious visitor on top of Joey's frequent disappearances made me think she really was up to something she didn't want us to know about.

"At least he doesn't look like a drug dealer," I said. "Although . . ."

"Although what?" Clare asked.

"He could be *buying* drugs."

Clare gasped. "You think? He looked so middle class."

I shrugged. "I just don't know."

Clare took out her cell phone. "I'm calling her. If it's something innocent, she'll tell me." She put her phone on speaker and called Joey, who answered quickly. Clare told her that she was planning on making a barbecue for Dylan's birthday and wanted to be sure Joey was free.

"Of course I'm free," Joey said.

"You can bring someone if you want." Clare glanced at me. She looked so proud of herself.

"Who would I bring?"

Clare looked at me for help and I shrugged. "I don't know," she said. "Whoever you want."

"Maybe I'll invite Sheldon," Joey said, laughing. Something unintelligible followed.

"What was that?" Clare said. "It sounds like someone is there with you."

"No one is here with me."

"I thought I heard something."

"It's the radio," Joey said. "I'm listening to Dr. Joy."

"But it sounded like a man," Clare insisted.

"It's a call-in show. Listen, I'm kind of busy now. Can I call you back?"

When I pulled into the mall parking lot, Clare was still obsessing on Joey's curious bearded man. But once we entered, the sensory assault of winding our way past Abercrombie & Fitch, the Gap, Waldenbooks, Foot Locker, Bath & Body Works, Express, Nine West, Old Navy, Dress Barn, Zales, B. Dalton, Ann Taylor, Williams-Sonoma, the Limited and Sharper Image on our way to the food court had lulled us both into a happy stupor. I was pretty convinced there was something piped into the air at the mall that made you believe with all your heart that the only thing standing between you and true bliss was a soft hot pretzel and a pair of dangly silver earrings purchased from a kiosk.

Clare, experiencing the same mall sickness as I, stopped in front of Victoria's Secret with a glazed expression in her eyes. The object of her fixation was a devil-red ensemble that consisted of a sheer, crotch-length garment with spaghetti straps over a matching thong.

"*Uh,* Clare?"

Silence.

"Is that something you're thinking of purchasing?"

She stared straight ahead.

"Clare? Honey? I've never seen you in red."

"Red?"

"Yes, red. As in the color? You haven't worn it since high school, when you paid Donna Lautato five dollars to do your colors and she said you were a summer."

"C'mon," she said, and walked so quickly inside I had to run to catch up with her.

Clare's shopping radar led her straight to the rack where the red ensemble hung. She quickly found her size and headed for the dressing room. I loitered in the shopping area, examining lace bras and filmy nighties. I'm not much of a negligee gal—and if I was, I'd be more drawn to satin than lace—but something white and pretty caught my eye. It was terribly sheer, the fabric delicate as vapor, with an empire waist and white ribbon straps. I put my hand beneath it and the material was so diaphanous I could see the crescents of my fingernails.

"Can I help you find a size?" asked a salesgirl who was a few sandwiches shy of a size zero.

"No, I, *uh* . . ."

"It would look great on you," she said, pulling one out and pressing it into my hand. Clare called me from the dressing room and I went to her, not even realizing I still clutched the sheer white nightie.

"What do you think?" Clare said, turning around to model the sizzling red ensemble for me.

What did I think? I thought that the way Clare looked in that thing was an indictment of modern society's insistence that bone and sinew define sexiness. Clare wasn't a hard-bodied, machine-enhanced ectomorph surgically altered to look more female, like our current crop of pop culture sex icons. She was a throw-back—a sensual, curvy, gorgeous woman. A 1950s pinup.

"I think Marc is going to have a coronary and collapse when he sees you in that," I said.

"You don't think my thighs look cottage cheesy?"

She seemed so serious I tried not to laugh, but couldn't help letting a snicker escape. "Clare, there isn't a straight man in the world you wouldn't stop dead in that."

"Really? You think it says 'Hot'?"

"I think it says 'Fuck me, big boy.'"

She sucked in her stomach and viewed herself from the side. "Is it too much?"

"I seriously doubt your husband will complain."

Clare's expression remained fixed, as if nothing I said got through to her.

"Don't you feel sexy in it?" I asked.

She shrugged and looked down. "I never feel sexy any-more," she mumbled.

"Why not?"

It seemed like an innocent enough question, but Clare reacted as if someone had just bombed her home. She burst into tears, covered her face in her hands, and slid down against the wall of the dressing room until she was curled in a ball on the floor crying.

I hesitated for a moment, trying to understand what I said that could have set her off. I crouched down. "Clare?" I said softly. "What's going on?"

She ran the back of her hand under her nose, a trail of mucus following behind. I found a tissue in my purse and handed it to her.

She looked up at me, her eyes red and wounded. "Marc cheated on me."

"Marc?" I said. "Are you sure?" It just didn't seem possible.

She nodded.

"How do you know? Did he tell you?"

She shook her head.

"Did you . . . walk in on something?" I shuddered. The thought of Clare experiencing what I did with Jonathan was excruciating to contemplate.

"No, but . . ." She cried silently into the tissue.

"But what?"

Clare blew her nose and wiped it clean. She took a deep breath. "A couple of months ago, Marc was in Houston on business and Sophie woke up with this terrible croupy cough. I was thinking about taking her to the hospital, but it was the middle of the night and I couldn't tell if it was just my anxiety running away from me, so I called his hotel room."

"And?"

"And . . . and a woman answered," she said.

Goose flesh rose on my arms. "What did she say?"

Clare folded over the tissue and wiped her nose again. "She said hello."

"What did *you* say?"

"I said hello back."

"And then what?"

Clare opened her own purse and found a pack of tissues. She pulled one out. "And then she hung up."

I paused to take this in. "And that's it?"

She nodded.

"Did you ask Marc about it?"

"No."

"Why not?"

"Because I wanted to be able to tell myself that I got a wrong number, or that Marc had been switched to another room and forgot to tell me. But I can't push it away. It keeps coming back. And all I can think is that I've failed in some terrible way."

Yes, I remembered that feeling. When I walked in on Jonathan and Savannah I felt that on some fundamental level it was my fault—that if I'd been a better wife, better lover, better artist, he wouldn't have cheated on me.

"Oh, Clare," I said. "This is not your fault."

"I used to be so pretty, Bev. Remember? And now I'm so fat and so old, like a mommy cow with expensive highlights."

I sighed. Part of me wanted to tell Clare that there was so much more to her than her appearance, but I knew it wasn't what she needed to hear just then. I stood up and grabbed her hands, bringing her to her feet. "Come here," I said, and dragged her to the door of the dressing room. I opened it a crack and scanned the sales floor. "You see that salesgirl over there?" I pointed to the tiny young woman who had helped me. "You're about twenty times prettier than she is."

"I am not."

"Okay, then thirty times prettier. And you see that woman in the spike heels?"

"Pucci's. She's stunning."

"Not compared to you."

"Liar."

I turned Clare toward the mirror and stood behind her, addressing her reflection. "I don't know what happened in that hotel room with Marc, but I know that you're a beautiful woman and that he adores you. But if you don't believe me, go ahead and buy this fuck-me-now nightie and look at your husband's face when he sees you in it. I think it'll tell you everything you need to know."

Chapter 15

Just two days later I was at Clare's house, sitting at the kitchen table drinking coffee and thumbing through one of her home decorating magazines while waiting for Dylan and Sophie to get home from day camp. Clare was at her Modern American Lit class and a contractor I hadn't seen was upstairs making more noise than I thought was possible without arena-sized speakers. He was, Clare had explained to me, remodeling the master bathroom. I couldn't imagine what was wrong with it to begin with, but it seemed that doing construction in one form or another was Clare's hobby. The house was in a continual state of metamorphosis.

The noise abruptly stopped and a few seconds later I heard the contractor's work boots trampling down the stairs.

"Clare?" he called.

I got up and walked toward the staircase, where I saw him descend. He was tall and lanky with a mop of dense, dark curls and looked like a young Marlon Brando, especially around the nose and lips. Dressed in tan baggy pants covered in dust and a faded green T-shirt that said Goode Earth Habitats, he reminded me of my ex. But the similarity stopped at the clothing. This guy had the bright eyes of someone with a profound capacity for happiness. I wasn't sure if I was attracted to him, but I wanted to be. I needed something to distract me while I waited to hear from that school in Las Vegas. And I needed someone to distract me from Kenny Waxman.

"She went out," I said to the contractor. "I'm her sister, Bev." Flirt, I told myself. For heaven's sake, *flirt*.

He wiped his hands on his shirt and we shook. His grip was firm, his palm warm and dry.

"Leo Carlotti," he said.

"Did you need something, Leo?"

"I had a question about the shower door she ordered. Do you know if it's here?"

I told him to look in the garage. He thanked me and went off in that direction, while I stood there chastising myself for not being able to think of some way to keep the conversation going.

I took a deep breath and followed him to the garage, where I found him standing in the middle of the immaculate floor, looking around.

"No shower door?" I asked.

"Nope."

"That a problem?"

"I'm not sure which one she decided on, and without the measurements I'm at an impasse."

Impasse. Fancy word for a contractor. I wanted to know more about this guy.

"I could try calling her husband at his office," I suggested, knowing full well Marc wouldn't have any idea what shower door Clare had ordered. But I congratulated myself for thinking of a way to get at least a few minutes with him.

He shrugged. "Can't hurt, I guess."

Leo followed me into the kitchen and I called Marc's office.

Fortunately, he was in a meeting and I was able to leave a message for him to call back.

"Do you . . . want to have a cup of coffee while we wait?" I tried to sound nonchalant and not at all desperate.

"That would be great." He smiled a pretty smile.

Gay? I thought for a second. No, not gay. Unless maybe. Shit. Clare and Joey probably had a special way to find that out within seconds, but I was at a loss.

I filled Clare's designer kettle with water from her designer faucet, and placed it on the designer stove. Then I put several scoops of designer coffee into an elegant French coffee press. I held up the bag of fancy coffee to show Leo. "I don't think there's one single thing in this entire house that's generic."

He laughed. "I get mine from the discount club."

Okay, so not gay then.

"What is Goode Earth Habitats?" I asked. "Is that the name of your company?"

He looked down at his shirt. "No, it's a charitable organization founded by a woman named Elinora Goode. We build homes for the homeless."

"*We?*" I asked.

He shrugged. "I got pretty involved after Hurricane Katrina."

"Oh my. That's so . . . noble."

Noble? What century did I live in?

He looked down, embarrassed. "Yeah, well. I'm good with my hands and don't have a lot of cash anymore, so I figured it was what I could do."

Anymore. That made it sound like Leo had an interesting history, as if there was a fallen empire in his past. And now he was just a good-hearted hippie type—the kind of person a lot of my artist friends wanted to be but were too self-absorbed to actually become. And maybe this was me being overly romantic, but the idea that he was unconcerned with having a lot of cash was endearing. An unambitious guy was a refreshing change. At least that's what I was telling myself. With Kenny and Joey so cozy, I was determined to be interested in this guy.

"So how does that work?" I asked, taking a designer mug from the designer cabinet. "Do you have to travel?"

"This job," he said, sweeping his hands toward the upstairs bathroom, "is mostly seasonal. So during the winter months, if I have enough cash saved, I go down South and help out."

"And where do you stay?"

"Someone usually puts me up."

"So you just sleep on someone's couch half the year? God, you're like Mother Teresa."

"Listen, I'll tell you the truth," he said, pulling out a chair and straddling it backward. "I love nearly every second of it. Imagine working really hard, I mean *physically* hard, which just releases all these endorphins, you know?" He looked off into the distance as if he were trying to picture it. "And if you screw up, which happens, no one gets pissed. I mean, not really pissed, because no one's there to make money. Everyone is just trying to get this very real thing done. And the people. The people are great." He tucked his curls behind his ears.

The kettle whistled and I poured the boiling water over the coffee in the French press. This guy was pretty intense, and possibly a little odd. But I was sucked in. I wanted to know more.

"And then, you know," he continued, "you get to see people move in. Old people. Young people. People with kids. And everybody cries. I mean everybody."

"Including you?"

"Especially me. Ha!" He drummed the table for emphasis.

"This is amazing stuff, Leo. Someone should be filming it, putting it on the news. I think people would be interested."

"Actually," he cleared his throat. "Actually, I'm writing about it. Kind of a memoir."

"You want to get it published?"

"Someday."

Aha. There it was. Call me a cynic, but I knew there had to be something not altogether altruistic about this guy. Not that I thought his heart was in the wrong place, just that I knew everyone harbored at least some sort of vanity. And I had found Leo's. Frankly, it made me more interested. Who wanted to date a saint?

"Are you hungry?" I asked.

He said he wouldn't mind something to go with the coffee, and I found some organic chocolate chip cookies in a package made from recycled paper. Clare would have been horrified, but I put the bag right on the table rather than arrange the cookies onto a serving plate. I pushed down the plunger on the coffee press and poured him a cup.

I watched as he drank his coffee and ate the entire bag of cookies without looking up. Then he asked for another cup.

I laughed. "You seem pretty hungry."

"Didn't have lunch," he said, still chewing.

I sat across from him, thinking I was doing a good job getting him to talk, but a lousy job flirting. I hadn't done anything to let him know I was interested. I wasn't even that successful in establishing eye contact. How did women steer the conversation in that direction without saying something stupid and embarrassing? Was I supposed to tell him he was *dreamy*?

"So what do you do?" he asked.

"I'm teacher. Or about to be one. I'm waiting to hear about a job."

"Cool. You married?"

"Divorced. You?"

"Never stayed in one place long enough to get married. One day, though. I could see being a husband and having kids."

"Yeah, kids are great." God, I sounded like an idiot. "I mean, that's why I'm a teacher now. I love working with children." *And that's why I want to be Miss America.* Sheesh.

"We should go out sometime," Leo said.

I heard a double honk from outside and bolted out of the chair, banging into the table and almost knocking over his coffee cup. "Oh! Clare's kids! But *uh* . . . yeah, we *should* go out sometime."

I rushed to the front door leaving Leo in the kitchen.

Seven-year-old Sophie got off the bus first, her face flushed red from the heat. Dylan, three years older, followed behind looking tired. I kissed the children hello and made them stop in the powder room to wash their hands before ushering them into the kitchen for snacks. Leo was standing by the sink, downing the last drops of coffee from his cup.

"Hello, Peace," he said to Sophie, messing her hair. He patted Dylan on the head. "Hello, Happiness."

I laughed, understanding that his nicknames were intentionally ironic. Sophie was a chatterbox in constant motion, and anything but peaceful. Dylan was a quiet kid and, today at least, a bit melancholy.

"Hi, Leo!" Sophie sang enthusiastically.

"Hi," Dylan mumbled.

"I need to make a Home Depot run," Leo said to me. "You think Clare will be here by the time I get back?"

"She should."

"And you?"

I smiled. "Maybe."

"Just in case, here's my card." He pressed it into my hand and leaned in for a whisper. "My home phone number is written on the back." He winked at me and patted my head like he did to the kids, and then he was gone.

Smiling, I stuck the card into the pocket of my jeans and turned my attention to the children, asking them about their day at camp as I searched the cabinets for the specific snacks they had requested—cereal for Sophie and an apple for Dylan.

"Courtney and Anastasia and Emma are my best friends at camp," Sophie said. "And the Cheerios are next to the granola, Aunt Bev."

"Got it," I said, and poured some into a bowl.

"At swim today I played with Beatrice and Tonya because we were in a group together and guess what? I was the only one who could swim underwater. And the swim counselor, Allison, said I could maybe move up a level next week."

"Uh-huh."

"And the juice boxes aren't in the refrigerator. They're in the cabinet under the fruit bowl. My counselor's name is Meg and she has a boyfriend."

"Sophie, honey, you're a force of nature."

"What's that mean?"

"It means you've been at this camp one week and you already have a bunch of best friends and know everyone's name. And I bet everyone knows yours too."

She smiled, satisfied, and I turned my attention to Dylan. I wanted to see if I could pull him out of his sullenness.

"Hey, you've got a birthday coming up, Dyl. Are you inviting any of your camp friends?"

"I don't know."

Clearly, it was up to me to keep the conversation going. "What was the best part of your day today?"

He shrugged. "Baseball, I guess."

"Oh yeah? Tell me about it."

"We were down two-one, and I hit a home run with two men on and we won."

Men. That killed me. "You must have been the hero of the day."

He smirked. "For *my* team, yeah."

I laughed, and pressed him to tell me more about camp.

"We did archery today," he said. "My first time and I almost got a bull's eye."

He was picking up, but there was an earnestness about this kid that made it impossible for him to hide how he was feeling, and I still felt like there was something tugging at him under the surface. I decided to try to lift his mood by making him laugh. I found an apple in the refrigerator and put it on my head.

"Archery, huh? Think you could shoot this?"

"Hold still," he said, not missing a beat. He pulled back an imaginary bow, closed one eye and released an arrow straight at me.

I put my hand to my face and doubled over, catching the apple before it hit the floor. "*Ow,* my eye!" I wailed in mock horror. "You shot my eye out."

Sophie squealed in delight.

Dylan smiled. "Sorry, Aunt Bev. Let me try again."

"Are you kidding? I only have two eyes." I made him stand against the wall and put the apple on his head. "My turn," I said.

Dylan stood straight up. I pretended to struggle with the tension of the bow as I pulled it back. I aimed right for the apple and released. Dylan grabbed the apple and bent in half.

"You got me in the gut!" he said. "I'm dying." He collapsed

to the floor and expired with all the melodrama he could muster. *"Oh! Ack! Argh!"*

He was genuinely hilarious, and the more Sophie and I laughed, the more he moaned and groaned and twitched in the throes of his last gasp. He signaled for me to come close enough to hear him whisper his dying words, which he croaked out. "Your . . . aim . . . blows." And then he closed his eyes and dropped his head to the side, the universal sign for croaking.

"What did you expect?" I said. "I'm blind in one eye, remember?"

Later, I tried to interest the children in an art project. Sophie was game, but Dylan only wanted to retreat into the playroom in the basement where his video games were set up.

"You sure you don't want to paint?" I asked. "PlayStation will still be there when we finish."

But I couldn't sell it, and he left us girls to our creative pursuit. When Clare got home with a few bags of groceries, I helped her unpack and told her that Dylan seemed a bit out of sorts. She said he'd been like that for a few days and she wasn't having any luck figuring out what was troubling him. She called into the basement to tell him to come up, and had to do so several times before he reluctantly trudged up the stairs.

"What?" he said when he faced her. Now his mood seemed dark, angry.

"I just wanted to see how your day was, sweetie." She reached into one of the grocery bags.

"It was fine."

"I got that spaghetti sauce you like," she said, showing him. "I'll make it for dinner."

"Did you get Mallomars?"

"Mallomars?"

He folded his arms. "They're my *favorite* cookies."

"I know that, Dyl, but they don't sell them in the summer."

"Why not?" he whined.

"Because the chocolate melts. I can't get them again until the fall." She drew a sack of oranges from a bag and put it in the refrigerator.

"That sucks!" he said, raising his voice. "That totally sucks!"

"We have other cookies, Dylan."

"I don't *want* other cookies!" he yelled, and ran back into the basement.

Clare turned to me, the color draining from her face. "This is how he's been. He's just angry all the time. I was hoping it would just pass, but now I'm getting concerned."

I couldn't blame her. It wasn't like him to be bratty. Something was troubling this boy, and someone needed to find out was it was. I wondered if I could be the one to do it.

I hung around for a bit, stalling, hoping I might get to see Leo again. I was just about to leave when I heard the doorbell.

"Hey, you're still here," Leo said when I opened the door.

"I was just on my way."

Clare came out of the kitchen, and I got the distinct impression Leo was checking her out in her tight cotton-candy-colored top. How could he not? She looked hot as hell. Instead of feeling threatened, I was glad for her. Clare, God bless her, needed to be ogled.

"How was your lit class?" Leo asked.

Clare grinned. "Very . . . dynamic."

"Who are you reading?"

I could have stuck around for the conversation, but I figured I'd let Clare discuss literature without feeling like her bookish sister was judging her. "I'm going," I announced to both of them."

"You'll call me?" Leo said.

Clare's eyebrows went up.

"I will," I said, and left.

Chapter 16

With our mother's birthday only a week away, my sisters and I decided to meet at Fortunoff—a local jewelry and fine gift store considered a Long Island institution—so we could chip in for something special. Joey was still being mysterious about her disappearances and hadn't said a word about the man with the red beard. Clare and I were determined to watch her closely for any signs of drug use. I was also burning to know if anything was going on between her and Kenny.

While Clare scrutinized some gold neck chains, I turned to Joey. "You hear from Kenny again? About the shoebox?"

"Didn't he tell you? His mother said it was probably in storage. Sam rented space from one of those self-storage places and moved a whole bunch of stuff there."

"What do you think of this chain?" Clare said, tapping her finger on the glass case.

Joey looked at the chain and snorted. "Boring."

"So was it in there?" I asked.

"I don't know," Joey said. "We couldn't find the key. Renee told Kenny it was a special key with an orange ring around the top, and that Sam kept it in his desk drawer, but it wasn't there."

"It's not boring," Clare insisted. "It's classic, elegant. Italian design, I think. I'll ask the saleswoman to take it out for us."

"We?" I said to Joey. "You went over there?"

"Last night."

Okay, fine. So Joey and Kenny were together last night. They had probably sealed the deal, picked up where they left off, rocked and rolled till dawn. I could handle that. I could. And anyway, what difference did it make? With any luck, I'd get a job offer from Las Vegas any day now and all of this would cease to matter. I'd be the new Bev. The Las Vegas Bev, with a new apartment, new friends, new clothes, new everything.

The saleswoman laid the necklace out on a square of black velvet.

"See?" Clare said. "See how it reflects the light?"

"Everything reflects the light in here," Joey said. "They probably have special bulbs or something."

"So what happened?" I asked Joey.

"What do you mean what happened?"

"When you went to see Kenny."

Clare picked up the tiny tag on the necklace with her manicured fingernails. "It's twenty-four karat," she said. "I knew it."

"Nothing happened," Joey said to me. We just fucked for a couple of hours and then shot heroin."

Clare and I both snapped our necks toward her. The saleswoman pretended she didn't hear, but I saw her ears flush.

"I'm kidding," Joey said. "Take it easy. We just talked."

Clare let out enough carbon dioxide to fill a greenhouse.

"About what?" I asked.

"He told me what a prick his father is. But Kenny's all fucked up over it. Part of him is sure his father is guilty. But part of him is hoping the body in the drum isn't Lydia's and that this whole thing will just go away."

"I see."

Clare picked up the gold chain. "What do you girls think?" she asked, trying to get us back on task. "Should we take it?"

Joey rolled her eyes. "We need something more exciting."

Clare held it to her neck to model it for us. "Look at it," she said. "It's beautiful."

"It's lovely," I said. "But Joey's right—we need something with more pop." I pointed to a hammered silver cuff in the next case. "Something like that."

"That chunky thing? Clare said. "It's so bohemian. That's an art teacher bracelet, not a mom bracelet."

Joey laughed. "She's right!"

"Well, what's *your* idea?" I asked Joey.

"How about a Star of David on a chain?" she said.

Clare and I looked at each other and shrugged, surprised that Joey came up with a pretty good suggestion. We went to the counter that sold religious jewelry and found an impressive assortment. I concentrated on the sparkly array, trying to get my mind off whether or not Joey was telling the whole truth about her and Kenny. As luck would have it, we couldn't agree on which one Mom would like, and I got caught up in the debate. Clare favored a gold star embedded with tiny diamonds, which I thought was fine, but not terribly exciting. Joey liked the one that substituted a heart for one of the triangles, which Clare thought was ghastly and I thought was just kind of weird looking. I liked the star with colorful gemstones in each corner and couldn't understand why my sisters thought it was juvenile. We kept looking, making the poor saleswoman show us every item they had, until we finally found one we agreed on. It was a delicate star with little sapphires and diamonds set in white gold that we all thought Mom would love. We paid and had it shipped to her at the Waxmans' address down in Florida, and then left the store satisfied.

Back at home, my sisters followed me to the front door, where I paused to look in the mailbox, even though I knew delivery came in the afternoon. It was, in fact, getting harder and harder to keep myself from checking the mail pretty compulsively for that job offer. To my surprise, there was a single small package inside in the box. I took it out and saw that it had a handwritten note on the front from Teddy Goodwin, asking me to pass it to Joey.

"For you," I said, handing Joey the package. I unlocked the door and we went into the house. Joey took it straight to the trash can and dropped it in.

"What are you doing?" I said. "Don't you want to see what it is?"

"I *know* what it is," she said. "It's a homemade CD with some song he wrote that he thinks I'll record, and he'll be the next Neil Diamond or something."

"Don't you at least want to listen to it?" Clare said. "Maybe it's good."

"I don't care if it's good," Joey said. "I'm not interested."

"Why not?" I asked.

"You'll hurt his feelings," Clare said.

Joey rolled her eyes and retrieved the package from the trash. "Fine," she said, tearing open the envelope and sticking the CD in her purse. "I'll listen to it. You happy now?"

"Why are you getting so upset over this?" I asked.

"Because everyone seems to think I should do whatever I can to get back into the music industry. But maybe I don't *want* to get back into it, did you ever think of that?"

I wondered if it was just fear holding her back, and I hated to see her let go of her dream for that. I thought of how many years I wasted running around pretending to be an artist, lying even to myself about what was in my heart.

"Are you worried about the temptations?" I asked.

"You mean drugs?"

"Yeah."

She laughed through her nose. "You don't get me at all, Bev."

"Because if that's it, if that's even a part of it, I understand. But you shouldn't let go of what's important to you."

"And also," Clare added, "remember that we're here for you."

"Okay, thank you Dr. Phil and Oprah," Joey said. "When I'm ready for a rousing chorus of 'Kumbaya,' I'll let you guys know."

"Don't be so snide," I said. "We love you. And you scared the living shit out of us for years. So if we seem to be watching over you like a couple of old aunties, cut us some slack."

Joey sighed. "Fine. But cut me some slack too. I'm going to rehab, doing exactly what I need to do. Don't worry so much."

Did Joey have any idea how hard that was after what we'd been through? The first time she disappeared, we filed a missing person's report, and then Mom, Dad, Clare, and I huddled together, crying, worried that she'd turn up dead. We didn't sleep, we didn't eat, and when we finally found her, strung out in Oregon with some junkie friend, I didn't know whether to weep with joy that she was still alive or strangle her till she was dead.

Clare suggested we all go out for lunch and Joey looked at her watch.

"I have to pass," she said. "There's someplace I need to be."

"Again?" I said.

Joey snickered and patted me on the noggin. "Don't you worry your pretty little head about it. I'll catch up with you guys soon." And then she was gone.

Chapter 17

Saturday was a glorious summer day, the atmosphere uncharacteristically clear for that time of year. No haze hovered between the heavens and the earth. It was just the white sun, the blue sky, and us fun-starved mortals. Leo and I decided it was a perfect beach day, and he offered to bring the beer if I brought a picnic lunch. So that afternoon found us side by side on a blanket, propped up on our elbows as we chatted from behind sunglasses, getting to know one another.

Since this was Jones Beach on a Saturday in early July, it was the farthest thing from a romantic scene of two lone lovers by the surf. We had little more than the seven square feet of space my blanket took up on the sand. Surrounding us were families with babies and children, groups of teenagers, grandmothers, grandfathers, and extended families from every known ethnic group and then some. As Leo told me about himself, a round, hairy-backed man with a toddler on his shoulders walked by our blanket toward the water.

"Where was I?" Leo asked me.

"College."

"Oh, right." He went on to explain that he had left Oneonta a few credits short of his bachelor's degree because a friend of his was making tons of money working as a stockbroker and convinced him to take the exams required to become a "registered rep." So at twenty-one he was wearing a suit and working for one of those boiler rooms on Long Island, selling false promises to people who often couldn't afford to take the losses. The place was a snake pit, he said, but he got so caught up in the flow of money he very nearly lost his moral compass. Then one day, when it got impossible to lie to himself about what his company was really up to, he got in a fight with his boss over refusing to sell a stock that was sure to tank after they finished with it. He walked out and never went back.

"Best thing I ever did," he said. "Couple of months later the Feds shut the place down and two of the guys I worked with were indicted for stock fraud."

"So how did you go from a stockbroker to construction? Seems like an odd transition."

"Wasn't a straight line," he said. "After I left Parker Jameson, I sold cars and then mortgages and finally real estate. From there I got involved with this other guy buying handyman specials, fixing them up and flipping them for a profit." A brazen seagull landed a few feet from our blanket and walked toward us. "This what you're looking for?" Leo said as he tossed it a crust of bread. He turned to me. "What was I saying?"

"Handyman specials."

"Right. My father was a contractor, so it felt pretty natural. Still, I had to make a lot of mistakes before I knew what I was doing."

I turned onto my side to face him. He wore bright orange trunks with a Hawaiian print, and his skin was tan and smooth. A suggestive line of dark hair ran up his belly from the top of his bathing suit. His body was long and lean— and maybe a little too skinny—but I wanted to touch him. I propped my head on my elbow instead.

"Do you like it?"

"What?" He was looking at the ocean and seemed distracted by the shrieks of children jumping the waves.

"Your job," I said. "You like it?"

"It's cool doing something where you get to see a finished product when you're done, something you're actually responsible for."

"Interesting." I sat up and squeezed a puddle of sunscreen onto my hand, which I rubbed onto my chest and shoulders. I glanced over to see if he was watching. He wasn't. I followed his line of sight and realized he was looking at a sailboat in the distance. I looked down at my chest and back at the horizon. Hey, I wanted to say, I've got breasts here.

I cleared my throat. "I've had a few different jobs where I got to create a finished product, but it never lit me on fire. I guess I was in the wrong field."

"And the teaching thing?" he said.

I closed my eyes and pictured a classroom. I saw myself walking around the room as the children worked on something I had just taught. I'd stop to offer gentle comments here and there. A small face would look up at me with an expression that said, "Is this right?" The guilelessness of the look, the complete trust in my guidance, touched me in such a raw spot it caused a lump to swell in my throat.

"The teaching thing feels right," I said.

"How'd you come to it?"

I told Leo that after catching my ex cheating, it shook the foolishness right out of me.

He sat up and rested his elbows on his knees. His flat nose was already turning red. "Was that rough? The divorce, I mean."

"Yes and no. I think deep down I knew that marrying Jonathan was a mistake, but I kept telling myself I could make it work, that he was an artist and I needed to accept him for who he was. But it meant wrapping my life around someone who was exhaustingly intense and self-absorbed."

Leo watched as a beach ball landed a foot from our blanket. He picked it up and tossed it back to a small girl in a tie-dyed bathing suit who stood beside us, arms outstretched.

He turned back to me. "What were we talking about?"

Oh God. I'd been droning on. "Forget it," I said. "I just broke the cardinal rule of the first date. You're not supposed to talk about your ex."

"I don't believe in rules," Leo said.

"I'll bet you don't," I said. "You want to go for a swim?"

The water felt like ice against my flesh, and I tiptoed in carefully, my elbows out so I could keep my arms dry as long as possible. Leo dove right into a wave and swam several few feet out.

"C'mon!" he called.

"Give me a minute!"

Even as a child I needed to get used to the water slowly. The cold of it felt like torture, and I had to deal with it inch by excruciating inch, until I summoned the courage to bend my knees and let my body submerge up to my shoulders.

I looked toward Leo and saw a high wave between us. I swam toward it as fast as I could so I could get over it before it crashed. I just made it.

"Water feels great!" Leo said, taking my hand and leading me farther out.

Though we were nearly fifty feet past the shoreline, the undertow pulled out and we were able to stand with our heads above water. We jumped together as a gentle swell rose and passed. A larger one rolled in and flooded beneath us as we floated. It was lovely being out this deep, past the point where the waves broke, just enjoying the rhythm of the tide as it pushed and pulled, with the sounds of the other beachgoers blending into the background, enveloped by the ocean's steady song.

As a kid, I coveted being out this deep. I remembered eyeing the swimmers beyond the whitecaps, envious of how relaxed they seemed, enjoying the peaceful rolls of the waves without fear of being pummeled.

Sometimes, when the dads were at work, we would go to the beach with the Waxmans, and Kenny's mom always brought Lydia along so she could watch us kids while she and my mom "coffee klatched," as she called it. One particular day, I was in the ocean with Kenny and Clare while Lydia played with little Joey at the water's edge, making footprints in the wet sand and then watching as the water rolled in and erased their impressions.

The three of us bigger kids were laughing and jumping the waves. Occasionally they were big enough to knock us down, especially if we were talking and not paying attention. Clare and Kenny seemed to take it in better humor than I did. I hated the surprise of finding myself submerged and then breaking the surface with a stinging pain in my nose. But I stuck with it, continuing to watch the swimmers farther out, who floated gently over the massive swells of the deeper water.

"You ever been out that deep?" I asked Kenny, as I pointed.

"Sure," he said. "Haven't you?"

I shook my head.

"Never?" he asked.

"We're not allowed," Clare said. "It's too far."

Kenny glanced over his shoulder at Lydia playing with Joey, and then at our moms on their beach chairs. "No one's watching," he said.

I looked at Clare, hoping she would put her foot down and

say something like, *We're already out too far*, but she just shrugged and said, "Let's go."

The two of them swam over the top of a wave while I treaded, unsure of whether to continue or retreat. I wanted so badly to be out there, but felt a terrible danger in passing the point where the tallest waves broke at their fiercest. I watched as just such a monster loomed over Kenny and Clare. But they dove straight inside it, their heads bobbing to surface beyond the foam once the whitecap broke.

"C'mon!" Clare called.

I couldn't see her expression, but I could hear in her voice that she was smiling, and that was what did it. I couldn't bear missing out on the fun.

I swam toward them using the undertow, watching as a wall of water approached them like a rolling mountain. It lifted them up higher and higher, and I heard Clare's faint laugh rising. As it approached me, morphing from a gentle giant to a violent white-capped beast, I knew what I was supposed to do—swim right through the middle of it. But I panicked at the thought of being beneath all that water, and I tried to swim over it, to beat the wave before it fully crested, even though it was already breaking as I approached. And then it happened. I was tossed under water with a terrible slam. Dazed, with my eyes shut tight in terror, I swam as hard as I could back to the surface. I could barely hold my breath; the wave had taken me by surprise, so I'd had no chance to fill my lungs. I kicked hard, anticipating the sweet moment where I'd break the surface and gasp in a huge gulp of air. I reached out with my hands like a blind person, knowing I'd be free of the water any second. Then a shock and a moment of incomprehension as I hit something hard. It was the ocean floor! I swam in the wrong direction.

A confused panic seized me and I must have opened my

mouth to breathe, because my lungs filled with water. A special kind of sickness came over me, like a sleepiness I could accept or reject. And then, before I got a chance to decide to fight or not, some unseen force grabbed me and pulled me up, up until at last I felt sweet air. I took a big, frantic gulp of it into my lungs, and as I coughed out water to replace it with oxygen, I heard the female voice of my rescuer.

"You're okay, dear girl."

It was Lydia.

I clung to her as she carried me back to my mother, my little bird heart beating fast against my ribcage. I felt Lydia's chest rise and fall in steady rhythm, like the sway of the ocean, and I knew I was indeed okay. It didn't occur to me then that she had saved my life. And perhaps she hadn't, perhaps I would have made it to the surface on my own, or some other swimmer would have yanked me out. But I think at that moment I understood for the first time how I could love someone I wasn't related to.

By the time Leo and I headed back from the beach it was early evening, and I was enjoying his company enough to want to prolong the date. But this was exactly the kind of situation that strained my social skills. We were both sandy, salty, and sweaty, and if I suggested dinner, it would mean stopping to shower at my house or his, and I just couldn't picture how that would play out, and whether or not he would assume it was a come on. I hadn't yet made the decision about whether I wanted to take this relationship to the next step. That was the point of spending more time with him—to decide if I liked him enough to sleep with him.

As we headed north from the shore in Leo's van, I wondered how my sisters would handle the situation. Actually, I wondered how *Clare* would handle it. Joey's approach was easy to imagine—she'd rip her clothes off and jump him. But Clare? I tried to channel her charm, picturing her sitting next to this dark, winsome guy. Most likely she'd flirt, dropping subtle hints that she wasn't quite ready to say good-bye. I opened my window. Leo had the radio on, drumming to the beat on his steering wheel.

"It's still so beautiful out," I finally said.

"Supposed to rain tomorrow."

So much for that approach. I put my hand on my stomach. "Beach makes me hungry."

"I'm still full from the beer."

Either I was really bad at this or Leo just wasn't interested. I decided I needed to be more direct.

"I had fun today," I said.

He glanced over at me. "Me, too," he said. Then he put his hand on my knee.

Okay, now what? I wished I had some sort of pocket translation dictionary for exactly what this kind of thing meant. I understood that he was attracted to me. That much was clear. But was this a come on, or just a statement? If I didn't react, would he take it as a rejection? If I did react, would he take it as a green light to his overture?

WWCD, I thought. *What Would Clare Do*?

"I didn't think we'd have much in common," I said, "but we do." There. A conversation starter. Not bad.

"Such as?" His right hand stayed on my knee, his left on the steering wheel.

"We both started out in careers that were wrong for us, and made a lot of misguided choices before winding up where we belong."

He nodded, thoughtfully. "Only, I think you have more of a commitment to yours. I'm still not sure if I'll stay in construction or wind up someplace else entirely. Maybe I don't have

one path, you know? I'm always thinking about what's next."
He laughed. "I think I'm kind of ADD, to tell you the truth."

Ah, that seemed to fit with everything he'd said. And maybe
it should have scared me off, but I thought that a distractible
guy, always looking for a diversion, might be exactly what I
needed right now.

He took his hand off my knee to change lanes, and then left
it on the steering wheel. Maybe it was because the idea of any
type of commitment was just taken off the table, but I was
feeling more at ease, and I figured the timing was right to ask
him if he wanted to have dinner together.

"What's on your agenda for tonight?" I asked.

"I was going to ask you the same thing," he said, "but I
didn't know how long a date you'd be up for."

Why on earth didn't he know that I was up for a longer
date? I'd been giving him every signal I could think of. I was
starting to wonder if maybe it was him and not me.

"I still have some energy left in me, Leo."

"Are you sure? You look upset."

"I do?"

"We can do this another time," he said.

I looked at him, trying to figure out if he was giving me the
brush off or if he was really just misreading me. "Why would
I be upset?" I said.

"You've been through a lot lately. Clare told me you passed
out cold when you found that body."

"I did," I said. "But that was days ago."

"I can't imagine what it must have been like." He shuddered. "The closest I ever came to something like that was
when my dog died. I was ten and I found him stiff. God, I was
a wreck."

"That must have been traumatic," I said, remembering the
summer our schnauzer, Stephanie, died. I was home from col-

lege and working as a camp counselor. As I was getting ready to leave the house my mother asked me to take Stephanie in from the backyard. I opened the door and saw that she wasn't on her tether. I glanced around and didn't see her anywhere. I called her name but she didn't come.

"She's not out there," I told my mom.

"She's not?"

"Did you tether her?"

"No," my mother said, biting her lip. "I was in a hurry and thought I'd just let her do her business and come right back in."

I shuddered, remembering what happened to Stephanie the last time I let her roam free in the yard. We both walked outside and called her name.

"I don't understand it," my mother said. "I just let her out ten minutes ago. Where could she have gone?"

I walked behind the shed because it was the only spot in the yard you couldn't see from the back porch. Stephanie was there, lying on her side, immobile. I rushed to her. She was alive, but barely. And instead of howling like she did that day when her leg got caught in the tether clip, she was quiet, panting in short breaths.

"Mom!" I screamed.

We rushed her to the vet, crying all the way. She wasn't a young dog, but I wasn't ready to lose her.

I sat in the back of the car cradling her in my lap as I whispered over and over, "You're going to be okay, girl. I promise." But when I put my hand in front of her mouth and her little tongue didn't slip out and lick me, I wasn't so sure.

"Please don't let her die," I said to Dr. Samalin, as he took her from my arms. She didn't seem to be breathing by that point, and they made us stay in the waiting room as they tried to resuscitate her.

A short while later, the doctor came out with his head bowed. "I'm sorry," he said. "She's gone."

I collapsed into my mother, not really paying much attention to what he said next. But later, when we told my father and sisters what had happened, I remembered that the doctor had said it was either heart failure or she had ingested something she wasn't supposed to eat, like insecticide. There was no way of knowing without a necropsy, which we just couldn't bear to do. And so we let the vet cremate her and were left to mourn together. The house never felt the same again after that.

"So," Leo said, bringing his hands together, "how about Chinese?"

Chapter 18

There aren't many ten-minute activities as rejuvenating as the after-beach shower, and I was looking forward to this one even more than usual. I had sent Leo away, and wanted to stand under a steady stream of warm water far longer than was necessary, washing away the sand and grime and memories, getting clean, clean, clean, to emerge a fresh, new Beverly Bloomrosen. After about two minutes, however, the water turned tepid and then cold, so I washed my dirty self as fast as possible and got out, shivering. I dressed quickly and went into the basement to see if I could discern any problem with the hot water heater.

It didn't take an expert to see that there was something wrong. The massive metal cylinder was sputtering and shaking, a steady stream of water pouring forth from a valve in the front onto the concrete floor of the basement.

"Shit."

I ran to the valve but couldn't find any way of shutting it off. A quick walk around the quivering machine didn't offer any further clues, so I grabbed a bucket and put it under the spout, and then tried to remember if my father had ever told me where the shut-off valve for the water main was located.

I couldn't find it in the basement or my memory banks. I picked up the phone and called Clare, who didn't know either. But she said she'd come over and help me look for it so we wouldn't have to bother Dad. Then I called the plumber whose magnetized business card was stuck on the refrigerator, and requested emergency service. They said it could be up to a few hours, and I got busy cleaning the water from the floor with towels and a mop.

By the time Clare got there, I had sopped up most it, and the hot water heater had stopped shaking and was only emitting a small trickle out of the spout. So we decided to just leave the bucket beneath it while we waited for the plumber to arrive.

Meanwhile, since Clare didn't have to rush home, we ordered Chinese food and gave Joey a call to see if she was free or pulling one of her vanishing acts.

An hour later, the three of us sat in the kitchen passing around cartons while we chatted.

"So how was your date?" Clare asked me as she spooned brown rice onto her plate.

"Bev had a date?" Joey asked.

Clare opened the container of Hunan pork and sniffed it. "With my contractor." She offered the carton to Joey. "Pork?"

Joey shook her head and reached for the egg foo young. "Cute?" she asked me.

I nodded.

"Get laid?"

"Hardly. He brought up dead dogs and I had meltdown thinking about Stephanie."

"My baby sister," Joey said, as if she had some kind of special right to the dog because she was the only one who didn't have a little sister. I always felt that my bond with Stephanie was the strongest and that she was, in fact, *my* dog. But I'll concede that we all probably felt that way. She was a hell of a dog.

Clare shook her head. "She wasn't even that old, poor thing."

"Did we ever figure out what killed her?" Joey asked.

"Vet said she might have ingested something she shouldn't have," I reminded her.

Joey raised her eyebrows. "Where would Stephanie have *accidentally* found poison?"

"Maybe there was insecticide on the lawn or the trees," Clare said.

"Or maybe she was murdered," Joey said.

Clare frowned. "You're joking, right?"

Joey shrugged and reached into her rice with chopsticks. "Remember how furious Waxman got when we let her run free in the yard?"

"And Mom *had* let her run loose that day," I added, picturing how it might have happened. I imagined Stephanie squatting by the fence that divided our property from the Waxmans'. Sam could have been watching from his kitchen window as her urine seeped through the ground to his precious lawn. He might have had some rat poison he'd been saving since the day he maimed her with the tether clip when he was sure no one was looking. He could have walked to the corner of his yard with some hamburger laced with poison, and fed it to our sweet little dog, who would have been grateful for the treat. I could imagine her stubby tail wagging as her pink tongue pulled the poisoned food into her mouth.

"I can't even think about this," Clare said, putting her hands on her head as if she wanted to block it all out. Poor thing looked like she was about to melt into something goopier than the brown sauce Joey was spooning onto her egg foo young.

I turned to Joey and changed the subject. "Did you ever listen to that DVD from Teddy Goodwin?"

Joey said she did. "Better than I expected. Nice refrain, crazy bridge. Really not bad." She shoveled a bite into her mouth. "You guys *have* to try this."

I reached for the carton, put some onto my plate and passed it to Clare, who broke off no more than a square inch for herself.

"Anyway," Joey continued, "I might record it for him, just as a favor to help him sell the song. I don't know. I haven't decided yet. Teddy's going to see if he can get some musicians together so we can practice, see how it goes. I didn't commit myself to anything."

"Why not commit yourself?" I asked. "What's the big deal?"

Joey shrugged and pointed to another carton. "Is that the General Tso's?"

The doorbell rang and I rushed to answer it. It was the plumber, and I led him into the basement to show him the hot water heater.

He stared at it and scratched his belly, which hung over his belt, straining against the buttons of his dark shirt.

"I'll have to check to be sure," he said, "but most likely it's the pressure valve."

"What does that mean?"

"Valve's supposed to open and shut automatically when the pressure builds up. But sometimes they break and the pressure just builds and builds."

When I got back to the kitchen my sisters were watching the small television that was bracketed to the wall above the table. Clare dabbed the corners of her eyes with a napkin.

"Fires in California," Joey explained when I sat down.

"Why are you crying?" I said to Clare as I picked up my fork.

She sniffed. "Those poor people. They lost *everything*."

If it was anyone but Clare, I might have asked if she was PMS-ing. Because while I understand that it's very tragic when people lose their homes, most of us can disassociate from the news enough to *think* it's a tragedy but not actually *feel* it. I guessed she was crying as much about her own life as about the strangers losing their homes.

"Sucks," Jocy said, putting a forkful of brown rice in her mouth.

"Don't be sarcastic," Clare said. "These are real people, real families."

"I wasn't being sarcastic," Joey insisted. "It *does* suck. But if you're so heartbroken over it, why don't you do something about it?"

"What makes you think I don't? Marc and I give to the Red Cross every year. And since Katrina and the tsunami, we've been giving even more."

"That's a start," Joey said.

"Oh, and I suppose you volunteer at a soup kitchen."

"As a matter of fact, I do."

This was news to me too, and I wondered if it was related to rehab. Perhaps they were encouraged to do volunteer work. Or maybe it was connected to some newfound spirituality, which I understood was a pretty common route for a lot of recovering addicts.

"When did this start?" I asked Joey.

"Couple months ago."

"Look!" Clare blurted, pointing at the television. "The Waxmans' house!"

Joey grabbed the remote and turned up the volume, just as

the image cut away from a video clip of the house on the day we discovered the body to a woman reporter in the studio, and we heard the tail end of what she said:

" . . . from several days ago. And today police revealed that while they haven't yet identified the body in the drum, they have confirmed that it was a young woman, and that she was five months pregnant."

Chapter 19

After my sisters left I felt too wired to sleep, and decided a nice warm bath would do the trick, perhaps even make up for the cold shower I had to endure earlier. I lit some candles, lowered myself into the tub, and closed my eyes. I didn't want to think about the young pregnant woman who had been murdered and stuffed into that drum. I certainly didn't want to think that it was probably Lydia. I just wanted to drift someplace peaceful.

To distract myself, I moved my fingers between my legs, remembering the charge I had felt when Leo put his hand on my thigh in the car. I was getting excited, but the image was as slippery as a bar of soap. I reached for it again and again, until at last it became clear that the attraction had dissolved, replaced by a vision that wouldn't be washed away.

Goddamn it, Kenny, I thought, *get the hell out of my head.* But he wouldn't. And so I let him into the bathtub with me, where he performed underwater feats that would make a sea monkey blush.

Afterward, I decided to finally try on the very short, very sheer white nightie Clare had insisted on buying for me at Victoria's Secret. I told her it was an insane extravagance—

and that I had no intention of ever wearing it—but she maintained that giving me a present would cheer her up, and so I relented.

I slipped it on over my head and turned to face myself in my bedroom's full-length mirror.

Okay then. This negligee was about as subtle as Patti LaBelle in concert. Maybe I just wasn't used to looking at my own body sexually, but the diaphanous fabric seemed to create extra contrast between the light parts and the dark, so that my belly was softened in lace but my nipples and public hair rang out loud and clear. Leave it to Victoria's Secret to create a nightie that makes you feel more naked than if you had nothing on.

I was looking at the price tag, deciding whether to return the thing, when I heard the doorbell chime three times in quick succession. It was eleven o'clock at night and I couldn't imagine who would be at my house ringing so urgently. I grabbed my robe and hurried down the stairs.

"Who is it?" I called

"He did it," came the voice from the outside. I opened the door.

"You're drunk," I said.

Kenny walked past me and went straight to the sofa. "Not as drunk as I seem," he said, dropping into it. "Surely not as drunk as I'd like to be."

"You heard it on the news, too?"

Kenny leaned forward, resting his elbows on his knees. I watched the veins in his hands engorge as blood traveled downward. His wrists and forearms became vascular too. Kenny's shirtsleeves were rolled up and it struck me that I had always thought there was something sexy about that. I guessed it was the unconscious masculinity of that particular section of anatomical real estate. Lots of men had vanity about their shoulders or biceps, but few considered the space from their elbows to their fingertips. It occurred to me that Kenny's nails, while clean, weren't manicured. Perhaps he wasn't that L.A., after all.

"Motherfucker really did it, didn't he?" he said. "Got her pregnant and killed her."

I sat down next to him and gently patted his back. "Yes."

"Did you know she used to sing to me when I brushed my teeth?"

"Lydia?"

"Some Hungarian song," he said. "I wasn't allowed to stop brushing until she was done." He leaned back and covered his eyes with his hand. I got the sense that he was trying to remember the tune.

"You really think it's her?" I asked.

"Don't you?"

"I don't want to believe it," I said.

"I know."

"Did you find the shoebox with her cards?"

"Not yet," he said. "Renee put it in a storage facility with a bunch of other stuff, but I couldn't find the key."

I suggested coffee and he agreed. When I came back into the room with two steaming cups, Kenny seemed to be getting it together. I handed him a mug, tightened my bathrobe belt, and sat down next to him. It hadn't escaped my notice that this was a familiar scene, and I didn't want to think about whether it would end the same way as it did the last time—with him in bed with Joey.

"It's like déjà vu all over again," he said. Even drunk, he could read my mind.

I nodded. He took a few sips of his coffee.

"I'm going to Florida," he said. "I need to ask Sam face-to-face where that key is."

We sat quietly for a few moments, sipping our coffee. I wondered if he was aware that our thighs were touching.

"When are you leaving?" I asked.

"In the morning."

I leaned back, settling into the couch. It was late and despite the caffeine, I was tired. Kenny put his arm around me. I let myself relax into him and felt like I could stay that way all night. It occurred to me though, that he would have other ideas. God help me, I wanted to. But how could I set myself up for that kind of hurt again? I couldn't. As long as he was in some way entangled with Joey, I couldn't.

"Kenny," I began, intending to make my position clear.

He kissed the top of my head and then tried to tilt my chin toward him. I didn't budge.

"I can't do this," I said.

"Sure you can," he said. "You lean your head back, I'll lean my face forward."

"You know what I mean."

He let out a long breath and removed his arm from around my shoulder. "I'm not sleeping with Joey."

"Yet."

"Why don't you get it, Bev? It's not Joey, it's you."

"Stop."

"It's always been you. Ever since we were kids—"

"Oh, please. Please don't start telling me I'm your Winnie Cooper."

"You *are* my Winnie Cooper."

I rolled my eyes. "I may vomit."

"Don't ever say 'vomit' to a drunk man."

"Which is why we're having this conversation to begin with—you're drunk."

"No. Well, maybe this much." He illustrated a small amount with his thumb and forefinger.

I stood. "I'm going to bed. You can sleep here if you want. There are blankets and sheets in the linen closet."

He rose, getting to his feet faster than I thought he'd be able to, and stood close enough to kiss me.

"I'll drive you to the airport in the morning," I began, but before I could finish, his lips were on mine. I didn't mean to return the kiss but I did. My mouth just couldn't help responding. I did, however, keep my arms straight down at my sides. There'd be no more than one kiss and then I'd go upstairs. Alone.

He moved the hair from my neck. "You're perfect," he whispered, which was exactly what he had said to me that night we were in high school, when the next thing he did was betray me. I took an awkward step back, not realizing my coffee cup was resting on my bathrobe belt. It tipped over and sent hot coffee down the lower half of my robe. I yelped in pain.

Kenny saw what happened and pulled off my robe as fast as he could.

"Are you okay?" he said, looking at my knee, which took the brunt of the hot liquid.

I touched it. Fortunately, the coffee wasn't scalding hot, so my skin was only a bit tender. "I'm fine."

"Are you—" he stopped abruptly. "Oh my God."

I looked down and gasped, realizing I was standing there naked-er than naked in my slut-sheer negligee. I tried to grab a pillow from the couch to cover up and he wouldn't let me.

"Please," he said, staring at my body. "I could die in a plane crash tomorrow."

I reached for my soiled robe and he threw it behind the couch. "Kenny," I protested.

He held my arms down at my sides. "Were you expecting someone?"

"No, I . . . I was just trying it on. The tags are still . . ." I felt my face burning in shame. "I was going to return it."

Kenny grabbed the tag and yanked it off in a blink-fast feat of prestidigitation.

"This thing was expensive!"

He pulled me close, his erection pressing against my crotch. He ran his hand from the outside of my thigh to the inside. He kissed me again.

"I'll pay you for it," he said.

I was outraged. "Pay me! What do I look like?"

"For the negligee." He laughed and ran his finger gently over the lace covering my nipple. "But if you really want to get into some kinky role-play . . ."

"You really don't have to pay for the negligee," I said.

He kissed my neck, my favorite spot. Without thinking, I tilted my head to give him better access. He nibbled on my earlobe as his hand slid to my backside, pulling me closer to him.

"Yes, I do," he said.

My breathing started to get faster. "You don't. Really."

He wrapped his fingers around one of the delicate ribbon straps and tore it off in one quick rip. The lacy fabric dropped, exposing my naked breast. "I do," he said, kissing my nipple and sending a jolt of electricity straight to my already damp outlet. The effect was catastrophic. I was no longer in control. It was the point of no return.

"Let's go upstairs," I said, panting.

"No."

"No?"

"We'll do it right here." He pulled off the negligee and pushed me onto the sofa. I was as wet as Jones Beach at high tide and wanted him inside me immediately. I helped him out of his clothes and into a condom with desperate speed, but he wouldn't be rushed.

"Easy," he said, and insisted on kissing and licking me until I was hyperventilating so hard I thought I might pass out.

"I'm not going to beg," I said.

He smiled. "You might."

He didn't protest when I got him into a position where I thought *he* might wind up begging.

"Say 'please,'" I said, as I flicked him with my tongue.

"I'll say anything you want."

I flicked him again. "That didn't sound like 'please.'"

"Please," he said.

"What?"

"Please."

"Excuse me?" I said. "Not sure I heard you."

He grabbed me by the shoulders, flipped me onto my back, and got on top. I opened my legs. He started to enter me but stopped. I waited. Nothing happened.

"Oh, I get it," I said. "This is when I'm supposed to beg."

"Only if you really want it."

I grabbed his ass. "I do."

"Excuse me?" he said, imitating my voice. "Not sure I heard you."

"Please?"

"You're going to have to do better than that."

"Pretty please?"

He shook his head in disapproval.

I leaned toward his ear and in the softest whisper, told him what I did in the bathtub and how I'd been thinking about him. I went into exquisite detail about what I imagined he'd done to me.

And then he did.

Chapter 20

The next day, after I took Kenny to the airport and was still floating around in a postcoital fog, I got a phone call from Clare, who said she and Marc were going out to dinner with another couple on Wednesday night, and wanted to know if Leo and I would join them.

Leo. I'd almost forgotten about him.

"I don't know," I said. "I'm not even sure how I feel about him."

"That's why you *date*, Bev. To find out if you like someone. Besides, I really need you there. This couple drives me out of my mind."

"Why? What are they like?"

"I don't want to scare you off."

I laughed. "I didn't realize this was a favor."

"I might slit my wrists if I have to spend an evening with these people without a buffer. Don't make me beg."

I had to smile at that. "Why don't you just blow them off?"

"I already did like four times. And Jade, the wife, was on a PTA committee with me and her son is friends with Dylan. I can't avoid her."

It was hard to think of Leo when my head was so filled with Kenny that I was imagining his reactions to every mundane activity of my day. This was no good. I was too old to be thinking like a lovesick pubescent. Maybe a date with Leo would be a good diversion—something to help me snap out of it.

"Can I wear jeans?" I asked.

Clare tsked. "I'll take you shopping."

"This would work," Teddy Goodwin said, folding his short arms.

He and Joey had surprised me by popping in and walking straight into the living room. They had bad timing. Clare was on her way over to pick me up so we could go to Nordstrom's together. Apparently, I couldn't be trusted to select an appropriate outfit on my own.

"What would work?" I said to Teddy.

"We're looking for a place to rehearse," Joey explained. "Teddy is putting a band together so we can record his song, but we need someplace to practice. He remembered that the living room here is square—a good shape for acoustics—and wanted to scope it out. So what do you think, Bev?"

"Looks square to me," I said.

"I meant about letting us rehearse in here."

"When?"

"I have to see when everyone's available," Teddy said.

The phone rang and I picked it up assuming it was Clare. But it was my mother, sounding just a bit hysterical.

"The police are here," she said. "They want to talk to Sam."

"Calm down," I said. "I *told* you they were coming."

"But he's not *here*. He's disappeared."

"Oh no."

Joey interrupted, "What is it?"

"Sam Waxman," I said, my hand over the receiver. "He's missing and the detectives are there."

Her face lit up. "Sheldon? Can I talk to him?"

I rolled my eyes at Joey and listened to my mother explain that Sam had gone missing once before, only to be discovered walking along the edge of the highway behind their development. This time, though, he wasn't there. Kenny had arrived from New York just a short while ago, and was already driving around looking for him.

Mom's voice changed to a whisper. "The police seem angry. Your father is talking to them by the front door now, promising he'll call them the second Sam shows up."

"Maybe you should let the police help search for him."

"I think they *are* going to search for him, Bev, whether we want them to or not."

"How's Renee?"

"She's in the kitchen, crying. The detectives questioned her for over an hour. They talked to your dad and me too." She paused. "And Bev?"

"Yes?"

"I hate to ask this, I really do. But . . ." she stopped.

"But what, Mom?"

She lowered her voice even more. "Do you think he really did it?"

I looked out the window at the Waxmans' front lawn and pictured Sam standing out there with his hose. He had one of those trigger nozzles and would park himself in the middle of the yard for hours. We called him the human sprinkler. Back then, it didn't occur to me to wonder what he was thinking as he stood there spraying and spraying, week after week, all summer long. But now, it seemed almost sociopathic. All those hours he could have been playing ball with his son, or helping his nervous wife around the house, or even involved in a more normal hobby, he just stood there. What was going through his mind?

"It's just so hard to believe such a thing," my mother added.

I thought about Stephanie, who Sam probably killed because she peed on his lawn a few times. Would such a man hesitate to kill a woman whose pregnancy could destroy more than a few square inches of sod?

"I don't know, Mom."

I waited for her to respond, but she was silent.

"You still there?" I said.

"I'm here, darling, but I'd better go now. I think they need me."

I told her to take care, and when I got off the phone I noticed that Clare was in the driveway, honking. I'd been too distracted to hear.

"I have to leave," I said, trying to usher Joey and Teddy outside.

"Do you mind if we stick around for a few minutes to check out the acoustics?" Joey asked. "I promise to lock up on the way out."

"Knock yourself out," I said, and gave her a spare key, as she had lost hers eons ago. "Just give me some warning before you decide to pop in and rehearse, okay?"

"Of course," Teddy said. "Of course we'll give you warning."

Apparently, only a few hours after he had gone missing, Sam Waxman turned up in a hospital, confused but not hurt or injured. According to what my mother told me, someone had found him wading in a canal, tossing pieces of bread to nonexistent ducks. He wasn't able to tell anyone his name, so he was admitted to the hospital as a John Doe. It was local police who had called Renee Waxman to tell her they had located her husband in the Boca Raton Community Hospital.

On hearing this news, a part of me wondered if he was being cagey, planting seeds for an insanity defense like that mobster, Vinnie "the Chin" Gigante. But was Sam lucid enough to pretend to be crazy? It was too paradoxical for me to figure out on my own, especially as I hadn't seen him in years and didn't have a real sense of how far gone he was.

I wanted to call Kenny to talk to him about it, but hesitated. The thought of hearing his voice again made my capillaries dilate and spill over with whatever hormone it is that makes teenagers so obnoxiously obsessive about their love lives. The rational side of me was at war with this force, trying to combat it with arguments of how self-destructive it was to be feeling this way. But it was a losing battle. The force was using its secret weapon of cloaking itself behind semi-rational ideas, like the fact that I needed to talk to Kenny to find out what was really going on. And that maybe, just maybe, he actually needed me.

"I was just going to call you," he said, instead of hello.

"I heard they found your father. Is he okay?"

"He seems fine—physically, at least. But they want to keep him a few days to run tests."

I kicked my shoes off and sat down on the couch. It still smelled like Kenny and me. "And mentally?"

He sighed. "Hard to tell. One minute he's fine, the next he's Uncle June."

I recognized the Sopranos reference but didn't laugh. Kenny just sounded too serious. "You think he's playing up the dementia?"

"I'll tell you this much. When the police asked for a sample of his DNA, he had the sense to refuse."

I grabbed a throw pillow and held it against myself. "Can he do that? Refuse?"

"He can if they don't have a warrant for it. But it's a futile gesture. They'll be back with one in a few days."

It didn't surprise me to hear that the police wanted a sample of Sam's DNA so they could determine if the baby was his. I imagined them hauling him off in handcuffs as soon as the results were in.

"I'm sorry you have to deal with all this," I said.

"I'm okay," he said. "I'm more worried about my mom. She vacillates between hysteria and catatonia. And I'm worried about your mom, too."

I sat up straighter. "Why?"

"She got dizzy today. Your dad took her pulse and said it, was probably just low blood pressure, but he wants her to take it easy."

Great. Something else to be anxious about. "She left me a message about your dad, but she didn't say anything about that."

"She probably didn't want to worry you. I'm sure she's fine. And your father is keeping a close eye on her."

"I feel so useless here. Is there anything I can do to help?"

"I can think of a couple of things, but they involve your various and luscious body parts."

"Stop," I said, laughing.

"You don't mean that."

"Stop means stop," I said anemically.

"In your case, it usually means 'that feels so good I can barely take it.'" There was a moment's pause. "Are you alone?"

"Why?"

"Tell me what you're wearing."

I hugged the pillow tighter. "Is this the conversation we're going to have?"

"Sure," he said. "If you're game."

"I should probably go."

"Wait," he said. "Just wait. And you don't even have to talk. Just listen to my voice."

Chapter 21

The next day I went to Clare's to watch her children, and I came prepared with an art project that I hoped would get Dylan to give me some clues as to what was going on with him. Before the children got home, though, I went upstairs to say hello to Leo, who was on a ladder installing a skylight in the bathroom ceiling.

"Hey," I said, looking up. He looked sweaty, dirty, and, I have to admit, adorable.

Leo looked down and smiled. "Hi," he said, and went back to adjusting the window. I watched the clouds move past his head. Then I looked at his butt, which was just above eye level. Cute as it was, I just wasn't interested. After the fireworks display with Kenny, nothing else could light my candle. I wondered if it was altogether fair to go on the date with him that Clare was pushing me into. I knew she needed me there to run interference with this Jade person, but I didn't want to lead Leo on. He was really such a sweetheart. Maybe I could find a way to back out of the whole thing. Clare would understand, wouldn't she?

"Clare tells me we're going out Saturday," Leo said.

So much for backing out. "I didn't know she'd already told you."

He climbed down from the ladder and wiped his hands on his pants. "Her friend Jade sounds like a piece of work."

"We don't have to do this if you don't want," I said.

"Naw, it's okay. I don't want to leave Clare in the lurch. Besides, maybe it'll be a trip. We can make fun of Jade after we leave."

I smiled and we stood there awkwardly for a moment. He seemed to be getting ready to kiss when, blessedly, the camp bus honked. I said good-bye and ran downstairs to meet the kids.

It was a blazingly hot day, and even Sophie seemed wilted when she got off the bus. I ushered both kids into the cool house, found a bottle of organic lemonade in the refrigerator, and poured them each a tall glass.

"Listen," I said as they drank, "I need your help with something. I got this idea for an art project that I want to do with my class when I'm a teacher, but I'm not sure if it's going to work okay. Would you guys be my guinea pigs and try it out? I'd really appreciate it."

"Sure, Aunt Bev!" Sophie said.

Dylan squinted at me. "What is it?"

When they finished their lemonade, I cleaned and dried the table, and then I handed each of them a sheet of special rainbow-striped paper I found in a teaching supplies store. Though I had been shopping specifically for something to help tap into Dylan's troubles, I couldn't resist buying a large enough supply to actually use in a classroom. A few packages of paper, I reasoned, wouldn't be that hard to take with me to Las Vegas. Of course, I didn't stop there. I wound up buying a supply of the funny-face pencils that were the current grade school craze, some reward stickers I hadn't seen before, a pack of die-cut bookmarks that said, "I am a book worm!" and a Nevada poster that listed every salient fact, such as major industries (tourism, mining, hydroelectric power), population

(2,495,529) and motto ("All for our country"), as well as some nonsalient information, like the state flower (sagebrush!) and the state fossil (ichthyosaur). This, of course, was as much for my own edification as my students'.

I took a sheet of rainbow paper for myself, and demonstrated that I wanted Dylan and Sophie to draw a big square with a black crayon and then color it in, so that almost the entire page was a big, waxy mass of black. After they did that, I gave each of them a tool, which was just a small wooden stick with a point. I instructed them to scrape a drawing into the black mass, so that the rainbow colors showed through.

"I think it would be cool to draw a secret scary thing," I said, "something that frightens you but that nobody else knows is scary. How does that sound?"

"You mean like a tree?" Sophie said, holding up her fingers like claws.

"Sure. Trees can be pretty scary."

"But not leaves."

"Right, leaves are our friends."

Sophie got right to work drawing her spooky tree. Dylan started with something I couldn't identify. First he outlined a big square, and inside that a slightly smaller square. Beneath it he drew a rectangle he filled with tiny squares. He drew a small oval next to it, and I finally figured out that it was a computer with a keyboard and mouse.

I got a bad feeling in the pit of my stomach as I wondered why he thought the computer was a frightening thing.

"Good computer, Dyl," I said. "Are you going to put something scary on the screen?"

He nodded and scratched out a long shape that quickly resembled a hammer.

"Is that the kind of hammer you use to fix something?" I asked. "Or is it a weapon?"

"It's a killer hammer," he said. "A mad scientist created it on the computer and it came alive. And now, if you try to type something on the keyboard, it comes out and smashes your fingers."

"I wouldn't want to use *that* computer!" I said.

After the children finished their drawings, I thanked them for helping me and asked if they wanted to make another one. Sophie was eager, but Dylan said he wanted to go downstairs and use his PlayStation. I gave Sophie another page to work on, and walked Dylan down into the basement. When we were out of Sophie's earshot, I made him look at me.

"Is there something on the computer that scared you?" I said.

He shrugged.

"Did you go into a chat room? Did you have an instant message conversation with a stranger? Did somebody say some inappropriate things to you?"

He shook his head.

"What, then?"

"I don't know." He looked down, his dark lashes dramatic against his fair skin.

"You can trust me, okay? I only want to help you."

He was silent.

"Did you accidentally click on a bad Web site? Did you see something you weren't supposed to see?"

"It wasn't a Web site." There was a tiny constellation of pale freckles on his nose, which just broke my heart. As rugged as he was athletically, he was still at such a tender age.

"But you saw something bad? What was it?"

He took in a jagged breath and let it out. I knew I was getting very warm here. "Somebody was IM-ing with my mom," he said.

"Who?"

He shrugged. "A man."

"What did he say?"

Dylan led me to the little office off the playroom where they kept their computer and sat down in front of it.

"Sometimes she forgets to close the window after she IMs with someone," he said as he put his hand on the mouse and clicked. He opened and closed a few windows. "It's not here today, but look." He opened Clare's instant message manager, which showed her entire list, including the people who were not currently online.

"That's him," he said, pointing the cursor at a screen name. "Hammerman223."

"You saw a conversation between this guy and your mother?"

"*Uh-huh.*"

"What were they talking about?"

"Sex and stuff."

This was the last thing in the world I expected from my sister, and I thought there just had to be some logical explanation. "Are you sure?"

"Yes."

I sat down in the side chair and swiveled Dylan around to face me. "Listen, I can't explain what you saw, but I know your mom, and she loves your dad very much. I just . . . I want to promise you that everything's okay."

I hoped I wasn't lying and paused, waiting for him to respond. He nodded, noncommittal. I realized, of course, there was only so much I could do. Clare was the one who would have to talk to him and assure him everything was all right. I leaned in to hug him.

"It was brave of you to tell me. I'm proud of you."

When Clare came home a short while later, Sophie ran to greet her. I called Dylan up from the basement, where he was slaughtering bad guys on his PlayStation. I was glad that he actually shut it off and came upstairs.

"Hi, Mom," he said.

She kissed him on the top of the head. He didn't pull away, and Clare glanced at me, beaming. I thought she was getting ahead of herself. Dylan's crisis hadn't passed—it was just on hiatus.

"How was your day?" she asked, releasing him.

"Fine."

"Did you get some time for free swim?"

"Yeah." He went to the refrigerator.

"We need to talk," I said softly to Clare, and gave her a look to let her know it was serious.

I went into the backyard and sat on one of the children's swings while Clare spent some time with Dylan and Sophie. After a while, she came outside and sat on the swing next to mine.

"What's up?" she said.

I took Dylan's folded up drawing from my pocket and handed it to her.

"What's this?" she said, looking at it.

"That's what Dylan drew when I asked him to make something secret and scary."

She cocked her head to get another angle on the picture. "I don't get it."

It was hard for me to say the words, so I waited a few minutes to see if she could figure it out on her own. But she just stared at the picture, her pretty brow knitted. I finally took a deep breath and got it out.

"Clare, who's Hammerman223?"

Her face turned white. She dropped the picture to the ground, where a breeze picked it up from beneath and danced it across the yard to the fence.

"Are you having an affair?" I asked.

She got up off the swing and tucked her hair behind her ears. "No," she said, and folded her arms defiantly. Then she put her head down and mumbled, "Not yet."

"What are you saying?"

"Don't judge me for this, Bev."

"You can't be serious."

"Why not?"

I couldn't believe what I was hearing. "Do I need to spell it out?" I held up three fingers and ticked them off, "Marc, Dylan, Sophie."

"No one has to know."

I pointed to the drawing stuck to the fence. "Hello! You haven't even *done* anything yet and you've traumatized your kid."

Her jaw tightened. "I'll deal with that."

"How?"

"It's not your concern, okay?"

I had to believe that a part of Clare wanted me to talk her out of it. Why else would she have told me? Surely she didn't think she would get my blessing.

"If you think that phone call to Marc's hotel room gives you license to cheat, you're making a huge mistake."

"It's not about that. You wouldn't understand."

"I understand that you have a whole life here, and you'd be risking *everything*."

Clare rolled her eyes. "You're only saying that because—" She paused.

"Because what?"

"Nothing."

"Say it."

She bit her lip and then exploded. "I'm not Jonathan, okay? This has *nothing* to do with you!"

"Don't be an idiot. I'm not talking about me. I'm talking about your family. How can you do this to them?"

She pointed a manicured finger in my face. "You have betrayal issues, Bev. Don't project them onto everyone else."

She was so maddening I wanted to strangle her. "Spare me the pop psychology. I have *reality* issues. I don't want to see you lose your family."

"I can take care of myself."

"Apparently not. You're being a bonehead about this!"

"A second ago I was an idiot and now I'm a bonehead? Make up your mind."

"Stop. You're being childish."

"And you're being superior! You think you know better than me about *everything*. But you don't know what it's like to feel like nothing—less than nothing—when suddenly someone is in your life who thinks you're beautiful and smart and desirable." She tried to hold back tears, but they spilled over her lashes and down her cheeks.

"Clare this is just stu—" I stopped myself. "You can't take a midlife crisis and whatever paranoia it's fueled and turn it into an affair. You'll ruin your life. You're better off getting a boob job or a facelift or whatever it is women in this town do when they're feeling unattractive."

"Is that what you think I need?"

"I didn't mean that."

"No, you meant that I should just stick to being a stupid, rich, mindless housewife."

"I meant that if you're going to be selfish and self-absorbed, at least find an outlet that doesn't hurt anyone."

Clare's eyes filled with fury. "Selfish and self-absorbed! How dare you! You think you know what my life is like? You don't even know what selfless *is* until you've been a mother. Have you ever gone three straight nights without sleep, trying to comfort a colicky newborn, and then gotten out of bed at five o'clock to drive your husband to the airport? Have you ever nursed a hungry baby until your nipples were bloody and scabbed? Have you ever gotten a urinary infection from holding in your pee an entire day because your husband and kids needed you to be three places at once? I give *everything* to my family. My own needs take a backseat to Marc and the kids every time. In fact, I pay so much attention to everyone else that I don't even know who Clare *is* anymore!"

"That doesn't entitle you to an affair," I said.

"Says who?"

"Sometimes I think being born beautiful was the worst thing that could have happened to you."

"Meaning what?"

"You think everything is supposed to *come* to you. You think you're *entitled* to feel desirable, no matter what it costs."

"I'm done," she said, and turned her back to me.

I grabbed her shoulders and turned her around. "Is it worth it?" I said. "Even the best sex in the world–"

"It's not just about sex."

"Of course it isn't."

She pulled away. "Don't patronize me."

I grabbed her by the arms this time, intent on getting through to her. "What is it, Clare? Are you falling in love with someone?"

She turned her face from me.

"Are you?" I repeated.

"Go away." She wrested herself from my hands and turned her back to me again.

"Who is it, Clare?"

She didn't answer, wouldn't turn around. But she didn't move, either. She just stood there. I walked to the corner of the yard and retrieved Dylan's drawing. I held it in front of her face.

"I can't let you do this," I said. "Look! Look how much you've hurt Dylan already."

She started to cry. "I'm an awful person."

I rubbed her back. "You're just confused."

"I don't know what to do," she said.

"Yes you do." I released her and put the drawing in her hand.

She stared at it. "I screwed up."

The back door opened. "Mom?" Sophie called. "Dylan spilled Gatorade."

"I'll be right there," she said.

"Make this better," I said to her. "Promise me you won't sleep with this guy."

She folded Dylan's picture into neat squares and nodded, then kissed me on the cheek and walked toward the house.

Chapter 22

"I think this table is drafty. Don't you think this table is drafty?"

So spoketh Clare's friend Jade, just as the six of us had settled into our chairs at a fancy seafood restaurant on the North Shore. She had straight pitch-black hair that was so shiny she could have starred in a Pantene commercial. I didn't know human hair could glow like that without special lighting.

"Seems fine to me," Leo said.

"I'm right under the air-conditioning vent," Jade said. "And that table has a better view of the water." She waved a slender but well-toned arm at the hostess who had seated us. "Excuse me!" She was so loud other diners turned to stare. "Do you think we could switch to that table?"

The hostess came back, and the lot of us picked up our things and moved to the table Jade preferred.

"I'm much more comfortable," Jade said as she settled into her seat. "Much."

I sensed that the final "much" was to quiet any objections over the switch, as if the degree of Jade's comfort was the determining factor in any decision.

Leo leaned into me and whispered, "This one's a *hoot*."

"So what do you do, Leo?" Jade asked as she touched her necklace, ostensibly making sure it was where it was supposed to be. I gathered, though, that the gesture was designed to ensure that her diamonds escaped no one's notice.

"I'm a contractor," he said. "I'm remodeling Clare and Marc's master bathroom."

I expected a disdainful reaction from Jade, but instead she gasped dramatically, her kohl-lined eyes widening as her hand went to her heart like she had to stop it from beating right out of her chest.

"A contractor! I had no idea!"

I glanced at Clare to try to get an idea as to why Jade would act like meeting a contractor in the flesh was more shocking than discovering a long, lost twin. Clare closed her eyes and gently shook her head. She seemed to know what was coming.

"Randall and I just bought a massive old house in Upper Brookville," Jade continued, "and we're renovating every inch of it. Don't even *ask* what we're going through."

"I wouldn't dream of it," Leo said.

Clare and I exchanged subtle smiles. Of course, it went right by dear Jade.

"I ordered granite countertops for the kitchen," she said, "and *three times* they came in wrong. Three times!"

"Bummer," Leo said. "Can you pass the rolls?"

"And we're still waiting for the marble tiles for the floor in the butler's pantry. It's been . . . I don't know. How long ago did we order that, Randall?"

Randall shrugged. "A month ago?"

She tsked and waved him away with her hand. "More like four months ago." She leaned in conspiratorially toward Leo. "He doesn't remember *anything*."

A waitress approached to take our order for drinks. All the requests were pretty straightforward until she got to Jade, who asked for a Grey Goose Seabreeze, "but tart, with extra grapefruit juice, and a lime not a lemon, in a martini glass with no ice."

Leo and I both glanced at Clare, who seemed pained by Jade's display.

"You should stop by and see the house sometime," Jade said to Leo. "And you too, Bev. You'll just die when you see what's going on there. We were hoping to move in this September, but I honestly don't think there's a *chance* it'll be ready."

"So you're homeless?" Leo said. Proud of himself, he rocked back on his chair, balancing it on the two back legs.

Jade laughed like Leo's remark was the funniest thing she'd heard in decades. "Oh, I like him!" she said.

Poor Clare looked like Jade was making her more miserable by the moment, so I tried to think of a way to steer the conversation in another direction.

"Speaking of homeless," I said, "have you ever heard of Goode Earth Habitats? Leo does a lot of volunteer work for them."

"Whereabouts?" Randall asked Leo.

"I've been helping out in New Orleans," he answered, "but the organization is national. They're even going to be doing some work in the Bronx soon."

"What was the name of that charity we worked for last year, Clare?" Jade said. "Harvest something?"

"It was two years ago," Clare answered.

"Was it? Well, it sure was a thankless task, wasn't it? Remember how they left our names out of the newsletter?"

"Did they?"

"You don't remember that? You were more upset than *I* was."

"Tell me more about Goode Earth Habitats," Clare said to Leo. "Can anyone get involved?"

"They're always looking for volunteers," Leo said. "If you have time to pitch in, I'm sure they'd be thrilled to have you."

Jade laughed again. "Like she has time in her schedule to build houses! Between the kids and the house and the PTA, she barely has time to return a phone call. Clare, I don't know *why* you insist on doing the laundry yourself. That's why you have a housekeeper."

Marc put his arm around Clare. "She's very particular about laundry."

Clare reached for the bread basket, took a roll, and slathered it with butter. A bad sign.

A short time later the waitress came with our drinks. I noticed immediately that Jade's drink was in a highball glass, and I was curious to see how she would handle it. I rooted for her to make a show of accepting it graciously, even if it meant listening to her brag about how magnanimous she was. But no, not a chance. Jade looked down at the glass set in front of her and held a pointed finger high above it, as if she didn't want to get close.

"What is *that*?" she asked.

"Seabreeze," the waitress said. "Didn't you ask for a Seabreeze?"

"In a *martini* glass," Jade said.

"Oh, right. I'm terribly sorry." The waitress picked up the glass. "I'll be right back."

She wasn't even out of earshot when Jade leaned in toward the table and said in a stage whisper, "What an *idiot*."

I cringed. "I'm sure it was an honest mistake."

Jade rolled her eyes. "Honest but stupid."

"Easy, tiger," Randall said, patting her hand.

"Oh, you're right," Jade said. "I'm just pissy because of all the mistakes I have to deal with every single day on the new house." She turned back to Leo. "Would you believe that they actually put in a *door* where we asked for a window? I mean, have you *ever*? They can't get a single thing right if I'm not there watching over their shoulders. Tell me, how could something like that happen? How could a contractor put in a door where there was supposed to be a window?"

"Sounds like a crossed wire," Leo said. "It happens."

"But why does it have to happen to *me*?" Jade said. "And every single *day*."

"Maybe a black cat crossed your path," he answered.

"I *do* seem to have bad luck," Jade said.

"Perhaps it's your karma," Clare offered.

Whoa. I hadn't expected my nonconfrontational sister to say what most of us were thinking. And while I was delighted by the remark and curious as hell to hear Jade's reaction, I was concerned for my normally charming sister. I hoped she had kept the promise she made to me in her backyard and was able to move on. I glanced at Marc, who seemed as relaxed as ever.

"My karma?" Jade said. "What does that mean, Clare?" She turned to her husband. "What does she mean?"

"Nothing," Clare said. "I didn't mean anything. Excuse me. I have to use the ladies' room."

Clare grabbed her purse and headed toward the back of the restaurant.

Jade watched her leave, staring at Clare's handbag. Either she was too dim to be offended, or so distracted by accessories that it overshadowed everything else. She gasped. "That's the new Fendi! My God, it's stunning." She turned to me. "I don't know if you know this, Bev, but your sister has *exquisite* taste. In *every*thing. Everyone else I know uses a professional decorator, but your sister does it all herself and her home is just *lovely*. You wouldn't even know it's not professionally done unless you had a trained eye. And even then. Even then you might not know. That's how good Clare is."

"And she's broadening her horizons these days with an American Lit class," I said. "Are you a big reader, Jade?"

"With my schedule? You've got to be kidding. Only you single gals with no kids have time to read."

How sensitive. How very, very sensitive to rub in the fact that I was the only woman at the table who wasn't married with children. As if being single at thirty-five with no prospects for having a family was exactly where I wanted to be.

The waitress brought back Jade's drink in a martini glass and set it in front of her. *"Ah,* that's better," Jade said. She picked it up and watched as her bracelets slid down her elegant wrist. For a moment, Jade seemed lost in reverie, like an artist admiring a landscape, only she was gazing upon her own delicately manicured fingers holding the smartly shaped glass of pinkish liquid. She closed her eyes and took a sip. *"Mm,"* she said. "Perfect."

Leo picked up his beer and took a gulp. "So what do you do, Randall?" he asked.

"Uh . . . I'm in finance."

"Stocks?" Leo asked.

"I'm involved in several ventures," Randall said.

"He started out as a stockbroker," Jade said. "But now my man's a tycoon. I love that word, *tycoon.*" She laughed as if she made a hilarious joke. Her husband seemed irritated. He took a breadstick from the basket in the center of the table and snapped it in half.

"I'm not a tycoon," he said.

"Fine," she said to Leo and me, contorting her face into a clown's version of sarcasm, "he's not a tycoon."

Randall asked Marc a question about the scotch he was drinking, and Jade excused herself to the ladies' room. Leo leaned into me and whispered, "I thought Randall looked familiar, but now I realize where I know him from. He headed the only brokerage on Long Island sleazier than Parker Jameson. He was indicted, Bev. Spent a couple months in jail and was fined half a million dollars."

"Are you serious?"

"As a felony."

"He doesn't look like he's suffering now."

"Nope. He lost his license, but I'm sure he's found other ways to rip people off. And you want to know something else? Princess Jade wasn't always dripping with diamonds. From what I heard, she used to be his manicurist."

"He had a manicurist?"

Leo gave me a look that said, *You have to ask?*

A few minutes later Jade returned, jangling her bracelets and trying very hard to make her expensive breasts bounce as she took her seat.

"Where on earth is your sister?" Jade asked.

"She wasn't in the ladies' room?"

"No."

Marc was surprised. "Maybe I should look for her," he said, starting to rise.

"I'll go," I said. "She probably just stepped outside to use her cell phone to call the sitter. I'll be right back."

I stepped out the front door of the restaurant into the warm night and smelled the breeze off the Long Island Sound. I looked to the left and right and didn't see Clare. Then I headed around back to the parking lot, and found her sitting on the hood of her car, her shawl under her butt.

"Hey," I said as I approached.

She got up off her shawl and unfolded it so that it was big enough for both of us to sit on, then parked herself on top of it again. Even depressed, Clare didn't want to dirty her clothes.

"You okay?" I asked.

She shook her head.

I sat next to her and put my hand on her back and waited for her to say something, but she was silent.

"Jade's a piece of work," I said.

Clare shrugged and stared off into the distance.

"She's an asshole and a show-off," I said. "Such a tiny speck of a person she has to make a big show to feel like she exists."

Clare exhaled through her nose. "It's not her."

"Is it . . . Hammerman?"

She shrugged.

"Talk to me," I said.

Clare lay back on the car so that she was facing the sky. I did the same. In that remote section of the North Shore, there was little ambient light, and stars dotted the black ether like someone had poked holes in the sky with darts. The night was quiet except for the buzz of cicadas and the occasional car *whooshing* past.

"Thing is," Clare explained, "Jade has so much, and yet she's always miserable. She complains about everything."

"Petty," I offered. "Ungrateful."

"But am I really that different?"

"Oh, c'mon, Clare, you're nothing like Jade."

"Aren't I? Look at me, Bev. I have everything Jade has, and yet I don't appreciate it. I just feel . . . empty."

"You're still upset about hearing a woman's voice in that hotel room."

"Of course. It's all pieces of the same puzzle—the same blank puzzle. Put them together and what have you got? Nothing. Just a boring, shallow middle-aged woman who used to be pretty."

"Oh, honey. Are you back on that?"

"Pretty is all I ever had, Bev. Even if you're right that I haven't completely lost it, so what? It's only a matter of time."

"You're wrong."

"I'm right. Every day it's another wrinkle. Every month it's another pound."

"I mean about pretty being all you have, Clare. It's simply not true. You're generous, compassionate, honest, and clearly not a shallow twit like that Jade. You think she would ever take a literature class to improve herself? Trust me, when Jade feels empty, she doesn't go to college, she goes to Saks."

"You think too highly of me."

"No way. You're my sister. I'm probably more critical of you than I am of anyone."

I expected a smile, but her face was immobile.

"Really, Clare, give yourself some credit. How many women in your position are trying to expand their minds?"

"I'm not sure my motives for taking that class are so admirable."

"What do mean?"

"Nothing."

Clare stared straight up into the sky, and in the moonlight her profile looked milky white against the darkness, colorless yet beautiful, like some glamorous old movie still of Ingrid Bergman.

"Tell me," I pressed.

She was quiet for a moment, but I let her be. I sensed that she was trying to put something into words. I wondered what it was about taking the literature class that made Clare feel guilty. Was it possible she enrolled in the course to impress someone other than Marc, like her mysterious online friend? Or was I letting my imagination run away with me? Maybe Clare was simply enjoying the idea of taking time for herself— time away from her kids—and was feeling guilty about it.

"Do you think about Lydia?" she finally said.

"Yes."

I put my head back down and gazed at the stars. I tried hard to imagine there was such a thing as an afterlife, that Lydia's soul might exist somewhere in that vast distance, and that she got to love her little baby for all eternity.

"I'm such a piece of shit," Clare said.

"You're not."

"I should be grateful I'm alive."

"Are you . . . keeping the promise you made about not having an affair?"

She went quiet for a moment and I got a terrible feeling in my gut. "Clare—"

"Don't lecture me," she interrupted. "I'm doing my best."

"What does that mean?"

She stood. "Let's go back inside."

Chapter 23

After dinner, Leo and I got into his van and exited the parking lot. I struggled with how to end the date, wondering what I would do if he asked to come inside. Did I owe him any kind of an explanation? And if so, what would I say?

I looked over at him and saw that he was gripping the steering wheel tightly, his lips moving as if he were talking to himself. He glanced over at me, and I understood that he had been rehearsing what he wanted to say.

"What is it?" I asked, hoping it wasn't a proposition.

He took a deep breath. "I haven't been completely honest with you," he said.

"No?"

"I should have said something earlier. I'm sorry."

What was he getting at? "If you're seeing someone else . . . ," I said, and stopped, wondering if I was projecting.

"It's not that. Not exactly. I mean, there is someone else, but I'm not seeing her. That's why I didn't tell you. I thought I could get over her but I can't."

I was confused. "Is this about an ex-girlfriend?"

He glanced back at the road. The car in front of us had slowed down but Leo was still accelerating. I had noticed before that he was what I call a "late braker," which indicated a strong Brooklyn influence. Either he learned how to drive there, or learned from someone who learned how to drive there. I instinctively pressed on a nonexistent brake, holding my breath the whole time. Leo finally slowed only inches from the car in front of us.

"We never went out," he said. "I'm just totally hung up on her. I can't get her out of my head. I thought I could, but I can't."

"Have you pursued her?"

I waited for an answer while he changed lanes and then made a right turn, but he was silent. Finally I said, "I'm sorry. You don't have to answer."

"It's not that, it's . . . she's married."

"Married?"

He nodded. "Fucked up, right?"

I shifted uncomfortably. The air-conditioning vent was blowing right in my face and I redirected it, wondering how he could have gotten close enough to a married woman to fall in love. That kind of thing usually happened in an office setting, where you were thrown together every day all week long. But the only women Leo saw on a regular basis were the housewives he did remodeling for.

Then a thought hit me like a two-by-four and I started connecting the dots in my head. The way he looked at Clare in her pink top. How she had carefully orchestrated having him at dinner tonight. And then there was her cryptic insistence that her motives for taking the Modern American Lit class weren't pure. Was it possible she took the class to impress someone? Someone with aspirations to be a writer? And oh dear God! Leo was a carpenter—a *hammer man*.

As much as I didn't want to believe it, I had to face the truth. Leo was Clare's mystery man. He was Hammerman223.

"Leave her alone," I muttered.

"What?"

"Just don't go after a married woman." I leaned over and shut off the air conditioning.

"I'm not. I'm trying to keep my distance, trying to get my mind off her. And you're so wonderful, Bev. I thought if I went out with you I could distract myself and maybe even forget about her."

Sure. What better way to get over someone than to go after her sister? A chill of nausea swept over my flesh. How on earth did this happen again? Was it my destiny to get mixed up with guys who had intimate connections to my sisters? Surely this was a sign from above that moving as far away as I could was the right choice for me.

And then another thought occurred to me. I was smack up against a chance to save my sister's family. If I slept with Leo, there was no way he and Clare would have an affair. She'd consider it déclassé to sleep with a guy her sister had gone to bed with. After all, what kind of trailer trash, spandex-wearing, Jerry Springer reject would sleep with a guy who had porked her sister?

Okay, so the irony wasn't lost on me. I knew I had done just that with Kenny. But in my defense, the porking in question had happened nearly two decades before. Surely there was a statute of limitations for these things.

I opened my window and felt a rush of humid air. Was it really okay to do to Clare exactly what Joey had done to me all those years ago? Was it okay *not* to? If I had the power to keep my sister from ruining her life, and all I had to do was sleep with an utterly adorable and sexy guy, did it make sense to turn my back?

I imagined what would happen if Clare had an affair with Leo and Marc found out. Their marriage would be over. These two, who really loved one another, would spend the rest of their lives nursing their wounds. And the children. Everything they knew would be ripped out from under them.

I knew, of course, that some kids did fine with divorce, and that some of the most screwed-up children were, in fact, the products of intact marriages. But I also knew how insidious the effects could be for an eager-to-please kid like Sophie, who would probably appear to be a model child until it was time to have an adult relationship of her own, and how devastating for a kid like Dylan, who internalized everything so deeply. It could be a prescription for disaster, and I didn't want to see that happen to this family. There was just too much at stake.

I glanced over at Leo again. His lips were so red. He'd be lovely to kiss. And his hair looked so soft, those dark curls so appealing. I could do this. I *would* do this.

Problem was, I lacked that damn flirtation gene and didn't know how to go about shifting his focus from Clare to me. I pictured Joey fluffing her hair and arching her back, and couldn't imagine pulling it off without looking like I was doing a poor imitation of a porn star. And Clare's charming smile and easy laugh eluded me entirely. I couldn't figure out how someone could turn this conversation in a seductive direction.

With Kenny, it was always so easy. The second I had a sexual thought he could see it as clearly as a swallowed key on an X-ray. I looked at Leo, but he was still stuck in his own private agony. If only he knew that I was just as hung up on Kenny as he was on Clare, I could break through.

Then I realized I had been ignoring the obvious. Why not let him know, in some subtle way, that we had this in common? I ran my fingers through my hair as I tried to figure out how to do this. Then at last I had an idea.

"So you were using me," I said, stirring his guilt to the

surface so I could skim it right off. "To try to get your mind off her."

"I guess I was," he said. "I'm sorry."

"Don't be. I was using you too."

He blinked. "You were?"

"There's this guy," I said, picturing how sexy Kenny looked in the airport with his rolled up shirtsleeves and a bag slung over his shoulder. "He's wrong for me in every possible way and yet . . . it's like a virus I can't get rid of."

"Like a fever," he said.

I nodded. "But then I met you and I found myself so attracted and I thought, 'This is perfect.'"

"Yeah, that's how I felt too."

"So I don't know, Leo. Are we stupid to let each other go for the sake of relationships that are all wrong for us?"

He went quiet, mulling that over. I leaned forward and switched on the radio, hoping for something seductive, but it was Carrie Underwood belting out something about Jesus. I switched it off.

"You think we should give this a shot?" he asked.

I hugged my arms against my body to try to create some cleavage. I wore a scooped neck top Clare had picked out for me, but had rejected her advice to wear a push-up bra. Alas, I needed all the help I could get.

"I don't know," I said. "It's so hard to figure out what's right."

He glanced at my chest. "*Uh,* yeah."

"Maybe you should come in and we can talk about it."

When we reached my house, he parked the car and leaned across the seat to kiss me. It was a gentle peck, soft and sweet. I smiled and he kissed me again, this time deeper. I noticed that a neighbor was playing loud music, and I guessed it was some recent high school grad throwing a wild party. By the time we got out of the van the music had stopped, but we weren't paying much attention. We had worked each other into a frenzy, kissing and groping as we approached the front door, fumbling with buttons before we even reached it, so we wouldn't have to waste any time getting naked.

I somehow managed to find the keyhole, even though my eyes were closed in ecstasy as Leo's body was pressed hard against mine. And then, just a second before I got the door open, there was an explosion that didn't come from inside my body. It was music, so loud the doorknob literally vibrated in my hand.

"What the hell?" I said, as I pushed it open.

There, in the middle of my living room, was my sister Joey, backed up by a full band, including Teddy Goodwin on the keyboard. The massive amps faced the front door and nearly knocked Leo and me on our asses.

"Oh my God!" I screamed over the music. I couldn't even hear my own voice.

"Joey!" I screamed. "Joey!"

She had her eyes closed and didn't see me. And she certainly couldn't hear me. Teddy acknowledged my presence by waving from behind the keyboard. He smiled, as if he assumed I was delighted to be witnessing this rehearsal.

"I'm sorry!" I screamed to Leo.

"What?"

"I'm sorry! I had no idea they were doing this tonight!"

"What?"

I looked at Teddy and sliced my finger across my throat to indicate that they should cut the music. He took his hands off the keys and spoke into the microphone. "Hold up."

The music stopped and Joey looked from Teddy to me and smiled.

"Hey, Bev!"

"What the hell is going on?" I asked.

"What do you mean? I *told* you we were going to use this place to rehearse. You said it was fine."

I gritted my teeth. "You said you would call me first." I turned to Teddy. "You promised."

He bit his lip. "Oops."

"What's the big—" she looked at Leo and stopped. "Oh, I see. You want us to leave?"

"That would be nice."

"Wait a second," Leo said. And then to me, "Can I talk to you for a second?"

I stepped outside with him, figuring he was going to ask me to come to his place instead, but he said, "Maybe I should just take a rain check."

"No!" I blurted, knowing that if we didn't do it that night I would lose my nerve. Or worse, that he'd make a move on Clare and she'd say yes. "I mean," I said more softly, "I have something upstairs I really want to show you."

Of course, the only thing upstairs I could think of showing him was my very sheer, very sexy, and very ripped negligee. I imagined finding a needle and thread when Leo wasn't looking and rushing into the bathroom to mend the thing.

Leo agreed, and went upstairs to wait for me while I ushered the band out of the house as fast as I could. Then I locked myself in the bathroom to put some quick stitches in my negligee. When I finally came into the bedroom dressed in my white-hot nightie, Leo was lying down with the sheet pulled up to his waist.

"What do you think?" I said, modeling for him.

"Fancy."

Fancy? I was prancing around the room in Victoria's Secret's sluttiest fuck-me nightie and all he could say was "fancy"?

Okay, so some guys just prefer naked. I pulled off the negligee and climbed into bed with him, where we made sweet, gentle love. And I didn't think about Kenny once. Okay, maybe once. Or twice. Three times at most. But that was only because he took so long that it was hard for me to stay focused. Point is, when he woke up at 6:00 a.m. and said he had to leave for work, he had a smile on his face and I felt my plan had worked.

Later, as I was getting out of the shower, I thought I heard a female voice singing downstairs. I opened the door a crack and listened. Someone absently hummed a tune that sounded so familiar and ancient it was almost as if it existed in some primal memory.

"Joey?" I called out.

"Sorry!" she yelled. "Did I wake you?"

I slipped on a bathrobe and went downstairs. Joey was standing in the middle of the living room with her hands on her hips, looking around.

"What's going on?" I asked.

"We're missing a cable from one of the amps. I thought I might have left it here."

From my vantage point, I could see it under the couch. "There," I said, pointing.

She bent and picked it up, and then draped it around the back of her neck like a prayer shawl. At that moment I realized what tune Joey had been humming. It was the Shema, an ancient Hebrew prayer that religious Jews chant to declare their faith.

"How was your night?" she asked.

I sat down on the soft armchair, sinking into it. "I think I did something really bad."

"You didn't stuff Leo in an industrial drum, did you?"

"Not funny."

"What, then?"

I stood. "I need coffee."

I went into the kitchen and Joey followed behind. I was silent as I made the coffee, thinking about how to tell her what I had done.

"C'mon," she said. "Spill it."

"I slept with Leo."

"Duh."

"I slept with Leo to stop him and Clare from having an affair."

Joey pulled out a chair and straddled it. "This is getting interesting."

"He's in love with Clare," I said.

"Did you tell him to get in line? Everyone's in love with Clare."

"This is different. She's in love with him too. And she's planning to sleep with him."

Joey's mouth opened. "Get *out!*"

"It's true."

"How do you know?"

"She told me. But it was only because I confronted her about it. Apparently, they were having cyber sex and she forgot to close the window on her computer. Dylan saw the whole thing."

"Shit."

"Yeah. Shit."

"So you fucked Leo to distract him from Clare?"

"And also to keep her from pursuing him. I know how it can derail your interest when the guy you like sleeps with your sister."

Joey raised her arms toward the heavens as if asking God what she should do with a sister who wouldn't let go of something that happened nearly two decades ago. "C'mon, that was different. I was stoned."

"I know," I said. "That's why what I did was much worse. I knew exactly what I was doing. It was . . . Machiavellian."

"But you weren't doing it to hurt her. You were doing it to protect her." Joey rose and opened the cabinet where we kept the breakfast cereal.

"Still. What kind of person does something like this? It's . . . am I evil?"

She pulled out a box of Honey Nut Cheerios and brought it to the table. "Of course not," she said, shoving her hand into the box.

"Clare will think so. It's going to drive her to the brink. It was cruel." Clare had a way of crying that tore at my soul. Imagining that I caused her pain on purpose was excruciating.

"Bev, you're being awfully hard on yourself. You think you're supposed to be above making stupid, emotional decisions, but you're not. Intellect has nothing to do with the heart. And yours has been broken for so long you don't even realize it." She dropped a handful of cereal into her mouth.

"What does that mean?"

She dusted her hands on her pants. "It's human nature to replay the events in our lives that have caused us the most pain."

The coffeemaker started whirring. It sputtered and water began to drip through the grinds.

"You studying psychology or something?" I asked.

"The recovery process. Sometimes we go pretty deep. Anyway, I have to leave."

"Aren't you staying for coffee?"

"Can't." She kissed my forehead. "You'll work it out. I have faith in you."

That made one of us.

I avoided calling Clare that whole day, and when Leo came by at night, I decided to drown my guilt in hormones. We ordered a pizza, and got so worked up while waiting for it to be delivered that we had sex on the kitchen table.

We were just pulling our clothes back on when the phone rang. I assumed it was the delivery man calling to say he couldn't find the address, but I was wrong. It was my father, and he sounded upset.

""Is everything okay?" I said, as I tucked in my shirt.

"Fortunately, they have some excellent hospitals in this area, so you don't have to worry."

My father's cryptic communication about a dire emergency was almost too much for me to take. Why couldn't he ever just get to the point?

"Who's in the hospital!" I snapped.

"Your mother."

Chapter 24

The only advantage to flying from the oppressive humidity of New York in the summer to the oppressive humidity of Florida in the summer is that you don't have to worry about winter coats jamming those overhead bins. I slid my travel bag right in and pushed the door shut until it clicked. Joy.

I took my seat by the window and belted myself in, hoping I wouldn't get a chatty seatmate. I wasn't in the mood for small talk with a stranger.

My father had told me that my mother passed out in the Waxmans' kitchen while making him a slice of toast. Arrhythmia, he had said. Something about nodes in the heart not sending the right signals. By the time he called me she had been thoroughly tested, and except for this circuitry glitch, her heart was healthy. Apparently, it just needed an electrical jolt now and then to keep it running, and so they were putting in a pacemaker and were trying to get her onto the schedule for surgery tomorrow.

Dad assured me Mom's life wasn't in danger and that I didn't need to make the trip. But I figured that if my mother was as healthy as he said, they wouldn't have scheduled the surgery so fast. I booked a flight for the next morning. Clare, of course, had the kids and couldn't leave, and Joey's rehab program required daily attendance, so it was just me.

A young woman hooked up to an iPod sat down next to me and I breathed a sigh of relief. She'd have no interest in talking to a boring old gal like me when she had her music to keep her company. I gave her a half smile and turned my face to the window.

At take-off, I watched as the ground below us disappeared beneath a haze of white. Then I pulled down my tray and put my paperback on it, but a couple of paragraphs in I got too drowsy to go on. My night with Leo hadn't afforded me much sleep, and I desperately needed a nap. It was a bumpy flight, and I fell into a very light slumber—the kind of semi-consciousness that allows the captain's announcements and other interruptions to break through.

A short while later I heard a flight attendant taking drink orders and opened my eyes. The girl next to me ordered a Diet Coke, loudly, without taking off her earphones. I asked for coffee and the flight attendant said someone else would be coming through with hot beverages.

"Thanks," I said, and half grinned at my seatmate just so she wouldn't think I was rude. But oh dear God, it was like I had dropped a box of Mentos into her Diet Coke. She pulled her earphones off.

"I know it's like totally retarded to drink soda in the morning? But, like, I could never get used to coffee? And caffeine's caffeine, right? Now I'm like a total Diet Coke addict. My friends call me a coke fiend." She laughed at her joke.

"We'd probably all be better off with orange juice," I said with a smile. I picked up my paperback to hide behind, but the girl looked at the cover and gasped.

"Are you reading Neil Gaiman? Oh my God! My roommate *loves* him. My roommate from college? We're not roommates now because it's summer but we'll room together again in the fall? At Binghamton? God, I should call her and tell her the person sitting next to me is reading Neil Gaiman. But we're not allowed to use our cell phones on the plane, are we? Until we land? But oh my God, I *have to* call her. I think it's going to be a while before you get your coffee? They're like all the way down at the end of the aisle? I think I have gum in my purse. Do you want gum? God, my purse is a *mess*. Did you see her hair? The flight attendant's? I mean the color? That kind of very blond blond with no highlights? My roommate dyed her hair that color just before school ended. Like what do you call that? Almost platinum, right? So retro. I'm thinking of getting highlights. But like, chunky?"

And so it went for the rest of the flight. By the time we landed I was having trouble having a coherent thought that didn't seem to end with a question mark. If these people would like move? I could get my bag? From the overhead bin?

I had told my father not to bother meeting me at the airport, as I'd planned to rent a car and meet him at the hospital. But when I exited the gate, I heard someone call my name and looked up.

"Kenny," I said, shaking my head to mask the jolt of joy that shot through me like I'd been defibrillated. "You didn't have to come get me."

"Shut up, you idiot." He gave me such a long hug I didn't think he was ever going to let go. "I'm glad you're here," he said, and then finally released me.

He smelled divine, freshly shaved. And he looked beautiful, of course, but there was a tension around his eyes that I hadn't seen before.

"You okay?" I asked.

"I am now." That smile.

Despite what I had said, I was glad he came. There's something about being met at the gate in an airport that makes you feel like you matter in this world. He took my bag and led me to the exit.

Transplanted Floridians will insist that their summers aren't any hotter than New York's, but as soon as we exited the terminal, I knew I wasn't in Long Island anymore. The atmosphere was wet, thick, and furnace-hot.

"Swamp air," I remarked.

"Swamp air?" Kenny echoed. "I think they're in Terminal Two."

By the time we crossed the road and walked the length of the long parking lot to his car, I was sticky with sweat, and the interior of his rental car made it even worse.

"*Ugh,*" I said. "Couldn't you park in shade?"

"No worries," he said. "Once I get this baby on the highway for ten minutes, it'll be a frigid eighty-two in here."

The car was too uncomfortable for me to think about the fact that I was alone with Kenny again. My whole focus was on trying to get some air between my clothes and my skin to bring my body temperature down.

"You booked a room at the Marriott?" he asked.

Kenny was staying at a hotel because my folks were in the spare room at his parents' house. The night before I had called to find out the name of the place so I could make a reservation there. He had told me there was plenty of room in his bed, but I'd just spent the night with Leo and the whole thing just felt too slutty. Besides, I was going to Florida to be there for my mother, not to carry on with Kenny Waxman.

Kenny asked if I wanted to stop at the hotel for a shower before going to the hospital. I pictured showing up in my mother's antiseptic hospital room grungy and damp with sweat, and told him I thought I'd better.

He clicked on the radio and I told him I'd heard from my father that Sam was in the same hospital as my mom.

"Is he okay?" I asked.

"Fine," Kenny said as he tuned past static to find a station.

"Then why are they keeping him?"

He stopped tuning when he found an oldies station playing the Stones' "Sympathy for the Devil." "Nothing major," he said. "My theory is that as his age, the more tests you run, the more things you find. His blood sugar is borderline, his cholesterol is high, and he has tachycardia."

"Tachycardia?"

"Rapid heart rate."

I tsked. "I know what it *means*. I just thought older people had *slow* heartbeats."

"They do, except when the police are closing in to arrest them for murder. Then their pulse picks right up."

I wasn't going to judge Kenny for using humor as a defense mechanism. Why should I? He was going through so much, and if it helped him cope, it was a handy tool.

"Have you been visiting him?" I asked.

"Yeah, sure. In between rounds of golf with O.J. and Robert Blake, I make chitchat with my dad."

Okay, so he was getting a bit sarcastic with me. I wasn't going to make an issue of it.

I turned the air conditioning vent to face me and was blasted with lukewarm air.

"What about the key to the storage unit?" I said. "You were going to try to find out where he hid it."

"That's been less than successful," he said. "I spent half the conversation trying to remind him that he even *has* a storage unit. If he has any idea where the key is, he's not talking."

"You think it's an act?"

"Either that or he's made a decision to let go of his faculties so he doesn't have to deal with anything. But I'm not inclined to give him the benefit of the doubt."

I sat quietly for a minute, trying to think of something helpful to say. Finally, I asked if he had spoken to Alicia Goodwin about his father.

"Why would I?"

"She's a psychologist. I thought she might have some insights."

He took his eyes off the road to look at me. "Please tell me you're kidding."

"Why would I be kidding?"

"C'mon. You're testing me, aren't you?"

"I don't know what you're talking about," I insisted.

"You're telling me Alicia Goodwin is a *shrink*, and you expect me to accept this without making a joke?"

I laughed in spite of myself.

"Where does she work?" he asked. "A halfway house?"

"Kenny," I chided.

"Does she specialize in patients with a *short* attention span?"

"Stop."

"Or people with a *low* libido?"

"Enough!"

"When someone makes a referral, do they say, 'I have little patience for you'?"

"Are you done?"

"I'm just teasing," he said. "I think it's great that she's a therapist. Teddy must be proud of her. I'll bet he loves to show her off at parties." Kenny cleared his throat and imitated Teddy's voice, "Have you met the little woman?"

I appreciated that he wanted to make me laugh, but I was getting uncomfortable. His PC button may have been stuck in the off position, but I felt guilty laughing at Alicia, who had been so kind to me after I passed out.

"Sorry," he said. "Sometimes it's like trying to quiet a case of the hiccups."

When we got to the lobby of the hotel, I veered to the right toward the front desk, and Kenny, who was carrying my bag by the shoulder strap, went to the left.

"Elevators are this way," he said.

"I have to check in."

"Your room won't be ready—check-in's not until four. You can shower in mine."

I squinted at him and stopped in my tracks. Was I being set up? Was this Kenny's way of getting me naked in a locked room? I felt too sweaty and disgusting to even think about it. Besides, how could I do that when my mother was in a hospital bed waiting for me?

When Kenny saw my hesitation he sighed. "Take it easy, champ. I wasn't planning on jumping your bones when you were on your way to visit your mother in the hospital." He hiked the bag up on his shoulder and headed toward the elevator. "I was going to save that for later."

The hotel lobby was well air-conditioned, and by the time we reached the elevator my perspiration had dried and I'd caught a chill. Kenny pushed the button for his floor and I rubbed down my upper arms against the goose bumps.

"You're cold now?" he asked.

"I'm fine."

The elevator doors slid shut, sealing the two of us in there alone, and I felt the air change, as if the ions were dancing invisibly around us, electrifying the atmosphere. My entire body felt the charge, which sensitized my nerve endings. The slightest touch, I knew, would spark a storm. I kept my eyes off Kenny, staring down at the floor, but felt his heat and smelled his aftershave. I had no control over my own thoughts, and I imagined him pushing me against the wall and pressing his body against mine.

"This way," he said, when the elevator doors opened.

I took a deep breath, let it out slowly, and followed him. Regardless of his promise, I knew that once we got into his room all bets were off, and that he'd start pawing me the second he shut the door.

He pulled a key card from his pocket and slid it into the door slot. A little green light flashed and Kenny pressed on the door lever and pushed it open, standing back while he held it for me.

"Thank you," I said, sidling past him.

The room had that pleasant hotel smell of faint air freshener, and the decor was contemporary and orderly. There was a king-sized bed in the middle, with an armoire and television facing it. On the other side of the bed, nearer the window, was a small sofa and coffee table. Opposite that was a small writing desk with a T-shirt draped over the chair. Kenny's sneakers were under it.

"Do you want me to put this in the bathroom?" Kenny asked, holding up my bag.

So he was really going to be a gentleman and not lunge at me? I was so surprised I didn't answer right away.

"Yes? No?" he said.

"*Uh,* sure."

I locked the bathroom and decided to take a quick shower so I wouldn't be tempted to think about Kenny on the other side of that door while I was naked. But by the time I soaped myself up, all bets were off. I imagined him picking the lock and letting himself in. I closed my eyes and tried to put clothes on him, but they kept dissolving. And then there he was— naked, and hard as wood. Suddenly it wasn't me soaping my body, but him, his hands everywhere. He'd put his mouth on mine and kiss me while he reached around and grabbed my slippery ass. I'd feel him enter me slowly, gently, while I grabbed onto his broad back.

There was a loud bang on the bathroom door.

"Bev?" Kenny shouted. "I'm running downstairs for a soda. You want one?"

"No, thanks."

"Okay, I'll be back in a minute."

I finished my shower and dried off, and then I availed myself of the tiny bottle of complimentary body lotion. I wrapped myself in one of the big plush towels and pulled the makeup kit from my travel bag. I just wanted to put on a little blush and mascara, but the mirror was fogged, so I opened the bathroom door to let out the steam. Kenny had returned already. He was sitting on the bed with his back to me, drinking a diet soda and talking on his cell phone. He seemed kind of agitated.

I left the door open while I applied my makeup, occasionally glancing at him in the mirror as I tried to hear what he was saying. The bathroom fan made it impossible. That is, until he stood, flipped his phone shut, and shouted, "Goddamn it!"

"What's the matter?" I asked, coming out of the bathroom and holding tight to the towel wrapped around me.

Kenny was pacing, angrily. "I thought I had that fucking job sewn up, but my agent told me she just found out another guy came into the picture."

"What does that mean?"

"Apparently there's only 'room' for one of us." He used air quotes to illustrate his disdain. "And that talentless fucker used to work for Jon Stewart."

"You know the guy?"

"He's a dick."

"Is he funny?"

"Not even a little."

"So what are you worried about?"

"Did you hear what I said?" Kenny shouted. "He worked for *Jon fucking Stewart*!"

"Don't get mad at *me*."

Kenny angrily pulled off his white T-shirt and threw it on the floor. He grabbed another shirt from his drawer—a red one—and started waving it as he talked. "The guy ass-kisses his way into every job. Never wrote a single funny line in his life, but has a résumé I'd *kill* for."

His threw the red shirt on the bed and sat down. "If I don't get that job my career is *fucked*." He balled his fists and banged his knee. This, I knew, was the flip side of his funny. If Kenny wasn't coping, he was angry. There was no sad and disappointed, no sullen and melancholy. He was either fine or he was furious.

I should have remembered that Kenny's temper needs to run its course and that I simply could not comfort him, but I felt like he needed me, and so I approached.

"You'll probably get the job, Kenny. Letterman wants somebody who can write funny jokes, not someone who can kiss his ass."

He sneered. "How would *you* know?"

"Because you don't get that successful by surrounding yourself with sycophants."

"The great and powerful Oz has spoken," he said.

"Don't be so sarcastic."

"Why not?"

"Because it's mean and it makes you sound like . . ."

His eyes got wild. "Like my father?"

"I'm sorry. I shouldn't have said that." I sat down on the

bed next to him and rubbed his bare back to try to soothe him.

He grabbed my wrist. "Don't do that unless you mean it."

I stood, but he didn't release me.

"Let go," I said.

He stood too, still holding me tightly by the wrist.

"Do you want to fuck or not?" He put the index finger from his free hand between my breasts and hooked it around the towel. The slightest movement and it would give and fall to the floor.

"Don't do this," I said.

He didn't move either hand. He just put his face into my neck and kissed it. Then he licked it. I shivered. He breathed into my ear, "Well?"

My head rolled to the side. "Well what?"

"I'm still waiting for an answer." He nibbled my earlobe.

My breathing started to quicken. "What was the question again?"

"Do you want to fuck or not?" His finger tugged the slightest bit at my towel.

Every cell in my physical being said yes. My flesh was ignited and my crotch pulsated in anticipation.

"No," I said.

"You sure?"

I paused. It was the moment of reckoning and I couldn't make a decision.

"I don't know," I finally said.

That was all he needed. He jerked his finger forward and my towel fell to the floor. Within seconds he had me pinned to the bed by both my wrists while he sucked and bit my nipples. I writhed against him, moaning, expecting the excruciating ecstasy of anticipation to continue until I was begging for mercy, like last time. But he kicked off his pants quickly, rolled on a condom and entered me hard, his eyes black and unfocused. He thrust angrily, holding onto my breasts while he pushed and pushed as if trying to hurt me, until one final violent plunge so deep he succeeded. I cried out and he was done.

He rolled off of me and covered his eyes with his arm. "I'm sorry," he said, but remained hidden. He wouldn't even look at me.

I got out of bed without speaking and went into the bathroom to clean off and get dressed. When I came out, he was asleep, his mouth open, his arm still covering his eyes.

I put my travel bag on my shoulder, grabbed his car keys, and left.

Chapter 25

The hotel concierge gave me easy directions to the hospital, so I was able to follow them . . . despite the fact that mascara dripped into my eyes as I drove. Goddamn him. I knew, of course, what I was getting into with Kenny. I knew about his temper, but it wasn't supposed to be like this. He wasn't supposed to take it out on *me*.

It felt like a betrayal of the worst kind. Worse than when he'd slept with Joey back in high school. Worse than Jonathan's infidelity. It was more personal than those. I was right there in the room with him and I didn't matter as much as his anger.

How could he? I thought his feelings for me were bigger than that. What an idiot I'd been.

I parked the car in the hospital's visitor lot and took a look at my face in the rearview mirror. It was a mess—red and puffy from crying, mascara dripping down my cheeks. Cleaning off the black streaks with a tissue I'd dug out of my purse did little to help. My nose and eyelids had that swollen look of someone whose heart had been kicked and beaten.

I went through the big glass doors of the hospital into the open lobby and barely got a second look. I guess they were used to seeing people cry. I tried to use that to center myself and gain some perspective. As trampled as I felt, it wasn't as if I'd lost someone I loved. Or was it? No! I refused to give in to the melodrama of that thought. I was not in love with Kenny Waxman. I was not.

I stopped in the ladies' room and wet some paper towels with cold water, pressing them against my face in an effort to get the swelling down. I didn't want my mother to know I had been crying because she might worry that it meant her prognosis wasn't as good as she'd been told. Afterward, a check in the mirror demonstrated only the tiniest improvement.

My face, I decided, needed a little more time to get back to normal. So I went into the gift shop determined to spend a few mindless moments inspecting silly knickknacks. The trick was to distract myself so I wouldn't start crying again, as if overpriced teddy bears, snow globes, and collectible figurines could push Kenny to the back of some mental shelf in my brain where I wouldn't notice him.

The gift shop had a few personal hygiene items, so I bought a tube of mascara, since I had left mine in my bag in the car and needed another application. For my mother, I chose an African violet in a trophy-shaped planter inscribed "World's Greatest Mom."

Back in the bathroom, I did the cold water trick again before applying the new mascara. I had some lipstick in my purse, so I rubbed a bit onto my cheeks before running it over my lips. Standing a couple feet back from the mirror, I thought the result wasn't bad. I looked good enough to pass. I flipped my clean hair over my head, ran a comb through it, and flipped it back. I was ready.

I smiled broadly as I entered my mother's room. "Hi, Mom!" I chirped.

She was watching TV with the sound too low to hear, and turned to face me. "Beverly! I told your father not to make you come."

"He didn't *make me* do anything." I leaned in and kissed her on the cheek. She smelled clean and powdery.

My mother held my face in her hands and looked at me. "What's the matter?"

What in the world had made me think I could fly in under Mom radar?

"Nothing. I'm fine. I bought you a plant. Where do you want it?"

"You're not fine. You were crying. Not over me, I hope—I feel as healthy as a young colt."

"You look great, Mom." I glanced around the room. There was a curtain dividing it in half, with Mom's roommate hidden on the other side. The walls were a pale blue and the two bedside chairs were upholstered in purple vinyl. I imagined someone thought it was cheerful, but it was a wasted effort. There was simply no way to make a hospital homey.

I glanced up at the television. Oprah was on her couch talking to a woman in a bright suit. I tried to listen for a second and realized the voices didn't match up with the mouth movements.

"Mom? Are you listening to *Oprah* dubbed in Spanish?"

She picked up the remote and looked at it. "I can't figure how to work this thing. All the channels are in Spanish."

"Did you call someone?"

"No, it's all right. I don't mind."

I tsked. This was so like my mother. She didn't want to bother anybody, so she was in bed watching television in a language she didn't understand.

"Mom, you're *paying* for this. You're entitled to watch it in English."

She waved away my concern. "There's nothing to watch anyway." She clicked off the TV and patted the empty space next to her. I put the plant on her nightstand and sat.

"Did you see Kenny?" she asked.

"He picked me up at the airport," I said, pretending to be interested in the controls that worked her bed.

My mother leaned forward and moved a lock of hair from my face, forcing me to make eye contact. I quickly looked away so she wouldn't press me. I didn't want to have to answer any questions about the past couple hours of my life.

"So when is your surgery?" I asked.

"First thing in the morning. Thank you for the plant. It's lovely."

I shrugged. "Are they letting you get some rest?"

"You know what they say—the hospital is the last place in the world you can get any rest. Seems like someone comes in to poke at me every fifteen minutes."

"You're not nervous, are you? Dad said it's a simple procedure."

"The whole thing is ridiculous. I feel perfectly fine. I wanted to wait until we got home to have this done, but your father insisted."

"Where *is* Dad?"

"He'll be back, soon. He went down to visit Sam, who's been alone all day. Renee was too distraught to get out of bed today. *She's* the one who should be in the hospital. She's a wreck, Beverly. Thank God Kenny is here. He's a great comfort to her."

"Uh-huh."

"Who knew he would grow up to be such a mensch?"

"Mm."

"I honestly don't know how he's holding it together. This has to be harder on him than anyone." She lowered her voice to a whisper. "His own *father*. Can you imagine?"

I nodded, trying to think of a way to change the subject. My mother grabbed a tissue from the nightstand and wiped her nose. I grabbed one too and dabbed under my eyes.

"How do you and Dad face Sam, knowing what he did?" I blew my nose.

My mother patted her hair while she thought about her reply. "It's like two different people, Beverly. The senile old man in that hospital bed is not . . . not the same Sam who could have done that terrible thing."

But he is, I wanted to say. He *is* the same Sam.

The phone rang, and my mother picked it up, saying *hello* with the drawn-out theatrical intonation women of her generation reserved just for answering the telephone. I wondered if they were taught it in school when they were young, or if it was some affectation they learned from the movies.

When she heard who was on the other end, my mother's voice went back to normal. It was clear she was speaking to Renee, whom I surmised was feeling better and ready to make a trip to the hospital. When she got off the phone, my mother asked me if I would mind running down to Sam's room and getting my father. Renee needed a lift to the hospital because she wasn't able to reach Kenny. Of course, that was just as well since I had his car.

"You want me to go to Sam Waxman's room?" I asked, feeling a shiver.

"Yes, dear. It's just two flights down."

"But—" I stopped. It hadn't occurred to me until that moment that I'd ever have to face Sam Waxman again, and the thought was making me hyperventilate. "Can't we just call down there?" I said.

"Do you know how much they charge for calls? It's robbery."

"I'm sure Dad will be back any minute. Why don't we just wait?"

My mother fluffed a pillow behind her back. "I'd go down

there myself," she said, "but they don't let patients get on the elevator without a nurse."

"How about if *I* just go and pick up Renee?" I said, rummaging in my bag for the car keys.

My mother sighed and clicked on the TV. The news was on in Spanish. "If that's what you want, dear," she said, turning her attention to the unintelligible broadcast.

I stood, the weight of guilt tugging at me. I wished my mother would get angry and yell at me, tell me I was being a sniveling little twit. But just bearing it silently—the way she always did—was more than I could handle.

"Okay," I said, rolling my eyes as I dropped Kenny's keys on her nightstand. "I'll go get Dad."

As I walked down the corridor to the elevator thinking about seeing Sam Waxman face-to-face, my body began to float away. I was disassociating, growing taller and taller as I moved away from the sound of my own footsteps. I couldn't tell what force was propelling me forward. It simply didn't feel like I was the one making my legs move.

At last I reached the elevator, which was larger than the average prison cell and not much faster. I had plenty of time to study the framed "Patients' Bill of Rights" posters on either side of me, though the language made my eyes glaze. Two doctors behind me talked about lab hours and a woman in front of me holding a stuffed penguin looked lost and tense. She turned and asked me if I knew where the children's ward was. I shrugged, and one of the doctors behind me answered, explaining that she needed to go back down to the lobby and take another bank of elevators.

I was only in a hospital once as a kid, when I had broken my leg badly and required surgery. I was six and don't remember much about the accident, except that I had gone over the handlebars of my bicycle, and that my father had been the one to take me to the hospital. The only thing that was vivid about the whole experience was my humiliation at having to go into a stroller when I got home. I wasn't able to walk for a week, and I guess I was so small they didn't bother with a wheelchair. One day, when I was sitting in the backyard with my mother, a group of kids were playing in Kenny's yard. This was before we had a fence, so I had a clear view. They yelled over that they were playing "family" and said I could be the baby, since I was in a stroller. I was hot with shame, but I agreed, because my loneliness was unbearable.

The kids came and got me, wheeling me across the grass to Kenny's yard. I was happy for company, but the kids tired of the game after only a few minutes and ran off to play something else, leaving me there alone. I cried for my mother, but she had gone back into the house and didn't hear me. After a few minutes Lydia came out the back door and asked me what happened.

"Shall I take you back home?" she said after I told her. "Or will you stay and keep me company? I'm feeling very lonely today."

We went inside and had cookies drenched with syrup, and played checkers. She told me over and over how happy she was that I was keeping her company. I went from feeling abandoned and miserable to lucky and proud. Lydia would have made a wonderful mother.

When we finally reached the second floor, the elevator stopped without opening. I glanced around at the hospital staffers in the car to see if they were concerned that we were stuck, but their expressions were unmoved. Finally, the elevator gave a little hiccup and the doors slid slowly open, making my stomach cramp into a knot. I didn't want to exit.

"Second floor," someone in the elevator said. The woman holding the stuffed animal moved to the side and I stepped out.

Waxman was in room 244, and the arrow on the wall directed me to the corridor on my left. I walked down the hall listening to the sound of my heels on the hard tile floor bringing me back into my body as I ticked off the room numbers I passed—238, . . . 240, . . . 242. . .

There it was: 244. I stood outside the doorway for a few moments, breathing in the hospital smell, which reminded me of that crisp synthetic scent you get when you open a Band-Aid wrapper. I listened for my father's voice from within, but all I could make out was the hum of electronics and the low murmur of a television. Slowly, I peeked my head inside and looked toward the bed, where I saw a husky man with thin red hair combed over a shiny bald head—definitely *not* Samuel Waxman. But it was a double room like my mother's, with a drawn curtain separating the two halves. I listened carefully, and didn't hear any voices coming from the other side of the curtain. *Maybe I don't even have to go in,* I thought. Maybe I could just go upstairs and tell my mother he wasn't there.

"You looking for Waxman?" the red comb-over man said.

I hesitated, deciding how to answer.

"Who's that?" came a familiar voice from behind the curtain. It was him. "Who's there?"

His voice. It sounded so ordinary, so benign. For a moment, I doubted my assumptions about his guilt. This was Sam Waxman from next door. He couldn't possibly have murdered a woman and stuffed her body in an industrial drum. Or my precious schnauzer, Stephanie. Who could be so evil? Certainly not the little man who was once so tender he had searched all over to buy me a tiny gift I had coveted.

I was no more than nine at the time. Our families were vacationing together in the Berkshires. In the lobby of the hotel there was a giant Christmas tree that mesmerized me. I thought it was so grand and yet delicate I couldn't get enough of it. But I felt guilty coveting something so Christian, so I tried to admire it when no one was looking. One ornament in particular captured my attention. It was tiny Santa inside a glass ball, and one day I got so caught up in looking at it I didn't even hear anyone approaching. But suddenly Mr. Waxman was by my side. He whispered, "I like Christmas trees too," and I felt relieved to know it was okay to admire it. And as if that wasn't enough, after we got home he gave me a present when no one was around. It was a Santa ornament just like the one I had admired on the tree.

The red-haired man in the hospital bed cleared his throat to get my attention. I took a deep breath.

"It's Bev Bloomrosen," I said to the curtain. "I . . . I was looking for my father."

"Who?"

"Bev? I waited for a reaction. "Beverly? Harold's daughter?"

"He has to see your face, sweetheart," the redheaded man said. "Go on in."

I hesitated, unable to move.

"Don't be shy," the man said. He cocked his head toward the curtain. "He won't bite."

I swallowed hard and walked across the room, aware of a dampness darkening the armpits of my pale shirt. When I reached the opening in the curtain, there he was, all alone, sitting straight up in a bed folded into a right angle. He looked smaller than I had remembered—his sallow skin drooping past his chin as if he had shrunk beneath his flesh—but exactly the same in every other way. There had been no transformation from man to monster.

I stared at his hands, transfixed by the very humanness of his aging flesh and liver spots.

"Who are you?" he barked.

I looked into his eyes to see if I could discern a lie. Was it an act or not? "I'm Beverly, Harold and Bernadette's daughter."

"The rock star?"

"That's my sister, Joey. I'm Bev."

"Harold's daughter is a rock star." He looked me up and down. "You're no rock star."

"I'm looking for my father," I said. "I thought he was here with you."

"Who's your father?"

"Harold. Harold Bloomrosen."

Mr. Waxman folded his arms. "Let me hear you sing something."

"I'm not a singer. I'm Beverly. Remember? You gave me a Christmas ornament once."

There was a flash of recognition in his eyes, and I could see that he remembered.

"Christmas?" he said. "What are you—a gentile?"

He was lying, but why? Why would he lie about something so harmless, something that revealed a kinder, gentler Sam Waxman? I looked at his eyes and got a white-cold chill. Suddenly, I knew.

"My God," I said. "You didn't *buy* me that ornament. You stole it. You stole it right off the tree."

He hesitated for a moment and then waved off my comment. "Forrester Inn," he said. "Filthy place. We should have gone back to Grossinger's."

"You remember," I said.

Our eyes met and I understood that he was back, that he knew who I was. For one fleeting second, before he glanced away, I could see it there in the darkness of his pupils—the icy evil that had been able to murder an innocent young woman. My insides began to roil.

He peered past me, squinting in mock anger. "Rock star, my ass. Harold's little girl is blond."

I pictured him hammering down the lid on the industrial drum, our beautiful Lydia dead inside. Murdered. By this man. I could see him dusting his hands after rolling it under the house, his task complete. What did he do next? Walk inside and ask his wife what she made for dinner?

"I'm *Beverly*." I pronounced it angrily and distinctly.

He picked up his remote control and turned on the television. I grabbed it out of his hand and pressed the Off button.

"I'm Beverly," I repeated, my face inches from his.

"Get out of my room, miss."

"Beverly," I said, looking intently into his lucid eyes.

"Whatever your name is, give me back my remote."

I held the remote control over the pitcher of water next to his bed. He eyes went from my hand to my face and back to my hand. I let the remote drop into the water, where it landed with a dull splash. I leaned in closer to his ear.

"I'm Beverly," I said again, "and I know what you did."

Chapter 26

After leaving Sam Waxman's room, I leaned against the wall in the corridor, shivering. I had just been face-to-face with a man who murdered someone, and it left me sick with shock.

A nurse wheeling a large machine down the hall stopped when she saw me. "Are you okay?" she asked. "Do you need assistance?"

"Bathroom," I blurted, feeling a rising nausea.

She moved her cart to the side and took me by the elbow to the nearest ladies' room.

I thanked her, then pushed my way into a stall. A violent spasm seized my stomach. I didn't vomit at first, but broke out in a cold sweat that felt like nothing except death. Trembling, I dropped to my knees and put my face over the toilet, praying for the release of regurgitation. My hair fell over my face, and when I looked past it into the water, I saw the dark reflection. It looked so much like what I had thought were fibers floating on top of the brackish liquid in the industrial drum, that for a moment my clouded mind lost the thread of reality and a colorless human hand rose above the surface, looking exactly as pallid and clammy as I felt.

The vision startled me and made my stomach seize again.

But this time it was forceful enough to push up bile, and I vomited into the toilet—a glorious and terrible purge.

I sat against the cold tile wall for a few minutes before getting up and approaching the sink. I lathered my hands and the bottom of my face, as well as the tip of my hair that had been nicked with vomit. After rinsing and spitting, I swallowed some water to wash the burn from my esophagus. I realized, then, that it would probably do me some good to put some food in my empty stomach. First, though, I had to head back to my mother's room to tell her I hadn't found my dad.

Trembling and depleted, I headed back to the elevator and up to the fourth floor. As I approached the room, I heard a faint male voice and was happy that my father had turned up.

"There you are," I said as I entered. But the second the words escaped my lips I realized that it wasn't my father's voice I had heard. I covered my mouth with my hand as if I could take the sentence back.

Kenny stood and faced me. "Bev."

I froze. It hadn't occurred to me that he might show up despite my having taken his car. How shortsighted of me not to realize he would simply call a taxi.

"What happened?" my mother asked. "You look terrible."

I remained at the doorway, unable to take a step into the room. "I never found Dad."

"Are you okay?" Kenny asked.

I gave him a cold stare and said nothing. Then I turned to my mother. "I don't know where he could be."

"He probably went to get a cup of coffee," she said.

There was an awkward silence, and it seemed like Kenny was searching for something to say.

"I'll go look for him in the cafeteria," I said, before he could speak. "And if he's not there, I'll go to pick up Renee."

"I'll come with you," Kenny said.

I put my hand up. "No!"

"Don't be silly, Beverly," my mother said. "Let him come with you. You don't even know the way."

"I'll figure it out." I picked up the keys I had left on the nightstand and turned to leave, but Kenny rushed toward me. He put his hand on my shoulder before I got out the door. I turned, trying to give him a dirty look, but my eyes burned from the effort of holding back tears.

"Wait a minute, champ," he said. "It's *my* rental car, remember?"

"You want to go pick up your mother?" I said. "Fine." I forced the keys into his hand, and then sat down in the vinyl chair by my mother's bed.

Kenny hesitated. "Come with me, Bev," he said. "Please? We need to talk."

"I have nothing to say."

"Do you want me to apologize right here in front of your mother?"

"No!" God, he was impossible.

"Then come with me."

I looked to my mother, hoping I would see something in her eyes that would show me she was on my side. And there it was, as clear as rainwater. She had picked up on my neediness and would protect me in any way she could. I moved from the chair to the edge of the bed and put my head on my mother's shoulder. She put her arms around me and I started to cry.

"You'd better just go," she said to Kenny.

Later, my father gave me a lift back to my hotel and insisted on walking me inside, even though he was hobbled by a walking cast and a cane. After I checked in, I told him to go back and rest, and I went up to my room alone.

I noticed that it was set up exactly like Kenny's room, with just the slightest variation in neutral colors. I dropped the key card on the dresser and collapsed on the bed, realizing it was evening already and I had never answered the hunger pangs that had jabbed at me earlier and, in fact, hadn't eaten a thing since the morning. I considered dialing room service, but I was so exhausted I decided to close my eyes for a few minutes first. I was desperate for a short nap. Maybe even a long one.

I lay down right on top of the bedspread feeling so leaden it was like gravity itself was pulling me into a thick, dreamless sleep. Sometime later, when someone knocked hard on the door of the room, I was disoriented. I couldn't figure out what time of day it was and why I was being awoken. I stumbled to the door and stupidly swung it open without asking who was there.

It was Kenny, carrying a pizza box.

"I thought you might be hungry," he said.

I stood for a moment, blinking, letting myself wake up and understand who he was and what he was doing there. The smell of the pizza wafted through the cardboard and nearly made me salivate. Almost without thinking, I grabbed the box from his hands.

"Thanks," I said, shutting the door with my hip. I walked over to the little table in front of the sofa and put the box down.

"Bev," he called through the door. "That was a peace offering. Open up."

I lifted the lid and took out a slice, devouring it greedily while I stood. It was hot and so delicious. Who knew they had such good pizza in Florida? This was real pizza. Brooklyn pizza.

"C'mon, Bev. At least give me the chance to apologize."

I sat down on the sofa and put my feet up on the table next to the box.

"Go away," I said with a full mouth.

"I'm hungry too, you know."

So what, I thought. I had worked my way down to the crust and was chomping through it.

"Look, I know I was an asshole," he said. "I'm sorry. Sometimes my temper gets away from me. Can we just talk about it?"

What was there to talk about? I believed he was sorry and I didn't care. It couldn't erase that he was someone capable of treating me like that.

I sucked my fingers clean and took another slice from the box.

"Bev?"

My hunger losing its beastly edge, I became aware that a napkin would be a good idea. There were none around, so I grabbed a tissue from the end table and used it to wipe my face.

"Can I have a slice, at least?"

I burped.

"What?" he said.

"Go away!"

"Not until we talk."

I picked up the remote and clicked on the television as I tried to relax and eat the second slice. *Entertainment Tonight* was on, which seemed like the perfect mind-numbing prescription. Problem was that hearing about celebrity breakups and which nightclub-hopping young actress had anorexia was so boring to me that it left my mind free to wander places I didn't want it to go, so I clicked around, aware that Kenny remained outside my door, saying something or other I couldn't make out. It was getting on my nerves.

Finally, I finished my slice and took another, placing it on a sheet of hotel stationery. I closed the pizza box and brought it to the door, balancing it on one hand.

"Here," I said to Kenny as I swung the door open. "Thanks for the pizza. Now go away."

"Don't do this, Bev," he said. I let the door shut and hesitated there for a moment.

"Okay," I heard him say quietly. "I'm leaving. But I'm sorry. I'm sorry for hurting you."

I listened to him walk away and then went back to the sofa to have my last slice. But a lump had found its way into my throat and I couldn't eat another bite.

Chapter 27

The next morning my father picked me up at the hotel so that we could sit together while waiting for my mother to come out of surgery. To pass the time, we brought bagels and coffee, as well as a couple of newspapers.

With sofalike cushioned benches affixed to the walls and an assortment of movable chairs so that families could gather in neat little groups, the waiting room was meant to be a comfortable place to hang around while sweating and fretting. A few televisions hung overhead, providing diversion, or at least a background hum for people too nervous for idle chatter.

Even though I had been assured my mother's operation was low risk, I was anxious about it. At least I think I was. It was hard to tell *how* I felt, as a numbness had settled in, fogging my brain. I guessed it was just emotional overload, but I felt as if someone had spiked my coffee with Thorazine or sneaked into my room during the night and performed a secret lobotomy. In any case, I floated in a kind of haze, unable to process all that was going on.

I tried to focus. "How long should this take?" I asked my father as I fished a covered container of coffee out of the bag for him.

"She probably won't be lucid for quite some time. They're big on morphine drips now. Used to worry more about addiction to painkillers. Now it's all about pain management."

I sighed. "You didn't answer my question."

"What?"

"How long will the surgery take?"

"About an hour or two."

I glanced around the room. A family of mostly obese people sat in another corner of the room, watching television, occasionally reaching into a box of Dunkin' Munchkins. The woman in the middle held a tissue and dabbed at her nose. On one side of her was an elderly man I presumed to be her father. On the other side sat a teenage boy playing a handheld electronic game. Two boys just a bit younger sat on the floor in front of her watching television. I could tell they were all worried about their loved one in surgery, and I wanted to tell them it would be okay. I didn't know that, of course, but I felt like whoever was in that operating room would fight like hell to get back to this family. Who wouldn't be pulled by that kind of love and support?

The woman said something to the teenager and he got up and brought over the box of treats.

"Would you like one?" he asked.

"That's very kind of you, thanks," I said, and reached in to find a little chocolate ball glazed in sugar.

He offered the box to my father.

"Did you know that Krispy Kreme was in the South for many years before going national?" my father said.

The boy blinked. "These are Dunkin' Donuts."

"Do you *want* one, Dad?" I asked.

He shook his head, and the boy went back to his mother, whom I thanked from across the room.

"Would it kill you to just say 'no thanks'?" I said to my father.

"You're in a mood."

Was I? I supposed enough emotions roiled beneath the surface to account for the snippiness with my father. I made a
promise to myself to try to keep a lid on it.

I picked up the local section of the newspaper and started
reading a story about a small child who had called 911 when
her diabetic mother passed out, thus saving her life. I felt like
I'd been reading that same child-as-hero story my whole life,
and I wondered why people couldn't seem to get enough of
such a recycled tale. Why was the idea of a young child saving
an adult so captivating? It had to be more than the charm of
precociousness and the novelty of reversing roles. Did we just
love the thought of rising above our own helplessness to save
the day?

My father was sitting back on the sofa, his cast leg resting on
the table in front of him. He scanned the newspaper through
the reading glasses on the edge of his nose. I knew that he was
coping with both Mom's situation and the Waxmans' drama
in his own way—by filtering everything through his intellect.
That was the wall around his tender heart. I reached over and
gave his arm a squeeze.

He looked up at me. "She's going to be fine," he said.

The waiting room door opened and a nurse came in. My
father looked up at her expectantly, but she walked over to the
Dunkin' Donuts family and addressed them in hushed tones.
The woman with the tissue nodded thoughtfully. I hoped they
were getting good news about their loved one's surgery. After
a few moments the nurse left and the family conferred, looking relieved. I let out an extended breath.

I read the paper for a while longer without much interest.
When my father finished and folded up his section, we traded.
Still, I couldn't focus. I got up and walked to the window,
which overlooked another part of the hospital building. Look-

ing down, I could see a section of the parking lot and some palm trees planted around it to provide some shade from the scorching Florida sun.

The door to the waiting room opened again and I looked up, hoping it was someone coming to fill us in on the progress of my mother's surgery.

It was Kenny.

I stayed where I was. Kenny glanced quickly in my direction and approached my father. They shook hands and spoke for a few minutes about my mother's surgery before Kenny approached me.

"I know you still hate me," he said. "But since you accepted the pizza, I thought you might accept this."

He handed me a shopping bag. I looked inside and saw a box of charcoals and a sketch pad.

"I never see you sketch anymore," he said. "You used to enjoy that. I thought it might help pass the time."

I pictured Kenny thinking hard about something he could get for me that would be meaningful, and then driving around greater Boca Raton looking for an art supply store. It was a thoughtful gesture, but I wasn't going to forgive him. I couldn't. Still, I accepted the gift with a quiet "Thanks" and took a seat.

"You can draw a picture of me with fangs if you want. Give me mean, crazy eyes. Hell, make a life drawing and miniaturize my . . ." he held his hands in front of his crotch.

He was trying to make me laugh but I just felt embarrassed. I didn't need everyone in the room to know I'd seen him naked. I shushed him, and he smiled at me, holding his thumb and forefinger a half inch apart to indicate how small I should make him. I rolled my eyes and pulled the sketch pad out of the bag. Kenny took the seat across from me.

I wasn't yet sure what I was going to draw—only that it

wasn't going to be Kenny. I took out the charcoals and put them on the seat next to me.

It had been a very long time since I sketched, and I didn't realize until that minute how much I'd missed it. It had always been a kind of meditation for me, but I gave it up during my marriage to Jonathan because he had been so dismissive of my work. "It's fine," he would say. "It's just not *art.*"

I closed my eyes for a few moments trying to conjure an image. And then, there it was, as vivid and precise as could be. I opened my eyes and started drawing. I began with a heart-shaped face with a high forehead, framed by unruly curls. I took my time with the large almond-shaped eyes spaced far apart, and gave richness and depth to the irises, being sure to leave a crescent of white space where the light reflected. The nose was long, but smooth and straight. The mouth was all Hollywood—broad and smiling, with dark lips and big white teeth. The cheekbones were also cut like a movie star's. I worked and worked, stopping occasionally to hold it at arm's distance for a better perspective. When at last the face seemed done, I shaded an area around it, leaving a halo of light. I was a little surprised by the final image, as I expected the eyes to look as happy as the smile, but there was a sadness in them. Was that clumsiness or my subconscious at work?

Still, I was pleased with it and turned the page around to show Kenny, who had been sitting quietly the entire time.

He stared at the picture silently, and I just waited. I thought the likeness was good, but was my memory playing tricks? Would he recognize this face?

Finally he said, "It's her. It's Lydia."

I nodded.

Kenny looked somber, and I worried that I had angered him with this drawing. But there was no fury in his eyes—only a softness, which touched me. I still wasn't forgiving him, but I couldn't help feeling sad for what he'd lost. I was sorry I'd drawn her. I considered ripping out the page and tearing it in half.

"Can I have it?" he whispered, his hand on his mouth as if he were afraid to even ask.

I carefully tore it from the pad and handed it to him. "It'll smudge," I said, "so be careful."

"I should have bought fixative, right? I forgot about that."

"Hairspray will do in a pinch, if you can get your hands on some."

"You need hairspray?" said the heavyset lady. She rummaged in her purse and pulled out a travel-sized aerosol can. She smiled and her whole face looked so different, so pretty. I hadn't noticed her complexion before—it was milky smooth.

Kenny thanked her and took the hairspray. He shook the can, pulled the cap off, and held it about an inch from the picture.

"Stop," I said. "It's not good to get that close."

"It can be," he said, "if you give it a chance."

I rolled my eyes and made him give me the hairspray. I wasn't going to have this conversation. "Just let it dry," I said as I sprayed a fine mist over the page, "and then it should be set."

He put his hand on my arm. "I really am sorry."

"I know." I gave the lady back her hairspray and thanked her again. She told me her name was Doreen and that her husband was having double-bypass surgery, even though he was only forty-four.

"I have three kids," she whispered, her eyes lit with fear.

"I'm sure the surgeon is very skilled."

She nodded. "The nurse said it was going well."

She looked like she needed a hug, so I gave her one.

I heard the door open behind me and turned to see if another nurse had entered with an update for either of us. But it was Renee Waxman, followed by a male aide pushing Sam into the room in a wheelchair. Renee pointed to an empty spot next to my father, and the aide parked the wheelchair there and then left.

I glanced at Kenny, whose jaw tightened. He said hello to his mother, and then took a seat near the window with his back to his father.

"How are you feeling, Sam?" my father asked.

"I think I left the water running," he said.

My father took off his reading glasses. "What water?"

"The hose. The goddamned hose."

"There's no hose," my father said. "You're in the hospital. Remember?"

Sam's eyes were unfocused. "It'll flood the tomatoes,"

"The tomatoes are fine," Renee said.

"They'll get flooded. I forgot to shut off the hose."

Renee glanced at my father and shrugged. "I shut it off," she said, "just before we left." She sat back, satisfied.

"You? You *never* shut off the water. Never do a damn thing. Can't even clean up your own messes."

Renee looked like she would cry. "Just relax, Sam," she said, her hand hovering over her mouth. "Everything is fine."

"Who are all these people?" he said angrily, as if he was accusing us of something.

"You know Harold, of course," she began, "and that's his daughter, Beverly. You remember Bev?"

"The drug addict."

"That was Joey," my father said matter-of-factly.

"Who's that man next to her?"

"That's our son, Kenny," Renee said.

"Right. Another drug addict. And who are those fat people?"

His voice carried clear across the room and I cringed. Kenny looked furious. He rose and approached his father.

"Shut the fuck up," he said quietly though closed teeth.

Sam looked at Renee. "What did I say that was so bad?"

I turned to Doreen. "I'm so sorry."

She waved it away.

"Beverly, let me see what you drew," my father said. I could tell he was eager to change the subject, but I didn't want to bring the page over to that side of the room.

"It's nothing, really," I said.

"It's not nothing," Kenny said. He picked up the drawing and brought it over to my father, who held the page out and stared at it.

"Oh," my father said, his face changing. I thought I detected a chink in his emotional armor, but he quickly recovered. "It's fine work, Bev."

"May I see?" Renee asked.

I glanced at Kenny, unsure what to do. He shrugged and took the picture from my father.

"Here," Kenny said, handing it to his mother.

I tensed waiting for her reaction. She stared at it for a few moments and then silently handed it back to Kenny. She opened her purse, extracted a tissue, and blew her nose.

"Let me see it," Sam barked.

Kenny's body looked as rigid as a marine's. He held the drawing with two hands right in front of his father's face.

"Recognize this woman, Sam?"

His father stared hard.

"It's Lydia," Kenny said. "You remember *Lydia*, don't you?"

Sam's eyes bulged. He swiped at the picture and Kenny pulled it away, but not before his father's hand had brushed over it. Kenny looked at the picture and then turned it toward me.

"Didn't smudge!" he said triumphantly, like he got a chance to protect Lydia and succeeded.

Sam leaped from the chair and pulled the page from Kenny's hand. "I don't know this woman!" he yelled. "Don't tell me who I remember!"

Kenny tried to grab it back but Sam ripped the page in half and dropped it on the floor before sitting back down in his wheelchair. I think I gasped.

"Well that's *perfect*," Kenny said, his voice rising. "Maybe Bev should draw her again so you can kill her a third time!"

"You're crazy," Sam muttered.

Kenny rolled his eyes.

"This man is a drug addict!" Sam said to Renee, whose sniffles had turned to sobs.

"Sam, don't," she said.

"Get me out of here," Sam said, trying to turn his locked wheelchair around. "I left the water running."

Frustrated that he couldn't move the wheelchair, Sam got up and walked toward the door. It opened just before he reached it, and Sam was face-to-face with a familiar-looking man it took me a moment to recognize out of context.

"Hello, Sam."

It was Detective Miller. Behind him was Detective Dunn. I'd nearly forgotten they had flown down to Florida a few days before.

"What are you doing here?" Sam asked.

"We went looking for you in your room, and an orderly told us where to find you."

"What do you want now?" Sam said. "I answered all your stupid questions."

"We want a sample of your DNA."

"I already told you. You can't have my goddamned DNA."

Detective Dunn produced a document from his pocket. "We have a warrant, Sam. You have no choice in the matter."

Kenny held his hand out and Dunn passed him the document.

"I don't give a fuck about your warrant!" yelled Sam.

It was shocking to hear Sam Waxman curse like that. He seemed nothing like the man I had grown up next door to. I glanced behind me at Doreen's kids, who were staring, wide-eyed.

"I'm not giving you shit," Sam said as he tried to pass Miller.

"Actually," Kenny said, "I think they just need saliva."

No one laughed.

"You have no choice, Sam," said Miller, who blocked the doorway.

"Just cooperate and it'll be over in a few seconds," Dunn said. "But if we have to force you down we will."

Renee was wailing. "Do what they say, Sam! I don't want them to hurt you."

Sam turned, his eyes filled with the terror of a trapped animal. He looked around like he was searching for a quick escape. And then, seeing none, he closed his eyes and his body loosened. It was over and he knew it. The air in the room seemed to change, as if someone had pulled the plug on the atmosphere's electrical current. I glanced over at Kenny to see if he noticed it too. His head was down but he must have sensed it because he raised his eyes to meet mine. Yes, it was obvious to both of us. Sam's hope had just vanished.

Sam Waxman approached his wife and took her hand, an unspoken intimacy passing between them. It seemed to me that in some very personal way, he was saying good-bye. Then he let himself fall into his wheelchair with a lifeless *thump*. Miller got behind him and grabbed onto the handles.

"What are you going to do to him?" Renee asked.

"It's just a simple cotton swab inside his cheek," Dunn said. "We'll do it in his room."

Miller unlocked the wheelchair and pushed it toward the door.

"Sam," Renee said as they passed. But she stopped. What was there to say?

"The water is running," Sam said feebly, as if keeping the charade going was a habit he just couldn't break.

Renee collapsed against Kenny in sobs.

Chapter 28

Later, after my mother was released from recovery and sent back to her room, Dad and I relaxed in the chairs beside her bed, waiting for her to be lucid enough to talk. Her surgery had gone smoothly, but as my father had predicted, she was on strong painkillers that kept her on the stupid side of zonked.

I touched her hand and asked her how she felt.

"Glrg," she said.

Dad switched on the television—it was still playing in Spanish.

"They never fixed this?" he said.

"I'll see if I can find someone to take care of it," I said. "I need a walk anyway." I leaned in toward my mother. "I'll be back in a little while, Mom."

"Frlmp."

"I love you too," I said, and kissed her forehead.

I took my pad and charcoals and left, fully aware that it wasn't just the exercise I was after. I was still reeling from that scene with Sam Waxman and needed to clear my head.

After stopping at the nurses' station to report what was going on with my mother's television, I wanted to take a walk outside so I could find a pleasant, shaded bench somewhere to sit down and draw. But the local landscape made finding such a spot unlikely, and sitting on the hood of someone's sun-baked car in the parking lot to sketch a palm tree didn't strike me as an especially pleasant diversion, so I went down to the hospital cafeteria, got myself a cup of coffee, and took a seat by a window overlooking a small, tidy garden.

I opened the pad and studied the static arrangement of tropical greenery. It wasn't much to look at, and I tried to imagine enlarging it, making it just a little wilder, putting a bench in the middle.

I started to draw, wondering who I would place on the bench. When I got to that part, I let myself go and a female form emerged, her face turned away. I stopped to think about how I wanted to position the rest of her body. When a pregnant woman carrying a container of yogurt walked by, I put my charcoal back on my female figure, giving her a swollen belly, her hand resting on the lower part, connecting to the life within.

As I worked, I thought about what would happen next with Kenny's family. The lab results from Sam's DNA would probably come back in a few weeks, proving he was the father of Lydia's baby. They would arrest him, then. There would be a media frenzy, and poor Renee would be hounded. Then there would be a lengthy trial, and she'd have to testify. So would Kenny. Perhaps my family would too. I tried to imagine my father on the witness stand.

"How long have you known the accused?"

"We used to play bridge together."

I looked at my woman on the bench. Her head was turned, so I followed her line of vision to consider what she might be looking at. Out the cafeteria window, the garden had sculpted shrubbery in that spot, which didn't seem right at all. I needed something with more vitality. Water, I thought, and started sketching a pond, letting it reflect the lushness around it.

I imagined Renee's reaction upon hearing the guilty verdict, which I saw as inevitable. The evidence against her husband was overwhelming, and since Johnnie Cochran had already gone on to meet the Big Judge in the sky, there was no lawyer on earth who could get someone that guilty acquitted. Sam Waxman would not get away with murder.

The trial, I figured, would be in New York. But where would I be? In the desert, motivating a classroom full of kids? What if the job didn't come through? Would I still be on the East Coast, getting messy with art projects as class after class filed in and out of my table-filled room? Could I possibly be happy there, or would the constant reminders of my failures keep me on edge?

I heard the scrape of a chair moving and looked up. It was Kenny.

"Mind?" he said, lowering himself into the seat next to mine.

"Do I have a choice?"

"Not really."

He put a bottle of Poland Spring on the table and held his open bag of miniature pretzels toward me, giving it a little shake so I would understand he was offering me some. I took a few.

"What are you drawing?" he asked, popping a pretzel in his mouth.

I shrugged and turned the page toward him. He stared at it for a few moments and then nodded.

"You put her in paradise," he said.

"Her?"

"Lydia. You created a serene and perfect little world around her."

I turned the picture back around and looked at it. "Is that what I did?" It hadn't even occurred to me that I was drawing Lydia again.

Kenny took a gulp of his water and put the bottle down. "Sam's being released today. Told his doctor he wants to go home."

"I'm surprised. I thought he'd want to continue playing up the idea of being sick."

Kenny ran his hand through his hair, which looked so shiny in the florescent lights of the cafeteria that I wondered how a painter could capture that luminescence on canvas. He wore a blue oxford shirt—rolled up at the sleeves, natch—and the way the color reflected in his eyes was disquieting. I pulled myself out of it by looking away. I didn't need to be thinking about Kenny's shiny hair or his bright eyes.

"Guess he wants to spend his remaining free time at home." Kenny stared out at the little garden. "Anyway, I should get going. I have my parents' car today and I want to run it through a car wash before I pick them up. I don't want my dad to lay into Renee for letting dust settle on his precious Crown Victoria."

"You're driving them home?"

He nodded. "That should be a fun trip, right? Not the least bit awkward. I'm sure my father will be thrilled to spend a little quality time with me and Mom." Kenny downed the last drops of water. "Want to come along for the ride? Act as a buffer?"

I tried to think of something I'd rather do less than be in that car with Sam and Kenny, and all I could come up with was that scene from *Marathon Man* where Laurence Olivier is torturing Dustin Hoffman with dental tools.

I shook my head. "Can't."

"C'mon," he said. "Your mom's unconscious, and your dad

is probably engrossed in a fascinating article on congenital malabsorptive diarrhea in the latest *New England Journal of Medicine.*"

Did he think that accepting the sketch pad meant I'd forgiven him? "Forget it, Kenny."

He stood. "If you change your mind, I'll be in that circle by the front entrance at four thirty."

"I won't."

When I got back to my mother's room, the television was blaring away in English, and contrary to what Kenny predicted, my father was not reading a medical journal. He was, however, so enraptured by something on the History Channel that he didn't notice me come in.

"Dad? How is she?"

"Rommel had an ulcer."

"Huh?"

"These World War II documentaries always get that wrong. They said that Rommel was at El Alamein when Montgomery attacked. But he was in Germany when the battle started—in the hospital with an ulcer."

"I'm sorry to hear that, but I'm more concerned with Mom."

"She's fine. She'll be coming out of it soon."

"Did you know Sam Waxman's being released today? Kenny is taking him home."

"Can you do me a big favor, sweetheart? Can you tag along and pick up your mother's white and green nightgown? She told me to bring it today and I forgot."

"What's wrong with the hospital nightgowns?"

"You know your mother. She won't want to stay in a hospital gown one second longer than she has to. Be a good girl and fetch it so that your mother's not disappointed when she wakes up."

"But— " I started, and stopped. The guilt button froze me in place. I tried to push past it to find any possible argument I could make against running this errand. I opened my mouth, knowing there was an effective protest in there somewhere, if I could just manage to get it out.

My father lowered the volume on the television. "You look like you want to say something."

I sighed. "What drawer is it in?"

"I knew you'd come," Kenny said when I approached. He was sitting on the hood of the car in front of the hospital.

"Don't flatter yourself. I'm tagging along to pick up my mother's nightgown."

"I once tried picking up your mother's nightgown. She slapped me." He patted the spot next to him. "Sit with me. I just had it washed—it's clean and cool."

I did what he said, and I realized that the last time I sat on a car with Kenny Waxman was more than twenty years ago. I didn't feel much of a connection to the person I was back then, but when I looked at Kenny's profile, I remembered one particular day when he'd worn the same expectant expression.

We were only nine and were perched on his mother's car as we waited for his father to arrive with Stella, a German shepherd mix Kenny had chosen at the North Shore Animal League a few days earlier. His parents had been promising him a dog for years and finally came through for his birthday. This was the day the dog's shots had been completed and she was allowed to be picked up. Mr. Waxman was getting her on his way home from work. Kenny was so happy he beamed.

Our small feet dangled off the hood of his mother's car as Kenny and I squinted into the evening sun waiting for his father's car to round the corner. Finally we saw the dark green

Impala pull up, and we jumped down, holding our breath as we watched Mr. Waxman get out and shut the door behind him. He headed straight for the house without even looking at us.

"Where's Stella?" I asked, confused.

He waved my comment away. "Bad idea, a dog," he said. "Mrs. Waxman doesn't like a mess."

Without saying a word to Kenny, he walked in the front door, leaving us there, stunned. I looked at Kenny, who went white. I thought he would break right in half. I put my hand on his shoulder and waited for the tears to start, because I knew that even a boy would cry hard over an injustice this tragic. But Kenny's eyes were dry and pale.

"Maybe he'll change his mind," I offered.

"He won't."

I was so confused by the lack of emotion that after I watched Kenny walk into the house I peered into his father's dark car to see if there was something I had missed. Maybe the dog was really there after all. But the car was as empty and as lonely as any space I'd ever seen.

Kenny's adult face was still inscrutable, but I knew how much pain it hid. I followed his line of vision to the hospital doors. They opened, but it wasn't the Waxmans—it was an elderly woman patient being pushed in a wheelchair to a waiting taxi. The old lady rose slowly and said something to the nurse behind the chair, who opened the cab's door. Frail and shaky, the woman sank into the vehicle's backseat, and the nurse handed her a paper shopping bag, which I assumed held her belongings. As the cab pulled away from the curb, I saw the old white hand wave from the dark interior. I hoped she was going home to more than a dying houseplant and a hungry cat.

I looked at Kenny to see if he was watching the taxi, but his eyes were unfocused as he stared straight ahead.

"What are you thinking about?" he said, as if he could feel me staring at him.

"I thought you could read my mind."

"I'm losing my powers. The Crown Victoria is my kryptonite."

"I was thinking about Stella," I said.

"Stella, the talking German shepherd mix whose tail wagged hard enough to knock over a small child? It was love at first sight."

"Did you say *talking* German shepherd?"

"Yup."

"She talked?"

"Uh-huh."

"What did she say?"

"How the hell should *I* know? I don't speak German."

Kenny's mother soon appeared, walking beside another aide pushing Sam Waxman in his wheelchair. Once they got past the sliding doors, the aide stopped and Sam pulled himself out of the chair.

Sam looked at Kenny and then turned to his wife. "Where's Harold?"

"With Bernadette," she said. "I told you. She just had surgery and I couldn't ask him to leave."

"Where's *our* car?" Sam asked.

"This *is* our car."

"Then why do we need a driver?"

"I've been too nervous to drive since . . . well." She looked at Kenny for help.

"It's no big deal," Kenny said, opening the back door. "Just get in."

His father paused and I feared there would be a showdown. I could see in his eyes that letting his son drive him home constituted some sort of defeat, but Renee stepped in, playing the incompetent housewife so her swaggering husband could have something to latch onto.

"Don't be too mad at me when you see how dry the grass is," she said, sliding into the backseat. "One of the sprinkler heads is broken."

Sam turned toward Kenny. "Give me the keys," he said, opening his hand.

"Can't. They took away your license, remember?"

Sam folded his arms. "I'm not getting in the goddamn backseat."

"It's okay," I said. "I'll sit in the back."

"Bev," Kenny interrupted.

"It's okay. Really."

Kenny rolled his eyes. He got behind the wheel and slammed the door shut. I slid in next to Renee, the interior hotter than I had expected. She leaned forward as Sam got into the car.

"Maybe you can hose down the lawn when we get home," she said.

He didn't respond. Kenny started the car and turned the AC on full blast. He pulled out of the front circle and drove toward the exit.

"It'll feel good to sleep in your own bed, won't it?" Renee continued.

He still didn't respond.

"Sam?"

Nothing.

"He's not answering," Renee said, her voice rising. "Why isn't he answering?"

"There's nothing to say," Sam snapped. "Just leave me alone."

"Isn't this special?" Kenny said to me. "All of us together like this?"

Sam pointed a finger at Kenny. "You're not allowed to speak."

Kenny laughed. "I'd say 'try and stop me' but I'm afraid I might wind up in an industrial drum."

Oh no. Kenny was gearing up for a fight. I readied myself for an explosion from Sam.

"Kenny, please," his mother said.

"You think that's funny?" Sam said.

Kenny passed a slow car, accelerated. "Not especially. But maybe I can do better. Let's see. My father is so guilty." He paused. "C'mon, Bev, help me out. How guilty is he? My father is so guilty they're going to lock him up and throw away the whole penitentiary."

"They should lock up drug addicts like *you*," his father said.

Kenny turned his face toward me. "See where I get the comedy from? It's in my *genes*, baby."

"Keep your eye on the road, dear," Renee said, and then addressed her husband again. "He doesn't do drugs anymore. That was a long time ago."

"Once an addict, always an addict," Sam said.

"I was never an *addict*," Kenny said. "I just got high a lot so I wouldn't have to deal with you. Once I was out of the house I donated all my drugs to needy children."

"Children?" his mother said, alarmed.

I patted her hand. "He's kidding, Renee." I wanted to change the subject and seized the opportunity to take another shot at finding out where the key to that storage facility was. So I asked Renee, knowing full well she was mistaken about where Sam had left it. I was playing to his obnoxious ego. I figured if she gave me the wrong answer he might want to step in and correct her.

"I thought it was in the top desk drawer, dear," Renee said, "but Kenny told me he looked there."

I waited a beat for Sam to pipe in but he didn't. "Do you

have any idea where it is, Mr. Waxman?" I said, leaning forward. I was hoping he'd forgotten about our hostile exchange in the hospital.

"What?"

"Mrs. Waxman thought the key to your storage unit was in the desk, but it's not there. Do you know where it is?"

"The key with the orange ring around the top," Renee interjected. "Do you remember where you put it, Sam?"

"I didn't touch any key," he said.

Renee looked at me and shrugged. I sat back, deflated. We all fell into a prickly silence again, which was preferable to the excruciating conversation between father and son.

"Hey, remember Stella?" Kenny suddenly said, and I wanted to smack him on the back of the head. Why was he looking for a fight?

"Stella?" his mother said. "Who's Stella?"

"That dog you promised me."

Renee wrinkled her brow like she was trying to remember. "Was that the dog from the shelter?"

"Filthy mutt tried to bite me," Sam said.

Kenny exploded with laughter. He laughed so hard he practically choked and had to smack the steering wheel to try to calm down.

"It's not funny," Sam said.

This made Kenny laugh harder.

"Stop it!"

"Really, Kenny," his mother said. "I don't see what's so funny about this."

Kenny caught his breath. "The lady at the shelter said *one* thing to me about that dog. When Stella came running to me, her tail wagging like mad, the lady said, 'This dog is a great judge of character!'" Kenny lost it again.

"Let me out of this car!" Sam said.

Kenny ignored him.

"Pull over! I'm getting out!"

"You don't think that's funny?" Kenny said.

"I said pull over!"

"We're in the middle of a highway," Kenny said. "Keep your pants on . . . if you can."

Sam grabbed the steering wheel with both hands.

"Hey, let go! Are you crazy?"

"Sam!" Renee shouted, as we both braced ourselves against the front seat for impact.

The car veered toward the shoulder and I felt the tires bump along the ridges.

"Motherfucker!" Kenny yelled.

Sam was pulling so hard on the steering wheel the blood rose to his angry face.

"Goddamn it, Sam," Kenny said. "You want to commit suicide, do it on your own time. Don't take us all with you."

The road curved to the left and Sam relaxed his grip to let Kenny get control of the car before we careened off the edge. But right in the middle of the bend, Sam grabbed tight again and yanked the wheel to the right.

The last thing I remember hearing as we flew off the road toward the embankment was the sound of Renee screaming.

Chapter 29

When I awoke I was in another moving vehicle, but this time I was lying on my back and a dark-skinned man in a white jacket was crouched over me, doing something painful to my legs. I moaned.

"Beverly?" the man said. "Can you hear me? You were in a car accident, but you're okay." He wrapped something around my arm. The environment confused me. I blinked a few times, trying to get my thoughts to gel, but nothing happened. I could see and feel and smell, but couldn't attach a thought to anything.

A familiar-looking man spoke. "You hit your head so hard. We were worried you wouldn't wake up."

I reached up and felt my head. There was something on it I tried to pull off.

"That's just a bandage," the first man said, gently pushing my hand away. "You'll need to leave that alone for now."

Something loud and shrill in the background made it hard to concentrate.

"What's that noise?" I asked.

"It's a siren," the man said. "You're in an ambulance."

"My cows hurt."

"Cows?"

"You know, my legs. The bottom of my legs."

"I think she means calves," the blond man said.

"You have some first- and second-degree burns," said the other man. "Not too bad. You got lucky—the whole car burned up and could have taken you with it. I just applied some local anesthetic so they'll feel better soon. Do you know what day it is, Beverly?"

"Tuesday? Saturday?"

The men looked at each other.

"Do you know who I am?" the familiar-looking man said.

It occurred to me that I did, but I couldn't find his name. "You were driving."

"That's right."

"You were my next-door neighbor."

"Yes."

"Have we fucked?" I asked. "I remember fucking you."

The men looked at each other. "It must be a concussion," the other man said to him. "Sometimes a little temporary swelling leads to loss of inhibitions." He squeezed a bulb-shaped thing and the cuff around my arm got very, very tight.

"Are you a doctor?" I asked.

"Paramedic," he said, releasing the pressure.

I tried to sit up. "I remember something!"

"Easy," he said, pressing me down.

I lay there and tried to piece together what happened. There was a car accident. It was like flying, but when we hit ground the car rolled over and then I must have blacked out. I heard someone calling my name over and over but I couldn't respond. There was a fire. I heard people screaming to stay away from the car, but I couldn't move. Then someone pulled me out. He must have risked his own life to save me. I tried to picture him and all I could discern was that he was a stranger in a blue uniform.

"How's the cop?" I asked.

"What cop?" asked the paramedic.

"The one who pulled me out."

The ambulance made a sharp turn and both men held onto me. We slowed down a bit and the blond man turned my face to him. "Do you remember my name?" he said.

"Jonathan?" I guessed, knowing it probably wasn't right, but it was the only name that came up.

"No, not Jonathan. Ken. I'm Kenny."

"Right, Jonathan was my husband. He was such an asshole."

"Yeah, well . . . he's not the only one. I'm thinking of starting a club."

"I'm going to take a nap now." I closed my eyes.

"Stay with us, Beverly," the other man said. "Stay with us."

In the hospital, someone wearing a paper mask worked on my forehead. He wore green scrubs and it seemed to take forever.

"You'll be as pretty as ever," he said. "I'm not even giving you sutures—just butterflies. You won't even have a noticeable scar."

Butterflies? I pictured pretty monarchs alighting on my head. But he was pressing so hard it didn't make sense. Then I figured it out—he must have been giving me a tattoo of butterflies.

"I think I'd rather have a scar," I said.

"Why?" He glanced at me through his magnifying glasses and his eyes looked huge.

"It would be less noticeable."

"Less noticeable than what?"

"A butterfly on my forehead. I'll look like an idiot."

"They're just little bandages that hold the skin together so it can heal. We call them butterflies because of the shape. You understand?" He finished what he was doing and pulled off the paper mask to reveal large, hairy nostrils.

"You should do something about that jungle," I said.

After that, they ran a bunch of tests, including something called a CT scan. I was getting more and more annoyed at all the poking and prodding and getting wheeled from one place to another. Finally, they brought me to a room and told me to get some rest.

Later, when my father came in, I pushed the bed's remote control button until I was upright.

"Am I okay?" I asked, thinking he looked very serious. "What did they tell you?"

"Do you remember anything about the accident?"

"Dad, am I *okay*?"

"You have contusions on both medial temporal lobes."

"What does that mean, exactly?" I fluffed the pillow behind my head.

"A little swelling that's causing a loss of inhibitions and dysphasia. As soon as it subsides, you'll be fine. They're keeping you here overnight as a precaution. Do you want some water?" He picked up the pitcher by my bed.

"I have a loss of inhibitions and dysphasia?"

"You're not filtering your thoughts like you normally do, and you're having some trouble with word retrieval."

"I know what you mean, I just didn't realize I was having a blemish."

He put down the pitcher. "You mean a problem?"

"What?"

"I think you mean *problem*, not blemish."

Problem, of course. Why on earth did I think the word was *blemish*? My father sat in the chair next to my bed. He was right. I was having word-retrieval problems.

"Am I going to get better?"

"In all likelihood."

"You mean there's a chance I won't?" I felt a panic forming like a solid thing deep in my center. "Dad," I said, "I can't . . . what if . . ." I was getting so agitated I couldn't get the words out. The thought that I might have to go through life stupid and inarticulate terrified me. I wasn't especially pretty. I wasn't especially talented. I wasn't even especially charming. All I had was smart.

I remembered going to an aquarium show when I was a kid. We were on a family vacation, and the kids were allowed to sit on the bleachers right up front, where we were almost certain to get splashed.

Before the show began, a man in a wet suit addressed the crowd, teaching us about marine life. At one point, he asked the kids if anyone knew what the largest species of dolphin was called. My hand shot straight up, as I had read the brochure and knew the answer. But the man looked right at Clare, with her silky blond hair and beautiful face. He didn't even seem to notice that my hand was up and hers wasn't.

Clare shrugged. "Porpoise?"

She was wrong. My hand shot up higher. The man pointed to a tiny boy in an Elmo shirt who had his hand up.

"Giant!" the boy said.

The man laughed. "Not giant. Anyone else?"

I practically pulled my arm out of its socket to get him to notice me. I knew I could make an impression if he just gave me the chance. But he went from kid to kid, exhausting all the cutest ones before he finally called on me.

"Orca, the killer whale," I said.

A few people tittered, assuming I was wrong. But the man said, "Yes!" and called me down by his side for a funny award ceremony where he gave me an Orca T-shirt while pretending not to see the whale rising out of the water behind us. I felt vindicated. I wasn't blond and I didn't have cute freckles or a winning smile. But I was the only one who knew the answer.

I looked at my father, tears spilling. "Smart is all I've got, Dad."

He patted my hand, and I waited for him to tell me I'd be fine, that everything would come back.

"Your mother is doing quite well," he said.

Later, when both my parents came to visit me, I was floating in a placid sea, as a nurse had given me a blue pill for anxiety. My mother wore a hospital nightgown and slippers, and held tight to my father's hand.

"The neurologist was here," I told them. "He said I was improving. Said I'll be fine in a few weeks, but might notice it's worse when I'm tense. I'm not tense now, though. How are you, Mom? You look good. You need some lipstick, though."

"I'm fine, dear. I think we'll both be discharged tomorrow. Do you feel okay? How are your legs? They told me you got burned."

"Hurt a lot at first, but it's better now."

"Do you remember the accident?" She shuffled to the chair by my bed and sat down.

I closed my eyes to think. "I know I wasn't driving. I know there were others."

"Four of you," my father said.

"Is everyone okay?" I asked.

"Everyone is fine," he said. "Sam and Renee got a little scraped and bruised. Kenny somehow managed to dislocate his shoulder."

"Right, Kenny." I pictured his sublime naked body from behind. "What an ass!"

My father nodded. "I heard you had some sort of falling out, but he's really a very decent guy."

"What?"

"He'd like to visit you. Is that okay?"

By the time a dinner tray was delivered I was hungry enough to eat hospital food. Or so I thought. When I pulled the plastic hood off my plate, even my lowest expectations weren't met, as I was greeted with a cold, gray sliver of chicken breast, a few waxy green bean sections, and two small round potatoes with shriveled skin.

"This isn't even *food*," I said out loud.

The other bed in my room was empty, so there was no one there to hear my complaint. I tore open the package of melba toast and munched on it unhappily. A few minutes later Kenny walked into my room trailing the most delightful smell. One arm was in a sling and the other carried a white paper bag, which he put onto the tray in front of me.

"What is this?" I said as I opened the bag.

"Corned-beef sandwich." He took the seat next to my bed.

I gasped. "I *love* corned beef!"

"I know."

I took the oversized sandwich out of the bag and unwrapped it. I handed him half.

"You have it," he said.

"If *I'm* going to have corned-beef breath, *you're* going to have corned-beef breath. How else are we going to kiss?"

He grabbed the half I was offering and took a huge bite, never breaking eye contact. I pushed the tray away from my bed and sat with my legs folded in front of me, the wax paper on my lap.

"Sit with me," I said.

Kenny sat opposite me on the bed and we devoured our sandwiches in silence. I ate mine in about three bites, then washed down the lump of corned beef and fresh rye bread that clogged my gullet with the ice-cold Diet Coke he'd brought. I watched him eat, my nerve endings tingling. I wanted so badly to kiss him, to be naked with him, to feel his divine hands—or hand, as one of them was incapacitated—exploring my flesh like it was the softest velvet.

"Are you done yet?" I asked.

He laughed. "What's your hurry?"

"I want to kiss you."

"Now?"

I nodded. He wrapped the remains of his sandwich in the wax paper and put it on my nightstand. Then he leaned in and gently kissed me on the lips.

"More," I said.

He smiled. "I like you when you're uninhibited."

"Good." I untied the string at the back of my neck that held my hospital gown in place.

"Bev, don't."

"Why not?" I said, and yanked the thing off. I lunged, and kissed him deeply on the lips. A second later we were horizontal with me on top.

"We can't do this," he said. "Anyone could walk in."

"You're already hard," I said, putting my hand on his crotch. "We can do it fast." I pulled open his zipper.

"Bev, no," he said, grabbing my hand. "We'll do this after you get out of the hospital. I promise."

I pushed my crotch into him. "Please!" I said. "I want you inside me. I want your cunt!"

He smirked, trying not to laugh.

"What's so funny?"

"Never mind," he said, carefully pushing me back onto my

pillow. He got off the bed and pulled my nightgown over me, his eyes so tender I felt like a well-loved child.

"You're such a sweet, gentle guy."

"Yeah, that's me. Sweet and gentle."

"No wonder I love you."

He leaned in and kissed me on the lips. It was heavenly. I reached for his good hand and pushed it up under my gown until it was on my breast. He left it there and kept kissing me. His breath started to quicken and the sound of it excited me. I was flooded with sexual memories . . . on the couch in my house, when he made me beg . . . upstairs in my bedroom, where we did it a second time, and a third . . . in his hotel room, where he. . .

"Stop!" I said.

"What's the matter?"

"I remember." One memory came back followed by another and another. Kenny assaulting me in junior high. Kenny sleeping with Joey after leading me on. Kenny taking his anger out on me in his hotel room. They were different scenes but the same emotional refrain again and again. He hurt me. He was supposed to love me and he hurt me. I put my hands on his shoulders and pushed him away. He grabbed the injured side and yelped in pain.

"Rapist!" I said, trying to hurt him back by resurrecting the name I'd called him in junior high.

"No, Bev. It wasn't like that."

"Get out of here!"

"Bev, please. Listen to me."

But I couldn't. I wouldn't. I balled my hands into fists, closed my eyes tight and howled like a wounded dog.

Two nurses came running to the room and asked what was wrong.

"Make him go," I said. "Please, make him go."

Chapter 30

As the plane circled LaGuardia Airport waiting for clearance to land, I thought about the holding pattern of my life. With no job, no boyfriend, no gravitational pull from my family, there was simply no place for me to alight.

When the plane finally touched down, I still felt so afloat I couldn't manage to get out of my seat. Why should I? What was waiting for me? Two sisters who thought everything I did was a mistake? A cute carpenter who was sleeping with me to get his mind off someone else, someone I just happened to share a fair amount of DNA with? The only thing I had to look forward to was a letter from a school in Las Vegas. And what if I didn't get the job? What if they were only interested in the younger, fresher, more moldable candidates? It would mean staying in New York and finding another apartment just like the one I'd left. Soon enough, I'd be dating guys like Bart Flaum again, attending family events where everyone tsked as I walked by, whispering how I'd once had so much promise.

"Buh-bye," I heard the flight attendants say over and over again. "Thank you for flying Delta. Enjoy your stay in New York."

When the last of the passengers had gone, I saw the flight

crew staring at me as if the woman in 12A with a bandage on her head was someone to be wary of. Fearing they thought I had some kind of agenda, I rose, plastered a smile on my face walked toward the front of the aircraft.

"Good-bye," I said in my most charming voice. "Great flight—very smooth. My flight down had so much terrorism."

The two flight attendants looked at each other and I immediately realized my mistake.

"Turbulence, I mean! Not terrorism. Well, buh-bye!"

Mortified, I hurried away. The neurologist at the hospital had warned me that the dysphasia could come and go for weeks, explaining that anxiety would exacerbate it. He hadn't warned me, though, that the stress-induced malapropisms might be bad enough to get me arrested.

When I got back home, there was no letter from the school district in Las Vegas. There were, however, three messages from Leo. My first inclination was to brush him off. After all, the seeds for derailing Clare's plans for an affair had been planted. All I had to do to reap the fruit was find the right time to let her know Leo and I had slept together.

But after moping around the house for a few hours with thoughts of Kenny insinuating their way into my subconscious as regularly as an insipid love ballad in rotation on a lite-music radio station, I changed my mind. I needed a distraction from Kenny Waxman.

So I agreed to go out with Leo the next night, and settled in to relax and regroup. A few minutes later Clare called, saying she and Joey wanted me to meet them for dinner. I begged off, and Clare tried getting me to change my mind. But I was resolute. Alas, she deployed her secret weapon, the thing that would harass, harangue, badger, cajole, and annoy until it wore me down. She had Joey call. I knew better than to put up a fight, and an hour later pulled up at the address she had given me.

The restaurant Joey had chosen was nestled deep inside a huge place called Veronica's, which billed itself as an "entertainment universe." The main attraction, which you had to walk through to get to the restaurant, was a casino-sized video arcade, which assaulted my already frazzled nerves with electronic whirrs, dings, clangs, bangs, pops, blasts, and buzzers, combined with flashes of light and glints of chrome. It was overload for my neural pathways, and they shut down like a tripped circuit. I made my way to the restaurant Joey had described and was happy to discover that it felt like a quiet oasis.

"*Ew*," Clare said when she saw me. "You're wearing that shirt!"

It was true. I had on the ugly beige shirt I had rescued from the trash when Clare decided it was an aesthetic offense.

"I didn't have a chance to unpack yet," I said, "and this was one of the only clean things I didn't bring down to Florida. Is it that bad?"

"Only if you don't like the color of rotting flesh."

Joey snickered. I rolled my eyes. Fine for Clare to say something like that to me, but God forbid I made a comment like that to her. It was as if Clare had permission to be touchy about her appearance, while I was expected to be above it. Truth was, I thought I looked kind of cute in the baby doll sleeves, and maybe even tan against the pale color of the shirt. It hurt to think I looked gross, and I considered pulling out my mirror and reapplying my lipstick, but didn't want to deal with the conversation that might spark.

The waitress came over and took our drink order—soft drinks for Joey and me, a white wine for Clare. She also handed each of us a game card for the arcade, which was apparently included with dinner in the restaurant. When she walked away, my sisters proceeded to ask me about the car accident, of which I remembered very little.

"Dad said Sam caused it," Clare said. "Do you think he was trying to kill all of you?" Her eyes were wide.

"Just Kenny," I said.

"He really wanted to kill him?"

I shrugged.

"Twisted," Joey said.

Clare reached across the table and took my hand. "You're feeling okay?"

If she was so concerned, why was she compelled to drag me out when I was tired. "Fine," I said, and pulled away.

The waitress brought our drinks and took our dinner order, and then Joey asked me what I thought of Veronica's.

I looked around the room. Giant posters of fifties-era movie stars, including James Dean, Marilyn Monroe, Sal Mineo, Rita Hayworth, Sandra Dee, Tab Hunter, and Elizabeth Taylor, adorned the walls, and the servers dressed in costumes that included Capri pants for the girls and rolled-up jeans for the boys.

"The restaurant's okay," I said. "But that arcade! Did you see who hangs out there?"

Clare nodded. "It seems like we're the only women here."

Joey sipped her club soda. "That's not so bad, is it? Maybe Bev will find someone to get her mind off Kenny."

"Please, there's not a guy here over twenty-two. In fact, there's not a guy here who looks like he doesn't live in his parents' basement and read comic books."

"Why does Bev want to get her mind off Kenny?" Clare asked.

Joey looked at me. "You didn't tell her?"

I shrugged. It wasn't something I particularly wanted to

talk about. The only reason I had told Joey was because I wanted her to know I was done with him. It was my way of giving her permission to hook up with him if she wanted to.

"What happened?" Clare asked.

I picked up a foil packet of butter and tested it for softness, just to have something to do. They both waited for me to say something.

"Kenny had angry sex with Bev," Joey finally said.

Clare looked from Joey to me. "Angry sex? What does that mean?"

I opened the packet and buttered a raisin roll I pulled from the bread basket. "It means I'm never sleeping with him again." I bit into the roll and made a face.

"Why are you eating that?" Joey said. "You *hate* raisins."

She was right. I put the roll onto my bread plate and passed it to her. Just then, our waitress came with another round of drinks, which we hadn't ordered.

"From the gentleman over there," the waitress said, pointing to a table behind me.

"Those guys have been staring at Clare since we got here," Joey said.

I turned around and saw three young men who couldn't have been more than twenty. They all had that messy hair that started in IT departments among goofy-looking nerds and eventually became geek chic. They waved at us. I ignored them and turned back around. Joey arched out her chest and waved back.

"Don't encourage them," I said.

But it was too late. They got up and quickly approached our table.

"Thanks for the drinks, guys," I said. "But this party is girls only."

The tallest one, whose self-esteem seemed unaffected by

the angry red pimples on both his cheeks, put his arm around one of the other boys and said, "Too bad. Corey here is in mourning and could use some comforting."

"Shut up, Jackman," Corey said, pushing his friend's arm off his shoulder. He had big dark eyes and seemed genuinely angry.

"What are you ladies doing after dinner?" Jackman asked.

"Not sure," Clare said. "But maybe we'll catch up with you later, okay?"

He leaned forward "What's your name?"

"Clare."

"Okay, Clare," said Jackman. "We'll be in the karaoke bar."

"There's a karaoke bar?" Joey said. She looked excited.

"It's new," he said, looking right down Joey's low-cut top. "I hope you'll meet us there."

"Maybe," she said.

He picked up Joey's hand and kissed it.

"Bye guys," Clare said. She smiled, and all three looked like their knees would buckle.

"Bye, Clare!" said the tall one. Then he winked at Joey. "See you later."

"Bye, Clare!" said the other two.

I watched them walk away and turned to my older sister. "You still think you've lost your looks, Clare?"

She shrugged. "We're the only women in this place. Of course we're going to get hit on."

"Not *we*," I said. "You. Well, you and Joey. I'm chopped liver, apparently."

"It's that shirt," Clare said.

"It's her attitude," Joey corrected. "She doesn't put her shit out there." She wagged a finger in my face. "You really should put your shit out there."

"For three underage geeks?" I said. "I don't think so."

"In general," Joey said. "You should put your shit out there *in general.*"

"Please. My shit is right where it belongs." I looked at Clare for support, but her expression was unyielding.

"I agree with Joey," she said. "You think it's beneath you."

"What? That's ridiculous."

"You think showing some cleavage will lower your IQ or something," Joey said.

"And that wearing pretty colors means you're shallow."

Why didn't they understand? It wasn't that I thought I was better than them. It was that I couldn't compete on their playing field. I was doing the best I could.

I stood. "I need some gas," I said.

My sisters looked at me strangely and I realized my mistake. "Air. I need some air," I said, and walked off.

"Bev," Clare called after me but I didn't stop. I exited the restaurant for the chaotic assault of the center hall arcade. I wandered up and down the aisles, lost in the noise and lights of the games until my stomach vibrated from the tumult. After a while, I became disoriented in the space and couldn't tell which direction the restaurant was in or where the front door was. Not that I really cared. I needed a diversion.

At last I noticed an arcade game that called out to me. It was called Megasaurs and was set up like an open booth. Inside was a bench facing a huge screen with realistic-looking prehistoric monsters. Instead of joysticks or buttons, players got to hold large automatic weapons designed specifically for dinosaur extinction. I sat down, slipped in my game card and started shooting. I was terrible at first, getting outsmarted by the giant lizards at every turn. But after a while I got the hang of the gun and started wiping out entire eras of the gargantuan creatures. *Pow pow pow.* Ankylosaurus, plateosaurus, brachiosaurus, stegosaurus, diplodocus: dead. I was up to the Cretaceous period, wiping out the dreaded Tyrannosaurus rex when I sensed another person slide in next to me. I didn't glance up. I couldn't. A pack of velociraptors was moving in from behind, and they had speed. The buggers dispersed as I fired shots into the group. I had to be fast, fast, fast. But they were too much for me, and a slippery one quicker than a lightning bolt sneaked up and ate me.

"Shit," I said.

"Having fun?" It was Joey.

I let go of the gun and sat back. "I needed to work out my hostilities."

Clare entered on the other side of the booth and sat down. "Can we play?"

"What about dinner?" I asked.

"We told them to keep it warm," Joey said.

"I'm really sorry," Clare said. "I guess we were kind of obnoxious."

I nodded.

Joey pushed her game card into the slot and set up the game for three players. "Thing is," she said, "we're probably a little jealous of you."

"Of *me*? I don't even get noticed half the time."

"You don't need to," Clare said.

The game sprang to life and a dinosaur came charging at us. I shot it quickly for a hundred points.

"You're the lucky one," Joey said.

"Nonsense." A brachiosaur appeared from behind a hill. "Shoot, Clare!"

She squeezed the trigger and the dinosaur blew up. Did they really think being the smart one made me lucky? It only meant that my family had unrealistic expectations for me. I would always be a disappointment. Always.

"You guys are the lucky ones. No matter what you do, Mom and Dad think you walk on water." I shot a stegosaur.

"You think I have no pressure," Clare said. "You think all I have to do is look pretty and keep a neat house and I've met everyone's expectations for me."

I glanced away from the screen to look at her. That was exactly what I thought. Another stegosaurus appeared and charged right for me. Joey blew its head off.

Clare let go of her gun and looked back at me. "The problem," she said, "is that when I get wrinkles or gain ten pounds I feel like a colossal failure. And then I hate myself for being so shallow. Of course, I can't talk to anyone about it without getting that eye-roll thing—*oh, poor Clare can't fit into her jeans and thinks the world is coming to an end.* So I try to make myself feel better by buying a new pair of pants or redecorating the house. It works for a little while and then . . . I don't know." She paused and it seemed like she was fighting the urge to cry. Finally, she cleared her throat. "Then a guy comes along who makes me feel appreciated for being exactly who I am, and it sends me into a spin." She looked back at the screen. "A brontosaurus!"

"Diplodocus," I corrected. She couldn't grab her gun fast enough so I shot it. I looked back at her soft, sad eyes. "I'm sorry if I seem unsympathetic sometimes," I said.

She shrugged, ready to move on. "I know."

I wanted to give her a hug, but just then a giant T. rex ran toward us, its ferocious mouth wide open. All three of us shot at it, but it was Joey who blasted a hole in the beast.

"Good work," I said.

"Of course. While Clare is busy getting attention for being gorgeous, and you're busy getting attention for knowing the difference between a brontosaurus and a whateverasaurus rex, I'm left singing for my supper."

"What does that mean?" I asked.

"It means that you two can weep all you want about how hard it is being pretty or smart. But I had to become a freaking *rock star* to get any attention in our family."

"That's not true," Clare said.

"It's not? Would you like to know the *one* time Mom and Dad ever told me they were proud of me? It was after the MTV awards. And I think they were more impressed that I met Michael Jackson backstage than they were that my group's video won best direction."

I let go of my dinosaur blaster. It had never before occurred to me that Joey's drive to be a star was powered by the same fuel that compelled me to go to art school. It was the most basic sibling rivalry. We were all simply competing for our parents' attention. How utterly childish.

I put my hand on her shoulder. "I didn't know," I said.

"Fuck it," she said. "In the scheme of things, it's nothing. People are starving, sick, and homeless. Besides, my French fries are getting cold. We should get back to our table."

Chapter 31

After dinner, we headed over to the karaoke bar, which had an orange neon sign above the entrance that said "Betty's." Inside, it was more crowded than I had expected and, as I discovered once my eyes adjusted to the dim lighting, it was where the girls were. No wonder Jackman, et al. had headed in this direction.

When we entered, a middle-aged man resembling Stanley Tucci was onstage, doing a fairly decent Elvis Presley impression. He seemed to be trying to move his hips, but they remained immobile. Instead, his shoulders twitched right and left in a way I found somehow endearing. He was trying so hard. A woman I presumed to be his wife was cheering from a table off to the right, her eyes bright with affection. There were a few empty seats in that area, and I wanted to steer my sisters in that direction. Besides the fact that they were some of the only other people in the place old enough to remember a time when *American Idol* wasn't the name of a television show, they seemed like a fun couple.

Joey put her arms around Clare and me and announced that we should do a song together. "Something extra corny."

"Count me out," Clare said.

"But you have to," Joey said. "You don't want to disappoint

your adoring public, do you?" She pointed to a table where the three boys from the restaurant were sitting. They waved, signaling us over. There were three empty chairs at their table—one between each of them.

"Just what we need," I said.

Joey tsked. "Don't be such a wet blanket."

Clare just shrugged and I decided to try another tactic.

"If we sit with them," I said, "it'll ruin their chances of meeting girls their own age."

"Big deal," Joey said. "They'll get laid another night."

I sighed, resigned, and we approached the table. We made our introductions, and learned that Jackman was the tall one's *last* name, but he didn't mind if we called him that. Corey, the one I assumed had recently been dumped, still looked pretty blue. The other boy was Anthony, though his friends kept calling him *Dawg*. He was quiet, which I had mistaken for arrogance in the restaurant. Up close, it seemed more like insecurity.

We sat down, and I found myself between Dawg and Jackman, who pushed a loose-leaf binder toward me.

"Here's the song list," he said.

I nudged it over to Joey, who sat on the other side of Dawg. She opened it and started scanning the plastic-sleeved pages. "Aren't you going to sing with me?" she said.

"I'll make you a deal," I said. "You don't ask me to sing and I won't ask you to draw."

Joey shrugged and turned to Jackman. "You guys going to sing?"

"Dawg's the one with the voice. Ask him."

We all looked at Dawg, who seemed pained.

"Did you look at the song book?" she asked.

He waved it away. "I'm not that good."

"It's a karaoke bar," she said, laughing. "How good do you have to be?"

Dawg nearly flinched, and I wondered why he was so uncomfortable. Was he just painfully shy, or was there more to it? He glanced away, his coal-dark eyelashes shielding him from being understood. But when he looked up, I got a straight gaze into his scared hazel eyes and saw something there I recognized. It was the same terrified look I saw in the eyes of a first-grade boy from my student-teacher days. The children had been assigned to draw their favorite animal character from a picture book the teacher had read, and this boy, whose name was Harrison, had said he couldn't.

"Just do your best, Harrison," the teacher had said, but his eyes got moist and he folded his arms, resolute.

I sat down next to him and drew a bird's head. I told him I couldn't figure out where to put the beak and he pointed. I gave him the pencil.

"Can you do it for me?"

He drew a beak with the same gentle slope as the one in the book, which was so sophisticated for a child that age I thought it might have been a fluke. Then he put in a single dot for the nostril just where it belonged in that profile view, which surprised me. Children that age never applied such detail. He handed the pencil back to me and I prodded him further, asking what kind of body we should give the bird. When we were done, it was a picture no one would have believed a six-year-old had drawn. The boy was gifted. I understood that it embarrassed him to be so different from his classmates. He wanted to hide his gift so he wouldn't stand out.

Dawg, I guessed, was a lot like Harrison. He wasn't ashamed that he couldn't sing. He was ashamed that he *could*. This was a boy who had a beautiful voice and was afraid to show it.

"You should sing with Joey," I said to him. "A duet. I don't think she wants to be up there all alone."

"I don't know," he said.

Going with my hunch, I leaned over and whispered in his ear, "Her voice touches everyone who hears it." If I was right, Dawg would respond well to the idea that he wouldn't be the only one up there with talent to spare.

He looked at me and blinked. Did he think I was exaggerating?

I leaned in closer to be sure no one would hear. "Remember the song 'Tiger Attack'?"

He nodded and I pointed to my sister. "That's Joey Bloom, the singer."

His eyes widened. I put my finger over my lips to indicate that he shouldn't tell anyone.

I leaned back in my chair. "Sing with her."

"Yeah, sing with me," Joey said, and scraped her chair closer to his so he could see the song book with her.

The two of them put their heads together and I could see him warming up to her, even getting excited about the idea of performing with another real singer. They went through page after page, finding songs that were *maybes* until they were almost at the very end and Joey smacked the book.

"That one!" she said, tapping at a spot on the page. "Do you know it?"

Dawg smiled, and Joey ran up to the emcee at the front of the room to put their name and selection on the list.

"Stanley Tucci" finished his Elvis impersonation, and someone named Amanda was introduced. She was about twenty years old and absolutely adorable. I glanced over at Jackman and he looked like his eyes would bug out of his head. Corey's expression didn't seem to change much, and Dawg was busy yakking with Joey about who would sing what part of whatever secret song they had chosen.

Amanda sang something awful by one of those girl pop

singers I can't keep straight, and did a decent enough job of it. Jackman hooted and howled as if the girl could sell out Madison Square Garden. She left the stage and went to sit with some girlfriends. The announcer introduced the next act.

"You should go talk to her," I said to Jackman.

"She's just a kid," he said.

I rolled my eyes. "She's about the same age as *you*."

"I like mature women," he said, and put his hand on my knee.

"Don't even think about it." I took his hand off my knee and wondered if he had already tried the same thing with Clare.

He leaned in toward me. "Do you have any idea how hot you are?"

"Do you have any idea how *old* I am?"

"Age is just a number," he said, grinning.

"So is temperature. Doesn't mean you can melt ice cubes in a freezer."

"But you're single, right?"

Jeez. This guy was relentless. I thought about lying, saying I was married to a comedy writer. Then I had an odd moment as I wondered why that particular lie popped into my head. Why wasn't my first thought about pretending I was still married to an artist?

"Divorced," I said, just to drive home the point that I was over-the-hill.

Jackman's eyes practically rolled back in his head. "Divorced! That is *so* sexy." He put his arm around me. I took it off. Since the term *cougar* had found its way into the vernacular, young men assumed whole new vistas of opportunities were open to them. I wanted to convince this kid I didn't belong to any species of warm-blooded mammal.

"Trust me, you're wasting your time. Why don't you go talk

to that cute Amanda? She's got a pierced . . . belly button."
It took me a second to find the right word, but I got it. My
dysphasia was definitely abating.

Jackman glanced toward the girl. I could tell he was thinking about it.

"Go on," I said.

"What would I say?"

Was this guy kidding? He was hitting on a thirty-five-year-
old woman and he didn't know how to approach a girl his
own age?

"Tell her you think she has a good voice." I couldn't believe
I was actually giving someone advice on how to flirt.

Jackman stood, glanced over the girl.

"Be brave," I said. "What have you got to lose?"

Jackman took a deep breath. "Okay." He turned and walked
toward Amanda's table. I saw him put his hand on the back
of her chair and lean in to say something. She glanced up and
smiled, and said what looked like "Thank you." They chatted
a bit more, and he took a seat at her table.

A few minutes later a group of girls singing together did
their big finish, and the emcee introduced the next act. "A
big round of applause now for Joey and Anthony singing
'Unforgettable'!"

Joey and Dawg got up and approached the stage, while
Clare, Corey, and I cheered. I glanced up and saw that Jackman, Amanda, and friends were cheering too.

The duo started their performance and the place went dead
quiet. Joey sang first, her voice so clear and pure I got chills
that started with goose bumps and ended with a sensation so
deep inside I teared up.

I looked around, embarrassed that a song could that do
to me. I glanced over at Clare and she looked about as pummeled as I felt. I hoped she wasn't thinking about Leo.

Dawg joined in the song and their two voices blended together like liquid. I wanted the sound to keep washing over me, but it ended too soon. I glanced around to see if everyone had been as moved as I, and the reaction was wild. The crowd howled and cheered. Everyone had loved the performance.

Everyone except Corey, that is. He sat stone still and pale, a distant look on his face. Then he got up and left the room.

"What's with him?" I shouted to Clare over the applause.

"I don't know. He was crying, then he just stopped and left."

Someone in the karaoke bar shouted, "Jo-eee! That's Joey Bloom from Phantom Pain!"

"Sing 'Tiger Attack'!" someone else yelled.

Joey shook her head and got off the stage with Dawg.

The crowd started chanting. "'Tiger Attack!' 'Tiger Attack!'"

"How about it, Joey?" the emcee said into the mike. "We've got the song."

The crowd went berserk, hooting and whistling. Joey looked at me and shrugged in a way that suggested she had no choice. I nodded my approval. Dawg sat back down at our table and Joey went onto the little stage.

"I promised myself I wasn't going to do this," she said into the mike.

"I love you, Joey!" shouted a guy in the back.

"I love you too, baby." She purred, giving him that sexy little grin that made guys crazy. "You people appreciate how utterly dorky it is to sing your own song in a karaoke bar?"

"Do it for Tyrone!" someone yelled.

Joey's expression changed as she thought about her dead friend. For a moment, she went silent.

"Okay, then. For Tyrone."

The music started and Joey let herself go, wailing through

the song, moving like she did in the video but reaching a more profound place with her voice than she had been capable of back when it was recorded. Clare and I, the two proud sisters, grinned like idiots.

Joey hit her final, famous note, and the crowd screamed like it was a rock concert, and even opened their cell phones to cast Joey in their appreciative light. When she got off the stage she was swarmed, and it took her more than a few minutes to make her way back to the table. She clearly enjoyed the adulation and I smiled, wondering if this was what she needed to remind her of how much she loved being a rock star.

When she got back to the table, Jackman had joined us again and had Amanda with him.

"Awesome!" Jackman said to Joey.

"You're the best," Amanda said. "My friends and me used to dance to your video at sleepovers."

"Thanks, guys," Joey said. "I'm still in shock from your friend Dawg, here. What a voice!"

Dawg beamed, his face metamorphosing as a new emotion took hold. "Call me Anthony," he said.

"Where's Corey?" Jackman asked.

Clare told him that he had walked out, clearly upset.

Jackman looked alarmed. "Not good," he said. "His mother just died like a week ago. We dragged him out tonight to try to cheer him up."

We all agreed to go look for him, and left the karaoke bar. Anthony, Jackman, and Amanda set off to check the restaurants, the bowling alley, and the restroom, while my sisters and I walked up and down the aisles of the arcade.

"We should check outside," Joey said, when it became clear he wasn't playing any of the video games.

We went out the front door into the muggy night air and

saw a lone boy sitting on the sidewalk out front, his back pressed against the building.

"I'm going to go talk to him," Joey said. "Go tell his friends we found him."

"Since when did Joey become a grief counselor?" Clare said to me as we walked away.

We found the others and took them back outside to where we had left Joey and Corey. They were deep in conversation and Joey held up her hand to wave us away. "We'll meet you guys back inside when we're done talking, okay?"

I was tired and eager to get home, but figured it would only be a few more minutes. After all, how long could Joey spend talking to a total stranger about the death of his mother?

I dragged Clare back to that dinosaur booth and challenged her to a two-player game, pulverizing her. For the next half hour we wandered halfheartedly from game to game, waiting for Joey to return. When we finally went back outside, she was still deep in conversation with the boy. It was another twenty minutes or so before she and Corey rose. She gave him a hug and he left.

"What were you talking about all that time?" I asked her.

"He was having a spiritual crisis."

"Were you able to help him?" Clare asked.

Joey dug her hands into the front pockets of her jeans. "I think so," she said. "He knew God hadn't abandoned him. He just needed to hear it."

"I'm really proud of you," Clare said, and gave Joey a hug. Then they both looked at me to see if I would join in the lovefest.

I rolled my eyes. "If you break into a rousing chorus of 'Amazing Grace,' I'll push you into moving traffic."

Joey put one arm around me, the other around Clare, and started to sing.

Chapter 32

When your heart and your ego have been shattered by a man you thought might have loved you, there are worse things you can do than go out on a date with a guy who's hung up on your beautiful older sister. For instance, you can agree to have the date at a romantic seaside restaurant, where you feel compelled to go through the motions and pretend you're having a wonderful time. Or worse, after dinner you can accompany the guy to a club where his friend is playing the guitar for a band that covers seventies classics, and then endure an hourlong conversation with the friend, who's more interested in finding out what it's like to be Joey Bloom's sister than in anything about you. Worst of all, you can end the date by inviting the guy inside and sleeping with him.

I'd like to say that being the smart one, I'd never do any of that. But alas, that's exactly where I found myself. It wasn't that the sex was bad, it's just that I was having a hard time concentrating. Maybe it was the slice of chocolate cheesecake in the refrigerator. That can be mighty distracting. Leo seemed to be having a grand old time, but my mind kept going back to the cheesecake, thinking about padding downstairs in my bathrobe after we were done. If Leo fell sound asleep afterward, which I suspected he might, I could have it all to myself.

"Feels so good," he said.

"So good," I echoed.

"God, I'm close!"

I closed my eyes and took a mental walk around the kitchen. Did I have any decaf in the house?

Jonathan, my ex, thought that decaf was the great Satan of hot beverages, and it pissed him off that it had become the default coffee at catered events. "It's not *coffee*," he would say. "They shouldn't call it coffee." And he would go off for an hour on how it was symptomatic of the great dumbing down of our society, how everything became blander and more diluted so as not to challenge the lowest rungs of taste and sensibilities.

I wondered if Jonathan was still sleeping with Savannah, and if they had any little schizophrenic artist babies crawling around the loft, making statements with their rice cereal. Jonathan and I didn't talk much about having a baby. I just always assumed the day would come. Most of our city friends who had kids waited until they were pushing forty, so I never felt tremendously rushed. After the divorce, I spent a few weeks in near panic worrying about my biological clock. Then I came to the decision that I was not going to let it become an obsession like it did for so many of my friends. So I made a pact with myself that if I wasn't married by age thirty-nine, I could have a baby on my own. It went a long way toward taking the pressure off.

Still, there was a part of me that measured every guy with the father yardstick. Leo loved kids and would probably make a splendid dad one day. The thought of it made me project the possibility onto the flat-screen TV in my mind. If I stayed in New York and took that art teacher job, would Leo and I keep dating? Could I see marrying this guy? Would that be too weird for Clare? I imagined a life where I took up a hobby that I could do while having sex. Scrapbooking came to mind.

"Almost there!" he cried.

Thank God. I wasn't getting any younger. And if I was going to stick to any sort of a plan about getting on with my life—starting with that chocolate cheesecake—we'd have to wrap this up. Fortunately, I could tell Leo was just about there and then . . . the phone rang.

Shit. The last thing this guy needed was a distraction. With his ADD it would derail him entirely. To my surprise, however, it had the opposite affect. His concentration increased. Leo grimaced and cried out, "The phooooone!"

He was done.

I felt like throwing a party. A chocolate cheesecake party.

"Are you going to get that?" he said, the very second he recovered. I thought he was kidding, but Leo rolled off me, picked up the phone, and handed it to me.

"Are you still mad at me?" said the voice on the other end. It was Kenny. I pulled the sheet over myself and sat up, looking at the clock.

"Why are you calling so late?"

"I'm at the airport—catching a late flight to New York."

"You're coming back?"

"I have news, Bev. *Letterman* called today. They're making me an offer. I'm flying in for a meeting tomorrow."

"I'm happy for you." It wasn't a lie. I wished him well. I just needed him out of my heart and out of my life.

"Listen, they're taking me out to lunch and I'd like you to join us."

"I don't think that's such a good idea."

"They told me I could invite someone."

"It's not that. It's . . ."

"C'mon, Bev. You're going to have to forgive me sooner or later."

Leo rolled over next to me and started snoring softly.

"I'm sorry. I can't."

"If you change your mind, we'll be at Nonny's on West Fifty-seventh Street at one o'clock."

"I won't change my mind."

Leo coughed.

Kenny paused for a moment and I felt a chill. "Is someone there with you?" he asked.

I hesitated, thinking about whether I should tell him the truth. On the one hand, it would surely end things between us. On the other hand, it was the cruelest way to do it. I drew in a breath.

"Yes," I said, "there's someone here with me."

I waited for him to respond. Nothing.

"Hello?" I said. "Are you there?"

All I heard was the sound of him breathing, and then a gentle click.

Chapter 33

Leo was still there the next morning when Linda Klein, the realtor, called with some news. Apparently, the Goodwins were still interested enough in the Waxmans' house to hire an engineer to evaluate it. It was, she said, a miracle that someone would be willing to buy a house that was the scene of a murder, and that we should "bend over backward" to accommodate them. The reason Linda called me was that she needed Renee's permission to let the engineer make his inspection, but every time she called the number in Florida she got disconnected. Sam, I figured, must have been intercepting the call and hanging up on her. I told her I would get right on it.

Sure enough, when I called the Waxmans' home Sam picked up on the first ring. I pictured him sitting on a floral sofa with the phone on his lap, not letting anyone near it.

"It's Bev Bloomrosen," I said. "I need to talk to my mother. It's important." I was being cagey. I thought if I asked to speak to my mother he might pass the phone, whereas if I asked for Renee he'd likely hang up.

"Who is this?" he said.

"Harold and Bernadette's daughter."

"The rock star?"

"*Uh* . . . yes." I thought it might be best not to argue.

"I saw you in that video. You looked like a whore."

"Can you just put my mom on the phone?"

"Are you calling about that damned key again?"

"My sister already found it," I lied, guessing Joey had tried to get him to tell her where the key to the storage unit was. I figured I might as well play along. Perhaps he was ready to give something up.

"It's fifteen, four, thirty-two," he said.

"What? What does that mean?"

"The combination. You don't need any damned key."

"It's a combination lock?" I said as I scrambled for a pencil and paper. "Fifteen, four, thirty-two? Is that right?"

"Who is this?"

"It's Beverly, Mr. Waxman."

"You're not Harold's daughter!"

"I am, don't you remember? You gave me the Santa Claus ornament?"

"Clare," he said.

"No, that's my older sister. I'm Bev. I was just in Florida with you."

"The car accident."

"That's right."

"He should have let you burn. I told him to. I said 'Let that bitch burn!' But he wouldn't listen."

I shuddered, thinking about the police officer risking his life to save me while Sam screamed from behind that he should let me burn. In fact, I almost remembered it. I could almost hear Sam's voice in the background.

"Is my mother there?" I asked. "I need to speak to my mother."

After breakfast, Leo and I got in his van and headed over to the storage facility to see if the combination Sam had given me would work on the lock. Maybe it was just my own eagerness, but I had a strong feeling about it. I was close to holding an actual sample of Lydia's handwriting that I could compare to the letter. The thought was at once terrifying and exciting. I wanted the truth, I *needed* the truth.

I told Leo to go straight at the light and he continued accelerating as if he didn't notice that it was red. I forgot he had that terrible habit of stopping short, and I once again slammed my foot down against an imaginary brake. My heel felt sore as I did it, as if I had injured it recently. When the van halted with a jerk, I remembered, in a vague sense, that I had slammed my foot down like that recently, only I had done it hard enough to hurt myself. When was that? I closed my eyes for a moment and envisioned it. I had been in the backseat of a car. Of course—it was the accident. Kenny had been driving and I was behind him with Renee.

When the light turned green and Leo stomped on the gas, the whole thing played back for me, as if the memory had been there all the time. Sam had grabbed the steering wheel, sending us off the road. I remembered seeing trees slap the windows and feeling like we went airborne. That must have been when the car flipped completely over, landing back on its tires. I must have passed out then, and when I came to, someone was shouting to me. *Bev! Bev!* I tried to ignore him and drift back into the black sleep, but he wouldn't let me. *The car's on fire!* He pulled at me. I looked down and saw flames. Sam was standing off by the side of the road, shouting for him to leave me alone, to let me burn, but he wouldn't. He reached in through the window and grabbed me. My leg was stuck and I couldn't get out. I screamed. *Don't worry*, he said. He put his arms under mine and tugged hard, but I was jammed. The interior seemed to light up then, and I realized it was because high flames shot up from the hood. I was terrified. People started shouting that everyone needed to back away from the car before the gas tank exploded. I thought he was going to leave me, then. I remembered thinking, *This is not how I want to die.*

The man pulled even harder and I tried to wriggle free, but it was useless—the front seat had fallen to the floor and pinned my foot. *It won't come out!* He told me not to worry, that he wouldn't leave me, and pulled so hard I heard something on his body pop. I thought it was over then. I was ready to die.

"Just go!" I said, but he didn't. And then, the floor under my foot burned away, freeing me. With his one good arm, he pulled me out. I was okay. The man in the blue shirt had saved me. But of course, it wasn't a police officer. It was Kenny. That was how he dislocated his shoulder—saving my life.

I looked at my watch. "I have to go to the Gotham," I said to Leo.

"What?"

"I mean the city. I have to go to Manhattan. I have to catch the next train."

"Why? I thought we were going to the storage place."

"Just drive me to the train station!" I yelled. "I have to be someplace. I have to get to Nonny's by one o'clock."

Chapter 34

As I sat by the window on a Long Island Rail Road train heading toward Penn Station, watching homes and the back end of local industry fly by, I worried about getting to the city in time to meet Kenny and the *Letterman* people having lunch. I was cutting it awfully close.

But I was more worried about whether I could get him to forgive me. Kenny had risked his life to save me. And what did I give him in return? Distrust, condemnation, even vindictiveness.

Yes, Kenny's temper was a bear, and sometimes it got the better of him. But he wrestled it relentlessly. In fact, when he hung up on me the night before, I could feel him caging the beast. Despite his hurt that I had slept with another man, he kept his rage to himself, protecting me.

I needed to blow my nose and looked in my handbag for a tissue. Finding none, I resorted to wiping my nose with the back of my hand. I didn't want to cry. But the tears spilled. After a few minutes a woman across the aisle and a row back approached, holding out a travel pack of tissues.

I took one and thanked her. She tried to hand me the whole pack.

"That's okay," I said.

She held onto the back of the seat as the train swayed. "I have more," she said.

I accepted it. "Thanks."

She looked like she was ready to head back to her seat, but hesitated. I could tell she wanted to know why I was crying.

"A man?" she asked.

I nodded.

"He hurt you?"

I thought about that for a second. "I hurt *him*."

"Then why are you the one crying?"

"I don't know."

She shrugged and went back to her seat. In fact, I did know. I was mad at myself and didn't know what else to do with the anger. It was, I knew, typically female to turn fury into sadness. Just like it was typically male to turn sadness into fury.

The windows of the train went black as we passed through the tunnel beneath the East River. We'd reach Penn Station in a matter of minutes. I looked at my watch. It was later than I thought. I wished I could get the train to move faster.

Choosing to take a taxi from Penn Station instead of the subway was a mistake. I thought I was doing myself a favor by ascending to the fresh air of Seventh Avenue, but I'd forgotten that there were two kinds of summer days in Manhattan—the oppressive and the unbearable. Today was the latter.

There were about a hundred people waiting on the taxi line, so I decided to start walking uptown and hail a cab on the way. The air seemed almost completely devoid of oxygen, and the sky was dark enough to threaten rain. But there'd been nothing in the forecast about it, so I hoped I was safe.

At Thirty-ninth Street, I felt a few drops. I looked up hoping to determine that they were drips from an air conditioner. By the time I crossed Fortieth Street, the sky opened in an angry torrent, and I dashed under an awning with a dozen other people. Water poured from the overhang in sheets, bouncing against the pavement and soaking our shoes. It seemed like the kind of downpour that might pass quickly, but even so, I didn't have the time to spare. I peered down Seventh Avenue to see if there might be an available taxi. The street was thick with the yellow cars, but none were vacant. And then, a miracle as welcome and spectacular as the Red Sea parting happened right before my eyes. A taxi slowed and stopped about ten feet from me, discharging a passenger. I made a mad dash, pretending I didn't see the old woman with a walker inching her way toward it. I forced myself not to feel bad about it. After all, I was in a hurry. She was probably on her way to a doctor for something malignant that was going to kill her regardless.

Okay, so Manhattan brings out the beast in me.

Traffic was a nightmare, and when we finally reached Nonny's, I overtipped the driver and sprinted to the curb. Standing beneath the restaurant's awning, I opened my purse and took out a compact mirror to survey the damage. I guessed I didn't look too bad for someone with wet hair plastered to her head and mascara dripping down her checks. I cleaned up the best I could and applied fresh lipstick. I looked inside the restaurant and saw Kenny sitting at a large table with David Letterman and a group I assumed was the writing staff. My heart started to pound in something like a panic attack. I tended to get stupid and tongue-tied around celebrities. Once, when Joey's career was at its peak, she dragged me to a barbecue in the Hamptons with her. She had neglected to mention that it was at Billy Joel's house, and I got so flustered that I spent the first hour holding onto a glass of wine and trying not to let anybody see my hands shake. I was in the process of putting it down on a table when a man brushed by and said "Excuse me." When I saw who it was, I dropped the glass and it crashed against the patio.

Billy Joel put his hand on my shoulder. I could smell his aftershave, the gin on his breath. "These parties never get started until someone breaks the first glass," he said kindly, and then signaled for someone to come over and clean it up.

I opened my mouth to respond and nothing came out. I spent the rest of the party hiding in the bathroom.

But that was not going to happen today. I'd be charming and normal. I'd tell David Letterman it was nice to meet him. I'd smile at Kenny and, with any luck, he'd smile back and invite me to sit down. Or maybe not. One thing I knew for sure: I was going to think before I uttered a single word. I would not risk being embarrassed by an attack of dysphasia.

Showtime, I thought, and pushed open the door. I walked toward the table, fixed on Kenny. God, he looked handsome. He felt me staring and glanced up. I guess the wet hair threw him for a second, because it took a moment for a flash of recognition to show in his face.

"Bev," he said, getting up.

David Letterman rose too, and I took a long, slow breath, trying to oxygenate my extremities, which were going numb. Every head at the table turned to face me. I went all pins and needles at that point. Calming down was out of my reach.

"I'd like you meet the freshly watered Bev Bloomrosen," Kenny announced.

The talk show host—looking thinner and tanner in person than he did on TV—flashed his iconic gap-toothed smile and extended his hand. "Lovely to see you," he said, as if I were a guest on his panel.

I was so flummoxed at the idea of standing before him in the flesh, blood and three dimensions, I went white. Smile, I told myself, and I think my face obeyed. I took his hand, and he kept shaking, expecting me to say something. I was aware of some quiet coughing as everyone waited for me to speak. I cleared my throat. *Say something quick and simple*, I coached myself. *Don't overthink this.*

"Same here," I finally announced. My own voice sounded far away. "I've always wanted to meet Jay Leno."

David Letterman dropped my hand and everyone froze in place as a postatomic silence seized the entire restaurant. Aware of my mistake the second the vibrations of my voice passed from my throat to atmosphere, I felt a panic rise up from the soles of my feet, bringing hot blood all the way to my scalp. I couldn't breathe. My face burned with shame. I wished some Richter scale phenomenon would shake Manhattan's skyscrapers and suck me down with the tumbling debris. *Please, God,* I thought, if the apocalypse is ever going to happen, let it be now.

I closed my eyes for a second, and when I opened them, everyone was still there, staring at me. I looked at Kenny, my salvation, but his face was covered by his hands. I counted two beats, waiting for him to look up and take me off the hook, but his embarrassment was so huge he stayed hidden. I turned and ran from the restaurant.

Now you've done it, I thought, as I raced down Fifty-seventh Street. Without thinking, I jumped onto the first bus I saw. I couldn't believe it. Any chance I had of getting Kenny to forgive me had just imploded. I had not only broken his heart, but had also humiliated him in front of his new boss. It didn't get any worse than that. I had ruined everything.

Chapter 25

"This is what God could have done if He'd had money."

That's what the famous wit George S. Kaufman had said to wealthy playwright Moss Hart when he beheld the exotic trees, lush plants, and colorful flowers of his collaborator's exquisitely landscaped property. He could just as well have said it about Clare's backyard, where the late afternoon sun cast long shadows across the designer stonework patio and onto the carefully manicured lawn, so verdant it was practically teal.

As if that weren't enough, the weather predictions for that afternoon had been right. By the time I found myself on Clare's property for the barbecue, the sky was a rich shade of late-day blue, the air temperature was Martha Stewart perfect, and the sun was welcoming the impending dusk with bright joy. If you listened carefully, you could practically hear it singing that "Wonderful World" song Louis Armstrong made famous. Oh, yeah.

When I arrived carrying the two ten-pound bags of ice Clare had requested and heard a sparrow in the dogwood tree joining in the festivities by singing its tiny little heart out, it was almost more than I could bear.

"Can't you do anything about that damned bird?" I said as I thrust the bags at Clare.

"You're in a lovely mood."

Her sarcasm was warranted. My mood was foul. I hadn't had a moment's peace since I ran from the restaurant in shame.

"Pour yourself a glass of wine," Clare said, pointing to a shaded section of the yard where a self-serve bar had been set up on a piece of wrought-iron furniture specifically designed for the function.

"Don't you need some help?" I asked. "You look so busy."

"My guests aren't permitted to help, you know that. Besides, Marta is back from South America."

"*Central* America," I blurted.

Clare rolled her eyes. "Maybe you should have two glasses of wine," she said, and went into the house.

A chilled bottle of Chablis stood sweating on the bar, and I poured myself a large glass before approaching Clare's husband, who smiled from behind a stainless-steel barbecue grill that was roughly the same size as my old apartment. At the far end of the yard, the children were running around, involved in some complicated game with a large orange disk that kept getting stuck in the trees. Most of the adults were either seated around the yet-to-be-lit fire pit or at a large table in the middle of the patio.

I peered over Marc's shoulder. On one section of the grill there was a row of chicken cutlets with perfect diagonal char lines. On the other side there were several fat burgers, two of which had large dollops of blue cheese melting down their sides. I started to salivate. The greasy meat patties taunted me, daring me to choose one of them over the prim white chicken breasts. It would, I knew, be stupid to go for the burger just because I was depressed. I never had Clare's hippy proportions, but I wasn't immune to gaining belly fat, and this was the just the kind of food that would settle into my gut and make me feel even worse. *Chicken*, I thought, go for the chicken.

"Jade is looking for you," Marc said.

"Jade?"

"Said she has a hilarious story she wants to tell you."

I grabbed a paper plate and held it out. "Let me have one of those blue cheese burgers."

Balancing the meaty sandwich on my plate, I made a bee-line for the buffet table where the condiments were situated and squirted an obscene amount of ketchup on my burger. I could have sat down at the table to eat like a civilized person, but I wanted to enjoy my feast in animalistic solitude. I took an enormous, ravenous bite. Ketchup, hamburger juice, and melted blue cheese oozed out of the bun and onto my hands. I was in pig heaven, and in the midst of licking the decadent liquid mess off my right wrist when Jade approached.

"There you are!" she said, way louder than she needed to.

I put the plate down and sucked my fingertips. "Hi, Jade." She wore a diaphanous sundress, patterned in swirls of swimming-pool blues and aquas, over a clingy white slip. It looked perfectly tailored to her perfect body, and I imagined it cost more than my last vacation.

"Is your friend Leo coming?" she asked, smoothing the fabric over her hips.

"Meeting me here in a little while."

"I have a hilarious story I wanted to tell the two of you."

I didn't want to hear her hilarious story. I wanted to go back to eating my burger alone. "We'll come find you when he gets here—"

"You know what? I'll just tell you now. What the hell, right? Life is short."

I glanced around. Was there no one who could save me? I picked up my burger and took another bite.

"Okay, so I stopped at Blackwell's on the way here, today," she began. "You know Blackwell's, right?"

My mouth was full, so I just shook my head.

"You never heard of Blackwells? Oh, Bev, it's the best bakery on the North Shore. Very expensive. Very, very. But you get what you pay for, right? Anyway, they have the *tiniest* parking lot and my car is *huge*. It's a Hummer."

"Naturally," I said, not surprised that Jade drove the biggest, showiest, most obnoxious, gas-guzzling, socially irresponsible car on the planet.

"It's out of this *world*," she said. "I know it's not everyone's cup of tea, but what can you do?" She grabbed my arm for emphasis, which made me want to growl; she was awfully close to my food.

"So anyway," she continued, "I stopped at Blackwell's to get these darling little French pastries they have because I *knew* Clare would love them. I mean, *I* don't eat pastries, but they're *so* pretty." She looked at my burger and I thought I saw saliva pooling beneath her lip. I angled my body away, trying as hard as I could to be subtle about it.

"Anyways, I'm trying to leave the parking lot and this blonde in a Hummer that's the same model as mine—only hers is bright yellow, which looked *ridiculous* with her hair—was driving down this narrow lane in the opposite direction. She wanted the spot I was passing but I couldn't move because she was in my way. So she signals me to back up and I'm like, no, *you* back up. And she's like, no, *you* back up. So I fold my arms because I'm like, I've got all day, sweetheart. So get this. She picks up a *book* to show me that *she's* got all day, and she starts reading it right there in her front seat in the middle of the lot!"

"Gee," I said, and took another bite of my burger, hoping her story would be over soon.

"I wish I had a book with me too, because it would have been so cool if I had started reading. But I had my cell phone, at least, so I held it up to show her, and then I called my sister and just started yakking and laughing and telling her how stupid the woman's hair looked with her yellow Hummer. Finally, she starts to inch forward and I'm like, where the hell is she going? She gets closer and closer to me like she's going to literally *push* my Hummer out of the way to get into the spot!"

I swallowed. "Where's Norman Schwarzkopf when you need him, right?"

"What?"

"General Schwarzkopf? Desert Storm?" Nothing registered. "I just meant it was like two tanks having a skirmish."

Jade clapped in delight. "Skirmish! What a great word. Yes, that's exactly what it was—a skirmish."

"So what did you do?" I asked.

"I backed up. What else could I do? *She* might not care if her car got dented, but *I* sure as hell don't want to have to drive around in a scratched-up Hummer. I have my pride."

"You didn't need a general after all," I said. "You knew exactly when to retreat."

"Retreat? Oh, I don't consider it a retreat. *She* was the one who was willing to dent her car. *I* behaved like a civilized person. As far as I'm concerned, I won, she lost."

"You don't think she's saying the same thing to *her* friends right now?"

Jade waved away my comment with a flick of her wrist. "You think too much."

Someone's got to pick up the slack, I thought, and shoved the rest of my blue cheese burger into my mouth, not realizing that it was just a bit too much to handle in one bite. I covered my mouth with my hand as I struggled to chew.

Fortunately, Jade was looking right past me. Suddenly, her eyes came to life. "He's *here!*"

"*Woo weer?*" I said.

"Leo!"

"*Weo?*" I picked up a napkin and wiped my hands and face. I had chosen this barbecue as the perfect opportunity to let Clare know about me and Leo so she would move on and forget about the idea of having an affair with him. I wanted to go to him immediately. "Excuse me," I said to Jade.

"I'll let you two have some alone time," she whispered. "But don't forget to share, okay?" She wagged her finger at me. "He's not a cheeseburger!" She squealed with laughter and walked away.

I greeted Leo with a kiss and linked arms with him, promenading around the yard as I told him about the conversation with Jade. The whole time, I kept my eye out for Clare, hoping she witnessed the intimacy. At last I saw her in the far corner by the hydrangeas, chatting with one of her guests. She was too deep in conversation to see us, so I brought Leo over to say hello.

At the sight of us, she looked stricken. But she recovered quickly and gave Leo a peck on the cheek.

"How nice to see you," she said to him.

"I hope you don't mind that I invited him," I said.

Clare forced a smile. "Of course not. Have you met my friend Harlan? He's the one who teaches my Modern American Lit class."

We made small talk for a few minutes, and then Leo and I excused ourselves. As we walked away, Clare called out as if something just occurred to her. "Oh, Leo! There's something I want to chat with you about later, when you have the chance."

"Sure," he said, trying to act casual. But their eyes met in a way that told me he knew exactly what she wanted to discuss.

Chapter 36

I was glad to see that Clare had invited Teddy and Alicia Goodwin, and after Leo went to the buffet table and piled a plate high with two pieces of barbecued chicken, one cheeseburger, one scoop each of macaroni salad and coleslaw, some grilled vegetables, a shrimp skewer, and an ear of corn, we took a seat at the table with them.

I asked the Goodwins if they'd made any progress toward getting an engineer into the Waxman house for an evaluation, and they told me the appointment was set. I imagined that if all went well, they'd be bidding on the house before too long.

Somehow, they had managed to hear back from Renee despite my phone conversation with Sam having gotten me exactly nowhere. It didn't even get me any closer to seeing Lydia's handwriting. Sam was either confused about that supposed combination lock or intentionally sending me on a wild goose chase. After dropping me at the train station, Leo had headed over to the storage facility by himself. Alas, he reported that the door had a padlock requiring a key. We were no closer to finding that shoebox than we ever were.

"I hope the house works out for you," I said to the Goodwins.

Teddy told me he had even more good news, but when I asked what it was, he was cagey, and said he'd be making an announcement later.

As dusk moved in, the air began to cool, and I wondered why Joey hadn't arrived. I didn't want to spoil the party by getting Clare nervous, so I kept my mouth shut about it. Meanwhile, Marc got the blaze started in the fire pit, and the children gathered round. He showed them how to thread marshmallows onto sticks and toast them, while Clare brought out a tray of chocolate bars and graham crackers to they could make s'mores.

I thought I heard Joey's voice and turned to see her entering the backyard. She was holding the hand of a man who had his back to me as he shut the gate behind them. He didn't have to turn around for me to know who it was.

Kenny.

Of course. It made perfect sense that he would run into her arms after I had hurt him and then rubbed salt in the wound by humiliating him in front of David Letterman. Still, seeing them together was as excruciating as that day in high school when I swung open the door of her bedroom to see if she had taken my nail polish remover again, only to discover the two of them naked on top of her lime bedspread. This time, though, I deserved it.

"You okay, dear?" Alicia Goodwin asked me. "You look pale."

"I'll be right back," I said, and slipped into the house.

Inside, I stood in a dark corner of the den by the back door and watched as Joey and Kenny made their way over to the table, where Alicia and Teddy greeted them. They laughed and chatted for a few moments, and I held my breath waiting to see if Kenny put his arm around Joey . . . or if she grabbed for his ass.

Before that could happen, Clare approached them and lis-

tened intently to something Teddy had to say. Then she nodded and called out to the whole party, "Can I have everyone's
attention? Our friend Teddy Goodwin has an announcement
he'd like to share with everyone."

The crowd turned from all corners of the yard to face Teddy
as he climbed on top of a low wooden table behind the fire pit.
Kenny and Joey moved in closer. Teddy began to speak.

"As many of you know, I've been writing songs for years
without any success, despite my connections in the music
business. But now, thanks to the help of my golden-voiced
friend here," he paused and pointed to my little sister, "that's
about to change. Joey was kind enough to record a song I
wrote several years ago called 'Craving You.' I had the opportunity to play the recording for the A and R guy at Ingenuity
Records and I'm happy to say that he wants to buy it!"

The crowd broke into applause, while several people called
out their congratulations. Alicia smiled and beamed.

"Wait," Teddy said, trying to get the group to settle down.
"There's more."

"Tell!" Joey shouted.

"Well, it has to do with you," Teddy said to her. "The guy
was blown away by your voice. He said you're twice the singer
you were back when you recorded 'Tiger Attack,' and he
wants to sign you. Joey, it's your chance for a comeback, with
a major label behind you."

Teddy grinned, expecting a huge reaction, and all heads
turned toward Joey. Despite the misgivings she had expressed
over re-launching her career, I thought for sure this news
would exhilarate her. This was huge, practically a guarantee
that she would be a rock star again.

I couldn't see Joey's face, but her body language said it all.
She was, quite literally, unmoved.

"Well, Joey?" Teddy said. "What do you think?"

She shrugged. "Thanks anyway."

"What?"

"Not interested." Joey leaned down, picked up a stick, and threaded a marshmallow onto it.

"Why not?" Teddy was incredulous.

"I have other plans." She moved closer to the flames and held her marshmallow over it.

Kenny folded his arms, and I got the impression he knew all about her other plans. It gave me a very bad feeling.

"What other plans?" Teddy said. "You mean with another label?"

Joey twirled her stick over the fire and pulled it out. The marshmallow was ablaze and she blew on it. "I love it when they're burnt like this."

Kenny approached and put his hand on her shoulder, then whispered something to her and she laughed. I think I could have handled just about any other reaction. But seeing them share a private joke was more intimate than I could bear, and I turned away. It was time for me to leave.

Upset as I was, I didn't want to leave without giving Dylan his birthday present. I hadn't seen him in the backyard during Teddy's speech, so I looked around the house for him. As I was climbing back up the basement steps, two boys ran into the kitchen to get another bag of marshmallows, and I asked them if they'd seen him.

"I think he took off on his bike," one of them said.

"His bike?"

He shrugged, and the two of them dashed through the door into the backyard.

I went out the front of the house, and sure enough the door to the garage was wide open and Dylan's bicycle was missing. What was that kid doing riding around by himself at night? I trotted to the end of the driveway and looked in both directions. No Dylan. I didn't want to panic, but this wasn't good. I jumped in my car to look for him.

I drove around the block, and then the next block and the next. I looped back and started the same thing in the other direction. Worst-case scenarios were nudging their way into my consciousness, and I knew that if I didn't find him very soon I'd have to alert Clare and Marc.

At last I thought I saw something in the distance. A boy sat on a curb, his bike lying in the street in front of him. His face was in his hands.

"Dyl?" I said, as I slammed my car door.

He tilted his head just enough to see that it was me.

"You all right?" I said when I got closer.

He shook his head without looking up. I sat down next to him and put my hand on his back. I could feel the ridges of his spine through his T-shirt. He'd been such a fat baby, with no neck and sumo thighs, that the transformation was dramatic. At two he was still a bit of a dumpling. By three he was so lean Clare had trouble finding pants that would stay up. Now, on his eleventh birthday, he was starting to add sinew to his bony frame, and it made me realize how fleeting these days were. Another summer or two and he wouldn't even think of himself as a kid anymore.

"Did you get hurt?" I asked.

He nodded.

"You fell off your bike?"

He nodded again.

"Let me see."

He lifted his head, and in the dim light I could see that he had cut his chin. I picked up his hands and turned them over. He had scraped his palms where he had caught himself falling. The worst, though, was a cut on the side of his knee, which bled profusely.

I took off my terrycloth sweater and used it to wipe the blood from his leg. Then I used it to make a tourniquet.

"That might need stitches," I said. "Let's get you home and cleaned up and we'll have a better idea."

"I'm not going home," he said.

"Why not?"

He folded his arms on his knees and put his head down. He sniffled.

"Did you have a fight with one of your friends?"

He shook his head.

"You can tell me," I said.

"I can't."

"Okay," I said, "but I have to wash your cuts so you don't get an infection. C'mon." I gently pulled on his arm to get him to stand, and he let me lead him to the car. I threaded his bike into my trunk, which I had to leave wide open as I drove slowly back to the house.

He didn't want to see anyone, so I surreptitiously steered him to the upstairs bathroom, where I washed out his wounds. I gave him a clean washcloth and told him to press it hard against the cut on his leg.

"If we can't get it to stop bleeding you're going to have to go to the hospital. It should probably get stitched anyway or you'll have a nasty scar."

He sat on the closed toilet lid and applied pressure to his leg. "I don't care," he said.

Voices from the backyard carried upstairs and through the window. I heard Marc calling his name.

"Dylan, please tell me what happened. You'll feel so much better."

He looked away, trying not to cry. My heart broke in half.

"They're probably going to have cake soon," I said.

He shrugged.

"I hope it's chocolate," I said.

"It is."

"Your mom let you see it?"

A dark mist passed over his face. His jaw clamped shut.

"Dylan?"

His face contorted into a grimace. I reached over and touched his hand. He whispered something I couldn't hear.

"What?"

"She *kissed* that guy."

"Your mom?"

"Ethan said he was faster than me, so we raced around the house and I saw them—on the side by the big tree. It was dark, but I saw." He took the washcloth off his knee. "I think it stopped bleeding."

I dabbed at the wound, which was starting to clot. "Dylan," I said, as I put antibiotic ointment on the cut and covered it with a large bandage, my hands shaking, "who did she kiss?"

He stood. "My dad is calling me."

I thought about pressing him for an answer, but didn't want to exacerbate his trauma. "Go on," I said, messing his hair.

I stayed in the bathroom for a few minutes, then went down the stairs thinking about what I might have to do to shake some sense into my knuckleheaded sister. Before reaching the landing, I heard voices coming from the den. I stopped and listened. I couldn't make out the dialogue, but one voice was a man's, and the other was Clare's.

I held my breath and walked as quietly as I could so I would surprise them. As I approached, I saw that the room was mostly dark, but there was no doubt who the two figures were—Clare and Leo. She was in the middle of taking her shirt off, pulling it up over her head.

"Clare!" I screamed.

She yanked the shirt away from her face and looked at me. "Bev?"

"What are you doing!" I tried to lower my voice and gain some control, but my heart was beating madly.

"Nothing."

"Nothing?"

She looked at Leo. "Should we tell her?"

"May as well," he said.

I felt a surge of adrenaline that made me want to strangle someone, but I couldn't decide whose throat to lunge for. What on earth was wrong with these two? How could they be so casual about this?

"Leo got me a position with Goode Earth Habitats," Clare said.

"What?"

"He told me they're starting to build some homes in the Bronx and could use volunteers."

"Volunteers?"

"They need people with her design skills," Leo said.

"Isn't it great, Bev?" she said. "It's chance for me to be useful. I'll be designing homes on a budget, helping underprivileged families. I'm so excited!"

Clare shook out the green T-shirt she had just taken off and turned it right side out. She held it up to show me the organization's logo. I realized that she still wore her black halter top. She had simply been trying the T-shirt on over it.

I rubbed on my forehead. "Listen, I'm not a fool, and I'm not falling for this."

"What are you talking about?" Leo asked.

"Dylan saw you two! He saw you kissing on the side of the house!"

Clare's face went white.

"Kissing?" Leo said. "I never kissed Clare."

"Liar!" I think there may have been froth forming at the corners of my mouth.

Leo looked at Clare. "What is she talking about?"

My sister put her face in her hands.

I glared at Leo. "Don't play dumb."

"It wasn't him," Clare said.

I studied Leo's face, but couldn't detect a single molecule of deceit.

"Then who did you kiss?" I asked Clare.

She fell into a chair and started to sob.

"Who!" I demanded.

She took an audible breath. "Hammerman!"

"But Leo *is* Hammerman."

"Who's Hammerman?" said Leo.

I looked at Clare and then back at Leo. His expression remained guileless. "*Uh* . . . I'm beginning to wonder that myself," I said.

"Harlan," Clare said. "Harlan Hammerman. My lit professor. He's an old friend—we went to college together."

"Harlan? That guy you introduced me to?"

Leo put his hand on my shoulder. "I think I'd better go," he said, and dashed from the room like it was on fire.

I sat down across from Clare, reeling. "I thought it was Leo. I slept with him to . . . oh, God."

"You don't have to worry, Bev. It's over. After we kissed he said he couldn't, he wouldn't. He left. I'll probably never see him again." Tears spilled down her cheeks. "My heart is broken."

Was she kidding? Dylan caught her in the act and she was concerned with her *own* heart?

"Wake up," I said. "Your *kid* is broken. What's more important?"

She took a jagged breath and covered her mouth, as if

she was just taking in the enormity of her mistake. "I really screwed up."

"You really did."

"Dylan," she said, her eyes registering fear. "My baby!"

"He saw it, Clare."

"I don't how to fix this. How can I fix this?"

"Talk to him."

"Can you help me?"

I stood, furious. How dare she act so recklessly and expect my help! "Clean up your own damned mess."

I went out the front door wanting to get away as fast as I could, but Sophie and two other girls came tearing around from the backyard, squealing.

"Everybody has to come into the backyard now, Aunt Bev. We're going to sing 'Happy Birthday.'"

"*Aw*, sweetie, I can't. I have to be someplace." I saw that her sneaker was untied and knelt down to double knot it for her.

"It has a big chocolate bar on top and blue flowers. And you know what else?"

"What?"

She leaned in and whispered, her breath as sweet as marshmallows. "Dad put on magic candles. The kind you can't blow out."

I stood and she looked up, her eyes beseeching me to change my mind. My anger melted into something like gooey chocolate. I put out my hand and she took it.

When we got to the backyard, Sophie made a dash for the table where the cake was set up. Leo approached me and put a drink in my hand.

"Everything okay?" he said.

"Not really."

As the crowd sang "Happy Birthday," Sophie and Clare stood on one side of Dylan and Marc on the other. They looked like the perfect family, but I caught Clare's eye and saw a Shakespearean tragedy's worth of toil and trouble there. I heard a splash, then, and turned around to see what it was. One of the boys had jumped into the pool, even though it wasn't a swim party. While everyone laughed at Dylan's futile attempts to blow out the candles, I walked toward the water. It was Jade's son, and he was doing the back float.

"I don't think you're supposed to be in the pool, buddy," I said.

I heard a melodramatic gasp from behind me and saw Jade running toward us in her high heels. "Max! Get out of the pool this minute!" she shouted.

He spit water straight in the air. "Why?"

"For one thing, you're not even wearing a bathing suit. For another, this is *not* a pool party. Where are your manners?"

"Come closer, Mom. I want to tell you something."

"Why? So you can pull me in? I wasn't born yesterday, young man. And I am *not* getting this outfit wet. It's couture." She adjusted the fabric over her designer buns.

Someone tapped me on the shoulder and I turned to see Joey.

"We need to talk," she said, trying edging me away from Jade and Max so that no one could hear us.

I didn't budge. "There's nothing to talk about."

Joey rolled her eyes. "You're pissed. Let's get it out in the open."

I clenched my teeth. "I am *not* pissed."

I started to walk away hoping to end the conversation, but Joey called out after me, "So it didn't bother you that I arrived with Kenny?"

I stopped and turned around, taking a step closer to my sister so no one could hear. "That depends. Are you fucking him?"

"Why? Are you in love with him?"

"No," I lied.

"So then what difference does it make?"

"None," I said. "It makes no difference."

"Fine," Joey said. "Then I'm fucking him."

"Good for you," I said, and tried to believe it. But the next thing I knew my hands were pushing Joey backwards into the pool. Stunned, she grabbed onto the only thing she could, which just happened to be Jade's hand, and as they went airborne toward the water, their four legs kicking at the air, I realized these two had something in common. Neither of them wore underpants.

Chapter 37

Joey's confession put me in a funk that wouldn't lift. And on Monday morning, following through on a promise I had made to myself as I drove home from the party, I called the principal in Queens who was holding a placement for me and told him to give it to someone else. It no longer mattered whether I was offered the position in Las Vegas. With or without a job, I was leaving New York.

After that, I called my old friend Holli Williamson, who had moved to North Carolina with her husband five years ago, thinking it would save their marriage to live someplace with less financial strain. Turned out their marital problems went beyond fighting over the price per pound for boneless chicken, and just a few months after they'd settled into their new home he left her for a twenty-four-year-old hair stylist and hadn't stopped spending since. Holli, meanwhile, resumed her teaching career and had been trying to convince me to move down there.

I filled Holli in on the job situation, leaving out the part about Joey and Kenny, and she was quick to repeat the offer she'd made in the past.

"I'll put you up for as long as you need, cookie. And if you want to work as a sub in my school until you find something full-time, you're as good as in. They're taking anyone with a pulse. I bring someone as cute and smart as you to the office and they'll name a building after me."

I heard a call-waiting click but I didn't take it. Joey had been trying to reach me since the party, but I was making myself unavailable. According to her messages, she had something important she wanted to tell Clare and me, and was hoping she could get us all together.

After finishing my call with Holli, I considered taking the phone off the hook so I wouldn't have to deal with more messages from my relentless younger sister. No doubt she'd keep at it until she got what she wanted, or died trying.

One summer, when we were both home from college, Joey got it into her head that she wanted to get high with me. I resisted because I had smoked pot a few times to disastrous results. But she wouldn't take no for an answer.

"I can't handle it, Joey," I had insisted. "I get paranoid."

"You won't get paranoid with this stuff," she promised. "It's giggle pot. I swear. Every time I smoke this I laugh my ass off. You'll love it."

Still, I said no. But she kept at it, day after day, week after week. The two of us were home a lot that summer, and pretty bored. Clare had already graduated and taken an apartment in the city. She worked in sales for a glossy women's magazine and was making decent enough money to spend her weekends in the Hamptons. I was working as a camp counselor and was home every day by four thirty. Joey and her band—an early incarnation of Phantom Pain that went by the name Meringue—were working only sporadically. One night, when our parents were out, I was particularly vulnerable. My date had stood me up and I couldn't think of a thing to do.

"You'll love this," Joey said. "I swear. For once, trust me."

"No."

"Why not?"

"I'll hate it."

"You won't."

"I will."

"It's giggle pot. What do you have against giggling?"

After about an hour of that, she finally wore me down, convincing me there was no possible way I'd get paranoid from this pot. Joey lit the joint, and we lay side by side on lounges in the backyard, passing it back and forth. By the time she snuffed out the burning paper of the spent roach, I realized that I'd been lost in the stars for some time, and it made me nervous. Who was I? Where was I? *You're right here on this lounge on Earth,* I reminded myself, as I balled and unballed my fists, testing for tingles.

"Shit," I said, sitting up and swinging my legs over the side of the lounge. I rested my head in my hands, praying to come down fast and trying to get my bearings.

"What's the matter?" Joey asked.

"I'm so stoned."

"Stoned is good."

"Not this stoned. We have to get out of here."

"Why?"

"Because Mom and Dad will be home soon and they'll know it. I can't act straight. I just can't." The very thought of it made me panic.

She tsked and pulled open a bag of Doritos. "You'll be fine. Mom and Dad know shit." She stuck her hand in and grabbed a few.

"They'll know!" I stood, my fear escalating.

"Would you chill, for fuck's sake?" She was chewing her chips and I thought she looked so utterly absurd that a child would be able to tell she was high.

"Let's go someplace," I said.

"I'm too stoned to drive. Have some Doritos." She shook the bag at me. "They're *awesome.*"

I grabbed one and chewed it, the crunch reverberating through my skull. How did people not lose their minds from the noise of chewing? I wondered if some people in mental institutions had been driven there by crackly foods messing with their brains. I swallowed and pushed the salty taste around my mouth with my tongue. I licked my lips and grimaced.

"What's the matter?" she said.

"My tongue is too big."

Joey laughed.

"That sounded really stoned, didn't it? See? I can't hide it. I need to get out before Mom and Dad come home. I can't face them. Let's go for a walk." The need to leave felt as urgent as life and death.

"Did you hear something?" she said.

"Are you trying to make me more nervous?"

"*Shh,*" she said, and rose from her lounge chair. "I thought I heard something." She walked along the perimeter of the yard as I watched in a panic. Was someone out there? It was a black night and I couldn't see a thing.

"Let's go inside," she said.

"No! Mom and Dad will be back *any minute.* I need to *leave.*"

"I can't," she said.

"Why not?"

"Someone might be out there."

"Who?"

"I don't know," Joey said. "It's too dark. But I heard something."

"We'll take a flashlight," I said.

"What if they're hiding in the bushes?"

"Why would they be hiding in the bushes?"

"So we don't see them."

"You're being ridiculous!" I said, pulling on her arm. "Let's go."

"I'm not going *anywhere*."

"Now who's being paranoid?"

We went on and on like that, our respective fears escalating the fight. I was too nervous to stay. Joey was too nervous to go. We didn't stop shouting until we heard a noise from outside, which I knew was my parents' car, but Joey assumed was someone who wanted to kill us.

"Where are you going?" she said.

"To bed! I can't face them like this."

Joey ran up after me and joined me in my room, as she was too scared to stay alone. And so it happened that Bernadette and Harold Bloomrosen came home one summer evening at nine o'clock to find their two college-age daughters asleep in bed.

The next morning, when I rolled over to see Joey still huddled next to me, black mascara smudged down her cheeks, I had two words for her.

"Giggle pot?"

Of course, from there it became shorthand for any of her claims I didn't believe.

The phone rang again, fraying my nerves. I assumed it was Joey, but when the answering machine picked up, I recognized Kenny's voice. He was calling from his apartment in Los Angeles. He had gone home to tie up some loose ends, and had just heard from Linda Klein, his parents' realtor. The engineer hired by the Goodwins could only come this afternoon, and Kenny wanted to know if I could go over there and let him in. He'd be there any minute.

I picked up the phone.

"Okay," I said.

"Okay?"

"I'll go over there and let him in."

Kenny paused, trying, I assume, to assess the clipped tone of my voice. "You all right?" he asked.

"Perfect," I said, and got off the phone as fast I could. I grabbed my sketch pad and went to the Waxmans' house to await the engineer. I sat down at the kitchen table and opened the pad, doodling abstractly as I thought about what to draw. When the doorbell rang I rushed to it, expecting some nerdy-looking guy with a clipboard, but it was Clare and Joey.

"What are you doing here?" I asked.

"Good to see you too," Joey said.

I rolled my eyes. "What do you *want*?"

"Did you get my messages? I have some news to share."

"It's not a good time. I'm waiting for the Goodwins' engineer."

"Please. This is important."

"Is it about you and Kenny?"

"No, it's about me."

I paused, still blocking the doorway, not quite understanding why I was so furiously opposed to hearing what it was Joey had to say. Her expression was earnest, and that angered me even more. I *wanted* to be mad at her, to have a goddamned good reason to shout and slam the door in her face. Finally, I just stepped aside.

"How did you know I would be here?" I said as she walked past me into the living room.

Joey lowered herself into the gold-toned wing chair facing the sofa. "I'll get into that," she said.

Clare sat on the couch and patted the spot next to her. We were to be Joey's audience. I remained standing, my arms folded.

"You're not going to sit?" Joey said.

I shook my head.

"Suit yourself," she said. "I wanted to explain why I was so cagey at the party when Teddy made his announcement."

I guessed this was going to take a while and compromised by resting my butt on the arm of the sofa.

Joey leaned forward and laced her fingers. I got the sense that she was launching into a rehearsed speech. Her curls looked especially shiny, and I resented the hell out of it. I imagined her shopping for a new styling product, which struck me as particularly competitive, as if spectacular talent, rock star status, and having Kenny wasn't enough. I felt lank and dull. Outshined. I stared down at my feet and listened.

"You know that Tyrone's death was like a tidal force in my life," Joey began. "It changed everything. It didn't just send me to rehab, but made me examine the big issues. And I mean *big*." She paused here as if to make sure we were as rapt as she needed us to be, but I didn't look up.

"Go on," Clare said.

Joey took a breath and continued. "Rehab didn't just get me sober, it helped me focus on something I'd been trying to ignore for so long: God."

"God?" Clare said.

"I always knew there was a higher power at work," Joey said, "but it's easy to forget when your ego is riding a coke buzz or your id is swimming in malt liquor."

Clare made a gagging noise and I glanced up. "You drank *malt liquor*?" she said.

Joey shrugged. "I drank whatever anyone passed to me, so who knows. Point is, it's amazing that I was able to stray so far because I can feel God everywhere. Especially when I sing. Rehab helped me reconnect with that. Not that it gave me any real answers. In fact, it was more helpful in providing questions—

lots of questions. So I started meeting with Rabbi Orn-
stein once a week." She was referring to the clergyman who
had led the congregation we'd attended most of our lives. "It
was . . . illuminating. The more we talked, the more I felt like
I wanted a holier life, but didn't know quite what that meant.
I only knew that I wanted to find a way to use my talents to
help people."

"I understand," Clare said.

"And then we found poor Lydia in that drum. It shook me
in about a million ways, stirring a lot of the same feelings
I had when Tyrone died, but there was more. I won't bore
you with the whole story, but the crux is that I thought a lot
about Sam and the path he chose, and it made me realize I
was being pulled in the opposite direction—toward a life of
service and goodness. I mean, why not, right? Why not help
fill people's hearts with love if you can?"

She waited for a reaction from us—from me, really, as I
hadn't said a word—but I just looked up at her and then at my
shoes again, eager for her to get to the point. I didn't know exactly where she was going with this, but as the minutes ticked
by without the engineer showing up, the bad feeling in my
stomach grew.

"So the rabbi put me in touch with Jacob, *Cantor* Jacob.
He's a wonderful man and we've become close friends. He's
also become my teacher."

Clare smacked my knee to get my attention. "I bet that's the
guy with the red beard."

Joey looked confused. "How did you know he has a red
beard?"

"We'll tell you later," Clare said. "Finish what you were
saying."

"Okay," Joey said, "so here's my big announcement: I'm
going to sing in temple. I'm studying to be a cantor."

"A cantor?" Clare said.

Joey beamed. Clare jumped from her seat and hugged our little sister. "I'm so proud of you!" she said. "In a million years . . ." She let the thought trail off as the two of them waited for a reaction from me. This was the big moment where I was supposed to let go of my anger and rush into my sister's arms. It was Joey's happy ending. She had beat her demons and was embracing God for real. But there was something about the scene that was all wrong to me. I rose from my perch and walked to the front door, as my sisters stared. I opened it and looked up and down the street.

"Where is he?" I asked.

"Where's who?" Clare asked.

"The engineer." I looked at Joey. "He's not coming, is he?"

Joey took a step toward me. "No."

I put my hand up to stop her. "You got Kenny to lie to me?"

"You wouldn't take my calls, so I asked him to intercede. It was the only way I could get you to hear my news. I didn't think you would mind once you heard my announcement."

Just when I thought the betrayal had reached an impossible peak, Mr. Honesty had agreed to trick me. I imagined Joey phoning Kenny for sympathy when she couldn't get me to answer her calls. He may have been angry enough with me to suggest the deception. Or perhaps Joey had been able to talk him into it. Either way, by the time they got off the phone they were probably laughing about how easy it would be to deceive me by appealing to my sense of responsibility.

"I really want you to be proud of me, Bev," Joey said. "Maybe I don't deserve it. Maybe I spent so many years screwing up that it'll take another few years to earn back your respect. But if you're just a little bit proud of me, it would mean so much."

I looked at Clare, whose eyes beseeched me to rise above my hurt, be the bigger person, understand that our baby sister had finally emerged from her self-destruction and it was a glorious and beautiful moment.

Joey stared at me, her eyes the same clear shade of blue they'd been as a child. The stupid haze of drugs was gone, as was the cynicism. All I saw there was my innocent little sister wanting my approval. She ran her fingers through her shiny curls, which bounced right back into shape.

"You're proud of her, aren't you?" Clare said.

They waited for a response, but I had nothing to say. I opened the door to leave.

"She doesn't want to admit it," I heard Clare say to Joey, "but Bev loves you."

They both looked at me as if certain I would soften, but I shook my head and stepped outside, letting the door shut behind me.

Chapter 38

On Friday, I sat across from Clare at a local diner. I had asked her to lunch because I wanted to tell her—face-to-face—that I was leaving New York.

She put her cell phone on the table and opened the diner's gigantic menu. I was pacing myself, waiting for the right moment to spring the news on her. She picked up her phone again and looked at it.

"Are you expecting a call?" I asked.

"Kind of."

"How cryptic," I said. Why couldn't she just tell me who she was waiting to hear from? I opened my menu to scan the massive array of selections.

Clare stuck her fork into the coleslaw the waitress had left on the table and shoveled some onto her bread plate. "Look, don't be mad, but . . . I asked Joey to join us."

I closed my menu. "Clare, you *know* I don't want to talk to her."

"Calm down. She wasn't home. I left a message."

"If you're thinking about orchestrating a reconciliation, forget it."

"I couldn't even if I wanted to. She's been missing since she told us her news."

I opened my menu again and flipped the pages. "I wonder if the chicken salad wrap is any good."

"Did you hear what I said?"

"Heard. Don't care."

"Four whole days. I left like six messages."

"Boo-hoo."

"Bev . . ."

"If she was dead the police would have sent a squad car to one of our houses by now. Relax."

"You aren't worried?"

"The part of me that worried about Joey simply doesn't exist anymore. Can we move on? Finish what you were saying about Marc. You were going to tell me what he said when you asked about the woman in the hotel room."

After the party, Clare had decided that the best way to help Dylan was to first come clean with Marc and tell him everything. Then they approached Dylan together to explain that sometimes grown-ups make mistakes, and Mommy had made a big one. But she would never kiss another man but Daddy again. And while Dylan seemed to be edging toward acceptance, Marc was another story.

Clare put her menu down and stared at me, as if she was trying to decide whether to push the whole Joey issue or just go ahead and answer my question. She sighed, resigned. "He told me it must have been a wrong number."

"Do you believe him?"

"What choice do I have? If I want to keep this marriage on track, I *have* to believe him."

I got that, I really did. Sometimes trust is nothing more than a leap of faith. A man in dusty coveralls passed our table, staring so hard at Clare that he nearly walked into a wall. She didn't seem to notice.

"And what about him? Did he forgive *you*?"

"He said he's trying but . . . I don't know if we're going to recover from this, Bev." She put her head down and tears fell.

I reached out and took her hand. "Of course you will."

"He left for Chicago on Wednesday—another sales meeting. Told me he wouldn't call me while he was away. Said he needed this time to think."

"What does that mean?"

"I don't know. He's supposed to come home tonight. I hope he does."

"You don't think he'd leave you, do you? Marc loves you. And it was just a kiss."

"I really love him," she said. "I'm such an idiot."

"Stop."

"He doesn't know if he can ever trust me again. And it's all my fault."

The waitress came over to take our orders and relieve us of the tome-sized menus. A bus boy slapped a basket of bread onto the table. I pushed the coleslaw closer to Clare and moved the bread closer to me. I'd miss these New York diners when I was gone. There was a lot I'd miss.

After lunch, I agreed to go with Clare to some new shoe store she'd heard about. I still hadn't told her my news. It was just too hard to dump on her when she was feeling so miserable and needy. Shopping, I thought, would be just the thing to pick her up.

The store looked a little too upscale for my budget, so I headed to the back, where sandals were on sale. The ones I had on were pretty beat-up and I thought it would be good to have a brand-new pair for my brand-new home, which could still wind up being in one of two states, North Carolina or Nevada. I found a strappy black shoe that I thought was kind of cute, and asked the saleswoman to bring it out in my size. Meanwhile, Clare examined a two-toned pump with an oddly shaped heel.

"What do you think?" I asked Clare, after I slipped on the shoes and walked to a mirror.

"I think we should take a drive to Joey's house to make sure everything is okay."

"I mean what do you think of these sandals?"

"They look like something from the back of your closet." Clare picked up a red open-toed pump and showed it to me. "This would look *hot* with that shirt," she said.

I was wearing a ruby-colored V-neck top that matched the shiny snakeskin shoe Clare held, and I knew she was probably right. I took it from her and examined it.

"I've never owned red shoes," I said.

"Then it's time."

I turned it over and looked at the price. *"Ack!"* I put it down on the nearest shelf but Clare snatched it right up.

"My treat," she said, waving it at the saleswoman.

I sighed. "Are you trying to bribe me?"

"It's a going-away gift," she insisted.

That stopped me cold. "You know I'm leaving?" I said.

"Of course."

"How?"

"The way you reacted to Joey. I don't think you would have done that if you were staying. It's almost as if . . . as if you *want* to be furious so you'll feel better about leaving. Part of you just doesn't want to walk out on the people you love."

I tsked, dismissing her observation. "That makes no sense. Wouldn't I be mad at you too?"

"You probably would be if I wasn't such a wreck. Your heart is too soft to pick a fight with me now."

I had to admit that she might have had a point. I remembered how furious I was with my parents right before I left for college. In particular, I recalled an utterly pointless fight over bath mats.

Clare's cell phone rang and she pulled it from her purse to answer it, but the call dropped. "I don't know this number," she said, looking at the caller-ID window. She called back to see who it was, and when the person on the other end answered, Clare looked alarmed.

"Someone called me from this number," she said into the phone. "I see. Okay, thank you."

"Who was it?" I asked.

"North Shore University Hospital, but the number sent me to the main switchboard, and they couldn't tell me who called. Do you think it could have been someone phoning about Joey?"

I swallowed against a lump as a familiar fear rose up. "If it was, they'll call back."

Sure enough, Clare's purse starting singing again as she paid for the shoes. I peered over her shoulder as she opened the phone, but it was a different number, and I recognized it. It was Alicia Goodwin's cell phone.

Clare had a brief and cryptic conversation, but her eyes told the story. Alicia had conveyed some kind of terrible news. Clare looked stricken.

"What is it?" I said.

"Alicia and Teddy just drove by the Waxmans' and there was a police car parked out front."

"In front of the Waxmans'?"

"No." Clare's hand went to her heart. "In front of ours."

When we screeched to a halt by the curb, Clare and I saw a squad car parked in front of my house . . . *our* house, the house someone looking for Joey's next of kin would wind up at. A uniformed police officer stood chatting with Detective Miller. We rushed over to them, and the officer opened his mouth to speak, but Miller held up his hand to silence him.

"It's Joey," he said to us, his face grim.

"No!" Clare said.

Clare screamed and I reached out for her, but I was the one who was falling.

Chapter 39

Detective Miller sped Clare and me straight to the hospital. Along the way, he explained that Joey was still alive, but that it didn't look good. Apparently she had smoked a large amount of crack cocaine, causing her blood pressure to skyrocket. This created such a buildup in her brain that a blood vessel burst. She was going in for emergency neurosurgery and the doctors had said to prepare the family for the worst.

I don't remember much about the trip after that, except that I kept apologizing to Miller and Clare.

My sister clenched her teeth. "Stop saying you're sorry."

"But it's my fault."

"It's not."

"She was clean. Everything was going so well. God, I may have killed her."

"She's not dead!" Clare cried. "Stop saying that."

When we reached the hospital, Miller escorted us upstairs, but we didn't get to see Joey. She was still in surgery, and we were shown to a waiting room and told a doctor would come out soon to talk to us.

The wait felt interminable. Clare and I got into a stupid fight over calling our parents. I wanted to wait until we had more news. She wanted to call them right away so they could make arrangements to come home.

"Do whatever you want," I finally snapped, and got up to pace the room, picking up magazines and slapping them down again, while Clare sniffled softly into her cell phone. My armpits were wet from nervous sweat and I was pretty sure I stunk.

Finally, a doctor in surgical scrubs came into the room, his mask resting below his chin. He was just a bit younger than my father, and had that stern look I had learned to associate with neurologists, the most somber of specialists. A diagonal line of blood marked his shoulder. Joey's blood. I tried to read his expression before he spoke, but he was inscrutable.

"Your sister is still in surgery," the doctor began.

"Will she make it?" Clare asked.

He took a breath, as if he had to regroup and start from the beginning. "It's not uncommon for a recovering addict to miscalculate and overdose. They tend to take the same quantity they were using when they quit, but their bodies no longer have a tolerance for the drug. In Joey's case, the cocaine increased her blood pressure so significantly it caused an intracranial hemorrhage. We're evacuating that now." He paused and pursed his lips. "There's no way to predict the outcome. We just have to wait and hope there's no further bleeding or swelling."

"If she lives . . . ," I began, but couldn't finish the sentence. I couldn't bring myself to ask if Joey's brain would be permanently damaged.

"I don't want to give you false hope," the surgeon said, anticipating my question. "The swelling caused by the hemorrhage is considerable. But let's focus on first things first. If she pulls through the next twenty-four hours, her chances of survival increase."

I turned to Clare. "She might not even live a day!"

The doctor told us they were doing everything they could for her, and we thanked him. As he reached the door, he stopped and turned back to us. "I know your father," he said. "A good man."

I nodded, but turned to ashes inside thinking about my parents. They didn't deserve to lose a daughter like this.

When I was in my twenties and announced my engagement to Jonathan, my family responded with guarded enthusiasm. I guess they had good reasons to doubt the prospects for our marriage, but I was crestfallen. Only Joey seemed genuinely pleased for me. Then, when she offered to throw me a bridal shower in her new Tribeca loft, I was swept away with gratitude. I wanted so badly to believe it would all work out that I managed to overlook the fact that her drug habit had escalated to the point where she was often barely functional. I gave her a guest list, and she took over from there, sending out the invitations, choosing a theme, hiring a caterer, ordering decorations, etc., and paying for it all with the royalties she was still reaping from "Tiger Attack." At one point Clare even complained to me that she wanted to help but that Joey insisted on doing everything herself.

When the big day finally came, I took a subway downtown to Joey's building, a warehouse that had been converted to massive apartments for a unique class of affluent New Yorkers—bohemians with cash. I had arrived fashionably late, figuring I would give my guests time to get there before me. Even though it wasn't a surprise party, I figured it would feel more like a shower if I arrived last. But when I got off the elevator on Joey's floor, my heart sank. There, standing in the hallway outside apartment 4E, was a group of about twenty women, including my grandmother, my mom, my sister, assorted female relatives of varying ages, and several of my closest friends, not to mention Jonathan's stern mother, two sisters, and his elderly Aunt Annabel with her oxygen tank and aluminum walker.

"I'm sure she'll be here any minute," Clare said when she saw my face, but it was too late. I had already burst into tears.

We stood in the hall for another half an hour before we began discussing alternatives. Finally it was decided to move the whole party to Jonathan's mother's apartment uptown, but only about half the guests agreed to make the trip. The others left me with their gifts and went on their way.

Joey later gave an excuse about getting tied up at a business meeting and said we should have just asked the super to let us in, as if the screwup wasn't her fault but ours. I knew it was the drugs, of course. We all did. And I was utterly furious. Looking back now, though, the most vivid part of the memory was Joey's earnestness about the planning, and how hard she was working to make me happy. I'm not taking her off the hook for the decision she made—then or now—but I understand that addiction is an insatiable beast. Rehab may have taught her to cage it, but it never goes away. A recovering addict has to master that part of herself that's always fingering the key, waiting for an excuse to open the gate. Stupid of me to assume Joey had managed that. Stupider, still, to be the catalyst.

Joey survived the surgery, but emerged in a coma. No one could tell us when she might wake up, if ever.

Lying in that bed, machines monitoring her vital signs, Joey looked like a shell, like someone who merely bore some physical resemblance to my little sister. The large white bandage on her head made her look small and waiflike. But the skin around her eyes was dark and papery, and her cheeks were hollower than I'd ever seen them. Clare collapsed into me.

"They have a tube in her throat!" she said.

I patted her back. "To help her breathe."

"But her voice! When my friend Sondra's mother had surgery on her shoulder, the breathing tube damaged her vocal chords. You have to tell them to take it out!"

Clare was hysterical and I didn't think it was the right time to mention that Joey's singing voice was the last thing we needed to worry about right now. So I just told her to go home and be with her family, and promised I'd sit vigil all night.

"I'll call if there's any change," I said.

"Will you talk to her? Will you try to get her to wake up?"

"Of course."

After Clare left, I scraped the side chair over to Joey's bed. I couldn't hold her hand because there was a monitor on her fingertip, so I stroked her cheek and spoke to her.

"Joey? It's Bev. I'm here. You have to wake up." I watched carefully, but there was no movement. I gently squeezed her arm. She didn't respond. I leaned in and started to whisper.

"You have to wake up so I can tell you I'm sorry."

I heard voices and looked up to see a doctor and nurse come into the room. They introduced themselves and explained that they would be checking on Joey throughout the night. They consulted her chart and the monitors. The doctor took a penlight from his pocket to check Joey's pupils.

"She'd been clean a whole year," I said, desperate for them to know she wasn't some drug addict living on the street. "She's studying to be a cantor."

The doctor nodded, and I wondered if he understood I was begging him to save her.

On my request, the nurse turned off the lights on her way

out. Sitting there in the dark, listening to the ventilator and watching Joey's chest rise and fall, I felt crushed with loneliness. I touched her shoulder.

"Joey?"

I closed my eyes and tried to picture her awake, propped up on pillows. I imaged her clear blue eyes, her smirk, the tiny vertical scar under her left eye that looked like a wrinkle when she smiled.

I opened my eyes again and touched the tape around her mouth that held the breathing tube in place, wondering if her subconscious could sense pain.

"I'm supposed to keep talking," I said, "but I feel like an idiot when you don't respond. Can you move your pinky or something?"

I poked at her small finger.

"I don't know what to say. 'I'm sorry' sounds so anemic when you're watching your sister . . ." I stopped myself. Did I really think she was going to die? "You're going to be fine," I said, knowing it was important to sound positive. "You're going to wake up and be a cantor and have a great life. It'll be just like before. But you have to wake up and open your eyes. You're the only one who can do it." I rose and went to the other side of the bed so I could hold her hand. There was no chair on that side so I knelt.

"I know you don't want to die, Joey," I whispered. "That's why you called Miller before you passed out. But you're going to have to fight for it. And who does that better than you?"

I suddenly felt so tired. I went back to the chair and reclined, staring at the acoustic tiles in the ceiling as I listened to the hypnotic rhythm of the ventilator and heart monitor.

"I know you wanted to hear me say I was proud of you. And I was. Of course I was. I should have said I love you. I was being mean and stupid. I just . . . you know, I was angry about Kenny." I stopped and pulled a tissue from the box by the side of her bed and blew my nose.

"But that's over. If you wake up and want to spend the rest of your life with Kenny, it's fine with me. Who cares? I mean, maybe I'll still be a brat about it, but so what. We only just got you back. Don't leave us now . . . *please.*"

I went on and on like that all night, saying anything that popped into my head. I talked about what it was like when she was born and Mom and Dad brought her home from the hospital. I didn't remember, of course, but my parents had told stories of how Clare and I fought over her. And then, of course, how we fought with each other just to get our mother's attention when she was busy with the baby. I told her how much she annoyed me with her singing when I was trying to do my homework. I asked her if she remembered how she made me promise not to tell our parents that the janitor from Dad's office exposed himself to her. I confessed that I broke my promise on that, because I was so worried. I told her I was the one who broke her sparkly green belt that summer. I told her I never liked her friend Fran who always thought everything was so funny, and that Phil Janks, who she had such a terrible crush on in seventh grade, had told me he thought she was cute. I shouldn't have kept that from her. It was jealous and petty. I told her that I used to brag and brag to my friends about how talented she was, and how I was so proud of her that I cried the first time I heard her song on the radio. I told her how terrifying it was when her drug habit got so bad she cut herself off from the family. I told her we had family meetings about her, and that Mom was so upset she thought the worry would kill her.

"I was so mad at you for hurting her like that. I thought you were so selfish. I guess . . . I don't know. We all took it so personally, as if we thought you were *trying* to hurt us."

By the morning I was so talked out I had no voice left. After the sun came up, more hospital staff members had paraded in and out of the room, doing the same tests over and over. Elena, one of the night nurses, brought me a cup of coffee before her shift ended. She told me to go home and get some sleep, but I wasn't ready to leave.

A short time later a team of people came in to take Joey for another CT scan. I stayed behind, too exhausted to move, too confused to figure out what to do next. When I heard my parents come in, their travel clothes creased from the flight, I was groggy and nearly asleep. They hugged me and said I should go home and get some rest. I didn't want to leave, but my mother insisted.

"Take a nice bubble bath and get some sleep," she said.

"I must smell like a sewer," I said. "I'm sorry."

She stroked my hair. "Don't apologize."

I opened my mouth to tell that I had a lot to apologize for, but couldn't find the words. So I blew my nose one last time and went home.

On my way inside I grabbed the mail. Mixed in with the usual stack of bills, catalogs, and junk mail was a single white envelope bearing a yellow forwarding sticker. It was addressed to me, of course. I stared, blinking, at the Las Vegas, Nevada, return address, waiting for the significance of the letter to have some kind of emotional impact on me. At last, I took it upstairs, dropped it into a dresser drawer unopened, and got into bed.

I thought exhaustion would overtake me quickly, but the thought of being woken by a terrible phone call from the hospital was giving me a most unwelcome adrenaline rush. Finally, after tossing and flailing about the bed for over an hour, I took the phone off the hook and drifted into a fitful sleep. One disturbing dream after another plagued my rest, locking me in a sleep cycle so close to the surface of consciousness that a lucid thread followed me from room to troubled room. At last, two of my dream selves discussed the situation right in my bedroom. The me that was asleep in bed said it was guilt that caused the nightmare anxiety, while the other, who was hovering by my bedside, insisted it was death itself. Sleeping Bev said that sounded too much like the Hollywood version of death, where the hooded Grim Reaper appears in the person's bedroom, holding a scythe. Then, in a horrifying moment, the sleeping me realized that the other presence in the room *was* the Grim Reaper. I understood too, that if I looked deep into the blackness of the empty hood, the face of the person being called would appear. I covered my eyes, believing that if I didn't see Joey's face she wouldn't be dead.

"Bev! Bev!" cried the angel of death, trying to get me to look. The presence was so real and terrifying that I awoke with a start to realize someone was really in my room. It was Clare.

"I tried calling," she said, her hand gripping my shoulder.

I sat up, shaking off the dream to understand what was really going on. Clare was in my bedroom, her face pink and blotchy from crying. I looked at the clock. I'd been asleep for six hours—enough time for anything to have happened. I looked back at my sister, knowing she wasn't the Grim Reaper, but may as well have been. With a somber face, she delivered the grave and startling news.

Chapter 40

The funeral service was held at the grave site. It was a bright summer morning, and though the sun hadn't yet had a chance to heat the atmosphere, I was starting to perspire in my dark blazer. My narrow heels dug into the soft earth, and I lifted one foot and then the other, hyperconscious of every mortal sensation. When the rabbi finished his eulogy and offered the mourners the chance to bid their final respects by emptying a shovelful of dirt into the grave, there was a moment of hesitation where no one came forward.

I squeezed my mother's hand and wondered if she was thinking about the last funeral we had been to together. Hard to believe it was only a year since Joey's former band member had died. Our whole family had gone to the memorial service, and as we sat watching Tyrone's poor relatives collapse in grief, all I could think was, *This could be us.*

We only knew Tyrone through Joey, but his family and the minister made it their business to let everyone learn about the boy he had been before his downward spiral. One by one, the mourners got up to tell stories about the sweet, funny, talented little boy they so adored. By the time the service had ended, every one of us had fallen in love with him and were grieving with as much agony as his family.

But where were my stories about Joey? My mother squeezed my hand back, and I wondered if the physical gesture could yield some sweet memories. But only the bitterest droplets emerged. It seemed like Joey and I had spent our whole lives in stupid conflicts. I remembered our teenage fights, and how furious I was when she pounded at the bathroom door while I showered, yelling that I was taking too long. I shrieked at her and she shrieked back. I remembered being furious with her for borrowing my things without asking. Once, when we were young, she took my favorite chapter book outside to read. It was a wonderful fantasy about a boy who turns into a bird and saves a kingdom. Joey was only seven, and it was too advanced for her. So she got quickly bored and left it there on the patio. It rained that night and my book was ruined.

When I discovered it, I cried with all the melodrama I could muster, wailing that Joey was never allowed in my room again. Of course, she didn't listen, and that night when I went upstairs I found all of Joey's favorite picture books laid out on my bed as an offering. I picked up a Dr. Seuss book and opened the cover. Inside was the familiar personalized bookplate that was in all of her books. The imprint said, "This book is the property of Joanna," but she had crossed out her name in blue crayon and written "Beverly." I picked up the next book and it said the same thing. So did the next and the next. She had done it to every single book, even *Where the Wild Things Are*, her favorite.

It was a perfect eulogy story. I blew my nose and hoped I wouldn't be needing it any time soon. Joey, thank God, was still alive, albeit comatose. This was Sam Waxman's funeral.

As Clare explained to me that day in my bedroom, Sam had been struck and killed by an oil truck after he once again wandered onto the interstate behind his condo development. No one knew for sure whether it was the Alzheimer's disease or suicide, but since it happened the day before the police were to announce the results of his DNA test and reveal that he was, in fact, the father of the dead woman's baby, most of us assumed he had killed himself rather than face his guilt.

It took a few days for Kenny to make arrangements to have the body flown up north for the funeral. Renee was a wreck, of course, and I worried what would happen to her if, under the circumstances, Sam wasn't allowed a Jewish burial. But I learned that even if Sam had left a suicide note, Jewish law allows a religious burial if the suicide resulted from mental illness. One more thing Sam Waxman had gotten away with.

Renee took a weak step forward as Kenny assisted her toward the grave. "It's okay," she said to her son, letting him know she would do this on her own. Renee took the shovel from the rabbi and pushed some dirt onto the casket. She turned to the mourners, holding up the shovel for whoever wanted to go next.

Some murmurs and coughs rippled through the crowd, and I thought that if she gave it another moment someone would have stepped up. But the hesitance alone was enough to push poor Renee over the edge. She threw down the shovel and her eyes lit with a wildness I'd never seen in her before

"You all have no right to judge him!" she cried, pointing an accusatory finger at the crowd. "No right! *God* will judge him! Only God! Because he knows . . . he knows . . ."

Kenny stepped toward her and Renee collapsed into him, crying.

"It's okay, Mom," he said, leading her away from the gaping hole.

My father hobbled forward in his walking cast and grabbed the shovel. Following his lead, the other mourners stepped forward one by one to offer the grieving widow this final respect for her husband. At last, the rabbi said the final prayer, in Hebrew and then in English.

His final words were, "Surely goodness and mercy shall follow me all the days of my life; and I shall dwell in the house of the Lord forever." Here the rabbi paused and we joined him in the final *"Amen."*

The next day Clare and I found ourselves alone in the hospital room with Joey, as our parents were busy helping Renee get through her day of receiving visitors. The results of Joey's daily CT scans were always the same—there had been no further bleeding and the swelling in her brain was receding little by little. Still, the doctors offered no definitive answers on when, if ever, she might wake up.

Clare and I sat side by side looking at Joey, who seemed to lose more weight every day. I worried that if she kept getting thinner, there would soon be nothing but a skeleton with flesh lying in that bed.

"Too bad they can't put a hot fudge sundae in one of those things," Clare said, pointing to the bags on the IV pole.

"Should we tell her about Sam?" I asked.

"I already did, but try again."

I leaned in, resting a hand on Joey's bony shoulder. "Hey. Joey. It's Bev. Listen to me. Sam Waxman was definitely the murderer. DNA results came back and proved he was the baby's father." I paused, waiting for a response. Clare took Joey's hand and I continued. "But there won't be a trial because Sam is dead. Did you hear what I said, Joey? Sam Waxman is *dead.*"

"Oh!" Clare cried out, startling me.

"What is it?"

"I think her hand moved."

Clare opened her own hand, showing me Joey's resting upon it. We both started down at it.

"Do that again, Joey," I said. "Move your hand."

Nothing.

"It's us," Clare said. "Me and Bev."

"Bev and *I*," I corrected.

Clare tsked at me but I smiled so she'd know I was kidding.

"You hear that?" Clare said to Joey. "You can't leave me alone with her. She's such a pain in the ass."

We focused on that hand, trying hard to discern the tiniest movement, when we heard something. A moan. We looked up at Joey's face. The breathing tube was still in her throat, but her head turned from side to side as she tried to make sounds. Joey was waking up.

Chapter 41

Two weeks later found me cleaning and straightening, getting the house ready for Joey's homecoming. My parents, who were now back home to stay, had gone to the hospital to pick her up. After those first initial sounds, the doctors removed Joey's breathing tube, and she groaned in a voice so quiet and hoarse it wasn't recognizable. It sounded like she was saying words, but most of her mutterings were indecipherable. The first word we really understood was *"Thirsty,"* and soon after that she started responding to yes or no questions, though her answers were often more automatic than truly cognitive. One such conversation went like this:

"Hi, Joey. It's Bev. Do you know where you are?"
"Yes."
"Where are you?"
"Rowaauh."
"I'm here too," Clare said. "Do you know who I am?"
"No."
"I'm Clare. "You're in the hospital, Joey. Do you know what happened?"
"Yes."
"Can you tell us?"

"There's a white dish in the sink."

"There's nothing wrong with her," I said to Clare, "she's just turned into Dad."

Then, one day when my mother and I were at her bedside, Mom asked if she wanted a sip of water. Joey said, "Yes," and then sucked from a straw Mom put to her lips. When she finished, her expression was confused. She touched the bandage on her head as if she were just discovering it. "Shit," she said, looking at us, "was I in a motorcycle accident?"

My mother gasped and I was so overjoyed I couldn't help laughing. "No," I said, "you OD'd and needed brain surgery."

"You don't have to sound so damned *happy* about it."

And that was it. From there, the language came tumbling out, though we celebrated with reserved joy, unsure of how complete Joey's recovery would be. For her part, Clare obsessed on Joey's voice, which remained a faint whisper. And though I kept reminding her that it was the last thing we needed to worry about, I was alarmed when the occupational therapist told me that after a week of working with Joey there had been no improvement, and that she could eventually need surgery on her vocal chords. She might, it seemed, never regain her old voice.

I tied two dozen yellow and white helium balloons to the lamppost out front and then came back inside to hang the Welcome Back Joey banner I had made with poster paints on a roll of craft paper. I stood back to admire my work and thought the place looked festive enough for a party, though we hadn't invited anyone except Kenny and Renee, as we didn't want Joey to be overwhelmed. However, Detective Miller had called that morning to ask if he could come over with some sort of big surprise he had promised Joey. Of course, I told him he was welcome. And though I was overjoyed that I got my baby sister back, a familiar jealousy began to roil inside.

Besides a second chance at life, Joey would get to choose from two wonderful men vying for her attention, Kenny and Miller.

Then, as if awakening from my own coma, I remembered the letter from Las Vegas sitting unopened in my dresser drawer. I took the steps two at a time and hurried into my bedroom. The sealed envelope was right where I had left it. I took it out, coaching myself that I'd be okay no matter what it said. There was, after all, a substitute teacher position in North Carolina that I could have just for showing up. Still, I wanted this so badly. I was ready for my very own classroom, for a sea of eager faces putting their trust in me, for the desert air, for ubiquitous swimming pools, for living in a city filled with people who believed in the fresh start as much as I did.

I carefully opened the envelope and unfolded the contents. "Dear Ms. Bloomrosen," began the cover letter, "It is my pleasure . . ."

Ecstatic, I scanned the letter quickly for the particulars. It outlined the starting salary, the benefits, school holidays. I was so excited I almost overlooked one critical fact at the bottom of the letter: the deadline for getting the signed contract to them was tomorrow.

I didn't spend more than ten minutes looking over the document that would seal my fate. I signed in ink and folded it into the enclosed envelope. Then I rushed out the door to our local FedEx office.

Clare, Marc, Dylan, Sophie, Kenny, and Renee were there when Mom and Dad arrived home with Joey. She was still bone thin, but was walking on her own now and the light was back in her eyes. She smiled as she crossed the threshold to the house, enjoying the attention.

"I should OD more often," Joey said in her new whispery voice.

"Don't joke about a thing like that," our mother said. "It's not funny."

"It's a *little* funny," Kenny said. "She just needs to work on her delivery."

Inside, Joey asked the heavily sedated, nearly catatonic Renee Waxman how she was doing.

"My husband is dead," she said.

"I know," Joey answered, giving her a hug. "I'm so sorry."

Renee's eyes stared into the distance, unfocused. "I made such a terrible mistake."

"It wasn't your fault," Joey said.

"No?"

"We all know how much you loved him."

"He was very good to me."

Kenny rolled his eyes and walked out of the room. "Anyone want a cold drink?" he called over this shoulder.

"Such a terrible way to die," Renee muttered.

"He didn't suffer," my father said.

Renee looked up as if she was surprised to see him there, surprised, in fact, that anyone had heard her.

A short while later, when we were all settled into the family room, a tray of beautifully arranged cookies (courtesy of Clare, of course) on the table before us, the doorbell rang. I ran to pull it open and saw Miller standing before me.

"Hi," he said to me and the gang assembled in the living room.

"Hi, baby," Joey whispered.

"Are you all ready for my surprise?"

"I thought it was just a surprise for Joey," I said.

"Oh, I think you'll all enjoy this," he said. "I'll be right back."

I watched as he dashed to his car at the curb and opened the passenger door. A middle-aged woman in a yellow top and tan pants got out. He walked her toward the house, and as she neared, I realized she looked familiar, though I couldn't quite place who she was.

And then, as she stood before me, I knew.

"How beautiful you've grown up," she said and smiled.

I reached out and touched her hand to make sure she was real. Her skin was dry but warm . . . and alive. And then at last I said her name.

"Lydia!"

Chapter 42

Five weeks later, as I sat on the hood of my car waiting for the moving truck to come, I held tight to my new cell phone. This time, I wasn't going to take any chances. I was moving out—getting a new place, a new number, a new area code. I'd need this phone.

I glanced down the street, past the activity at the Waxmans' house, where another moving truck was parked at the curb. Alicia Goodwin waved and caught my eye. Beyond her, inside the dark maw of the truck's interior, I could see stacked cartons, an emerald green sofa, a table turned upside down like a dead beetle—everything the Goodwins were moving in to their new home.

"How's it going?" I called.

Alicia said something to one of the moving men and then jogged over to me.

"I guess you're all packed," she said, when she reached me.

"Just waiting for the Allied truck."

"You're feeling okay about all this?"

I nodded and smiled. "It's the right decision." I used my hand as a sun visor and glanced toward what I would never stop thinking of as the Waxmans' house. "Where's Teddy?"

"Inside, bossing the men around."

I laughed. "Good for him."

"Will you be sure to say good-bye before you leave?"

"I will," I said, but jumped off the car and gave her a hug, just in case. "Anyway, I'll see you when I visit my folks."

She squeezed my hand and went back to what she was doing.

It hadn't been very long since Sam had died and we found out that Lydia wasn't the woman in the drum, but so much had changed since then.

It turned out that Lydia had been living in relative peace since she left the Waxmans' house over twenty years ago. I say "relative" peace, because she harbored a dark secret in her heart that didn't stop haunting her until she heard on the radio that Sam Waxman was dead.

It seemed that Lydia had accidentally witnessed the aftermath of Sam's deed. She was in the backyard weeding Sam's garden when she heard a terrible commotion inside. A woman screamed, a door slammed. Lydia ran in through the mudroom, stopping to grab a baseball bat for safety. There was no one in the house so she went into the garage, where she saw Sam holding the lifeless body of a young woman she had remembered meeting. It was Halina, a sweet young girl from his factory. Sam was dragging her onto a tarp, and her face was covered in blood. Lydia screamed in fright, and held up the bat, quite sure that Sam would have killed her too if she didn't defend herself. As it was, he threatened to come after her if she ever told a living soul, and she believed him. She fled immediately. And even though she went from working for a family in Connecticut to becoming a practical nurse at a hospital in Westchester—eventually marrying a radiology technician and having a family of her own—she kept her word.

"I was a coward," she said to us that day in my parents' living room, her accent softened from years of speaking English. "I'm so sorry. But I feared for my safety and my children's."

Crying, I threw my arms around her and told her it was okay. I was so happy she was alive.

Renee had become so hysterical at the sight of Lydia that my parents brought her back to her house to get some rest. Marc, not wanting the children exposed to the drama of the situation, took them out back to play. So it was just Joey, Clare, Kenny, and me with Miller and Lydia.

"What made you come forward now?" Clare asked.

"I heard on the radio that Sam has been killed, so I called the police right away. I wanted them to know, and so I told the truth at last, I saw. He killed that poor girl. I can never forget. There was so much blood. And then . . . when I came in with the bat, he dropped her to the floor like trash. I dream sometimes about that sound when she hit." She covered her ears as if she could hear it still.

"You poor thing!" Clare said.

Miller explained that when he spoke to Lydia and learned that she lived just over the bridge in Westchester, he decided that he would drive there and get her as soon as Joey was out of the woods. "I knew you would all want to see her," he said.

By that point, Clare and I had both hugged her and blubbered and hugged her some more. Only Kenny kept his distance. I think the shock of discovering Lydia was alive was more than he could bear. It was so much to take in at once—his father's death, and now this. But when I glanced over at him standing next to the chair his mother had vacated, I saw something I never expected to see. Kenny was crying.

Lydia put her arms out. She was crying too. "Oh, my dear boy," she said, and they hugged.

One by one, Lydia asked each of us about our lives. She wanted to know more about Kenny's career and Clare's children. She was happy to know that Joey planned to devote her life to helping people find their way.

"If I can't be a cantor," Joey said in her slow, breathy whisper, "I'll find something else. I know there's a path for me."

"And the drugs?" Lydia said in that direct way she always had.

Joey looked down for a moment. "Addicts are supposed to tell you that's a day-to-day choice, and I guess it is. But right now I can't imagine I'll ever take that risk again. God gave me this gift of a second chance for a reason."

Miller put his arm around her and kissed the top of her head.

"You two make a couple?" Lydia asked, and I held my breath, waiting to hear what they would say and how Kenny would react.

Miller took Joey's hand and kissed it. "Yes," he said. "We make a couple."

Lydia smiled, and Kenny's expression was inscrutable. Finally, I couldn't take it anymore. "What about you two?" I said, pointing from Joey to Kenny.

Joey laughed, which came out sounding more like a cough. "There's nothing going on between me and Kenny."

"But you said—"

Joey bit her lip. "I did, didn't I? I thought by now you would have figured out I was lying. You're supposed to be the smart one."

"You were lying?"

"What did she tell you?" Kenny asked.

"She told me you two were sleeping together."

"Why would you say that?" Kenny asked.

"I just . . . ," Joey began. "It seemed like a good idea at the time. Bev, you were in such denial about your feelings for Kenny that I thought you needed a jolt. I wanted you to realize you were in love with him."

"And you thought telling me you fucked him would do the trick?"

"Did it work?"

Yes, I thought, but couldn't say it in front of everyone. Kenny was still furious with me for sleeping with Leo and for embarrassing him in front of Letterman. How could I confess my feelings in this room and publicly humiliate myself? I looked down, focusing on the red shoes Clare had bought for me.

"You didn't answer the question," Kenny said.

"Aren't you mad at me?" I asked him.

"I was."

"You're not now?"

"Bev, I get mad all the time. It's my cross to bear. But I come to my senses eventually."

I nodded and backed away. Kenny and I might have had some unfinished business to resolve, but I wasn't going to have some teary love scene with him in front of everyone, especially since any feelings between us were now moot. I was leaving, and that was final.

A short while later, Miller announced that he needed to get Lydia home, and so, after much hugging and kissing and promises to keep in touch, they departed. That left just Clare, Joey, Kenny, and me in the living room, and I realized it was time to announce my news. I told them the offer from Las Vegas had come through and I accepted.

"You can't be serious," Joey said. "You're leaving?"

I lowered myself into a chair. "It's done. I signed the contract and mailed it off."

Clare pushed a chair forward until it was facing mine and sat. "Can't you change your mind?"

"Are you going to make us beg?" Kenny said.

"I want you to understand," I said to him, "I'm not running away from you. I'm running away from . . ." I stopped and looked at my sisters, whose eyes were so tender I couldn't finish the sentence. Was I really running away from them? They loved me so much it felt like my heart was swaddled with their warmth. "I don't know anymore," I said. "I have a headache."

Kenny stood and addressed my sisters. "Bev is under the impression you see her as a loser. That's why she's leaving. She thinks you sit around waiting for her to fail."

"What can we do to convince you that's not true?" Joey said.

"She knows you love her," Kenny said. "She's just scared."

"Scared of what?" Clare asked.

The three of them looked at me and my whole stupid career flashed in front of my eyes. My failure as an artist, a photographer's assistant, a junior graphic designer, an assistant studio manager, a freelance illustrator, etc. My failure as a wife, a daughter, a sister.

"I can't keep doing this," I said.

"Doing what?"

"Failing."

"We all fall down sometimes," Joey said. "But it's pretty great when the people who love you are there to pick you up."

"All I *do* is fall," I said.

"Is that why you're leaving?" Clare said. "Because you're so sure you're going to fail again that you're embarrassed?"

I looked at Clare, stunned. Could she possibly be right? And if she wasn't, why did I feel like I'd been kicked in the chest? I realized, then, that it wasn't *their* opinion of me I was running from, it was my own. I was so sure I would fail again that I wanted to run away so that I could do it in private. *I* was the one who thought I was a loser. Clare held a box of tissues in front of me, and I realized there were tears spilling down my cheek. I wiped my face and blew my nose, then I looked down, fixing my stare on my shiny red shoes. I wondered what magic might happen if I closed my eyes and clicked my heels three times. But I knew. I'd open them and be sitting right here with these people who loved me. I looked from Joey to Clare to Kenny and I realized that running away would make sense only if I didn't love them back with everything I had. And I was much too smart for that.

Chapter 43

At last the moving truck pulled in front of my house and a man with a clipboard stepped down from the cab.

"Bloomrosen?" he said.

I jumped off the hood of the car. "That's me."

"We're taking you to East Seventy-seventh in Manhattan?"

Kenny had pulled some strings and found me a reasonable sublet on the Upper East Side. He had moved in to a gorgeous prewar on the West Side, and it was already clear that the whole idea of taking my own apartment was more of an emotional crutch than a practical necessity, as I was spending most of my nights at his place. Still, I convinced myself that the East Side address offered an easier subway commute to my job as an art teacher in Queens, which I'd be starting any day. It only took one phone call to Principal Perez to explain that I was very sorry but I'd changed my mind, and she should tear up my contract. She wished me luck, and said that if I ever decided to move to Las Vegas, she'd probably be able to find a place for me in her school.

Later, when the last of my things were being loaded into the truck and it was time for me to lock up the house, I decided to

do one last thing and give the Goodwins the spare key I had. I
went into the kitchen and reached for the green ceramic froggy
cup I had made in second grade. I was distracted, though, and
accidentally knocked it to the floor, where it shattered.

I kneeled down to pick up the pieces, as well as the loose
spare keys that had been stored inside. To my surprise, among
them was a small key with an orange ring—the type that
would open the padlock on a storage unit. I guessed either
Sam or Renee had given it to my parents for safekeeping and
forgotten about it.

One of moving men appeared at the door. "We're ready to
leave," he said. "Do you want to follow us?"

"Go on ahead," I said. "I have a stop to make. My sisters are
at the apartment—they'll let you in."

I drove over to the storage facility, excited to find that shoebox so I could give it to Kenny as a surprise gift. He'd be so
happy to see those old cards and letters from Lydia, especially
now that he knew she was alive and well.

It was an indoor self-storage facility that had giant corri-
dors lined with what looked like orange garage doors, each
with its own padlock. When I reached the Waxmans' unit, I
put the key in the lock and turned it. The U-shaped shackle
pulled out easily, and I stooped to grab the door by the bottom
and push it up.

The room, which smelled faintly of disinfectant, was tidily
organized. Against the back wall was an upholstered chair
with a small table next to it. If it weren't for the old television
resting on the seat, it would have looked like an inviting spot
for visitors. On the left there were odds and ends like a floor
lamp, a large bulletin board, curtain rods, framed prints, and
a folding table. On the right were file boxes and other cartons,
carefully labeled. Three of them said "Kenny" in black marker,
and I was confident I'd find the shoebox in one of those.

They were in the far corner of the room, and I had to push the small table out of the way to get to them. I noticed that there was an envelope on the table, held in place by a glass paperweight. There was something handwritten on the envelope, so I picked it up and read what it said: *Renee Waxman—Please open in the event of my death.*

Had Renee written her own obituary? It seemed such an odd thing for her to do. And why would she have left it here instead of in her home? Still, it wasn't my business. I put it back on the table, placed the paperweight where I had found it, and pulled out the cartons I wanted to search.

The first box I opened contained report cards, notebooks, and drawings from Kenny's childhood. I glanced at a few of the report cards, enjoying the teachers' comments. One said, *Kenny is a bright young man with an active imagination. He needs to work on keeping his jokes to himself when others are talking.* I smiled and closed the carton, pushing it back against the wall. The next box had the detritus of his team-sports days, including things it made no sense to save, like old shin guards and baseball mitts. There was a shoebox in the bottom of that one, and I pulled it out. Pay dirt. Inside were the yellowing cards and letters Lydia had written to him. I took it out and placed it on the table, then closed the carton and stacked it against the wall.

I put the shoebox under my arm and walked out. Before pulling the door shut, I stopped, thinking about that mysterious envelope.

I walked back inside and picked it up, turning it over to examine the seal. Sure enough, the old glue had given way, and I could easily slide the letter out without anyone ever knowing.

I lifted the television off the chair and set it on the floor so I could sit. Then I took out the letter, and read.

To whom it may concern,

On May 15, 1986, I did a terrible thing. I killed a young woman named Halina Olszewski. I need to explain how it happened, so you can know it was me and not Sam who did it.

I came home from the supermarket and heard her fighting upstairs with my husband. She was pregnant with his child and refused to get an abortion. He told her that if she had the baby she would ruin his life and mine. But she said she would never get an abortion, not ever. Then she told him she loved him, and I could see from the bottom of the stairs that she put her arms around him. I panicked, fearing he would leave us for her, and I was terrified for our lives. I ran up the stairs and pulled her off him. I didn't realize she would fall. But when she tumbled down the steps I thought maybe she would lose the baby and we would be okay.

But she hit her head so hard she didn't wake up. I told Sam we should call an ambulance, but he told me to leave. He said he'd take care of it and I needed to get out of the house so I wouldn't get in trouble with the police. I didn't want to go, but he insisted. When I got back, he said I had killed her. He made me promise not to tell anyone what happened, and said that if anyone ever found the body, they would assume he did it. He said he would go to jail for me. I'm weak, and so I agreed. He doesn't know I'm writing this letter, but I don't want to die with this secret because of what that could mean to my darling Sam.

I'm so sorry for what I have done.

Renee Waxman

Stunned, I sat there, absorbing the contents of the letter. Had Renee Waxman really killed Halina, or had Sam tricked her into thinking she had? If I gave the letter to the police, would they be able to perform forensics to determine if it was really the fall that had caused her death?

And what would it mean for Renee if I brought the letter forward? In one scenario, she goes on trial and goes to jail. In the other, she learns that's she's innocent, but that the man she had loved and believed in all these years had taken advantage of her in the most evil way imaginable. Perhaps it would be best just to leave the letter here in this storage space and pretend I never saw it.

I turned the letter over again and again, trying to decide what to do. I don't know how much time went by, but when I finally stood, my knees felt stiff. Had it been minutes? Hours? My sisters were back at my apartment waiting for me, and I was lost in time.

I folded the letter and placed it back in the envelope. Then I laid it on top of the shoebox, and carried them both out with me. I didn't yet know whether I would bring it to the police, but I wouldn't decide alone.

Acknowledgments

If a writer is extremely lucky, she finds a smart, patient and generous friend willing to read through her messy first drafts. And if that friend happens to be Myfanwy Collins, a gifted writer and insightful reader who appreciates commercial and literary fiction with equal enthusiasm, it's like winning the lottery.

My embarrassment of riches doesn't stop there. I have a cadre of writer friends who buoyed my spirits through the roughest months, believed in me more than I ever dared hope, and inspired me with their own brilliant work. This list includes Mark Ebner, Kathy Fish, Susan Henderson, Jordan Rosenfeld, Robin Slick, Maryanne Stahl, and many others.

To the friends I made online who offered their support—including my buddies from the Zoetrope Virtual Studio, the talented authors in the Girlfriends' Cyber Circuit, and the astounding women at CafeMom—my respect, affection, and gratitude.

Heartfelt thanks to the professionals who gave their valuable time to fill the sizeable gaps in my knowledge, including Barbara Bauer, Detective Robert Edwards, Deborah E. Franklin, Charlie Goldberg, M.D., Lee Goldberg, David Kudrow, M.D., Gary Levine, Lisa Palmieri, Detective Lieutenant Kevin P. Smith, Susan Sternberg, and Nicole Wiedenbaum. Any factual errors in this book reflect my own artistic license and not the quality of information I got from these fine folks, the true smart ones.

To the world's most patient and gentle editor, Carrie Feron, my thanks for believing in this book through all its drafts, and for offering such wise counsel along the way. Your guidance in helping this work take shape is beyond compare.

To the dynamic duo, Andrea Cirillo and Annelise Robey, you are my foundation. If they awarded agents medals for endurance, loyalty, and encouragement, you'd win in a clean sweep.

And finally, to Max, Ethan, and Emma, who outsmart their mama every day of the week, and to Mike, who will always own my heart, all of my love.

A+

AUTHOR
INSIGHTS,
EXTRAS, &
MORE...

FROM
**ELLEN
MEISTER**
AND
AVON A

A CONVERSATION WITH ELLEN MEISTER

When I take a break from my writing but can't drag myself away from the computer, I often gravitate toward an online forum called CafeMom. It's an amazing place, filled with women whose support and generosity awe me every day.

So when my editor told me I could include an interview in the back of this book, I turned to my CafeMom friends for help. What follows are questions they asked and my candid responses.

When did you start writing?

I knew from my tender teens that I wanted to be a novelist one day, but apparently I had more talent for procrastinating than for putting words on paper. It just always seemed like I had my whole life to buckle down and get it done. So while I did a lot of short story writing in college, I put off getting serious about it for years and years. After all, I had my career to worry about. And since that involved writing advertising copy, I was already exercising some of my creative muscles and enjoying a certain fulfillment from that. Then getting married and having kids took priority.

Sometime in the year 2000, I finally woke up and realized mortality was staring me in the face, and decided that it was time to get off my butt and reach for my dreams.

Was there a specific event that gave you a wake-up call?

I didn't realize it at the time, but looking back I understand that learning my closest friend had aggressive and possibly terminal cancer was probably the catalyst.

What happened to your friend?

She passed away before my first book was published. The last time I saw her, when the fight was over and she was receiving hospice care, I told her I was going to dedicate it to her. When she asked why, I couldn't even speak. How do you explain to a dying friend how much they mean to you?

Do you plan to write different types of books? An autobiography, perhaps?

Ha! I'm not nearly interesting enough for an autobiography.

What motivated you to write?

Stephen King talks about the fact that we write because we're good at it, and I think there's a lot of truth to that. Once you discover that there are certain aspects of this art that come easily to you, it's almost a compulsion.

Where do you get your ideas?

It usually starts with something like an itch—a thought that gets under my skin and won't leave me alone. If it turns out to be something I want to explore, I start to think about how it might work in a book. For instance, before I got the idea for *The Smart One*, I had this nagging thought that I wanted to explore something specific about the relationship between sisters. I kept wondering how much power our childhood labels had in determining who we became. The character of Joey occurred to me first because I'm so intrigued by our society's hunger for fame. Personally, I find the idea of being a celebrity utterly intimidating, so I'm very curious about what is in someone's childhood that would make them yearn for fame.

Does any of your writing come from your experience?

While my work is always fictional, aspects of my life creep in constantly. Once in a while I actually pull small pieces of real events. For instance, there's a scene in this book where the Bloomrosens' dog, Stephanie, winds up with the clip of her leash piercing the tendon of her hind leg. Most aspects of this scene are completely fictional, but as a child, I did once discover my next door neighbor's shelty in this terrible predicament. (Dog lovers, rest assured that the pooch recovered quite nicely.)

Usually, though, the bits of my own life that find their way into my writing reflect more of an emotional truth than a factual one.

What was your most life-altering event, and how did it change you?

Maybe it's too easy to say it was the birth of my first child, but I can't think of another moment that rivals that (unless it's the birth of my second or third child). After that moment, when your child is pulled from your body and held up, wailing, and you witness a new force of nature that didn't exist until that very second, you're changed forever. From then on, the world is both more glorious and more terrible than you ever imagined. It's like gaining five extra senses in one shocking burst.

Are any of your books based on "ripped from the headlines" events?

I think "inspired by" actual events is more accurate than "based on." People who live on Long Island might, for instance, recognize some of the facts surrounding the murder in this book. That's because I was indeed inspired by an actual event that happened just miles from my home. The body of a young pregnant woman was discovered in an industrial drum in a crawl space under a typical suburban split level. It was a terrible story of murder and betrayal, and since it happened so close to home I was as captivated as I was horrified. What could have motivated someone so like my own next door neighbors to have committed this crime? Once that seed was planted, I knew this was something I had to explore. My goal was not to write about the actual crime. It was simply the springboard for a completely fictional story.

Do you get feedback from friends and family before you submit a book to your editor?

I do. I'm very fortunate to have some writer friends who are as generous as they are talented, and I show one or two of them my work before submitting it to my agent or editor. With family, it gets a little trickier because there's an emotional component to the feedback.

How do you write? Do you outline a story or do you have a plot line and go from there?

Some writers are very conscientious about creating a careful outline before setting down chapters. Others start with a vague idea and let the story unfold organically. I don't think there's a right and wrong here—just different styles.

That said, I think a certain amount of flexibility is vital, even for writers who like to create a very detailed outline. Otherwise, you could wind up forcing your characters to say or do things that are unnatural to them.

For me, a combination approach works best. I start with a loose outline hitting key plot points that will get me to where I want to be. However, it becomes a very fluid document, as things shift and change as my characters reveal themselves and the story finds its pace.

When you are not writing your own books, who do you read?

First of all, I read all the time—whether I'm in the process of writing a book or not. I love to read, of course, but I also find inspiration in whatever pages I'm perusing. Even books that are utterly opposite in style and tone from my own writing have something to teach me.

And I do have favorite authors, of course, but I don't limit myself to this handful of writers. I love to discover new authors, and find it enriching to read all sorts of novels, from the darkest literary fiction to the lightest popular books.

Do you get pressure from friends and family to put them in a book?

No, I think they're afraid of what I might write!

Do the relationships of your characters mirror your life?

I don't set out to have my books mirror my own relationships, but I suspect my subconscious finds a way to sneak my issues in.

Does finding humor in your own life make it easier to write?

Finding humor in my own life makes it easier to live.

How, as a busy mom, do you find the time to write?

I tend to squeeze it in whenever I can—early in the morning before the kids wake up and during the school day. (Alas, I'm not a night person and can't compose a coherent sentence after sundown. So no writing for me after the kids are in bed.) Also, I find letting the housework go takes some of the pressure off. So if you ever drop by unannounced, you'll have to excuse the crud on the stovetop, the papers on the counter, the muddy boots by the door, the fingerprints on the walls, etc. etc.

How has having your books published changed your life?

Before I published my first book I drove a green minivan. Now I drive a red one.

What do you do when you get writer's block?

I think writer's block is just getting to a point in a story where you're not sure how to proceed. So I make notes. I just sit down and start to type every thought in my head, no matter how stupid or outlandish. I write down all the questions I have about the scenes and the characters, and list as many solutions as I can think of, and where they will lead the story. Eventually, the right answers start to reveal themselves.

What advice/tips would you give to fellow authors trying to break into the business?

One: write what you love. Two: don't give up.

Where do you write? Do you hand write or work on your computer?

I have a home office, which is really a tiny extra bedroom. I do my writing directly onto the computer, as I can never get my thoughts down fast enough when I write by hand. However, I like to do my line editing by hand on hardcopy. So when I'm ready to start nitpicking, I print out the manuscript and grab a red pen. Thank God for laser printers!

How did you decide who to dedicate this book to?

My parents and I have been through a lot together the past year, and so dedicating this book to them seemed like a natural.

Are the sisters based on you and your siblings?

Like Bev, I'm the middle sister. And while I like to think of myself as The Smart One, my sibs might object to that. (Heck, my lawyer brother might even sue.) Seriously, as pretty as my brother may be, I don't think he has very much in common with Clare. And it's a long stretch to compare my tone deaf (albeit delightful) younger sister to Joey. She does, however, ride a motorcycle.

How soon after finishing one book do you get started on writing the next?

Immediately. In fact, another writer once said that the best way to finish a book is to fall in love with your next idea, and that's how it works for me. I usually can't wait to get done so I can start on the next project.

Has the support you get from your family changed since you were published?

I'm pretty lucky in that my family has always believed in me. So I got plenty of support before and after I was published.

Did you sell your first book on your own or with the help of an agent?

I couldn't have done it without my agents.

The sisters in *The Smart One* have very distinct personalities. Would it be fair to say that, to a degree, each of these women share a small (albeit skewed) reflection of your own personality?

I think it's fair to say that all my characters share something with me. Before I can write and develop a character, I have to find some emotional common ground.

Does that mean it's difficult to create a character whose personality is very different from yours?

It's difficult only if I can't find that emotional connection. But if that's the case, I keep probing until I do find it.

Where you are living and with whom?

I live in the suburbs of Long Island with my husband and three children. (Would love to say there are some dogs running around, but alas one of the kids is allergic.)

Which one are you—The Smart One, The Pretty One, or The Wild One?

Depends who you ask.

We're asking you.

In that case, I'm The Cagey One.

QUESTIONS FOR BOOK CLUB DISCUSSION

A+ AUTHOR INSIGHTS, EXTRAS, & MORE...

1. As adults, Clare, Bev, and Joey seem to reject *and* embrace the labels of childhood. How has this conflict influenced each of their lives?

2. Since Bev always considered herself The Smart One, why did it take her so long to come to terms with her dream to be a schoolteacher?

3. How does the discovery of the body work as a catalyst for *self*-discovery in each of the sisters?

4. Bev feels that the teenage sexual encounter between Joey and Kenny was a cruel betrayal. How, then, does she justify setting out to do almost the exact same thing to Clare? Is there more to this act than Bev herself realizes?

5. Toward the end of the book, Joey slips so far off track she may have completely derailed her prospect of becoming a cantor. How does she remain positive despite this obstacle? Do you think she'll be successful in battling her addiction?

6. As Clare comes to terms with the fact that beauty fades, she has to redefine her self-worth. How do you think this will affect her relationship with her husband and children?

7. Is Kenny's anger more like an 800-pound gorilla or a monkey on his back? Do you think he can easily defeat it, or will it be a lifelong struggle? How do you think the resolution of the story will affect his temper and his relationship with Bev?

8. The most prevalent image in this book is water. Discuss the various forms it takes and what it might represent.

9. When Bev sees Sam Waxman for the first time since learning of the murder, she is transfixed by the "humanness of his aging flesh and liver spots." Why is this such a revelation to her?

10. At the end of the book, Bev discovers a secret Renee Waxman has been harboring, yet the author doesn't reveal whether or not Renee's assumption about the murder is correct. Why do you think this was deliberately left vague? How important is this detail to the story?

Photo bcredit

A former advertising copywriter, **ELLEN MEISTER** left the business world behind to raise a family and chase her fiction-writing dreams. She lives on Long Island with her husband and three children. This is her second novel.

www.ellenmeister.com

Ellen Meister